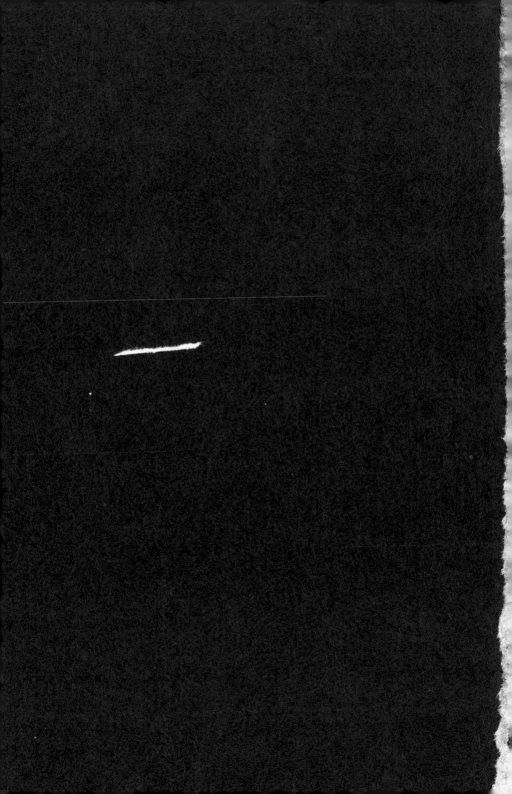

Souvenir of Cold Springs

Also by Kitty Burns Florey

Family Matters
Chez Cordelia
The Garden Path
Real Life
Duet
Vigil for a Stranger

Souvenir of Cold Springs

. . . . a novel

Kitty Burns Florey

COUNTERPOINT

WASHINGTON, D.C

Library of Congress Cataloging-in-Publication Data
Florey, Kitty Burns.
Souvenir of Cold Springs : a novel / Kitty Burns Florey.
    p. cm.
ISBN 1-58243-153-1 (alk. paper)
1. Women—Fiction. 2. Mothers and daughters—Fiction.   I. Title.
PS3556.L588 S6 2001
813'.54—dc21   2001028900

FIRST PRINTING

Jacket and text design by David Bullen

COUNTERPOINT
P.O. Box 65793
Washington, D.C. 20035-5793

Counterpoint is a member of the Perseus Books Group

10   9   8   7   6   5   4   3   2   1

This book is dedicated to my mother

Geraldine Goodson Burns

1910–2001

Though much is taken, much abides.

Tennyson, "Ulysses"

Souvenir of Cold Springs

Kerwin Family Tree

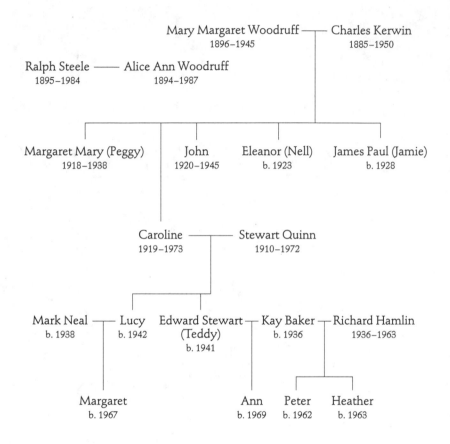

Mary Margaret Woodruff —— Charles Kerwin
1896–1945　　　　　　　　　1885–1950

Ralph Steele —— Alice Ann Woodruff
1895–1984　　　　　1894–1987

Margaret Mary (Peggy)　　　John　　　Eleanor (Nell)　　　James Paul (Jamie)
1918–1938　　　　　　　　1920–1945　　b. 1923　　　　　　b. 1928

Caroline —— Stewart Quinn
1919–1973　　　1910–1972

Mark Neal —— Lucy　　Edward Stewart —— Kay Baker —— Richard Hamlin
b. 1938　　　b. 1942　　(Teddy)　　　　　b. 1936　　　　1936–1963
　　　　　　　　　　　b. 1941

Margaret　　　　　　　　　Ann　　　Peter　　　Heather
b. 1967　　　　　　　　　b. 1969　　b. 1962　　b. 1963

Margaret

1987

ANYWHERE, Margaret thought. Chicago, Minneapolis, Denver, but preferably someplace warm. Honolulu, Acapulco, Saint-Tropez. On the subway, she recited the names of cities to herself, a rosary of places that weren't Boston. Palermo, Pamplona, San Juan. Miami Beach, for heaven's sake.

The T was cool and clammy; outside, the day was even colder. Daylight saving time was just over, all the trees were leafless, and the streets got dark at five o'clock. Buenos Aires, Palm Springs, Algiers. But anywhere, really. Paris, London. No, not London. Or would it matter? What were the chances of her running into Matthew in a city the size of London? And what would it matter if she did? Paris, London, Rome. Anywhere, anything.

She tried not to look at the other people in her car. She read the advertising instead. Vodka, beauty school, Jobfinders, beer. The procedure to follow in an emergency was posted by the door in both English and Spanish, and she read it over and over. Pull the ring and slide the lever to the left, then follow the instructions of the train crew. An emergency seemed imminent. It always seemed to Margaret that people on the subway at odd hours looked disturbed in some way. Mornings, everyone going to work, they were absorbed in their newspapers or not awake enough to make trouble, and at the evening rush hour they were blank-eyed and exhausted. But during less busy times—like now, four in the afternoon—they weren't a crowd, they weren't safe. They were separate individuals, thinking. They were all potential maniacs.

Q: And what about me? I'm on the subway. Am I a potential maniac?

A: A maniac *in potentia*. Potential comes from the same Latin root as powerful, so you are a paradox: a powerless potential maniac. And so not really a maniac at all. You don't have the energy to be a maniac. Your maniacal days are past. Remember that.

En el caso de una emergencia obedeczca las órdenes del equipo del tren . . . How beautiful things sounded in Spanish. Majorca, Madrid, Managua, Manzanillo, all those warm and maternal words, everyone speaking Spanish, the food fiery with chilis, the hot blue skies continuing into the evening, and then the long sweaty nights. Guitars. Bars. Men with cigars. The windows open to the stars. The doorways would be arched, carved into thick stone walls that were rough to the touch. Moorish. There would be flowers everywhere, everything red and yellow and lush, rampant green. She stared at an advertisement for shampoo that would make people want to smell her hair and thought: I've got to get out of here.

She was on her way to Cambridge, to see some people about driving their car to San Francisco. All right: San Francisco wasn't that warm, but it wasn't Boston, either. On the phone, the woman with the car—Mrs. Haskell, whose daughter at Berkeley needed their old

Toyota—had said, "I suppose you've heard Mark Twain's famous comment, that the coldest winter he ever spent was a summer in San Francisco." Margaret hadn't heard it. The only thing she could quote from Mark Twain was the last sentence of *Huckleberry Finn* about lighting out for the territory. She said she was thinking of doing that, and Mrs. Haskell had laughed tinklingly and said, "Oh, that's wonderful—the territory—because of course California still is in some ways such an uncivilized place, isn't it? I mean, compared to Cambridge."

She would drive the Haskells' Toyota to California, and she wouldn't come back. She could find a job, a neighborhood, people to live with. The main thing was to escape her parents and Roddie Smith and everyone else she knew and the cold city and the sidewalks full of dead brown leaves. The main thing was to chuck everything and start over.

At Park Street station, where Margaret changed trains, a young woman was singing. The song was a lament about a maiden fair, with rose-red cheeks and coal-black hair, the love that fades like the morning dew, the price you pay for a love untrue. No one was looking at the singer, though there were coins in the basket at her feet. Margaret dropped in a quarter: the price you pay for distraction. Then she leaned against a post and studied the singer—a mousy, overweight girl, who sang smiling. Her voice was shrill and powerful, like the voice of Joan Baez on an old record, echoing off the steel rafters and the mosaic walls, the posters advertising booze, the maps of the Red Line and the Green Line, the gleaming, frightening tracks—filling the subway station with (Margaret thought) madness. It was mad to stand there singing about lost love, singing for no one, singing for quarters. What could make her do that? Did she believe what she was singing? Did she wish as she sang that she had rose-red cheeks and coal-black hair? Had she experienced a love that faded like the morning dew? The station was strangely still, as if people were irresistibly, secretly listening. The voice was gorgeous, the song haunting. Margaret closed her eyes, and in the darkness the sound pierced her like a knife in her skin. When the Cambridge train came she was thankful.

All the way across the river to Harvard Square, she huddled in a corner of the car with her sunglasses on and the collar of her shirt pulled up around her ears. The thought of Cambridge still filled her with terror. She had dropped out of Harvard in April with her junior year unfinished. Officially, she was on leave. They would take her back, she knew. They longed to take her back. She felt Harvard's kindly, fatherly hands on her shoulders wherever she was, but it was worst of all at the Square. She never went there any more. Even going through on the subway was risky, and Porter Square, where she was headed, couldn't be more than a mile from Room 105, in Emerson, where she had disgraced herself. She always thought of it that way, probably because her mother had said, "Well, you've finally disgraced yourself," as if disgrace was what she had been waiting for since the day Margaret was born.

Buckingham Street was three blocks from the subway station, a street lined with plane trees, which her mother poetically called sycamores and which always seemed to Margaret to be diseased, their bark tumorous and scabbed. Number seventeen was a brick house with a fanlight over the door. As soon as she saw it, Margaret knew she wasn't going to be hired by Mrs. Haskell to deliver her Toyota to California. She imagined a patrician old lady, honest gray hair in a bun, flowers on a polished table, thin Yankee lips pursed in disapproval of Margaret's punky hair and purple nails. And now that Mrs. Haskell had had time to think about it, would the name Margaret Neal sound familiar? Wasn't there a Professor Haskell in the English Department? Would Margaret's disgrace have reached as far as Buckingham Street?

She passed by the house, crossed the street, and backtracked to Mass. Ave., where she turned in the direction of Harvard Square. She hadn't had her Daily Suffering yet. Not getting the Toyota wasn't enough. She had known that particular dream wouldn't come true. No: her Daily Suffering would be to walk through the Square. Maybe even stop in the Coop or get a cup of tea somewhere or stroll through the Yard, past Emerson. No, not that. Just the Square.

Q: Can I keep my sunglasses on?

A: Yes, even though it will be almost too dark to see by the time you get there. You'll see well enough to suffer. If you don't, you're honor bound to take off the sunglasses.

She was wearing a flannel shirt over a turtleneck and a long, deeply flounced skirt, tights, and lace-up boots. Everything black except the shirt, which was black-and-blue plaid. One of her mourning costumes of the second rank. And then the sunglasses. Earrings long enough to bang against her jawline when she walked. She looked at her reflection in shop windows: a dry cleaner, a liquor store, Erewhon, a craft store with a window full of patchwork quilts, rag dolls, duck decoys with every painted feather in place.

She pushed her sunglasses up on her head and studied herself against a pink-and-white quilt. How wholesome the quilt, how dolesome the Margaret. A woman in the shop smiled dubiously out at her, raising her eyebrows. Coming in, dearie? Want to buy a nice dead duck? Margaret pulled down her sunglasses and went on. She tried to think what she could do after she negotiated the Square. She could call Felicity, whom she hadn't spoken to since April, and arrange to meet her for dinner at Adams House, ha ha. She could call Roddie and get him to take her to a movie. She could ride the T back to Boston and walk around the city and get dinner someplace and see a movie by herself. She could go home. She could make a beautiful, hand-crafted, one-of-a-kind noose in decorator colors out of her mother's needlepoint yarn and hang herself from a beam in the attic.

Harvard Square was darkening. The cars had their headlights on, and the neon Out-of-Town News sign was red in the gray air. At the Coop corner she waited to cross. This was going to be uneventful.

She saw no one she knew, and no one looked at her. Dressed all in black, maybe she could disappear into the darkness. Cars zipped by. A homeless woman snored on a bench, surrounded by bundles. Someone played a banjo. A man with Reagan's picture on a stick was passing out bumper stickers that said NO MORE SHIT, and Margaret took one. A girl in a Stanford sweatshirt jogging by bumped into her and said, "Whoops." Just then, she spotted Felicity.

Felicity was crossing Brattle Street with a boy Margaret didn't recognize. They were deep in conversation, Felicity doing most of the talking, sticking her teeth in the guy's face as she always did when she got excited. "You know?" Margaret knew she was saying. "You know what I mean?" The boy nodded, grinning. He was unremarkable-looking, one of those people it was impossible to describe—the kind who get away with crimes. Well, officer, uh, brown hair, and some kind of eyes, I don't know, sort of average height, I guess . . .

She followed them across the street. He walked with his hands in his jacket pockets and Felicity held on to his arm. He was perhaps an inch taller than she, so that would make him five feet eight. Wait: was Felicity wearing heels? Margaret maneuvered until she could see. Sneakers, both of them. Okay, then, five feet eight. Brownish corduroy jacket, the same dead color as his hair. Narrow shoulders. The skinny drippy preppy type Felicity always said she despised. Behind them there were two women with shopping bags, then a caricature of a professor (gray crew cut, tweed jacket, briefcase), then Margaret. If Felicity and Mr. Blah turned around they would see her instantly. Margaret took off her sunglasses. The risk would be part of D.S.

Still talking, they turned into Au Bon Pain. Margaret stopped dead, and the crowd parted around her and went on, oblivious.

Q: Do I have to go in there?

A: Decide for yourself.

She imagined herself going in after them, ordering a greasy spinach croissant, following them to their table and sitting down nearby.

Or would they just be getting coffees to take out? Okay, she'd stand at the counter and order a cup of tea with milk in a loud, clear voice. Felicity would turn and look at her. Felicity would—what? Puke? Scream? Laugh? What could Felicity do that wouldn't be horrible in some way? Even if she sank to her knees on the phony Frenchy black-and-white tile floor and begged Margaret's forgiveness. Even if she pretended nothing had happened, yelped with joy, and hugged her.

No. Forget Au Bon Pain. Even for Daily Suffering, that was too much. She put her sunglasses back on and stood outside by the door. Here, in better weather, people sat at tables; here she had sat with Roddie, with Felicity, with fun fellow students, discussing professors and theses and movies and vacations and the weather. *Normal life,* she thought. Had that been normal life? She imagined herself being interviewed, at some point in the future, by some big-shot evening-news type. They are back in the Square—scene of her quaint youthful peccadilloes. She has a streak of gray in her hair, like Susan Sontag. She crosses her legs; her legs are spectacular; the camera pans back. She smiles off into the distance and says, *It seems so long ago. We were all so young.*

She looked through the window. Felicity and John Doe were sitting at a table eating pastries and drinking coffee, still talking. How could they have been served already? How long had she been standing there? She felt chilled with horror and also with the cold. I have to get out of here, she thought. I am going crazy for real.

A small wind had come up, and the sky was darker. She headed back toward the subway station. She took the bumper sticker out of her pocket and looked at it: NO MORE SHIT. Easy to say, but where else was there to go but home?

. . . . .

SHE WROTE to her cousin Heather, the only person she knew in California. Heather was twenty-five and had graduated from Berkeley and was working in San Francisco as a paralegal. Heather had been a fastidious teenager who spoke to Margaret only to give her advice about personal grooming. Head & Shoulders for dandruff but follow up with a good-smelling conditioner because Head & Shoulders smells like Lysol. Baby oil on your elbows but make sure you rub it in good or you'll get grease spots on your blouses. Hand lotion on your neck or else when you're old it'll get all stringy like your mother's. They had met a couple of times since then, at family events, and Heather seemed improved. The Thanksgiving before, at Aunt Nell's, they had had a long heart-to-heart about Heather's boyfriend, Rob, who was some kind of banker. Heather was getting tired of him. Rob was obsessed with the West Coast club scene, Heather said. Margaret thought that made him sound interesting, for a banker, but Margaret knew he couldn't really be interesting or he wouldn't be seeing Heather.

She rummaged through her desk for some decent paper to write on. She used her desk to store the junk of her youth, and she had to sift through letters and stickers and school papers and stuff about beekeeping, the English royal family, and the Boston Red Sox— some of her obsessions over the years, most of them from when she was eleven and twelve. Almost all the letters were from the Swiss pen pal she'd had during that time, Annette Brise. They were all in bad English; hers to Annette had been in bad French and quite dull: *ici ca va bien,* she always used to write, forgetting the cedilla. Margaret's mother had bragged so much about that correspondence that she had to end it, even though she liked writing to Annette and liked getting installments about Annette's crush on a boy named Denis: an affair of the heart, she called it.

She found some old stationery with her name and address printed on it, one of her mother's efforts to encourage her to keep writing to Annette. She took it downstairs to the kitchen, made herself a cup of tea, and sat looking at the sheet of notepaper, wondering what to say. Elegant black letters against cream, and the same address she'd had since she was seven, except for Harvard. It hadn't felt like her address for a long time: it was her parents' house, which meant that she was homeless. The *Globe* was folded up on the table; she could just see the headline, CONCERN FOR HOMELESS TOPS ON DEMS' CAMPAIGN AGENDA. She imagined Dukakis and Gephardt and Jesse Jackson getting together to buy her a plane ticket to San Francisco.

Dear Heather, I'm thinking of lighting out for the territory—namely California, preferably San Francisco. I'm getting fed up with the East, the weather, etc. What would you advise in terms of finding a job, a place to live, people? I have no money and will be lucky if I can get out there at all, but if I did— do you know anybody who needs a roommate? Do you have any ideas about where I could apply for a job? Are jobs hard to find? Around here, everybody has Help Wanted signs up. I mean waitressing, working in shops, etc. I'm not looking for demanding intellectual work. I'm sorry to lay this on you, I know you're busy, but you're my only contact out there. For any assistance you can give, the undersigned will be eternally grateful. Love, Margaret

She put it in an envelope before she could think about how stupid and desperate and pathetic it sounded, found the address in her mother's address book, and took a stamp from the monogrammed brass stamp dispenser her father had given her mother. She wondered if Heather had heard about her disgrace. Would her mother have told Uncle Teddy? No one would tell Aunt Kay because no one in the family was speaking to her, but her mother had these weird moments of intimacy with her brother, late-night phone calls with a lot of laughter, sometimes tears. Margaret wondered if there had been long-distance tears over her disgrace—or long-distance laughter, which would be even worse. She couldn't imagine her mother laughing over it: enough to make strong men weep, was one of the dumb things her mother had said. But what about weak men like Uncle Teddy? Enough to make weak men laugh, and then call Heather up and chuckle over it with her? I've got to tell you the latest about your cousin Margaret, she got involved with her English professor and then the guy dumped her and she had an abortion and a nervous breakdown and dropped out of school and got this weird haircut and has done nothing since April but sit around the house feeling sorry for herself and driving Lucy and Mark crazy. Isn't that hilarious?

No. Not even an alcoholic nutcase like Uncle Teddy, who wore a smoking jacket, sang Gilbert and Sullivan patter songs, and called her mother Pieface. Uncle Teddy wouldn't laugh; he would sympathize. His own life was full of similar disasters and humiliations. She should take off for Providence and get him to adopt her.

Boring though Heather was herself, Margaret always considered her lucky to be part of an interesting family—a father who wrote books and drank, an anorexic drug-addicted sister, a born-again redneck brother, a mother who had deserted them all. Compare that to being an only child with a mother whose main interest in life was keeping everything neat and a father whose idea of fun was to talk about how much it all cost.

She walked down to the mailbox at Cleveland Circle. She could take that walk in her sleep—often did, actually. Awake, asleep, there wasn't all that much difference. The sun shone grudgingly, and off in the distance a huge black storm cloud was riding in from the ocean. It was malevolent-looking, more like a mass of pollution than a natural phenomenon. As she watched it, the sun disappeared again, and she noticed that a similar cloud was approaching from the other direction. They would meet within the hour over Cleveland Circle, she thought. They would meet right over her head, and the heavens would open.

She mailed the letter, walked around for a while looking at the shops, and bought a copy of *House and Garden* at the AM/PM store.

Then she went into Eagle's Deli and ordered a cup of coffee. For her Daily Suffering she would walk home in the downpour.

Q: Is that good enough?

A: Probably not. We'll see.

She opened *House and Garden* and read an article about an English family with a hyphenated name who lived in a renovated Victorian horse barn. Their children were James, Charlotte, Alexander, Emma, and Tony. Charlotte was fourteen and had her own studio to paint in. Little Tony had his own playhouse, a hundred years old, with a thatched roof. The stables were like a palace. It would all be jolly good fun for the homeless: fifteen rooms, sixty acres, Hepplewhite beds, Chippendale chairs, antlers on the wall to hang hats on, everything dusted by servants, and, through the silk-curtained windows, views of the lime walk, the dovecote, the bell tower.

Margaret loved *House and Garden*. For years, she had given her mother a subscription every Christmas, until her mother refused to read it any more. She claimed it was a frivolous and decadent magazine. Margaret had asked her if it wasn't more frivolous and decadent to live that way yourself than to read about other people living that way. Her mother had said what nonsense, they didn't live that way, and Margaret had said that they would if they could, wasn't that what this house was all about? Antiques and china and expensive tea and those five-dollar cans of oatmeal imported from Scotland. Admit it, she said—you'd love it if I called you Mummy. And her mother had said you are an absurd, ridiculous girl, you are truly pathetic, you have lost contact with reality.

The rain started when she was halfway through her second cup of coffee, and she left without finishing it in case the rain stopped prematurely. It was a tentative rain, but she was glad to see that it increased as she walked. She put the magazine under her sweater and lifted her face to the clouds, which were now a solid gray mass over her head. In the west there was a window of blue. California, she thought. Water dripped down her neck. She wondered if her earrings would rust. Too bad: part of D.S.

She thought about Roddie, the only person who knew about Daily Suffering. He had said he would do it too, and he probably did for a while, but she was sure he wasn't doing it any more. Not that he didn't feel bad about it—he agreed with her that abortion was an important right for poor black teenagers, etc., but wrong for healthy young spoiled white women who had gotten pregnant through carelessness and a feeling of invincibility. They both knew they should have gone through with it, let the baby live, gotten married or at least had it adopted.

But Roddie didn't feel bad about it quite the way she did. If she knew he felt bad enough, she might want to see him. But he hadn't had the nausea and the swollen breasts, he hadn't had a little thing with arms and legs and brain scraped out of him, he hadn't bled buckets, he hadn't been told he was a disgrace.

This particular Daily Suffering hadn't seemed like much when she decided on it, but by the time she got home she was soaked through, her teeth were chattering, her feet were frozen. When she looked in the mirror her ears and her nose were bright red, the rest of her face dead white, her hair plastered down to her head like molasses. She thought with satisfaction that she had never seen anything so ugly. *Oh you lovely young thing.*

She ran a hot bath and took off her clothes, shivering. No heat until November first, that was her father's inflexible rule. She threw everything down the laundry chute, even though her mother had made her promise never to throw clothes down wet because of mildew. She stepped into the tub and submerged everything but her head. She had forgotten to take off her earrings, and they were cold against her neck. Even under the hot water, her feet and her knobby knees stayed bluish. She would never warm up. This would be the Ultimate Daily Suffering, to stay cold forever until she froze to death like her mother's aunt Peggy had: until her blood froze in her veins, her brain hardened like a flower after an ice storm, her eyeballs became marble eggs, her heart a Popsicle, her toes and fingers deader than wax . . . .

She ended up in bed for a week with a major cold. Her mother had been in Vermont taking photographs, but she got home just in time to keep Margaret supplied with vegetarian broth and fruit juice. She put the antique cowbell next to Margaret's bed for her to ring when she wanted anything—an old Neal family tradition. Her mother loved it when she was sick, Margaret could tell; it made her a dependent again, a mother's dream: a daughter whose biggest disgrace was her runny nose.

When her father was home, he answered the cowbell. He stood in the doorway and said, "Your wish is my command." To prove, contrary to all appearances, that he really did love her, he would go out and get her anything. Mocha lace ice cream, Soho black cherry soda, spinach croissants: nothing was too much trouble except normal conversation. He would bring her what she wanted, ask her how she was feeling, tell her to keep drinking liquids, and return to the basement where he spent his evenings caning chairs and refinishing furniture. He went to bed at 9:30 every night because he had to leave at 6:30 in the morning to avoid rush hour. He was a research physicist at a lab in Watertown. Her mother stayed up half the night and slept the mornings away. For a long time Margaret had wondered how they managed their sex life until it finally occurred to her that they didn't have one.

She and her mother looked at the Vermont photographs together—the usual product, just right for the annual calendar that was her mother's one claim to fame. This would be its eighth year: *Lucy Neal's New England Visions, A Portfolio for All Seasons,* it was officially called—a small but steady seller. Tourists loved it: arty black-and-white views of churches and birches, kittens curled up in baskets made by Native Americans, wheelbarrows, picket fences, village greens with harmless old cannons, hay wagons piled high with pumpkins.

"Pick two," her mother said. "We're looking for October and November." She sat at the foot of Margaret's bed, curled up like a kid. Margaret shuffled through the photographs and picked out one of smiling children in Halloween costumes and one of a broken-down fence and leafless trees twisted against the sky. Her mother frowned over them, her light curly hair falling in her face. She tapped her top teeth with one fingernail. Her fingernail was ragged, her cuticles bitten. Her lips were chapped, so she had smeared Vaseline over them. She wore a baggy blue sweater and faded jeans and a necklace made of moldy-looking greenish chunks of something. In contrast to the house, she always looked like a slob.

Her mother said, "I don't know, I don't know, I'm not sure about the trees. They're so depressing." She sighed, but Margaret could tell she was really in a good mood. There were times when her mother's unhappiness was massive and scary, a force that appeared out of the blue and permeated the whole house like poison gas. Margaret sometimes thought her mother must have a secret life that preoccupied her, that dictated her mysterious ups and downs—a lover in Maine or Vermont, where she took her photographs, or in New York, where she was always going to see her art director. When Margaret was feeling generous, she hoped this was true, though it was hard to imagine. Roddie, whose tastes were bizarre to say the least, thought her mother was good-looking.

Her mother asked, "What about the basket of acorns?"

"You did a basket of pinecones two years ago." Margaret had had the calendar in her room at Adams House. That November—the pinecone November—she had met Roddie. She had circled November twenty-ninth in red because that was the first time they had slept together. Big deal. She had thought it would lead to better things, but it had only led to a blob of blood and tissue thrown out with the trash at Cambridge Hospital. She counted back in her mind: Roddie hadn't called her in two and a half weeks. *Gloria in excelsis Deo.*

Her mother finally decided on the trees and the broken-down fence, and she praised Margaret's taste. For years, she had paid compliments meant to encourage Margaret's artistic talent. She thought Margaret should be a painter. Margaret hadn't painted in years, not since high school. She hated to think of the paintings she had produced, the lame attempts at drama and shock (a dead squirrel she found in the backyard that she painted in various stages of decomposition, a sequence of dead flowers in expensive cut-glass vases) and the cheap symbolism she sometimes attempted as a commentary on current events—like Reagan grinning on a television screen that was really a coffin. She knew she couldn't paint, even if her mother didn't have the sense to realize it. Or maybe her mother did, and encouraged her anyway because she was perverse, or because she wanted Margaret to be mediocre, or because she wanted Margaret to get off her butt and back in touch with reality.

Except that now she was exempt from getting off her butt because she had a cold. She wondered how long she could hang on to her precious germs. She thought about writing a poem, "To a Virus," the way poets used to write poems to mice and fleas. *Hail thou microscopic beastie. On my blood thou hast thy feastie.* It was pleasant to be sick. Her father ran errands for her. Her mother made hot toddies, lentil soup, custards. She framed a print of the trees and gave it to Margaret to cheer her up, propping it on the top shelf of her bookcase between the pottery vase full of chrysanthemums and the old-fashioned wind-up alarm clock.

Her mother's passionate quest for domestic perfection usually seemed to Margaret a form of insanity—everything relentlessly clean, tidy, and aesthetically pleasing, the whole house a monument to anal retentiveness. Or to her parents' empty marriage. Or her mother's vague but stifled creativity. Whatever. But when she was ill she liked it. Sunlight, flowers, neat bare surfaces—they made her feel pampered, like a movie heroine with a wasting disease, someone beloved who would be missed when she was gone. Everything was ready: the camera crew could move right in, wouldn't have to touch a thing. Just dab some makeup on her red nose.

She liked the tree photograph. It would be one of the things she would take to California, as a souvenir. It was perfect: dead-looking trees, photographed by her mother.

"It looks nice on the shelf," Margaret said.

"It's pretty bleak," her mother said dubiously.

"It's supposed to be bleak, Ma. November is the bleakest month."

Her mother smiled at her, as she always did at the hint of a literary allusion, any evidence that nearly three years at Harvard plus a home life rich in culture had done its work. "Are you reading anything good?" she asked. "Besides *House and Garden*?"

Margaret held it up, open to the stables people. "James goes to Oxford, Alexander's at Eton, and Charlotte's won the watercolor prize three years in a row at her school. And look—that's Tony's little playhouse."

"Please, Margaret," her mother said. "Let's not have our *House and Garden* argument again."

"I'm also reading *Middlemarch*."

"God—what's that? The fifth time?" Her mother used to be proud of her for reading it so many times. Lately it was worrying her. It was like when Margaret was eleven and used to read about keeping bees. She wrote to the Department of Agriculture and the National Beekeepers' League for pamphlets, and subscribed to an English publication called *The Apiarist*. Her Bible had been *The ABC and XYZ of Bee Culture*. At first her mother thought it was cute, an eleven-year-old who knew, and would tell you, that bees won't fly unless the temperature is at least 55 degrees Fahrenheit, that drones have 37,800 olfactory centers in each antenna. Then she started thinking it was weird, and kept trying to distract Margaret by buying her things: a boom box, a fish tank, a set of wooden chickens that nested one inside the other like Russian dolls, an *Alice in Wonderland* pop-up book from the Metropolitan Museum of Art that was much too young for her. Also, that was the summer they went to England. When the beekeeping craze was safely over, she heard her mother say to her father, "I suppose she gets *something* out of these obsessions," and for years afterward she wondered what she had gotten out of her love for bees besides a love for bees.

"Or the sixth?" her mother asked, picking up *Middlemarch* and squinting at the painting on the cover: a woman in a fussy Victorian dress, languishing in an uncomfortable-looking chair.

It was only the fifth time, but Margaret said, "Seventh."

At the end of the week, when she was beginning to feel better, a postcard came from Heather. Fast work: hard to believe, from a cousin whose busiest moments used to involve putting three coats of polish on each nail and drying each coat separately in a nail-drying machine she had conned Uncle Teddy into buying her. Margaret was glad she was home alone when the mail came; her plans were private, as Heather should have known. Margaret assumed she did know, and that was why she'd chosen to expose them on the back of a postcard.

She took the card up to her room to read it. In her tiny cramped printing, Heather said that if Margaret was serious about coming to San Francisco, she should get in touch with Rob at his bank, where they always needed teller trainees, though the pay was lousy. Heather and Rob were in the process of breaking up. Heather was living in a tiny studio apartment, but she might be able to put Margaret up for a night or two if she didn't mind sleeping on the floor. There was a P.S.:

As for the weather, you've probably heard Mark Twain's famous line that the coldest winter he ever spent was summer in San Francisco, so don't expect much.

Margaret turned the postcard over: a tinted photograph of a 1957 Chevy in front of a hot dog stand with carhops. She tried to visualize someone going into a shop and actually buying this card. Then she read Heather's tiny cramped printing again and decided the message was hostile. But it told her one thing she needed to know: avoid Heather like the plague. She ripped the card into four pieces and tucked them in her sweatshirt pocket.

Her mother was out at the supermarket, so she couldn't ring the cowbell. She blew her nose and went down to the kitchen to make tea. She hadn't had a cup of tea since she got the cold: tea with milk tasted terrible when you had a cold, like drinking mucus, and she hated tea plain. She put Heather's postcard down the garbage disposal and put on water for a pot of Jackson's Queen Mary, her favorite. While she waited for the kettle to boil, she stared at a photograph hanging over the sink: herself at fourteen—one of her more awkward ages—wearing a denim jacket and trying to look tough, but looking, in fact, harmless to the point of geekiness—which was why her mother had framed the thing and hung it on the wall. God forbid she should just thumbtack it up. That photograph was one of the million things Margaret wanted to escape. If she made a list of them, it would stretch from Brookline to San Francisco.

She carried the tea and a tin of shortbread cookies upstairs on a tray. She had planned to pig out on cookies washed down with tea and make a leisurely list of her options, but before she took three bites it was clear to her that her only hope was Aunt Nell—her mother's aunt, actually, a no-nonsense ex-schoolteacher who wore sandals with colored cotton socks and was probably a lesbian. Aunt Nell was the only one of her generation left, and she had all the money.

But Margaret hesitated to ask her, not because she thought her aunt would refuse but because she was pretty sure she'd agree. It made her feel guilty. What did the old lady have in her life? A cat. A

big old house full of stuff nobody wanted. Bran cereal and prunes.
Relatives who coveted her dough.

When Margaret was little she used to like going to Aunt Nell's
every year for the big family Thanksgiving dinner. She and her parents always stayed overnight. There was always a cat, that Aunt Nell
always named Dinah. There was an antique bed with pineapple
posts. There was the dusty attic where she could take the cat and
hide from her cousins. There was Aunt Nell's friend Thea, who kept
chocolate kisses in the pocket of her apron. There was Aunt Nell
herself, who at some point always used to tuck a folded ten-dollar
bill into Margaret's palm and say, "This is for you to spend, don't tell
your parents about it."

As Margaret got older she dreaded those reunions. Her cousins
always seemed to be going through unpleasant stages. After Thea
died, Aunt Nell became crabby, and the food wasn't as good. And it
was boring there—nothing to do but pet the cat or sneak away with
a book or be snubbed by Heather or watch Uncle Teddy get drunk.
She was still fond of Aunt Nell, and sometimes thought of going
up to Syracuse to visit her, but she never did. She couldn't believe
she would be anything but a burden, an awkward young niece who
didn't have a lot to say. After Thea's funeral, when they were all up
at her aunt's house eating lunch, Margaret had tried to tell her aunt
how much she had liked Thea, how sorry she was, and Nell had
been mean to her for the first time in her life—brushed her aside,
said it didn't matter, what good did anyone's sympathy do.

She sat on her bed and finished the tea and cookies. She tried to
empty her mind by staring at the alarm clock. The tick was so loud
she couldn't actually use the clock, and when she was eight years
old she had permanently stopped it at 8:13, which someone told her
was the time Lincoln was shot. She used to stare at the Roman-
numeraled face until she got double vision and began to feel dizzy,
and then she would close her eyes, open them, and something sig-

nificant would come into her mind. She tried it, but the only thing that came into her mind was the doctor who had scraped her clean, Dr. O'Something, she could never remember, trying to hide his disapproval behind an unconvincingly brisk manner, calling her "Ms. Neal," scribbling on her chart and refusing to look her in the eye.

Q: Should I or shouldn't I?

A: Go ahead. See if you can take advantage of an old lady on top of everything else you've done.

She went to the desk for more stationery and wrote:

Dear Aunt Nell, I wonder if you could lend me the price of a plane ticket to San Francisco. My parents are still mad at me for leaving Harvard, and I'm afraid to ask them for anything. In fact, I try to stay as unobtrusive as possible around here. I've been in touch with Heather, and she has promised to look after me, help me find a job, etc. But I can't make any definite plans until I have plane fare, which I figure is about $250, say $300 (one way), although I'll fly the cheapest airline possible and send you back any extra. I hate to ask you, but you've always been so good to me, not that that's a good reason, I don't like to impose on your goodwill, but I'm really desperate. I've had so much bad luck in Boston and vicinity that I just feel the need to make a fresh start somewhere. So for any assistance you can give, the undersigned will be eternally grateful. Love, Margaret.

P.S. Good luck with selling the house and your new condo. I guess we'll see you at Thanksgiving unless I'm in California by then—???

Margaret took the letter downstairs. She was definitely beginning to feel better. Writing the letter had helped, even though it might annoy her aunt to death and was riddled with lies. It wasn't true, for instance, that she was afraid to ask her parents for the money; the problem was that she was too proud, and she didn't want to endure the lectures that would accompany their refusal. And Heather wasn't going to look after her. And she wasn't planning to refund any extra money she might get beyond the plane fare. And she was going to do her best to avoid the usual family Thanksgiving. But a lot of the letter was true: her bad luck, her eternal gratitude, even *Love, Margaret.* She did love her old auntie.

She put the letter out for the mail carrier to pick up and went back to bed. She definitely felt better, but she was in an uncertain state, neither sick nor well, so that she didn't know whether or not the cold still qualified as D.S. or if she should find something else. Could Heather's postcard count? It had involved a certain amount of mental anguish. She decided to give her illness one more day, settled back into the pillows, and sank like a stone into the familiar troubles of *Middlemarch.*

. . . . .

SOMETIMES she dreamed about Matthew. She always thought of him as Matthew, though in real life she had never called him that. She had called him Mr. Nicholson like everyone else. The dreams were very boring. He was walking down a hall, usually with his back to her, his wild white hair flying around his head. He was sitting in an airport on a blue plastic chair, looking mournful, a suitcase beside him. Once she had a wonderful dream where he was in a garden smiling at her—at least, she hoped the smile was for her, but she realized when she woke up that it could have been directed at anyone.

Sometimes she woke up from the dreams missing him and humiliated. For a while after the abortion she thought constantly about being in bed with him. She had hated making love with Roddie, always. She never got to like it better, even back in the days when she liked Roddie's long dopey face and sweet smile.

With Matthew it had been completely different, in spite of the amount he'd had to drink. When Roddie was drunk he was a dead weight, half-asleep, and things were worse than usual. But Matthew had been wonderful. The booze hadn't made him tired, it had made him reckless and loving. He had taken such care of her; he had taught her to like sex the way he had taught her to like the Augustan poets. She had been nothing, and that long afternoon in his bed he had made her into something.

He was English. His wife had recently left him. He was at Harvard just for the year. He drank too much. He was forty-two. All this was common knowledge.

First semester, Margaret took his Age of Pope course; second semester she and Felicity signed up for Eighteenth-Century Prose. He used to invite his students to his apartment on Linnaean Street and serve them tea, with crumpets that were sent to him by his sister in London. They toasted them in the fireplace on long forks. It was like being in a novel by E. M. Forster or Evelyn Waugh. It was like being in the Bloomsbury group.

The day came when Margaret stopped by, alone, to drop off a paper, found him drunk, stayed to make tea and talk, and ended up in his bed. He had said, "Oh you lovely young thing, I should take you back to London with me." She remembered that perfectly: oh you lovely young thing.

Some days when she could think of no better Daily Suffering, she forced herself to relive it. First the good part, the afternoon of lovemaking: what he had done to her, what he had said, the light coming yellow through the drawn shades, the way he had murmured and held her, didn't want her to leave. *Oh you lovely young thing* in his beautiful accent. His funny cotton undershorts, his old-fashioned watch on the bedside table, his salt-and-pepper pubic hair. She had laughed at him, lovingly, and he had laughed at her, played with the tips of her nipples, used his tongue, and afterward there had been true peace, a state she had never experienced, and knowledge she had never had. Lying in that yellow room with Matthew, there was nothing she didn't understand. She was one of the enlightened, one of the elect.

She would go to England with him, become his mistress, and live in a state of continually renewed knowledge and pleasure and feeling. Her life had begun. Her life was a garden, like Twickenham—ordered and beautiful in a way she had always, before, assumed was closed to her.

She walked home in the misty dark. It was late March, and the trees in the Yard were coming into leaf. The streets were full of people who looked happy. There was a foggy new moon like a chalk mark on a blackboard. She had gone back to Adams House, told Felicity she had been at the library, and shut herself in her room so she could say it over to herself until she had it memorized, every move, every word, every touch of his hand on her skin.

And then nothing. He didn't answer her notes or return her phone calls. She went to his office during office hours and found he had canceled them. She rang the bell at his building on Linnaean Street and got no reply. He dashed out after class as if pursued by furies. It took her a couple of weeks to realize he was embarrassed by their encounter. He regretted it. He had been drunk. Sober, he realized he had screwed a student—like Abelard. She cried herself to sleep every night but tried to be philosophical: she had had her heart broken. She wanted to be a writer, and she knew tragedy was necessary. Eventually she'd be able to make use of it.

Then she missed a period and panicked—but her panic contained a kind of elation. This he couldn't deny. She knew it was his. Roddie: she hadn't seen Roddie in ages. She had been avoiding Roddie for—how long? Long enough. Roddie was no one. It was not possible that sex with Roddie could produce a baby. Sex with Roddie was like a frozen dinner: barely nutritious and certainly not creative. If she was pregnant, it was Matthew's baby. She pictured a little English child, a boy in a sweater and short pants, climbing over a stile.

She told no one. She missed another period. She had mild nausea in the mornings, which she hid from Felicity. She went out with Roddie sometimes but she wouldn't sleep with him. She reread *Middlemarch*. She cut classes and owed papers to everyone, including

Matthew. Her other professors hounded her for them; Matthew never said a word. She lay awake crying, trying to make a plan. The end of the semester was approaching. She knew he would be leaving for England soon. *I don't want to miss a day of the English summer,* he had said. *Oh you lovely young thing, I should take you with me.*

She finally confronted him in the hall before class because she didn't know what else to do. She clutched his arm, hung on to the rough tweed of his jacket, told him she was pregnant, asked him why he didn't want to see her. She had wept and been noisy. There had been students all over the place, shock and awkward laughter, Felicity and Alan and Jessie Henley and Peter Green and everyone else staring in amazement. He had said—she remembered this even better than *Oh you lovely young thing*—he had said, "My dear young woman, I haven't the faintest idea what you're talking about," and looked over her head at the collected crowd as if he expected them to save him. She had seen that look: fear was in it, and bewilderment, and incredulity not untouched with amusement. It was so convincing that she wondered if she was going crazy. She certainly felt crazy. Had she dreamed it all? Had she read it in a novel? His long kisses, the funny English undershorts with buttons, the ice melting in the whiskey glass beside his old-fashioned watch?

They took her to University Health Services, and a psychiatrist talked to her. Then she was examined by a physician. They did a pregnancy test. She was talked to by an abortion counselor. Then by the head of a women's group that wondered if it had a sexual harassment case. Then by the psychiatrist again, who explained that Professor Nicholson had had a vasectomy years ago, he had offered to call London and get the documents that would verify it—not that that was necessary, of course. Professor Nicholson was very concerned about her. He had been fond of her, she was one of his best students.

Her mother came, tight-lipped and red-eyed, elaborately kind at first but moving quickly to words like *disaster, disgrace.* Then Felic-

ity, who said, "I keep trying to understand you, Margaret. I keep trying to have sympathy for you. But I can't figure out how you could
act like that toward someone you supposedly liked and respected."
Then Roddie, who put his head in his hands and said, "Oh Christ,
this is going to wreck my whole life."

They took her from UHS to Cambridge Hospital, where Dr.
O'Whatever performed the abortion. She quit talking to Felicity,
and she told Roddie she couldn't see him for a while. She met with
a counselor who arranged for her to take a leave. It turned out that
on top of everything else she had a very mild case of mono. Her
father picked her up at the hospital and drove her home to Brookline, a ride across the river that was perfectly silent except for a
Mozart horn concerto on the tape deck.

. . . . .

RODDIE called and asked her to meet him at Lulu's. "For what?"
she asked.

"I just want to see you."

"For what?"

"Not *for* anything, Margaret. Just for the hell of it. Just to get
together."

"I'm not sure I see the point."

"Oh, for Christ's sake, then forget it," he said, and hung up.

She called him back and said, "All right. I'm sorry. I'll meet you
at Lulu's."

"For what?" he asked.

"I've got something to tell you."

"Good or bad?"

"Neutral."

There was a pause, and then he said, "I've been missing you."

"I've had a cold," she said, as if that explained why she hadn't
been missing him.

They met at Lulu's the next afternoon. Since she had left Harvard, they always met at Lulu's, a lunch place near the Museum of Fine Arts. The nearest school was Northeastern. The chances of her seeing anyone she knew at Lulu's were very small.

She wore her black jacket and black jeans: mourning costume of the first rank. She was late. When she arrived, Roddie was eating a hamburger at a table near the back. He half-rose when he saw her, then sat down again awkwardly. She took off her jacket and sat across from him. They exchanged half-smiles.

"Sorry about the hamburger," he said. He had never stopped feeling guilty because she was a vegetarian and he wasn't. She didn't say anything, just sat and watched him eat. A waitress came over and asked her if she wanted anything, and she ordered a cup of tea.

"Make it two," Roddie said. He finished his hamburger, wiped his mouth prissily with a napkin, and pushed his plate away. There were dribbles of blood and fat and ketchup on the plate. He dropped the napkin over it and said, "So what's your news?"

Now that she was with him, she didn't want to tell him. There was something about Roddie that made her feel as if she had died. It was hard for her to speak. Even to move seemed more trouble than it was worth. Every time she sat with him in Lulu's she felt she would sit there forever because she'd never have the energy to get up.

"It's not really much," she said finally. "I'm moving to California."

The waitress set two cups of tea on the table, scribbled out a check, and tucked it between the napkin holder and the sugar bowl. When she left, Roddie said, "Sometimes I wonder about you, Margaret. What do you mean, *not really much*? You're moving to California and that's no big deal? What do you mean, you're moving to California? To do what?"

She couldn't stand the way he got excited about things. Not the fact that he got excited, but the way he did. He always started out calmly—he knew he had a problem—but then his eyes popped, he spit saliva, he gestured wildly, his voice got loud and wobbly.

She sat silently, watching him. He waited for her answer, gave up, and went on. "I wish you would approach things like a normal person, Margaret. I wish you would just be honest and open and not be putting on this act all the time." He reached across the table and wound his fingers around her wrist. "You don't have to be supercool with me, you know. You can admit that moving to California is a very big deal. I don't understand this. Why are you moving to California all of a sudden, anyway?"

She looked down at his skinny, black-haired fingers. Her hand in his grasp looked pink and frail, a small trapped animal. She wiggled it but he held on tight, and she sighed. "I'm not even sure I'm going," she said. "It depends on whether my great-aunt sends me the money. She probably won't. I'll probably be stuck in that house with my parents for the rest of my stinking life. Forget California. Forget I said it."

He let go her wrist and put sugar in his tea, stirring it violently, and took a slurp off the top. "Do you want my advice?"

"No."

"Think it over. I'm a smart guy."

"No, thanks."

He looked at her in squinty-eyed silence, nodding his head as if she were some rare species he was on the road to figuring out. He was a double-concentrator in biology and computer science. He was doing his thesis on the comparative radar systems of *Myotis lucifugus,* otherwise known as the little brown bat, and its larger cousin, *Eptesicus fuscus.* One of his many minor interests was vintage rock-and-roll. He had recently sent an article to *Popular Culture Review* about the influence on the Beatles of old rock-and-roll songs—of "La Bamba" on "Twist and Shout," "He's So Fine" on "My Sweet Lord," "My Boyfriend's Back" on "Sergeant Pepper." A thousand and one nights listening to the Shirelles in Roddie's room at Lowell House.

He drank more tea, spilling it. "You know what's your real problem?"

"Yes. My real problem is how to get out of this city before winter."

"No," he said. "That is not your real problem."

They sat staring at each other. She didn't want to stare at Roddie—she hated the way he looked, couldn't believe she used to think he was cute—but she would have lost points if she had looked away. It occurred to her that she wanted to know what he would say. She cocked an eyebrow at him. "Okay, Roddie," she said. "What's my real problem?"

"Guilt."

"Uh-huh."

"I mean it. You're reeking with guilt over the whole mess, the abortion, everything."

"We agreed not to discuss it, Roddie."

"We agreed on that last April, for Christ's sake, Margaret. It is now October, in case you haven't noticed, and you haven't progressed one tiny bit. For six months you've done absolutely nothing."

"Not true," she said. "I've done plenty of things."

"Name one."

She thought. "I had a cold." He started to speak again, but she said, "Forget it, Roddie. I don't want to hear it."

"Well, you ought to hear it. You ought to face things a little better. Okay, you screwed up, you acted like a jerk, and you and I were stupid, and you had an abortion, and you dropped out of school. Let's face it. You've had a lot of problems."

"Okay," she said. "Let's consider it faced. Now can I go?"

"Margaret." He ran his fingers back through his hair. He needed a haircut. She had cut it for him months ago, and it looked like it hadn't been touched since then. She fingered her own hair, the stubbly strips shaved around her ears.

She said, "I think you should wear one dramatic rhinestone stud in your left nostril."

"Just shut up and listen to me. Let me finish." He slurped his tea again and banged the cup in the saucer. "I'm being serious, Margaret. You can laugh all you want, but I'm giving you good advice. You ought to go back next semester. You could take your usual course load and finish up your incompletes and you'd only be a semester behind."

He was doing it again, the staring eyes, the jabbing finger, his hair standing on end. Oh God: Roddie. She was supposed to be fond of him. *My boyfriend's back.* Right. How could she not be fond of him? He was her first, her only serious boyfriend. She had lost her virginity with him. She had gone to bed with him a million boring times. He had impregnated her, hard though it was to believe. He was brilliant, he was having an article come out in *Popular Culture Review,* she used to find him attractive, and, worst of all, he was in love with her.

"You'd only graduate a year late," he said. "If you keep on the way you're going, you're not going to graduate at all."

She smiled at him and said, "Oh horror."

He pushed back in his chair, and the table lunged toward her. Their teacups and saucers slid off and crashed to the floor. Roddie paid no attention. He said, "God damn it, you don't seem to understand that I feel responsible for you. What the hell do you think I'm supposed to do? I can't write my fucking thesis, I can't do my research, I can hardly go to classes, I don't sleep at night—nothing. I think to myself, can I call her, do I dare, is she going to hang up on me or what? All I do is worry about you, and you sit there and laugh."

He calmed suddenly, made a distracted gesture toward the cups on the floor, ran his fingers through his hair again, looking helpless. The waitress hovered nearby. People were watching them, warily. Margaret put on her jacket and started toward the door. She saw Roddie count out some money. "Sorry, sorry," he muttered, following her. They went out onto Huntington Avenue.

"Get away from me," she said.

"No," he said, and took her arm. "Margaret, this is killing me. You never think about what it's doing to me. It's all you, poor Margaret, she's got to punish herself, but you're punishing me too, damn it. I'm suffering, Margaret. I don't need to manufacture any fucking Daily Suffering, I've got it all built in. I'm going crazy because of this."

At the subway stop he let go of her arm. They stood in silence. I will not cry, she thought. He will not make me cry. He'll get over this. I'll be gone. It doesn't matter. She turned her back to him and stared down the tracks, unblinking.

He said, "Margaret?" She didn't answer. "Margaret?" She could see the T coming, way down the block. She concentrated on trees. There were plenty of them around the museum, most of them bare like those in her mother's photograph, but not bleak. The sky behind them was a brilliant blue that looked fake—dyed by some sentimental optimist. When the car came, she got on and looked behind her for Roddie, but he was gone.

. . . . .

SHE DID nothing but read. "You could occasionally do something more productive," her mother said. Her mother had also made several serious speeches about her going back to school. If not Harvard, then how about transferring somewhere else? How about Cornell? Her parents had both gone to Cornell, and had been hurt that Margaret wouldn't even apply. Or B.U.—nothing wrong with B.U. Maybe Uncle Teddy could get her into Brown for spring term. Or she could take a job for the rest of the year and start school again in September. Or at least do some volunteer work. One of the soup kitchens, a literacy program, tutoring in the schools.

Her mother's ideas ran down and finally ended with, "If nothing else, you could paint." Her smile eager, her eyes bright with stubborn hope.

Margaret hated it that they didn't force her to go out and get a job—though she knew she would hate the job even more. She didn't even have to do housework. They still considered her to be on the brink of some disaster: unbalanced, dangerous. They pretended she didn't revolt them, pretended she was their pet. After six months, her mother was still making all her favorite foods and doing her laundry. Her father was still coming up to her room when he got home from work and asking nervously, "So how's my girl today?"

She always said, "Oh, pretty good, Dad. Hanging in there," and he would do the fake grin he had perfected over the summer and say something like, "Hey—I see we're having tortellini for dinner. I'd better get down there and see how things are coming along."

She wished she had the guts to become anorexic or run away or join the homeless on Cambridge Common or at least go officially crazy. She imagined lunging at her father when he came in, making animal noises, slashing with her fingernails. Or tossing the bowl of tortellini through the dining-room window. She hated herself for wolfing down her mother's goodies, and for slopping around the house all day in her old sweatpants, reading. She was even beginning to resent the books she read: in them, things happened. Life went on. People went to work, dressed up, took walks, held conversations, got into their cars or their carriages and drove places. No one hung around in sweatpants and read about it.

She considered calling Roddie up and saying, "Okay, loverboy, let's get hitched." She considered showing up at his room with her wrists slashed, bleeding all over him: *this is what blood looks like, Roddie,* and she would smear it on his shirt, his face, his hairy hands. She considered calling him and saying she was in London, Matthew had sent for her, they were living together, and every night they went to the theater and then to a pub and then home where they screwed gloriously, royally, incessantly, so fuck you, buddy, fuck all of you.

She finished *Middlemarch* and reread *Portrait of a Lady,* and she tried and failed for the third time to get past page ten of *Less Than*

Zero, and she reread *The Beggar Maid* and *Mr. Bridge* and was halfway through *Mrs. Bridge* when a package came for her in the mail from her aunt Nell.

It was the size of a paperback book, and it was wrapped in brown and tied daintily with white string. Her heart sank when she saw it. It certainly didn't look like anything that was going to get her to California. She tried to think what it could be. Aunt Nell had a sarcastic side. A guidebook to San Francisco? A rubber frog? A photo of her favorite auntie? Whatever it was, it looked like Daily Suffering, neatly packaged.

No one was home, thank God, thank God. Margaret took the package to her room and cut the string with nail scissors. Under the wrapping was a box that had once held Christmas cards—gold bottom and stiff plastic top, with tissue paper inside: tissue wrapped around small hard objects.

Margaret began unwrapping them. A ring, a necklace, more tissue, other things—all small pieces of jewelry, like prizes in a kids' game. She thought at first that she was meant to sell it to finance her trip to California, but the stuff was clearly worthless: a cheap necklace of blue glass beads, another necklace of fake pink pearls, a brass chain with an ebony pendant in the shape of a half-moon, an enamel ring, a cat pin, two thin gold bangles, and a scarab bracelet. Junk.

Then she saw that at the bottom of the box there was an envelope, square and white, with her name on it in Aunt Nell's handwriting. Aunt Nell wrote in blue ink with a broad-nibbed fountain pen, so that the letters were shaded and the writing looked formal and old-fashioned. The *M* in Margaret bore a flourish like a flag blowing in the wind, the *t* was crossed with a plumed streak. Could Aunt Nell write her name with such conviction if there wasn't a check inside? If there was no check, wouldn't she write in small, apologetic letters?

She waited. She looked at the jewelry, piece by piece. The ebony pendant was rather nice—and black, so she could wear it with her mourning clothes. The gold bangles were okay, not exciting. She put the ring on her finger—blue enamel with little pink flowers and SOUVENIR OF COLD SPRINGS in yellow. Cute. Kitschy. So what?

The ring seemed familiar, seemed to have a vague unpleasant association, but she couldn't place it. She sat and stared at the way it looked on her finger, waiting. Then she studied her boldly scrawled name. Margaret. Margaret. Margaret.

The envelope, please.

Q: What's in it?

A: What you deserve.

She opened it. Inside was a folded piece of notepaper and inside that a folded check. The check fell out, still folded. Her stomach dropped, and she could hear her pulse beat. She read the note.

Dear Margaret, This is some of your great-aunt Peggy's old jewelry. I'm cleaning out the attic preparing to move, and I thought if anyone should get this, you should, since you're named after her and you look more like her every year. I don't think I'll have the family here at Thanksgiving this year. I'm between houses, and the place is in an uproar. Take care of yourself out in California, let me know how it goes, and don't let Heather boss you. I hope the enclosed will help. Best wishes to all. Love, Aunt Nell

Margaret twisted the ring on her finger, listening to the sound of her blood beating in her head. She looked at the folded check: a square of beige on her bedspread. If she never unfolded it she would never know. She would never have to do anything, ever. She could sit in her parents' house with the check unfolded for the rest of her life. The check would yellow and crumble and disintegrate, her sweatpants would fuse to her legs, she would go blind from reading, she would eat tortellini and ice cream until she croaked. They would have to cut Great-Aunt Peggy's enamel ring off her fat finger.

She touched the check—poked it, hoping it would unfold by itself and reveal its magic. It could be anything—twenty dollars toward her ticket, a hundred. *Hope the enclosed will help.* Aunt Nell was selling the old house and moving to a condo: did that mean she'd be feeling rich or poor? What did *help* mean? *Margaret* in blue ink with a flourish? A cache of worthless jewelry?

She began to think she was incapable of unfolding the check. She would have to take it to someone and get them to do it for her. Mrs. Niedermeier next door. The man at the bank. She twisted the ring around her finger. SOUVENIR OF COLD SPRINGS. How strange that the ring fit her so perfectly. Was that a sign? A sign of what?

She picked up the check and held it for a moment without unfolding it, thinking: *this is absurd, you are pathetic, if it's not enough what will you do, what will you do, you'll call Roddie, you'll go to Brown, you'll go back to Harvard and eat dirt, you'll go mad, you'll die, you'll die, you'll die. Oh you melodramatic jerk. Stop it, stop it.* Her stomach churned. She closed her eyes, unfolded the check, opened them.

It was a check for a thousand dollars. She put her head in her hands and cried for the first time since Emerson. She felt her heart begin to unfreeze. The ice melted in her veins. She would live.

Heather

1982

HEATHER had a bad flight from San Francisco—as if the Thanksgiving hordes weren't bad enough, there had been turbulence all the way, and her connecting flight in Pittsburgh had been delayed for two hours because of a bomb threat. By the time she got to Syracuse it was after ten. She checked into the hotel at the airport and called Aunt Nell's house from her room, which had a cockroach in the sink and mural over the bed of Indians creeping through a forest. Her father answered the phone.

"I'm not going to make it tonight," she said. "I just got in and I'm really tired. I checked into this Airport Inn place."

"Heather, for Christ's sake, why are you spending my money on a motel? I'll come over and get you. It's twenty minutes. We're all here waiting for you."

"Dad, I really feel lousy," she said. "I'm ready to pass out. Tell Aunt Nell I'm sorry. I'll be there tomorrow early, I promise."

"How early?"

"By noon. I promise. And I'll take a cab."

"This is completely unreasonable."

"I'm exhausted, I can't help it." She stared at the Indians. They looked like white movie stars in heavy makeup. They wore pony-tails and moccasins and loincloths. She heard her father say, "She's tired out, she's going to stay at the Airport Inn," and someone— Aunt Lucy?—said, "Oh Teddy, can't you put your foot down?"

"Dad?"

He sighed. "Yes, Heather."

"Has Mom called, by any chance?"

"What? Mom? No. Why? Is she supposed to?"

"Not really. I just thought she might."

"I very much doubt that your mother would call you at this number, Heather. Frankly."

"Okay. I just wondered."

"There's no way we can persuade you to come over here?"

"I'm half-asleep already, Daddy."

After they hung up, she picked up the roach with a tissue and flushed it down the toilet. In the mirror she saw that her mascara was smeared; she had black rings beneath her eyes, like a punk rocker. She removed the mascara with baby oil, washed her face, and rubbed in moisturizer. Then she took two Seconals and fell asleep before she could start thinking.

The next day they were all mad at her, of course. She was late because there was a snowstorm and it took the guy at the desk for-ever to get her a taxi. Then the taxi got stuck at Carrier Circle and they sat for half an hour while the driver told her his idea, which was that drug addicts should be rounded up and sent to reservations like Indians used to be. While they were going through withdrawal, they could be looked after by WACs.

"I figure the government could give the WACs the equivalent of combat pay," he said. "Assign them to, say, six-month hitches out there."

Heather sat looking at the snow and sucking on a Lifesaver. "Hmm," she said. "That's a good idea. Really creative."

"That way you not only get these characters off the streets, but you put the broads in the military to good use."

"Right," Heather said. "Brilliant."

"I think about this stuff a lot," the cab driver said.

They made slow progress, but she was, to say the least, in no hurry, and the city was clean and almost pretty in the new snow. They turned up Hillside Street, and her aunt's place looked like something on a Christmas card—the tall white house a bit shabby, maybe, but there were the clean new drifts of snow, the driveway flanked by white-frosted pine trees, a wreath on the front door. She gave the driver a nickel tip, and he stared at it said, "What kind of shit is this?"

She said, "You should be institutionalized."

"Fuck you," he said, and sped away.

Her father answered the door wearing white wool pants, plaid socks, and a black turtleneck sweater with a pendant on a chain around his neck. She clung to him for a moment, then kissed his cheek and said, "Wow, Dad, that's a weird outfit."

"Thanks," he said. "You should talk." They smiled at each other and linked arms and went into the living room where there was a weak fire burning. Dinah the cat sat washing on the rug. Heather's father poked the fire, and it flared brightly then subsided to a glow. "I'm so glad to see you, baby," he said. He sat down in the old easy chair; the cat jumped immediately to his lap and settled herself. "I was worried about you yesterday. I must have called the airport ten times. They finally told me your flight was delayed."

"There was a terrorist or something. And then just now I had this bizarre cab driver. A really sick guy. The world is starting to give me the creeps."

"I got so depressed when you didn't show up last night."

"Oh, Daddy. Can't you wait until I've been here a while before you start laying the guilt trip on me?" She sat down in a chair opposite him. "What's wrong with my outfit?"

"A bit preppy," he said. "Is this what you kids at Berkeley have come to? Monogrammed shetlands and penny loafers? You look like my girlfriend Patty back in tenth grade. You look like you're on your way to the hop."

"Everyone's wearing them. Back to basics, Daddy."

"Well, you look nice, anyway. You always look nice. You look like your mother."

"With you, I don't know if that's a compliment or not."

"Definitely," he said. "Definitely a compliment. How is the old girl? Where was she supposed to call from?" There was a glass of something colorless on the table beside him. He picked it up and drank. "And what made you think she was going to call, anyway?"

"I don't know, I just had a feeling." Tears stung her eyes, and she blinked frantically. "Actually, I'd kind of planned to see her on this trip, but she's gone to Palm Beach, presumably with one of those playboy types she hangs around with." She kept the tears back, but the threat of them was ominous: she had sworn she would keep her cool on this trip, in the face of no matter what. She changed the subject. "Peter's not coming, is he?"

"He's in Mexico with some friend of his. He'll probably come north for Christmas to see your mother."

Peter was a sophomore at a branch of the University of Alabama, where he had acquired a Southern accent and a rifle. He had taken Heather to a rifle range last Christmas. She spent a long, frightening afternoon watching Peter score bull's-eye after bull's-eye and talk to the men there about gauges and ammo and telescopic sights. He made her try some shooting, and she had been so scared of the noise and the way the gun kicked when she pulled the trigger that she felt sick and shaky for hours afterward. And Peter—she'd been scared of Peter, too.

She said, "I guess I'm supposed to spend Christmas at Mom's, but I'll come up to Providence and see you afterward."

"For New Year's?"

"I have to get back to do New Year's Eve with Timmy."

"And how's our boy Tim?" He tossed it off, but she knew he was hoping they'd get married when Heather graduated. He thought of Timmy as a solid, stable type just because he was in law school.

"He's all right. Same as ever, I guess."

"Sounds like a wild and torrid romance we've got here."

"He's all right, Daddy. We're getting along just fine."

"One of those towering passions that sweep all before it—a love for the ages."

"Cut it out," she said, but she had to laugh. "Where is everybody?"

He ticked them off on his fingers. "Two aunties, one great and one regular, in the kitchen cooking dinner. One deadly uncle down in the cellar attempting to fix the washing machine, which overflowed this morning. One arty great-uncle and his unsuitably young wife out in the studio looking for some precious artifacts he left behind when he scuttled away to England. One teenybopper cousin up in her room listening to the hideous music of her generation."

Heather listened. Something by the Police floated faintly down from upstairs. "Oh God," she said.

"Be nice to your cousin. She looks up to you as a role model."

"Oh definitely."

"And you should probably go out right now and say hello to Aunt Nell."

"I should. I will. She's mad at me—right?"

"Well—" He drained his glass and looked around distracted. "Maybe a little." He started to get up. The cat raised her head, looking alarmed.

"Let me." Heather went over to the cupboard by the piano where Aunt Nell kept the booze and returned with a bottle. "This?"

"Your auntie's blessed Tanqueray." He stroked the cat, and she curled up again. "Fill it to the brim—with gin."

She filled it halfway. "I don't know how you can drink straight gin."

"Like this." With jerky robot gestures, he raised the glass to his mouth. "See?" He drank and smacked his lips. "Piece of cake."

"Yuck."

"Actually, if you'd bring me a couple of rocks from the kitchen I'd appreciate it."

Her great-aunt Nell was bent over the turkey, basting, and her aunt Lucy was patting some kind of gray mess into a bread pan. When Heather came in, Lucy was saying, "Her art teacher says she has real talent, if she'd only apply herself."

Heather said, "Hi, everybody."

Aunt Nell straightened up, her glasses misted from the oven, and said, "Well. It's about time." She closed the oven door and set the timer before she went over to give Heather a hug. "I can't believe you went to a hotel when we had your bed all ready for you."

Lucy kissed her cheek and said, "Don't you look nice, Heather. I love your skirt. Is that real camel hair? And look at this." She touched Heather's sleeve. "It's sweet, with the monogram. But you look more like Cambridge than California. Doesn't everyone in California go around in jogging clothes all the time? You look very—what's the word? Pulled together. Something I've never been able to achieve." She looked down at her jeans and bare feet as if they puzzled her— as if she truly didn't know what the alternatives were. Heather was aware that her aunt Lucy took pride in the way she looked—thought it showed how spiritual and caring and socially responsible she was.

"I have a personal shopper who does it for me," Heather said.

Her aunt gave a dubious laugh, not sure if Heather was joking, then quit suddenly and looked worried. "Teddy was really upset last night. Wasn't he, Aunt Nell?"

"To say the least." Nell stood wiping her glasses on her apron. Heather could remember the apron from her early childhood: a red gingham skirt and white cotton bib embroidered with apples and pears. It was spotlessly clean and looked starched. Without glasses, Aunt Nell's eyes were old and squinty, pale blue. "He started on the gin right after dinner, Heather. He was so worried about you."

"Well, he's drinking straight gin right now, and I'm here, so it's obviously not my fault. I refuse to take the blame for my father's drinking."

"Nobody's talking about blame," Lucy said.

"Oh really." Heather poked at the bread tin. "What on earth is this?"

"It's for Margaret and me. Lentil loaf. It may not look like much, but it's very good. I hope you'll try it."

"You guys are still vegetarians?"

"Being a vegetarian isn't something you get over, Heather, like an illness."

"I know plenty of ex-vegetarians."

"Well, I'm not one of them."

"Get yourself a Pepsi, Heather," Aunt Nell said. "Mr. Fahey is still sending it over. I don't know how to tell him I never touch the stuff. Thea drinks it once in a while with rum in it."

They all laughed, but Heather was embarrassed by the mention of Thea. She was Aunt Nell's friend—companion—roommate: no one had ever inquired too closely, though Heather had once seen them embracing in the upstairs hall.

Heather let her laugh dwindle to a polite smile. "Where is Thea?"

"Down cellar with Mark working on the washing machine," Nell said. "That damned thing. I'm going to have to get a new one,

I guess, but I'm waiting until they go on sale at Sears. It's terrible to be a slave to your machines."

"At least it's just the machines making trouble this year," Lucy said. "So far, anyway. No family feuds."

Heather turned her back on Lucy and went to the refrigerator for a Pepsi. The name hung unspoken in the room: Kay. What Lucy meant was: now that Kay's not here, no one makes trouble, no one starts feuds. God forbid anyone should ask, how's your mother, Heather?

Aunt Nell glanced at the clock. "Mr. Fahey should be here any minute. And I wish Jamie and Sandra would come in from the studio. He's out there rummaging around looking for some old sketches of his. I told him I haven't seen them in years, but he insists they're there."

"Maybe he and Sandra are snowed in," Heather said. She put ice cubes in her glass and looked out the window. Huge white flakes drifted down, as if in slow motion. The studio was over the garage. She could see a light on. Then it went out, and she saw her great-uncle Jamie and his wife, Sandra, come down the steps and begin to struggle up the back sidewalk. They were joined in the driveway by Mr. Fahey from next door, wearing a red cap and a red-plaid wool jacket. "Nope—here they come," Heather said.

She was shy, suddenly, about meeting Sandra, and she got another ice cube from the refrigerator and took it in to her father and dropped it in his glass. He was sitting as she had left him, petting the cat. She noticed that the pendant around her father's neck was the head of a dog or a wolf with grinning ferocious jaws. "One arty uncle and wife are coming up the path with one ancient neighbor."

"So I hear." The back door slammed, there were exclamations in the kitchen, a nasal English voice that must be Sandra, old Mr. Fahey's cough. Her father said, "Maybe you should go up and get Margaret away from that degenerate caterwauling. God. When I was her age I was listening to *Iolanthe*."

"Yeah, but you're a wacko, Dad."

"I am not a wacko. I am a person of culture and refinement." He transferred Dinah gently to the rug and stood up. "Is Mark in the kitchen?"

"No."

"Then I think I'll be sociable. Your new English auntie is quite a tomato," he added, winking at her.

She watched him go, the cat trailing him. He never staggered, never acted drunk. She tried to figure out how much gin he had had. The green Tanqueray bottle was almost two-thirds empty. Some of that was from last night, of course, and the bottle may not have been full to begin with. But probably it had been.

She took the Pepsi and her bag upstairs to the room she always slept in, the cubbyhole next to where her great-grandfather had died and then her grandmother. As far as she knew, no one had died in this room. She took the barrette out of her hair and brushed it hard, and put the barrette back in, and took out her green wool dress and hung it up. Maybe she would die there. Let the dark devils come. She had death in her bag: the bottle of Seconal. She couldn't look at it without the thought crossing her mind. Wash them down with Pepsi, and—whammo: good-bye, Mom. So long, Daddy. Drink up, folks.

She burst in on Margaret in the middle of "Don't Stand So Close to Me." As far as Heather could tell, Margaret had been lying on the bed staring into space, but she jumped up when Heather came in and looked caught. "Oh God, Heather, you scared me. I didn't know you were here."

"Just arrived. How are you?"

"Okay. How about you?"

"Slightly alienated but otherwise okay."

"They were really mad at you last night."

Heather sat down on the bed. "So what else is new? How's it going? How's school and all that?"

Margaret propped herself up on her elbows and shrugged. Heather couldn't understand why anyone would dress the way her cousin did—worse than Lucy, who was just a slob who refused to take the trouble. Margaret obviously worked at it. She wore plaid pedal pushers over white tights, and a V-necked sweater striped in black and white. Her hair was bunched up on one side in a green rubber band. Her eye makeup looked like what Heather had removed in the mirror the night before.

"What're you in?" Heather asked her. "Tenth grade?"

"Yeah."

"How's geometry?"

"I did geometry last year. I'm in the accelerated program. This year I've got trig."

"Oh." Heather laughed. "Well, how's trig? God, I hated math."

"I kind of like it, actually. It makes things bearable. Just."

"Really." Heather searched for something else to say. Talking to her cousin filled her with a math-like boredom and despair. From where she sat, she could see out the window: still snowing. "God, what uncivilized weather. Can you believe that two days ago in California I was hiking in the mountains?" Margaret looked at her blankly, as if she wasn't sure what hiking was, or mountains, and Heather said, "So. What's happening in your life, Margaret? Do you have any boyfriends?"

"Are you kidding?"

"Does that mean yes or no?"

"No."

"You should do something with your hair."

"I do," Margaret said. "I put it up in this rubber band."

"Want me to French-braid it for you?"

"No, thanks. I really prefer it like this."

The tape ended, and Margaret turned it over. Oh God: Spandau Ballet. Must everyone be so predictable. Heather thought of her little sister, Ann, out at her new school in Michigan. Lambert Prep,

Ann's fourth school in three years. Each one was slightly tougher, like a series of trials in some fairy tale. At her last school, they weren't allowed to listen to music or use makeup. They wore uniforms and were allowed to leave school only if they were accompanied by a parent. Their letters home were supervised. Ann had run away twice, and when they brought her back the second time she said to the headmaster, "So kick me out, asshole. Who gives a fuck?"

Heather asked, "Could you turn that down, Margaret?"

"Oh—sure." Margaret turned the volume down to a whisper. "What about you? Are you still going out with that same guy? The one in law school?"

"Yes. Actually, we're living together."

"In a dorm? They let you live together?"

"No, in an apartment off campus."

"Wow. That sounds serious."

Heather laughed. "I give us two months."

"Why two months exactly?"

"What? Oh, I don't know. We're going to this big bash on New Year's Eve, for one thing. This dance. Strauss waltzes and champagne and pink balloons released at midnight. I'm on the committee, so I'm really obligated to show up with a date."

"Do you know how to waltz?"

"Of course."

Margaret stared at her. "You guys waltz? Wow. What is this—a new thing?"

"It's not that big a deal, Margaret. It's kind of fun, and it's very good exercise." She picked at the chenille bedspread. "Timmy's not crazy about it, actually, but what the hell."

"So—you mean you want to break up with this guy but you can't because you're on the committee for this dance and you've got like—tickets for it?"

"Yeah—that's roughly it. The tickets are fifty apiece."

"Fifty dollars?"

"And I have this dress."

"What kind of dress? A formal?" Margaret sat up, as if she were about to take notes. What a pain in the neck she must be in class.

"Well, it's long." Heather thought of what the dress had cost her—the hole it had put in her checkbook. It had been a mistake—all of it: tickets, dress, Timmy, life. There they'd be at the dance, herself in the dress, Timmy bored and refusing to talk to anyone. The hell with him. She would talk to Rob Berglund, her committee head. And after the dance she would tell Timmy: Happy New Year, the time has come. "And I've got long white kid gloves to go with it," she said.

"Oh my God." Margaret flopped back on the bed again. "This is another world. I don't think I want to go to college." She reached under the pillow and brought out a flat tin box. Inside were three neatly rolled joints and a book of matches. "Want some?"

"Actually, they sent me up here to get you."

"They can wait." Margaret held out the box. "Here."

"I'm not really into this stuff at the moment, Margaret."

"You don't do drugs out there?"

"Not really."

"Not even pot?"

Heather said, "Frankly, I've got better things to do." This was intermittently true.

"I suppose you can't get high and waltz at the same time." Margaret held out the box. "Come on. You don't have to be into it to smoke it once in a while. On special occasions, like when your relatives are bugging you."

"Oh, all right." The matchbook said Café Algiers in gold script on black. Heather knew that was a place in Cambridge. She wondered what Margaret's life was like. She struck a match and inhaled, passed the joint to Margaret. She hadn't smoked pot in a while, and she hoped desperately that it wouldn't make her sick. She still felt queasy from the breakfast she'd had at the motel.

Margaret inhaled like a pro and said, "Potent stuff, *n'est-ce pas?*"

"Where do you kids get dope?"

"My friend Tara's brother brought this back from Mexico."

"What a coincidence. My brother's in Mexico right now."

Margaret pretended to cough and pounded herself on the chest. "Excuse me, Heather, but I really can't stand your brother, if you want my honest opinion."

"I don't, thanks, actually."

They smoked in a slightly hostile silence. The dope was making Heather feel better, oddly enough, but it seemed wrong to her that Margaret had been the one to offer it—this teenage whiz kid who, except for the weird hair and makeup, looked like she should still be playing with her Barbies—except that she knew perfectly well Margaret had never played with a Barbie doll in her life.

"How's Ann doing?" Margaret asked.

Heather shrugged. She wasn't going to tell Margaret about Lambert Prep. "All right, I guess. They don't get a Thanksgiving vacation at her school."

"They don't? Wow. What is it? Reform school?"

"Ha ha," Heather said. "Not quite. Actually, my mother was up there a couple of weeks ago, but I haven't had a report from her lately. She's in Florida at the moment."

She had the postcard in her purse. Blue pool, palm trees, tanned people on chaise longues. The card read:

Honey, I'll miss you at Thanksgiving (so called) but when I get a chance at some sun I'm not about to pass it up. I'll be here 2 wks, then back to S.C., then who knows. See you Xmas I hope. I'll call. XXX. Mom

Margaret said, "I kind of miss your mother being here on Thanksgiving. She always livened things up." She chuckled. "Is she still casting spells on Uncle Teddy? I remember she had that voodoo doll she used to stick pins in. And she was consulting with some gypsy fortune-teller."

"God, Margaret—that was a joke. One of my father's weird routines." This was a lie: Heather had seen the doll. Her mother had mailed it to her father, a yellow-haired figure made out of one of his old shirts, stuck through with straight pins. Her father had opened the package and stared at it speechless, then he'd begun to laugh uncontrollably. Shortly after that he got his ulcer. Heather said, "My mother's bad, but she's not that bad."

"Oh well," Margaret said mildly, obviously sick of the subject. She squeezed out one more drag and crushed the remains in the tin box. She turned off the tape in the middle of a song. "I guess we should go down. What do you think of Sandra?"

"I still haven't met her. What's she like?"

"Sort of snobby. She hates America, especially Syracuse."

"Who can blame her?" Heather asked.

. . . . .

UNCLE JAMIE had found the old sketches he'd been looking for: pencil drawings from ten, twelve years ago of Heather and Peter and Margaret and Ann. He had set them up on the chair rail around the dining room, and they all exclaimed over them as they lit into the turkey and potatoes and lentil loaf.

Weren't they cute.

Will you look at little Heather—those eyes.

I know I've said this before, but Margaret's the spitting image of Peggy, you've really captured it in that sketch, Jamie.

As always, when Peggy's name was spoken, there was a melancholy moment of silence. Aunt Nell bowed her head, then looked up again at the sketches and said, "And Ann—the sweetest face."

Heather looked at small, blonde Ann, smiling out at the world. The picture gave her an actual pain between her breasts, like indigestion. Looking at the sketches of herself wasn't much better.

Uncle Jamie wanted them for a show of his drawings at some gallery in London. "You're going to put me up in a gallery?" Margaret asked. "These old pictures of me?"

"Why not?" Sandra said. She smirked around at the table. "I should think you'd be flattered, Margaret." Mawgrit, she pronounced it. Heathah, she had said when they were introduced. I've been dying to meet you, I hear you're the absolute hope of the family.

"I hate being conspicuous," Margaret said.

Sandra laughed. "Well, I hardly think any of your little friends are likely to stroll into a gallery in London and see your portrait there."

"No, but I can sympathize," said Lucy. "It's just knowing that you're on public exhibition. And it reminds me of those primitive peoples who don't want their photographs taken, they think it takes away a part of themselves. I really try not to photograph people unless I have their permission and explain to them exactly what they're getting into."

"But these are so sweet," Thea said. "They really express what childhood is all about."

"I do think pencil sketches are rather a different thing from photographs," Sandra said. "We really are talking about fine art."

Heather sighed. "There we were—innocent babes trusting our dear old Uncle Jamie to draw our pictures. Little did we know what we were getting into."

She had meant to joke, to lighten things up, but Jamie put down his fork and folded his hands tightly in front of his chest. "It seems to me that you're making rather a big deal out of nothing," he said stiffly. He jerked his head when he talked, like Sandra did, and little Britishisms were creeping into his speech—all those rathers. "This is a completely insignificant exhibit, and this is insignificant early work."

"Hardly, darling," Sandra murmured.

"I'm only including them because I was specifically asked to. I can easily leave them out. They certainly don't represent my best efforts."

"Could you all argue about it after dinner?" Nell asked. She passed the turnips across the table. "Here, Jamie. Please. Have some turnips."

"And let me give you some more turkey," Thea said. "I know you like dark meat, Jamie. And what about you, Heather? Did you get enough?"

"But it's a family tradition," Teddy said. "We always argue at Thanksgiving dinner. Come on. Don't stop there. Let's talk about Thatcher. Let's talk about Reagan."

"Oh God, don't get Teddy going on Reagan," said Lucy.

"What's the matter, Ted? You're not better off than you were four years ago?" asked Mark.

"Not bloody likely," said Teddy.

"And whose fault is that? Reagan's? Isn't there a more obvious candidate?"

Sandra broke in. "Reagan's a good man at heart, don't you think?" She cut a piece of turkey and put it in her mouth, still talking. "Getting on a bit, perhaps, but he's such an inspiring figure."

"He's a younger fella than I am," Mr. Fahey said. When Mr. Fahey chuckled he showed crooked yellow teeth, browning at their roots. "Spring chicken compared to me."

"He's an old fascist," Margaret said.

"Please," said Nell. "My dears. Don't start. My digestion isn't what it was."

"It's the meat," said Lucy. "It makes people aggressive."

"Then what makes you and Margaret aggressive?" Mark asked her. "Lentils?"

"Am I being aggressive? I thought I was being a model of self-control."

"Maybe it's the champagne," Aunt Nell said, looking tired. "Teddy, you should quit bringing champagne. It gets us all fired up. We should drink something milder."

"Pepsi," Mr. Fahey said, and they all laughed.

Sandra said, "I do think American holidays are fascinating. The idea of getting together for the sole purpose of overeating."

"Oh my God!" Lucy put her hands over her mouth. They all looked at her. Her cheeks flamed red. She gave a little laugh. "I just ate a piece of turkey. Just absentmindedly took it off the platter and put it in my mouth and chewed it and ate it. Oh God, I can't believe I did that."

"It won't kill you," Mark said.

"That's not the point. I haven't touched a piece of meat in—how long? Nearly eight years."

Heather said, "See, Aunt Lucy? What did I tell you? The world is full of ex-vegetarians."

"I'm not an ex-vegetarian, Heather. I'm—God, this isn't funny, it's terrible, I feel awful."

"Oh Mom." Margaret reached across Mr. Fahey to pat her mother's arm. They had exactly the same nose and mouth, Heather noticed. Tiny and prim. Lucy was actually prettier—though if Margaret would do something with her hair it would help a lot. "Maybe you should go rinse your mouth out with water," Margaret said. "At least you'll get the taste out."

Lucy stood up. Mark said, "Lucy, forget it, for Christ's sake. There's no need to make a scene."

Heather agreed: it occurred to her that Lucy had caused nearly as much trouble at these dinners as her own mother had. The year she had the miscarriage and went into hysterics. The time she made a long sermony public declaration of her vegetarianism that had given Heather and Peter a fit of the giggles. The time she insisted on organizing a sledding party no one wanted because she thought they all sat around too much. The way she always intervened when the kids fought, taking Margaret's side, making everything worse. Not to mention plenty of nasty exchanges with Mark. Why they stayed married to each other was anybody's guess.

"I'm not making a scene, Mark," Lucy said. "This is none of your business, anyway."

"It is if you keep yakking about it."

She left the room and they heard water running in the kitchen.

"I quite agree," Sandra said. She smiled at Mark. She thinks he's attractive, Heather thought. Good God. "A lot of fuss over nothing, if you'll pardon my opinion," Sandra went on. "Not that I don't think she has a point, in a way."

"I have to respect a strong belief," Aunt Nell said. "I can see where she'd be upset."

"Right on," Teddy said. "I don't blame her a bit."

"Really." Mark reached for the champagne bottle and poured some into Sandra's glass, then his own. "And what strong beliefs do you have, Ted?"

"I didn't say I had any. I just respect them."

"I thought you might have one or two."

"Nope. Want to pass that bottle over here, sonny? Anybody want more besides me?"

"There you go, Ted," Mark said, tapping the bottle with his finger before he handed it over.

"There I go what?"

"There's your strong belief. You believe in booze."

Nell said, "Mark."

Teddy looked at the champagne bottle, surprised. "Do I? No, I don't think so. Booze isn't a belief. It's more like a way of life. A whatchamacallit—coping strategy. Helps me cope with my in-laws, for instance." He poured more champagne into Sandra's glass and it fizzed and slopped over. "I don't mean you, of course, fair one."

"I wish you two would just cut it out," Aunt Nell said.

"Pepsi," Mr. Fahey said. "People should drink more Pepsi."

This time no one laughed. Thea said, "There's still a lot of turnips here. Can't I give anyone a second helping?"

Heather looked around the table, trying to sum each of them up in an adjective. Margaret: arrogant. Mr. Fahey: pathetic. Dad: drunk. Sandra: bloody. Mark: fascist.

Lucy returned, still looking flustered. Margaret asked, "Better, Mom?"

Lucy shrugged. She sat down and said brightly, "More peas, anyone? Lentil loaf? More potatoes?"

Heather asked, "What's the big deal, anyway, Aunt Lucy? I mean the whole meat thing. Turkeys, especially. These big ugly birds that don't seem to have much of a brain."

"Do you know how they raise those poor birds, Heather? In cages the size of a bread box." She held up her hands a foot apart. "They feed them hormones so they'll produce more white meat. They cut their beaks off so they can't peck each other."

"Makes sense," Mark said.

"I always buy free-range birds," Nell said. She patted her mouth with her napkin. "I have to go all the way out to that farm in Manlius."

"Okay—so what's wrong with that, Aunt Lucy?" Heather asked. "They have a short happy life, pecking each other like crazy, and then it's over. They don't know what hit them. They don't care."

"Like people," Teddy said.

"The birds are not the point," Lucy said. She picked up her fork again and took a bite of lentil loaf. Lucy: priggish. "We're the point, Heather. The whole process brutalizes us. All life is connected. We're not one thing and turkeys another."

"That's true, at least," said Mark. "There's more than one turkey at this table." He smiled over at Heather, as if he had scored a point for her.

"Har de har har," said Teddy. "Couldn't you just die?"

Aunt Nell said, "Please, Teddy."

"I suppose the worst of it is that it permeates our whole society," Sandra said. She had bright red hair, and she pushed at it with one plump hand while she talked. She had drained most of her overflowing glass of champagne. Nervous with Jamie's folks, Heather thought. That had been Timmy's excuse for not coming east with her: he said he couldn't handle meeting the family en masse like that. Heather tried to imagine him there. Timmy: what? She couldn't think of an adjective.

Sandra said, "It's almost impossible to avoid. I mean, on the plane coming over I read an appalling article on cosmetic testing—what they do to rabbits."

"You can buy cruelty-free cosmetics," Lucy said. "I could give you a catalog, Sandra. There's a place in Minneapolis that has really good products."

"But that's just a drop in the bucket, Lucy. Take shoes. Or try to buy a decent pocketbook that's not leather."

Lucy shrugged. "There are things you can do. I haven't bought leather shoes in years."

"But there are just so many places you can wear running shoes," Sandra said. "Or take the whole question of dairy products."

"Not me," Mark said. "I'll just take some more turkey, thanks. I'll eat that drumstick if no one else wants it." Heather passed it to him and put more white meat on her own plate. Fuck hormones. Lucy on the subject of meat reminded her of Timmy on the subject of acid rain. Not that they weren't right: they were right. But there was too much to worry about. If you even read all your junk mail you could go crazy: boycott grapes, save the whales, no nukes, adopt a starving Ethiopian.

Mark said, "This is a big treat for me, I'll tell you. I eat lentil loaf at home all year, and then I get my annual pig-out at Aunt Nell's Thanksgiving dinner."

"You eat meat every day for lunch, Dad," Margaret said. "And in restaurants."

"It's the principle of the thing. It's a relief not to have to feel like a sinner just because I like a nice drumstick. Some kind of leper. A pariah in my own family. Sometimes I think they let me stay around just because I pay the bills. I'm not sure I do anything else right."

They all looked at him with varying degrees of disapproval. Teddy was bad enough, but he usually made a joke and changed the subject before things got tense. Mark always went too far. On the other hand, he fixed washing machines when they broke down. On yet another hand, thought Heather, what must it be like to have a precocious fourteen-year-old pothead for a daughter. Or to live with Lucy, a saint who slopped around in jeans and baggy old sweaters. Though hadn't her father once implied that Lucy had a lover somewhere?

Margaret got up suddenly from the table and went over to Mark to embrace him. "Come on, Daddy," she said. "It's not that bad. You know it isn't." Across the table, Heather could see Mark's hand patting Margaret's shoulder, and Margaret humped over awkwardly with her rear sticking out. It occurred to her that this was a touching scene.

"There," Nell said. "That's better."

Jamie said, "What it comes down to is this: the more I see of people, the more I like dogs. Somebody said that."

"Some pain in the ass like George Bernard Shaw," Mark said, releasing Margaret, who went back to her seat with wet eyes and a little smile.

"Thurber, actually," said Teddy.

"Well, excuse me," said Mark.

Nell sighed. "Will someone pass me the turnips, please?" She took the dish from Sandra and said to her, firmly, "So. Speaking of dogs, do your parents still raise pugs?"

.   .   .   .   .

DINNER WAS the high point, Heather thought. Turkey and champagne and bickering were better than nothing. Afterward, it was just boring. Her father sat back down with the gin bottle. Thea escorted Mr. Fahey home, across the two driveways in the dark. From the kitchen, the dishwasher made its noise. Jamie put the television on loud. Sandra got out her knitting and started talking about the BBC. Everyone else sat slumped reading newspapers or magazines.

Heather sat on the floor looking at an old *Newsweek*. Margaret flopped down next to her and asked if she wanted to play Scrabble.

"Oh God," Heather said. "Live fast, die young."

Margaret tossed her hair back. "Well, what else is there to do?" She had taken the rubber band out, which helped some, but not much.

Heather raised her fingers to her lips and made a smoking motion. "Would you mind? I'll pay you for it if you want."

"Forget it," Margaret said. "Help yourself. Upstairs in my room."

"You're not coming?" Margaret shook her head. Heather said, "I just feel like unwinding. These gatherings get to me." She glanced at the television: a movie that seemed to be an idiotic modern remake of *The Lady Vanishes.* She said, "I wish they wouldn't always tamper with everything, damn it. I really love those old Hitchcocks, don't you?"

Margaret shrugged and picked up the *Newsweek*—pissed off, apparently. Heather sat for another minute watching her cousin read an article on Michael Jackson as if her life depended on it, and then she got up with a sigh and went toward the stairs, feeling peevish. Lucy was coming in from the kitchen.

"Oh—Heather," she said. "I was just looking for you." They stood in the hall, on the rug where Lucy had her famous miscarriage. A faint shadow of the bloodstain was still there. Heather could remember Lucy's screams, and Margaret crying and refusing to eat. She remembered how horrible it had been, her father saying, "All my sister wants is a couple of kids, is that so much to ask?" and his hand shaking when he poured his drink.

"I just wondered if anything was wrong," Lucy said.

"What do you mean—wrong?"

"Well, you seem a little—" Lucy shrugged and smiled, spreading her hands. "A little distant from all of us, Heather. I wondered if you were unhappy—if you could use someone to talk to."

"Oh, Aunt Lucy." Lucy means well, her mother always said.

Why did that sound like such a put-down? People always said *but . . .* after it. Heather looked at her aunt—not really her aunt, as Peter was always reminding her. The sister of their stepfather. The day they went to the rifle range, Peter had made a long speech about how he felt no loyalty to Dad or his family, and how Heather shouldn't forget he was Ann's father, but he wasn't their real father, and they should stop calling him Dad, anyway, and call him Teddy. And the family they should really be close to was their mother's, out in Illinois. They had grandparents and cousins they'd never seen. They should get Mom to take them out there, back to their roots. Not let Dad's family, Teddy's family, take over their minds.

Lucy stood there smiling at her. She had beautiful, sad eyes. Heather tried to imagine her meeting a lover. Would she go in jeans and old sneakers? And did she know Margaret smoked pot? At fourteen? Was that why she looked so sad?

"Is there anything the matter, Heather? School troubles? Romantic troubles?"

Heather said, "Not really. Just the usual."

"How's your mom?" Lucy was making her voice casual. "Have you heard from her lately?"

"Yes, I have," Heather said. "She's great. Fine." She paused. Lucy seemed to be waiting, and she felt mean not to say more. "I guess it's kind of Dad I worry about."

"Well, I can't say I blame you," Lucy said. "I worry, too. But he seems in good spirits, and I think he likes teaching."

"If he can hold the job."

Lucy looked sharply at her. "What makes you think he won't hold the job?"

Heather shrugged. "Drinking, for one thing. And—I don't know—is he writing? Don't they expect him to produce something at Brown? You can't live forever on your reputation. His book came out in—what? Seventy-three?" Her father's book, *The Kingdom Is at Hand,* was a work on religious cults that was considered definitive. Privately, he joked about freaks and zealots and crackpots, the Jesus, Jesus, come and squeeze us crowd, but what was remarkable in the book was his balanced sympathy with the groups he wrote about— that and what was always referred to as his limpid prose. "That sure wouldn't be enough at Berkeley."

"Well, he comes up for renewal in the spring," Lucy said. "We'll see then."

They stood in silence, looking at one of Uncle Jamie's paintings on the wall, a stark abstraction in blue and white that always looked to Heather like a woman in trouble, a woman at the edge. It seemed out of place in that stodgy old house: Heather could imagine it in her apartment, maybe on the wall over the teak desk. Lucy folded her arms and stared at it with her head on one side, as if she'd never seen it before. Then she sighed. "I don't know, Heather. The book is still in print, and still being talked about—that's something. As for his new one, I have a feeling it's on hold. He does do articles from time to time, but teaching takes a lot of his energy."

Heather realized her aunt was agreeing with her, that her father's job might be in danger, and her heart flip-flopped. It would be better to have a father like Mark, who did something boring and scientific and reliable. What would happen to Ann if Daddy lost another job, never wrote another book? What would happen to her and Peter? She imagined herself marrying Timmy so that her father could drink himself to death in the spare bedroom.

Lucy said, "Well, let's hope for the best." Heather smiled weakly, and Lucy put a hand on her arm. "Heather? Really. Are you all right?" She gave a hesitant laugh. "You know, we hardly ever see you. You're so far away out there in California. Sometimes I feel we don't really know you any more. But if you ever need anything, you know you can always come to us. Any of us."

"Thanks, Aunt Lucy." In spite of herself, Heather felt a lump come into her throat. She waited until it was gone. "I'm all right, though. Honestly."

Lucy patted her arm and smiled sadly, as if Heather had said her life was in ruins.

Dinah was curled up on Margaret's bed. She didn't stir when Heather reached under the pillow for the tin box. "Hi cat," Heather said. No response. She took the box to her own room, where she kicked her shoes off and sat on the bed, leaning against the headboard. She lit a joint—the bigger of the two—and inhaled. Immediately, she felt light-headed—maybe because she'd had a lot of champagne. She closed her eyes and let the smoke fill her lungs. She considered calling Timmy and telling him now: why wait until January? Except that she didn't want to talk to him—didn't even want to hear his voice. He was having dinner in Santa Rosa with his parents. Hello, is Tim there, well this is Heather. Just tell him I want him out of the apartment when I get back. Thanks. Click.

It was tempting. She imagined going home to find all traces of him gone: no ten-speed in the front hall, no sneakers in the closet, no Sierra Club poster on the bedroom wall—no more elk staring at them while they made love. No more making love: no more Timmy heavy on her, his eyes squeezed shut as if he didn't want to look at her, then rolling off, groaning, talking about all the work he had to do.

The joint went fast. She lit the other one. Found a five-dollar bill in her purse and put it in the tin box, rolled up. Surprise. Maybe Margaret would light it and smoke it—wouldn't even notice. She was spacey enough to do it.

Okay. No more Timmy. She would clean the apartment thoroughly—get rid of every last stray sock, every copy of *Mother Jones,* every damned used razor blade. Then she would call Rob Berglund. And say—what? Invite him over for a beer or something. And then what? Tears filled her eyes and rolled slowly down her cheeks. Hell, hell, bloody screaming hell. She didn't want Rob Berglund. An accounting major, for Christ's sake. Rob Berglund and his short, fat, pink, ink-stained fingers. Was it true that you could judge a man's penis by the look of his fingers?

She finished the second joint and butted it out in the tin box. Then she took the box back and replaced it under Margaret's pillow. The cat was still asleep, still unmoving, wrapped in her alien stillness. Hesitantly, Heather petted her; the cat stirred, then raised her head and yawned. Heather said, "Hey—cat." The cat blinked at her and curled up again. Heather stretched out on the bed. Dinah began to purr—a warm vibrating deep in her core—and Heather laid her face along the cat's soft flank and closed her eyes.

The house was very warm—an old lady's house—and completely silent, as if everyone downstairs had fallen asleep, or died; even the television was still. Heather lay there, half-dozing, and dreamed she was lying in the sun at some pool where a precision swimming team was performing. She watched the swimmers falter, heard their screams, watched them sink, one by one, still in formation, not knowing if she should intervene or if it was all part of the routine, and conscious always of the chenille bedspread, the purring cat warm against her cheek.

When she woke up, her contact lenses felt dry and her mouth had a bad taste. From downstairs, the television was loud again: she heard the Baroque music of a wine commercial. Her father said something, and there was laughter. In the bathroom she looked in the mirror; the pattern of the bedspread was imprinted on her cheek. She wet her lenses, and then she went into Aunt Nell's room, where there was a phone. She sat down on the bed and called Information in Palm Beach and got the number of the resort hotel her mother's postcard was from. She dialed it and asked for Kay Quinn, and the person at the desk said, "One moment, please, we'll ring that room for you."

While she waited, she looked around her aunt's bedroom. Ancient iron bed, saggy in the middle. Aunt Nell's bathrobe hanging over the bedpost. Ancient mirrored oak dresser. Starched dresser scarf embroidered with girls in sunbonnets. Hairbrush, nail file, hand lotion, tissue box, handleless china cup with pins in it. Index card on which was written, "Call about windows. Get elastic. Vaseline." Stuck in the mirror frame, one of Lucy's photographs: Thea laughing, her gray hair tied back with a red scarf.

Heather closed her eyes and hunched over with her head to her knees, the phone pressed tight against her ear. She felt vaguely, distantly ill—as if another person living inside her body was being sick to her stomach. Pregnancy, cancer, indigestion. Mom, I've got cancer, I haven't told anyone, I wanted you to be the first to know. No. Mom, I'm pregnant, what should I do, help me, help me.

When the phone had rung twelve times, the receptionist said, "We don't seem to be getting an answer in 406. Shall I keep ringing?"

Heather said, "Yes," and on the next ring it was answered by a voice that said, "Well, I'm obviously no match for this kind of persistence. Hello, for Christ's sake."

"Mom? Is that you?"

"Heather! God, I couldn't imagine who this could be, ringing and ringing on Thanksgiving evening. How are you, honey? All through chowing down with the relatives?"

"I didn't know if you'd be there," Heather said. She had never expected to reach Kay, and she felt suddenly, unreasonably happy. "I thought you'd be out eating dinner or something."

"I'm between events," her mother said. "In fact, I was getting ready to go out, which is why I wasn't inclined to pick up the phone. So how are you, honey? How's everyone? How's the old man?"

"Oh, everyone's fine. Dad's in top form as usual."

"Is he still seeing Marie, do you know?"

"I have no idea. He didn't mention her."

"Hitting the bottle?"

"Some." Heather settled back on her aunt's bed and studied her fingernails, picked at a chip in the pink polish. "He and Mark insulted each other like crazy at dinner, as always. Dad got in a few good digs. Then Mark and Lucy started in. You know. Typical Thanksgiving dinner. Uncle Jamie is here with the famous Sandra, and they're both being rather frightfully boring. And Margaret's gone punk."

Kay laughed. "Anyone mention me? Anyone regretting my absence? Tell me everything. Don't spare my feelings. Not that I have any, at this point."

"Well, Margaret was sort of fondly reminiscing about you. She was wishing you were here to liven things up. She has happy memories of when you used to put curses on Dad—that whole voodoo routine."

"I've been thinking of getting into it again, just for the hell of it." Heather heard her mother light a cigarette and inhale. "Not that your father needs any curses. Just being a member of that godforsaken family is a curse. Oh—Heather—" Kay laughed, a little gasp. "Do you remember that time Lucy said to Daddy that he's his own worst enemy, and Mark said not while I'm alive? Oh Lord—I can't stand Mark but sometimes he kills me." Heather listened to her mother's laugh, imagining her head thrown back, her eyes crinkling at the corners, her mouth open showing her perfect teeth all the way back to the fillings. "Oh well," her mother said. "That was ages ago. So tell me what's happening with you."

Heather told her about Timmy and the New Year's Eve dance, her problems with economics, her straight As in French.

"Well, that's marvelous," her mother said. "Now tell me one other thing, Heather—do you have enough money to fly down to Charleston for Christmas? If I'm in town?"

Heather's heart sank. "What do you mean, if you're in town?"

"Oh, I'll be there. Just pipe-dreaming. But you never know. Always hoping for that good old sunshine."

"One of these years we should go on a Mediterranean cruise or something together at Christmastime," Heather said.

"Mmm." Her mother made a sound that could have been a chuckle or smoker's cough. "My going on a cruise would probably depend on getting somebody else to pay for it. Of course, we could go and take our men friends. Is there something indecent about that? Or would it be fun?"

"Might be." Heather knew this would never happen. She tried to imagine Timmy agreeing to such a thing. Or Rob Berglund. She could just hear her mother on the subject of Rob Berglund. Her mother never introduced Heather to any of her men—Heather wondered sometimes if her mother really didn't have any, and just pretended she did to annoy Teddy. Heather had no idea if her mother's wild life, which she reported faithfully, did annoy him; her father kept a poker face when it came to Kay.

She went on, "But what I was going to say, Heather honey, was that I hope you've got the dough or can get it from Daddy or put it on Visa or something because there's no way I can send you an airline ticket this time. The fees at Lambert are insane, as I'm sure your father has told you. It's outrageous what those places get. And for what? I mean, it's not exactly Choate, is it? I mean, take the teachers. Mostly they hire kids just out of some two-bit special ed program who last maybe three semesters before they can't take it any more and move on. Rotten pay, I'm sure. I'll tell you who's raking it in—it's that goddam headmaster, who in my opinion is good for nothing."

Heather said, "How is she, anyway?"

"Don't ask me. Please. I'm on vacation."

"Dad wanted to know."

"Did he." There was a pause. "Well, I think she might actually last out the year. She hasn't tried to run away yet, and she's getting better about eating. They've got her on a new kind of medication for

the rest of it. There's a therapist who seems to have faith in her. Ann
likes her a lot, apparently. She swears she's going to turn over a new
leaf."

"Well, that's great," Heather said. "That's fantastic, actually."

"Isn't it. Isn't it just wonderful that my twelve-year-old daughter
isn't going to get kicked out of school again. That makes me very,
very happy. Listen, Heather, I've got to get going. People are waiting
for me."

"Oh—well, I'm glad I managed to catch you, Mom." Heather
got up off the bed and looked at her face in the mirror over the
dresser. She asked, "How's the weather down there, anyway? Are you
having a good time?"

"I'm having a marvelous time." Her mother sounded distracted,
as if she were dabbing on perfume, struggling into her satin coat,
fussing with her hair as she talked—half out the door to meet the
people who waited for her, whoever they were. Did they exist at all?
Heather wanted to ask, just to see what her reaction would be: what
people, exactly? What are their names? Where are you going?

Her mother said, in a brisk voice, "The weather is gorgeous. The
temperature was eighty-one today. We spent all morning at the
pool."

We: who is we? Heather thought of her dream of the doomed
precision swim team. "It's snowing here," she said.

"Oh dear. Typical. Well, I'd better get going, baby."

"Mom? Do you think Ann will ever be a normal person?" She
blurted it out—not what she had meant to say, at all—and, in the
mirror, her lips stretched out tight in a mask of pain. She put her
hand over her mouth. Tears filled her eyes, brimmed over, and ran,
black with mascara, down her hand.

"Oh, Heather, what a question at a time like this. How do I
know? I'm not God. Listen—I really, really have to run. I'll get back
to you about Christmas. I'm sorry, honey, but you can't imagine
how late I am."

Heather took her hand away from her mouth. "Here's my opinion," she said. "I think that eventually she's going to be fine." Her voice was perfectly steady. She pulled a tissue from the box and wiped her eyes. "I think this is something she's got to go through and she's going to end up surprising us all. She's going to really settle down and quit screwing around and get her head on straight. She'll even go to college, and then—oh, I don't know, she and I can room together, get jobs. Really. You wait."

Her mother laughed—a new, harsh bark of a laugh. "Listen to the oracle. What kind of voodoo are you dabbling in, sweetie? Well. Stranger things have happened, I guess. I've got to go. We'll have a good gossip at Christmas. You'll have to tell me all about sexy Sandra—and Margaret's shaved head."

"It's not shaved, actually. Just looks like shit."

Her mother laughed again, and they hung up. Before she hung up the phone, Kay always made a kissing sound. Heather kept the phone to her ear for a few seconds, and then she smoothed the bedspread and brushed her hair with her aunt's brush. Talking to her mother had made her feel better. She thought that was pathetic, even perverse. She should be too old to care. And her mother was a terrible mother, probably a terrible human being. But Heather definitely felt better. She went into the bathroom and fixed her eye makeup, and then she went downstairs and played Scrabble with Margaret.

Nell
1980

HE WAS to think, in the years afterward, that her real life, brief though it was, didn't begin until her brother Jamie said, "I saw you."

They were eating dinner. It was May 17, 1980, a Saturday. She was fifty-seven years old, Jamie was fifty-two—old bachelors, both of them, a schoolteacher and a painter. They had lived together in the same house, harmoniously enough, all their lives.

"I saw you," Jamie said. "I think you should know that, Nell."

She wasn't sure what he had seen, only that there was plenty in her life to see if you looked in the right places.

They were eating a vegetable stew with Thea's whole wheat rolls. Years later, Nell still remembered that, and that Dinah, their old black cat, lay striped with sunlight on the rug by the door. Nell put

down her fork and took several sips of water. Jamie picked up his
knife and buttered a piece of roll, but he didn't eat it. He sat looking
at it. She watched him. What a pathetic fellow he was, his shirt un-
ironed, the collar frayed; at the neck was a grimy triangle of under-
shirt. His shiny bald head was freckled like a fish. He had Dad's long
nose and Mother's prim mouth—their worst features.

"What do you mean, you saw me?" she asked, her voice hard.

He looked from the roll to his plate of stew—not at her. Whatever it is, he'll mumble it, she thought. Won't look me in the eye and
call things by their names in a firm voice.

"Saw me what?" she asked again.

"I saw you two in the yard." He mooshed around in the stew
with his fork as if looking for bugs. "I don't have to lay it out," he
said. "You know what I mean. This afternoon."

No: it wasn't terrible. It was funny. She had dreaded this for years,
and now she had to raise her napkin to her lips and smile behind it.
Poor Jamie. Poor baby. "We thought you were downtown," she said,
and the smile threatened to become a laugh. "Buying turpentine
and going to the library."

He shook his head, purse-lipped, unable to speak. He must have
come back early. He must have been up in the loft, painting. In his
blue work shirt and overalls, with his palette held high. He was drab
when he just sat and talked, or ate, or read library books in his favorite chair by the fireplace, but when he painted he was dramatic,
impressive, a god. His students worshiped him. James Paul Kerwin,
artiste extraordinaire. He painted only from photographs—he could
be commissioned from a catalog in the gallery of his New York rep-
resentative—and he invariably made his subjects happy. She imagined him backing away from the canvas to check the light falling on
the nose of some wealthy surgeon's wife, and catching a glimpse out
the window of his sister with her friend—her so-called friend—
her—Oh my God.

"What were we doing?" she asked him.

He snatched his napkin from his lap and threw it on the table. Half stood up, sat down again. Glanced at her and away. "I can't see what you've got to smirk about," he said. "It's not funny. It's disgusting. You had your arms around each other."

"We're friends, Jamie." The impulse to laugh receded. The word *friend* nearly brought tears to her eyes. Friends. My friend Thea. My dear friend, Thea Parsons. She had never had a friend until Thea— only Peggy and Jamie. One was dead, one might as well be. "We're very good friends."

He made a sound that signified disgust, as if he really had found a cockroach in his stew. "You're more than friends," he said. "Don't lie to me, Nell."

"I was getting to that," she said. "Of course we're more than friends. We're also lovers. We've been lovers for years."

He stood up and left the room before she finished the sentence. Dinah woke, blinked, then curled up again in a ball and slept. Distracted, Nell ate her stew, buttered her roll and took a bite. Had she really said that? To Jamie? *We're lovers. Lovers for years.* She couldn't help herself: she did begin to laugh. She pressed her hands to her mouth and giggled, and when she calmed down she loaded the dishwasher.

He was looking for an excuse to get mad at her: that was her theory. No one, not even Jamie, could genuinely be this disturbed to discover that his fifty-seven-year-old sister had a woman for a lover. He must have wanted to pick a fight—stir things up, like Teddy always did with Kay. "Life gets dull, Aunt Nell," Teddy said just before the divorce, when he and Kay were having one of their battles royal. But how absurd. She and Jamie were brother and sister, after all, not husband and wife, though they'd often been mistaken for an old married couple—something that always amused her but agitated Jamie. "Heavens, no—she's my older sister," he would say. Vain, silly little man, bald as a trout. "He's my baby brother," she sometimes got in first, to annoy him.

And life was never dull: that was Nell's firm opinion. It wasn't life that was dull, it was people like Jamie.

But really, he was absurd, and now he would be a problem with Thea, at least for a while, until he got used to the idea. He would be cold; she could just see it. He would say, "Oh—hello, Thea," when she came in, and then pointedly leave the room. He would disdain the rolls and cookies she brought as if they were poisoned. She imagined him perfecting his tight, polite little smile in front of the bathroom mirror.

Oh dear. She would have to call Thea. They would meet tomorrow to discuss it. Where? Not here. Brunch at the bagel place. Lie low for a bit. He's such an absurd person, Thea. I hope you won't be hurt by this, you know how he is, but he's good at heart, he'll get over it, promise you won't let him get to you.

When she came out of the kitchen, he was in the front hall with a suitcase.

"Where are you going?"

"I'm moving into the loft," he said stonily. He stood with his hands in his pockets, looking down at the suitcase. It was Dad's ancient leather one—of course. Jamie didn't own a suitcase, he had never gone anywhere in his whole life.

"Why on earth are you moving into the loft?"

He took one hand from his pocket and gestured. "I can't—"

She said, "Oh Jamie," and began to laugh again, but she was more appalled than amused. He really meant it. She had dreaded his ever finding out, but she had never expected this reaction. Shock and outrage, maybe. Disgust, too. But not rupture. Not a family feud. "Can't what, Jamie? What can't you do?"

"You know damn well," he said, mumbling.

"Wait—yes—don't tell me," she said. "You can't stay another minute in this corrupt house. Is that it? You're afraid I'll contaminate you? That if you live under the same roof with me for another minute you'll start chasing boys? Making a pass at the mailman?" She clasped her hands at her chest and said, "Jamie, you poor silly thing, look at you with your Daddy's old suitcase, how can you act this way, Jamie, at your age, at my age, what does it matter whom we love as long as we love somebody?"

He didn't speak. From the kitchen, the dishwasher made its customary noise: heena-wah, heena-wah. A perfect fifth. Jamie had been the one to notice, last year when they had it installed.

"Jamie?" She reached out to touch his arm. He moved away. "I'm sorry," she said.

She meant she was sorry for her last words. She knew he didn't love anyone, he hadn't had a woman in years, so far as she knew. Had he ever?

"Well, that's something," he said, sighing, and she knew he thought she meant she was sorry she wasn't like other women. He picked up his suitcase and moved toward the door.

"You are an ass," she said.

He left, closing the door gently. She moved from window to window, watching him. He walked briskly and purposefully, like a Fuller Brush man with a case full of samples, aware she was watching. He went down the front walk to the sidewalk, down the sidewalk to the driveway, down the driveway to the garage, into the garage by the side door that led upstairs. She saw the light in his studio go on. She imagined him methodically taking his stuff out of his suitcase. Summer pajamas, clean undies, shaving kit, library books. What would he do next? Turn on the radio and listen to *Evening Concert Hall*. Read his book on hermit crabs. Work on the surgeon's wife. Tuck himself into his little cot early. Then what? Cry himself to sleep? Masturbate, taking pride in his wholesome heterosexuality?

She remembered the fights he used to have with Caroline during the troubled year she had lived with them before she died. She had been, as Jamie put it, active until the end: he meant sexually active, of course. When she moved in she brought her big antique double bed with her—she hadn't wanted to sleep in the bed Mother and then Dad had died in—and there was always one of her men around, lounging in front of the TV, joining them for breakfast, sitting on the porch while Caroline posed against the railing—still gorgeous and sexy in her fifties. "I don't know what's come over me, Nell," she said once. "I never liked sex when I was younger. Back in my crazy prudish religious days. Now I can't seem to get enough."

Nell didn't mind. She had met Thea, and everything enchanted her—other people's love lives, especially. Even Caroline, whom she decided she had spent too many years disliking. But Jamie was in a state of perpetual agitation.

"She's promiscuous," he said to Nell. "She doesn't care who she brings home."

"How do you know?" Nell countered, thinking *whom*. "Maybe she cares a lot, maybe she's madly in love with all of them."

She liked Caroline's men. They were more fun than Stewart, Caroline's husband, had been. They were friendly and talkative, and they did things around the house—took down the screens, raked the leaves. More than Jamie did. And Nell liked their predictable, comfortable wit, based on insults and things they heard on TV. They always had the latest jokes, the one about Nixon, Mayor Daley, and Pope Paul in a lifeboat: it still made her laugh.

But Jamie hated every minute of her stay. "Slut," he finally called her, and she laughed at him. That was when he put the cot in the loft. It was also around that time that he stopped painting his beautiful, enigmatic abstractions and began doing portraits and making money.

When Caro died—suddenly, swiftly, of a heart attack—Jamie had told Nell he couldn't help it, he couldn't grieve, he was glad she was gone, and for a while Nell had hated him for those words.

As she watched, his light went out. After a minute she saw him leave by the side door. The old Chevy was in the driveway. He backed it out and drove down toward Wadsworth Street, the muffler growling. She stood in the front door watching the blinking red lights until they were out of sight, and then she stood there a while longer. Dinah came to rub against her legs. It was a soft spring evening. She could smell lilacs, earth, mown grass. She raised her arms above her head, clasped her hands and stretched. Then she picked up the cat and went inside to phone Thea.

.   .   .   .   .

NELL WAS fifteen when her sister Peggy froze to death on the ice in 1938. Peggy had been her best friend, the only person on earth she loved without reservation. When Peggy came home from California early in December, she and Nell went Christmas shopping together. They had bought Mother a pair of slippers, Dad a scarf, Jamie the drawing pen he'd been wanting. There was so much she could still remember perfectly—the pen nesting in its box against purple velvet, the soft pink slippers. What did they get Caroline and John? That was gone. But they had stopped at Wells and Coverly for the scarf, and Peggy knew the clerk, some girl she'd gone to high school with. Louise something? Lorraine? Afterward, they had cocoa at Scrafft's—cocoa with marshmallow—and Peggy told Nell all about San Francisco: the Golden Gate Bridge that was lit up at night like a necklace, the hilly streets of the city, the cable cars, the weird Chinese food. Aunt Alice had a cleaning lady. Uncle Ralph had a wine cellar. They had been good to her, taken her everywhere. Peggy made it sound like paradise, every minute an adventure, everything fun. She had loved California, but missed snow. It never snowed in San Francisco! When they told her that, she couldn't wait to get home.

When she died, a cold black hole opened up in Nell that wasn't filled until 1950, that first summer in England. No: not really filled until she met Thea, ten years ago in March.

Still, after more than forty years, she missed her sister. The night Jamie left, she lay in bed sleepless, back to back with Thea, remembering Peggy. How her first reaction had been a feeling of betrayal:

the unfairness of it all, that Peggy should come home only to die like that, just when Nell was finally old enough to be treated like an equal, when they went shopping together, talked late at night while Caroline was out somewhere, made plans for the summer when they would both be helping Dad at the store, how they would have lunch together, trade clothes, do each other's hair . . .

She never got over it. Time never made it any easier to bear. She had been cheated, robbed, betrayed. She had missed out. She could never explain the particular fascination Peggy held for her. Peggy, who wasn't pretty—not like Caroline—Peggy with her skinny legs and thick ankles, a long nose like Jamie's, and wispy hair that wouldn't stay put. And who was flighty, everyone said. They had always said it. Peggy was flighty the way John was a wise guy, Caroline was a beauty, Nell was smart, Jamie was artistic. What they meant was that you never knew what she would say or wear or laugh at. And then she decided college was boring, said she wanted to go to work and make some money. But first she wanted to see the world. So she took the train to California, and Aunt Alice and Uncle Ralph liked her so much they made her stay for three months.

But she came home for the snow. And she and Nell became friends, more friends than sisters, united against Caroline. And then Peggy went ice fishing with Caro's fiancé and froze to death in the middle of the lake, wearing her black coat with the frog closings and two pairs of black wool stockings and her red boots with the red-dyed fur around the tops and a striped stocking cap and a blue enameled ring no one had ever seen before. If she hadn't died, everyone would have said that was just like Peggy to go off with somebody else's boyfriend, to do something crazy like ice fishing when a blizzard was predicted. What a narrow escape, out there in the middle of it, she could have frozen to death. That girl has always been a strange one.

As it was, they all said how terrible it was, what a tragedy, poor Peggy, poor Ray, poor Mother and Dad, poor dear Caroline, poor young Jamie. When it was Nell who was really poor, Nell who had nothing.

She breathed deeply, adjusted herself against Thea. They wore their matching nightgowns: blue for Nell, pink for Thea. How silly they were. She smiled in the dark and reached for a tissue to dry her eyes. They didn't often get a chance to sleep together. She had been so discreet all those years! And partly, at least, for Jamie, that twerp. She blew her nose softly, but Thea heard her and turned over, hugged her around the waist and snuggled her chin into her shoulder.

"What's wrong, ducky?"

"That damned Jamie."

"Shh. Never mind." Thea yawned, her warm breath on Nell's neck. "He's a fool."

"I know he's a fool. But imagine how many people think like that. What a horrible world it is, Thea," she said.

"Ssh. No. No, it isn't, Nellie. No." Thea put her lips against Nell's neck and tightened her arm around her waist. With her other hand she lifted Nell's blue nightgown. "Not so horrible," she said. "Is it, my little Nell?"

. . . . .

IN THE morning they had their special breakfast. Cantaloupe. Whole wheat scones. The raspberry jam they made last summer. Poached eggs. Orange juice. Prince of Wales tea in the pot Nell bought in England. They sat in their bathrobes, eating and listening to the public radio station.

"He's so rigid, Thea. So intolerant."

"Maybe he'll change," Thea said. "Maybe this will be good for him. The truth can't do any harm."

"Jamie's not like other people," Nell said. "His reactions are not normal reactions."

"Maybe you don't give him enough credit."

Nell, lying awake after Thea went to sleep, had heard his car pull in at two o'clock. She would give a lot to know where he had been so late on a Saturday night. Jamie! Who spent his Saturday nights reading. But she would never ask.

She sighed and said to Thea, "Let's go to England again."

"When? This summer? Can I afford it?"

"You could if you economized, Thea."

Thea was impossible; she loved to shop, loved clothes. She was tall and slightly stout, and she favored long caftans, bold jewelry, gold sandals, bright scarves tied around her gray-blond hair.

"Is it worth it?" she asked.

"England's always worth it," Nell said. "Aging lesbians are a dime a dozen over there."

After all this time, the actual word still made them laugh. "But it's not as if we can walk hand in hand into a teashop," Thea said.

"Maybe certain teashops."

"But how will we know which ones? There should be some kind of newsletter."

"Or they should post a sign in the window. Lesbians welcome. Like the signs about dogs."

They were still laughing when Jamie walked in. "Whoops," Thea said.

"Good morning," said Jamie. He went over to the stove and turned on the kettle. He didn't smile and he kept his head unnaturally high.

"There's tea," Nell said.

"I think I'll just make coffee, thanks."

"Yes, you'd better. We might have put opium or something in the tea."

He threw down the coffee spoon with a clatter, turned, and went out the door, his mouth pursed up like a raisin. The door slammed behind him.

A Bach cantata came on the radio into the silence. They sat listening, then Thea said, "You shouldn't have, Nell. He was trying to be civil, I think." She got up to turn off Jamie's coffee water.

"Jamie's idea of civil is most people's idea of unbearable."

Thea leaned over Nell and put her cheek against her hair. "We should be patient with him."

"You're too good for this world, Thea." She took Thea's hand and kissed it. "You're a saint. Saint Thea. The first lesbian saint."

Thea laughed. "I doubt it." She sat down and poured more tea for them both. The music swelled: a soprano-alto duet. *O Jesu. O Meister.* Nell watched Thea listening to it with her mouth open, lost in the music. She thought: *she really is a saint, she is perfectly good, without her I would be an evil person.* She remembered the first time she saw Thea: the new history teacher, older than Nell, a big, bosomy woman with a sweet smile and that amazing hair. She remembered how she had been drawn to Thea right away, couldn't leave her alone, used to walk by her classroom just to hear her low, clear voice talking about the Greeks and the Romans. For ten years, she had been convinced that Thea had saved her from some sort of hell.

When the music stopped, Thea said, "Really, Nell, I think we're the ones who have to make the effort with Jamie. He's upset. We're happy. We can afford to be magnanimous."

"Oh, let's just forget him," Nell said. "If we're so happy, let's talk about something pleasant. Let's do England."

They were poring over their favorite guidebook—the student guide they preferred because it listed everything that was cheap—when Jamie returned.

They both looked up, without speaking. Jamie stood in the middle of the kitchen floor with his hands clasped in front of his crotch. The sun made his pink head shiny. He was wearing his seersucker jacket, wrinkled chinos, a clean white shirt, and his yellow tie with the regimental stripes. What a horrible outfit, Nell thought automatically. On the radio was harpsichord music. Perfect: she always considered harpsichord music effete and boring.

There was an awkward silence. "So, Jamie," Nell said at last. "Are you going to make coffee, or what?"

"I actually came in to make an announcement."

"Well, get yourself some coffee first."

"Maybe I will have some tea."

He sat down at the table. Nell and Thea raised their eyebrows at each other, and Thea poured him a cup. He put in milk and sugar, frowning so that he looked older than he was. Smile, Jamie, Nell thought. It takes ten years off your age.

"Scone?" She offered him the plate.

He shook his head. Too agitated to eat, she thought. This must be a major announcement. She would say that to Thea afterward: the way he acted, I thought he was going to tell us he was pregnant.

"Quite a coincidence," he said.

"What?"

He nodded down at the guidebook. "England. That's where I'm going."

"You, Jamie? You're going to England?" She couldn't believe it. Jamie had never been anywhere. He wouldn't fly and wouldn't sail. "There are only two ways to get there, you know," she said. "Astral projection doesn't count."

"I'm going to fly, Nell," he said with dignity.

"How wonderful," Thea said. "You'll love it, Jamie."

"That's your announcement?" asked Nell. "I can't stand this music. Anybody mind?" She got up and turned off the radio.

He cleared his throat. "I'm going with Sandra. We're getting married."

Nell and Thea stared at him, then at each other, then back at Jamie. He sat looking down into his cup, smiling slightly and trying not to, like a little boy who's just confessed to some harmless bit of mischief.

"Jamie? Am I hearing this right?"

His smile exploded. He looked ten years younger—at least.

"We're getting married over there," he said. "She called her parents last night. Woke them up. They're delighted. They live in Somerset. The wedding will be in their village church. And then we'll live somewhere in Cornwall, probably. Sandra loves Cornwall. She says it's a perfect place to paint. I'm going to concentrate on landscapes for a while—forget the damned portraits. If I invest what I've got wisely, I'll be in good shape financially. And of course Sandra will be working. She suggests I get drunk before I board the plane."

"Jamie, how marvelous," Thea said. She put her hand on his, and he smiled into her face. "What a lovely surprise."

"Wait. Wait just a minute," Nell said. "You are talking about Sandra Kilburn, your student?"

"Obviously."

"And how long have you two been—whatever. Involved."

"Not quite as long as you two have," he said—reproachfully, somehow, as if long involvements were particularly sinful. "Not for years. Months is more like it. Since last winter."

"Jamie—where? When?"

She was stunned. It was like the revelation of another plane of existence below the one she knew, a sinister shadow world peopled by strangers. And then she realized that Jamie must have felt the same when he saw her and Thea embracing on the lawn.

"The student-teacher relationship is often a highly emotional one, Nell," he said. "Especially in the arts. Sandra and I have become very close. She's an extremely gifted painter, as you know. Though of course her profession is that of art instructor in a school."

"Oh Jamie, don't be so pompous," Nell said. "This is wonderful news. I'm so glad. Do you mean to say that you two have been having a *relationship* up there in your studio? On that squeaky old cot? Since last winter?" She got up and went around the table to hug him. He smelled vaguely of aftershave—leftover from last night. That too was a secret. "And you're in love? And Sandra? She really—?"

Thea frowned at her and she stopped. Sandra was no more than thirty, an Englishwoman who had come over with her American husband. They had been divorced a year or so ago. Nell had met her a couple of times—a stocky redhead, not unattractive in a gym-teacher sort of way, with an accent that sounded overdone. She had once complained to Nell that in America you couldn't get milk with cream on top. *Cream you don't need, honey,* Nell had thought.

"Yes, believe it or not," Jamie said, squirming away from her embrace. "She loves me too. She's most anxious to get married. And she's very homesick for England. She's given notice at the school. We're going to leave as soon as we can get organized. In a month or so, we hope."

Nell sat down again. "Well, I'll be damned, Jamie. All I can say is, it's about time."

"I'll bet that's not all you can say, Nellie. I'll bet you two will have plenty to say when I'm gone."

They sat looking at each other, and then they began to laugh. Thea joined in, and the three of them spontaneously took hands, like people at a seance, laughing like maniacs. Nell thought: this should have happened years ago, all of it, the truth should have come out, all the truth. Thea was right, truth is better. She thought of Jack Wentworth, who had died of cancer last winter—of the night she had revealed to him, a man she hardly knew, the great truth of her life. She squeezed Jamie's hand and laughed with tears in her eyes. Then she saw that they were all crying a little, and that made them laugh harder and let go hands to wipe their eyes with napkins.

When they calmed down, Jamie looked at his watch and said, "I should be going. I'm picking Sandra up for church."

"Church?"

He grinned again—the new Jamie: easygoing, cheerful, a fiancé, a churchgoer. "Sandra goes to the Episcopalian church on James Street. She wants me to go with her so she can introduce me to the rector."

"My God," Nell said. "Jamie, you've been an atheist since—"

"Since Peggy died."

How shocking his rage and bitterness had seemed because he was only eleven. Little Jamie, the pet. "Forty-two years," she said.

"You don't have to believe in God to go to church with the woman you love," he said, and Thea shook her head, agreeing, her eyes misting over again.

Jamie stood up. "I want to say one more thing, Nell. Thea." He pursed up his lips again but it wasn't the same. He would always be different now: she would never see him as he used to be. And how had that been? She'd never known him, and vice versa. The thought came to her: *I don't know him, but I do love him*—old Jamie, her baby brother. She could remember him in diapers, Peggy changing him, saying baby shit looked like cooked squash.

"What, Jamie dear?" Thea asked. Sometimes she went too far.

Jamie looked at her anxiously. "I apologize for what I said yesterday about you two, Thea. I'm sure Nell told you how upset I was. It was a shock, I admit it. You think you know someone, and—"

"Life is stranger than you think, Jamie," Nell said, looking sharply at him. "And it's much more interesting that way."

"No, no, I know that, Nell. Don't get mad at me all over again. I had a long talk with Sandra last night. She's very tolerant, very— wise about things like this."

"English," Nell said, nodding at Thea. Thea smiled and, under the table, pressed Nell's bare foot with her own.

"And you were absolutely right, Nellie," Jamie went on. His voice was jerky, forced. He was doing his duty, making a speech. She imagined Sandra squeezing a promise out of him. *Jamie, my deah boy, you ebsolutely mahst a-pole-ow-gize.* "What you said yesterday. That as long as you love someone. And if things are a bit unorthodox, well—I mean, I know people will say things about Sandra and me. I'm more than twenty years older than she is. I'm practically an old man, and she's so—" He gestured vaguely, with his secret smile. "So I just want to say that I think it's fine about the two of you. Who am I to—" He stuck his hands abruptly in his pockets and jingled his keys. "As long as we're all happy," shrugging, and then beaming at them with his new, youthful grin.

They embraced him at the door, and when he was gone they made a fresh pot of tea and ate more scones. There were endless things to talk about. They decided that Thea would move in when Jamie left. They'd split everything fifty-fifty. Thea could stop paying her exorbitant rent; it would give her a lot more money; they could easily afford England. They could go over for the wedding. They could visit Nell's old friend Gillian Welsh, who was in a nursing home in London, and they could see the Turner exhibit at the British Museum. And they could buy Jamie and Sandra a wedding present over there and save shipping—get something arty in a craft shop. They said over and over that they couldn't believe it—old Jamie— what next? Finally, when two more pots of tea were drunk, when they couldn't stuff in another sip, another bite, when they had thoroughly hashed over Sandra and Jamie and the wedding and their trip and their new life and how unbelievable it all was, they began to believe it.

Except that a voice in Nell's head kept saying: it's too perfect, it can't last, I don't deserve it. She imagined herself alone someday, living in the house she had shared first with Jamie, then with Jamie and Caroline, now with Thea. How much harder it would be. How bereft she would be, how black the void. They both assumed, always, that Thea would die first. Nell had the constitution of a tank, the energy of a girl in her teens. Thea had ailments—all kinds, and she was past sixty. She had no gall bladder, no uterus, cataracts forming, arthritis in one foot. Breast cancer ran in her family, her mother and sister had both died of it . . .

Jamie was gone, Thea would die. Even Dinah—her fifth Dinah, after all—wouldn't live forever. And there Nell would be, alone. She'd have nothing again—just the relatives coming to see her once a year, at Thanksgiving. All that arguing. Teddy drunk, Lucy nursing her bad memories, Mark being alternately sarcastic and silent. And the kids—well, not really kids anymore. Not the sweet little people she used to cuddle. Heather primping in the bathroom, Margaret with her nose in a book, Peter such a smart alec—like that time he cursed Teddy, and Teddy didn't say a word, just poured himself another drink. Poor little Ann on tranquilizers and antidepressants, stuck away in those terrible schools, at the age of ten, eleven. Half the family vegetarians, refusing the turkey. Even poor old Mr. Fahey wouldn't make it to many more dinners. But Thea's empty place at the foot of the table would be the worst.

Thea bustled around the kitchen. Dirty dishes in the dishwasher, leftover scones in a plastic bag, tea leaves into the compost. She hummed the Bach cantata as she worked; she had a rich, pretty voice, slightly off. Nell sat in her chair watching her. She remembered the first time Thea had come to her house, an afternoon in early spring. They had sat in the living room and drunk sherry. A spar of sunlight lay across Thea's chest. Nell had raised her hand, and the gray shadow of her finger in the sun touched Thea. A phantom touching her breast, stroking it. Thea had noticed nothing. Nell had trembled with desire and then, in shame, clenched her hands together in her lap. Then that night they had talked, she had confessed everything, and Thea had touched her in just that way, the way Nell's shadow had. But not a shadow. A flesh-and-blood woman. The love of her life.

She wanted to tell Thea she was scared. She knew she was like Jamie in some ways—she had the melancholy streak that all the Kerwins seemed to have, and she was, underneath it all, timid and afraid of change. Afraid also that if Thea lived with her, got to know her that extra, intimate bit more, she would stop loving her.

To get rid of her fears, she joked. "Can't you just see Jamie as the perfect English gentleman? He'll wear tweeds and pick up Sandra's accent and write indignant letters to the *London Times* about people letting their dogs foul the footpaths."

"Poor Jamie," Thea said. "He's going to be a respectable married man soon, Nell. You shouldn't make fun of him."

"What nonsense," Nell said. "God wouldn't have created people like Jamie if he didn't mean us to laugh at them." And then, when they were going upstairs to get dressed, she caught Thea's arm and blurted it out. "You won't desert me, will you?"

Thea paused on the step above her. Even in her ratty old bathrobe she looked regal. And still beautiful, not a mass of wrinkles like Nell. It paid off to be a tad plump. Nell wanted to put her arms around her and rub her face against Thea's stomach, but she waited to see what she would say.

"Will you, Thea?"

Thea looked down at her and slowly shook her head. "Nell, you are such an ass." Nell blushed: just what she had said to Jamie. "Why would I desert you?" Thea said. "You're my whole life, you idiot."

She did put her arms around her, and they stood there like that for a few moments. Three years later, when Thea was dead, that was the morning she would keep remembering as almost the best.

They carried their work to the backyard and spread it out on the picnic table. It was term paper time, and they each had a stack of them to grade—Nell's on *Dubliners* and *The Wasteland,* Thea's on the fall of Rome and the rise of Christianity.

But it was a beautiful afternoon, hard to get going. Nell walked around the yard, deadheading tulips, followed by the cat. "What a relief it is," Nell said suddenly. "To have someone know. To tell someone. To say it!"

"Isn't it?"

They smiled at each other. Nell thought she would die of this happiness, she would fly up into the air she was so happy, the world was such a perfect place.

"Come here," Thea said. "Smell the lilacs."

They stood, sniffing, in front of the bush Nell's mother had planted in 1935. "My God, Thea," she said. "Do you realize Jamie has never lived anywhere but this house? Even when he was in art school he lived at home. He's never traveled, never gone away on a vacation. I'm trying to think if he's even spent a night anywhere else in his whole life."

"It's really a wonderful thing," Thea said. "At his age."

"At any age."

If someone had looked out a window, they would have seen what Jamie had seen the afternoon before: two aging women, one tall and plump, one tall and skinny—one in a long skirt and peasant blouse with her hair tied up in a scarf, the other in jeans and bright red socks and sandals, her gray hair frizzy and wild. They stood in the sunshine with their arms around each other.

Lucy 1978

THE PARTING with Jerome was bitter. Jerome had begged her to go to California with him—he couldn't make it without her, he said. He was a television producer with a small cocaine problem that she knew was getting bigger. Their affair had been going on for three years, but it wasn't until he asked her to go away with him that she knew she didn't dare commit herself to someone like Jerome.

When he saw she meant it, he had threatened to tell Mark everything. She had hit out at him, enraged. He had hit her back, and she had fled into the night and run all the way from his apartment on Mount Vernon Street to Park Street station, taking her purse with her but leaving her keys in the pocket of a jacket that hung over the chair in Jerome's bedroom. She had worried for days about those keys: should they have the locks changed? Imagining arriving home someday to find Jerome sitting at the kitchen table, laughing the way he did when he was high, ready to spill the beans. She had done nothing about it, of course: how could she? She told Mark the keys must have fallen out of the hole in her jeans pocket—showed him the ripped seam. Neither of them mentioned the bruise on her face.

The bruise faded. Every day she looked in the mirror and told herself that when the bruise was gone she would be over Jerome. It went from a deep yellowish purple, to violet, to pale purple, to nothing. It took about two weeks, and she still wasn't over Jerome—still missed him, still thought about him compulsively, was tempted to phone him, couldn't get any work done, cried the mornings away after Mark and Margaret had left.

She drove to Providence and told the whole sordid story of the breakup to Teddy, drinking tea and talking nonstop in the tiny bare kitchen of his apartment while he drank gin from a pint bottle. He let her finish, and then he said, "Oh Christ, Lucy," and began to cry.

She was flattered before she realized he was drunk. Then it became obvious that it wasn't her loss of Jerome he was crying for, it was himself. "You're so lucky," he said. "You had this thing with Jerome for three whole years. You've got that to look back on, at least." He tipped the pint up to his mouth but there was nothing left. He held it upside down and shook it. "Just like my life," he said. "Empty." He smashed the bottle hard against the side of the table. Glass flew in all directions.

Lucy jumped up. "Jesus, Teddy!" Shards of glass littered the floor, the tabletop. A piece glistened in her teacup like an ice cube. She imagined it in her eye. Reflexively, she looked for a broom, though she couldn't imagine that Teddy would have such a thing.

Teddy sat holding the jagged neck of the bottle. "Empty," he said. "And broken." He looked up at her, tears rolling down his cheeks, and they both began to laugh, out of control, holding their stomachs, wiping their eyes. Then they walked to a supermarket down the street and bought a broom and a dustpan, cleaned up the mess, and went out for pizza. Teddy had a long red cut on one finger and refused to put a Band-Aid on it—not that he had any Band-Aids. He said he wanted a visible reminder of what an asshole he was. He drank ginger ale with his pizza, and he apologized for his outburst and his self-absorption. He told Lucy she should have gone to California with Jerome.

"Okay, so it might have been hell," Teddy said. "But what's the definition of a good life if it's not the constant risk of hell?"

The next day Lucy called his old girlfriend, Marie Lindbergh, and asked her to get in touch with Teddy.

"Did he put you up to this?" was the first thing Marie asked.

"No," Lucy said. "But he needs you." She expected nothing from the call, and she wasn't sure she had the energy for it. She considered hanging up. And then what? What she really wanted to do was go upstairs and lie down, close her eyes, sleep until Margaret got home from school, and then help Margaret work on the chart she was making of the House of Windsor.

Marie said, "If he needs me he can call me himself."

"No, he can't, Marie. You know how Teddy is."

"Right. Crazy."

"He's not crazy. He's just got problems."

"Who doesn't? Teddy's always so special, his troubles are always so much worse than anyone else's. And you spoil him rotten, Lucy. You don't even let him make his own phone calls."

From the kitchen phone, if she looked out the window over the sink, Lucy could see the daffodils in bloom by the garage and remember the daffodils Jerome had bought her that last afternoon, four bunches of them at two-fifty each from a vendor on Charles Street—Jerome's grand gesture with a ten-dollar bill. Back at the apartment, they emptied a coffee can and stuck the flowers in it. Then they made love. Then Jerome made his proposal, she declined, they fought, she fled.

Lucy turned her back on the window and said, "I'm not spoiling him, Marie. Be reasonable. I'm just trying to help him. He's going through a bad time."

Marie snorted. "And coping with it in his usual fashion, I suppose."

"What do you mean?"

"Oh, come on, Lucy."

She could picture Marie—a crude caricature, she always thought, of the wholesome Swedish beauty: yellow hair, red cheeks, pink lips, blue eyes, big white breasts. Marie would be looking irritated, glancing down at her watch, drumming her fingers on a tabletop. Lucy had deliberately called Marie during what she knew were her working hours, so she would catch her home. Marie was a freelance journalist, like Teddy. Lucy and Marie had been friends during the time Marie and Teddy lived together, but Marie had always made her slightly uncomfortable. She always said exactly what she meant, and she never shrank from asking embarrassing questions: it probably made her a good journalist, but it made her a difficult friend.

"He only drinks when he's lonely," Lucy said. "If you went back with him he wouldn't do it."

"Is he drinking now?"

Was he drinking now. She didn't know what to say. He had certainly been drinking the day before. On the other hand, he had been chastened, had switched to ginger ale. And over pizza he had told her that the local Gilbert and Sullivan group had asked him to play Koko in *The Mikado.* He had been cheerful, had sung "Taken from the county jail" while they walked back to his apartment.

"Not really," Lucy said, hoping it was true. "Considering."

"Considering what?"

"Well, he's lonely. He's not working at the moment, and he really doesn't have any good friends in Providence since Dave moved to Iowa. He's living all alone in a studio apartment on Benefit Street. And he misses Ann like crazy."

There was a pause as Marie registered this, and Lucy felt the first faint surge of hope. Marie said, "Ann is still at that school, then? She's sticking it out?"

"She really likes it," Lucy said.

It was only a small exaggeration. Ann had been there since September—at Saint Basil's, somewhere on the Hudson, a school Kay had found when Ann became impossible for either her or Teddy to handle. *A Center for Caring Discipline,* was how the place advertised itself, and the entire first semester Teddy had ranted against it.

"They take a cold shower every morning at six," he told Lucy. "And then they run two miles, rain or shine or snow or whatever. And then they have breakfast, which is milk and porridge. Can you see Ann eating porridge? Running? Those fat little legs? And then they have classes from eight until four, and Latin is compulsory, and so is phys ed. And every night after dinner they line up and march into the kitchen to wash their own dishes. I mean, leave it to Kay to find a place where they wash their own dishes—Kay who wouldn't know a dishcloth from a clothespin."

Lucy did admit that the school sounded extreme—so stereotypically Dickensian, in fact, that she wondered if Saint Basil's was an institution devoted chiefly to irony. Mark said it was absurd, Teddy had to be exaggerating. Lucy called Kay, who told her coldly that it was a perfectly respectable boarding school, Ethel Kennedy had sent one of her children there, it had a dedicated faculty and a long list of distinguished alumni, and if Lucy was so concerned about it she could damn well help with the fees, and besides, what else were they supposed to do with Ann, what other fucking choice did they have, and tell Teddy he could quit involving his goddam relatives in his family's personal business.

Teddy said that Ann's compulsory weekly letters home had become gradually less outraged and hysterical as well as neater and better spelled. She still complained about the showers and the running, as well as the Latin, in which she was doing poorly, and the food, which didn't improve. Teddy still called the headmaster Kaiser

Wilhelm and wrote to him regularly, reminding him that Ann was only eight years old and protesting the effects of cold showers on her delicate constitution; the Kaiser wrote back with good reports of Ann, saying she was running the two miles with ease and hadn't had a cold all winter. Teddy grumbled, but his harangues stopped, and he settled down to simply bitching about Kay and wishing he had his daughter back. Not working. Living thinly off the proceeds of the book he'd written in 1973. Breaking gin bottles because his life was empty.

"Ann is doing great," Lucy said. "It's Teddy who's got problems."

"Those kids of his are his biggest problem."

"Heather goes off to college in the fall."

"Where?"

"Berkeley, probably."

"Ah. West Coast. I like that. And what about Peter the psychopath?"

"Peter's with Kay, of course. Permanently. He and Teddy can't live together, Marie, you know that. He's Kay's son, anyway, not Teddy's." Then she added, with the sense of playing a trump card she'd been hoarding up her sleeve, "Ann only comes home for two days at Thanksgiving and a week at Christmas, plus for two weeks in the summer, and Kay has her half that time."

"Lucy, you're not going to talk me into this." From the way she said it, Lucy knew Marie had been thinking about Teddy. Marie lived in Boston, but Lucy never saw her; the breakup of Marie and Teddy had been epic, and had reverberated. The last she'd heard, in a letter from Dave in Iowa, Marie was seeing some scientist from M.I.T. who was about to be tapped for a big job in Washington. *Seems a bit establishment for Marie,* Dave had written. *Sounds like a reaction against Ted, if you ask me.*

"Just call him, Marie. He could use a friend, if nothing else."

"You don't know what I went through with that kid."

"Yes, I do," Lucy said. "We all went through it."

"Honey, I lived there. I've still got a scar on my shin where that little animal threw a tape recorder at me."

The tape recorder incident was famous: Ann's midnight tantrum, Marie's intervention, the Sony portable hurled at her, the emergency room, the stitches. "I know, Marie. It wasn't easy for you."

"Easy! It was living hell. And I actually loved him, Lucy. I really did. I loved that schmuck."

"He loved you, too," Lucy said, though she wasn't positive that was true. "I get the feeling he still does."

"Oh shit."

"He's so lonely, Marie." Lucy pressed her advantage. "I feel so bad for him. I drive down to Providence every week or so, just to give him someone to talk to."

"Yes, but you're a fool, Lucy. You know that?"

Anger overtook her—not so much at Marie as at Teddy. The same anger she had felt when he broke the bottle: that her brother should put her through these things. Marie was absolutely right, she had spoiled him rotten. She said, "Okay, forget it, Marie. I'm not in the mood for abuse. I've got troubles of my own. I'm sorry I called."

"No—no, Lucy, I'm really glad to hear from you," Marie said, her voice suddenly warm. Because she'd won some minor power game? Because she was a genuinely good person? "Maybe I'll get in touch with him after all. I'm sorry to be such a pain in the ass about it. I've been going through a tough time myself, but I really kind of miss him. Give me his number, what the hell."

Lucy gave her Teddy's number, trying not to let her optimism get out of control. Marie would probably never call him; if she did, they'd argue and hang up on each other; if they did get together, it couldn't last. She remembered the brief time Teddy and Marie had lived together, nearly two years ago—the way Marie had relieved her of Teddy's burdens, had brought Teddy out of his depression following the divorce—had even, it seemed at first, been good for Ann. That had been a wonderful time, a perfect interlude in Lucy's life—

when was it? January to August, last year. Her best months with Jerome.

Briefly, she and Marie exchanged information about themselves. Lucy told her about the contract she had signed with the calendar people. Marie told Lucy about her breakup with the scientist and her interview with Pat Nixon for *Ms.*

"I asked her what keeps her going," Marie said. "I always ask people that. You get some interesting answers. You know—what gets you out of bed in the morning. Pat Nixon gave this perfectly awful laugh and told me it's the challenge of seeing if she's going to make it through the day. I didn't print that, of course. But it reminded me of you, Lucy."

"Me?" She was startled, thinking of Pat Nixon in San Clemente. The mighty fallen. Her husband walking on the beach in a business suit, making his stiff jokes, golfing with gangsters.

"It was the kind of thing you used to say when you were talking about leaving Mark. What's happening with you, anyway? Are you still seeing the cute guy with the beard? Are you and Mark still together, or what?"

"Still together," Lucy said. Remembering her long talks with Marie, Lucy felt embarrassment. In those days, she had been going to leave Mark, definitely, it was just a matter of time. "I broke up with the cute guy with the beard," she said, her throat constricting. "Too old to change, I guess."

"I have to admit I'm surprised. Whenever I think about you, Lucy, I always think: well, she's probably left him by now. Probably remarried to someone really great, some interesting guy, a trumpeter in a jazz band or a famous writer. John Updike, I think. Lucy's probably run away with John Updike by now."

Lucy laughed and touched her cheekbone where the bruise had been. The scene with Jerome came back to her: curses, threats, blows—all of it so unexpected, so particularly horrible after that unseasonably silky spring afternoon, their long walk, the daffodils.

And here she was with Mark. There were never any scenes with Mark. They didn't fight; they clammed up. It was one of the things they had in common—that, the house, their daughter. Also their long history of anguish, though that seemed very far away. Hard to believe they had ever turned to each other for comfort, made love frantically in hope of another pregnancy, wept for joy when Margaret was delivered safely. All those times in the hospital, Lucy weak and grieving, Mark holding her hand—Lucy looked back on them with astonishment: another world. After the last time (a boy, Jonathan, who nearly made it) she had thought she would surely die, drown in the blood or fade away from sorrow. *No more,* they said. Lucy had her tubes tied. That year, she stopped eating meat and started taking pictures again. They bought the house in Brookline, set up a darkroom. Lucy enrolled in the M.F.A. program at B.U. And she and Mark had gradually withdrawn from one another into what Lucy believed had been the true nature of their marriage all along, its naked reality: sterility.

"Sorry, Marie," she said. "I'm still hanging in there."

"Then let me ask you my question. What gets you out of bed every morning?"

"Oh Lord." She stood up and went to the stove to put on the teakettle. There were the daffodils against the green wall of the garage, the wind whipping them hard. The tight brown lilac buds, the tulips, the primroses exposed along the driveway—all of them being tortured by the wind. "That's a cruel question," Lucy said. "Don't ask me to answer it. Isn't it enough that I do get out of bed? Every single goddam morning of my life?"

. . . . .

WHEN THEY hung up, Lucy took a cup of tea and two aspirin into the living room and sat in the wing chair beside the fireplace. Mentally, she ticked things off. Teddy. Marie. Margaret. Did Mark get the tickets for the Red Sox opener. What else. Tomorrow the darkroom,

then lunch with Philip, show him the Maine photographs. What else.
Prune the roses. What else. What else. Run away with John Updike.

In February, when she was in the tiny town of East Waterford,
Maine, she had gone out for an early morning walk and seen moose
tracks: perfectly round, bisected like the peace signs from the sixties,
two pairs of them ambling up the muddy dirt road behind the inn
and then veering off into the snowy pine woods. She had waited
with her camera in the raw morning air, knee-deep in wet snow,
hoping to catch sight of a moose. What a shot for the calendar: that
bizarre and magnificent animal glimpsed through the bare trees or
silhouetted against a pale sky. She waited until her fingers and toes
were numb, rehearsing the description of the scene she would give
to Jerome when she telephoned him that night. She would tell him
about the tracks, the woods, the dirt road winding away beyond the
trees, the odd sensation she had in that deserted place of being
watched. He would admire her pluck, her dedication, her feeling for
her craft. Standing there freezing, she was overcome with love for
him and with the awful, fatalistic knowledge that it was him she
would leave—not her husband.

Someone—probably Marie—had once said to her, "Frankly,
Lucy, I don't see what you get out of your marriage." Lucy had
answered, unhesitatingly, "Safety, security," but when she was asked,
"What kind of security? Safety from what?" she had no answer. What
she meant went beyond the two words: what she meant was the
bond she and Mark had forged over the years in blood and sorrow.
We've been through so much, she would think to herself. And in the
Maine woods waiting for a moose that never showed up, or fighting
with Jerome in his apartment, or sitting in her pristine living room
with a headache, she still couldn't find an answer. She sipped her tea
and thought, prune the roses. Ask Mark about the tickets. Take the
lentil soup out of the freezer.

. . . . .

"YOU NEED another Jerome," Teddy said to her over pizza.

"Don't be cynical," she responded.

. . . . .

SHE HAD lunch with Philip Talner and brought along her photographs from Maine. Philip had been her photography teacher in graduate school and had helped her land the calendar job. He was older than she, long divorced, well known, proud of her small successes. They had lunch together every couple of weeks.

She met him at a restaurant on Newbury Street and saw immediately that he was upset and distracted. Their lunches made Lucy nervous: she always felt slightly on the spot with Philip, like a prize pupil in an especially demanding class. Things were complicated because he insisted on paying the check, and by the fact that once, in the darkroom, he had stood behind her, put his hands on her shoulders, kissed the back of her neck, and then said, without explanation, "Forgive me, Lucy."

It was typical of him. He was given to enigmatic utterances, to grand gestures followed by ambiguity. His students complained that they never knew what he really thought: he would critique a photograph harshly in class, then choose it for a student exhibit. He was a kind man, but he had picked one of Lucy's photographs for a show—a shot of a shabby elderly couple buying a cabbage at a farm stand—and given it the cruel title, *Vegetables.* Sometimes, when she felt she most needed guidance, he would refuse to say a word, and just when she'd thought he was disgusted with her work, he had recommended her for the calendar job.

She knew something was wrong because he didn't mention the portfolio under her arm. She put it on the floor against her chair. Philip sat looking sadly at the menu, raking his fingers through his thinning black hair, and then he began to tell her about his trip to New York to clean out his father's apartment.

Old Mr. Talner, Lucy knew, had been killed on the street during a robbery—stabbed by the boy who stole his wallet. It was the kind of death that was almost as disturbing to Lucy as that of her own mother. "I couldn't stand to look at his stuff," Philip said. "I gave every single thing he owned to Goodwill, including the dishes and his underwear and his books and some good pieces of furniture. I just had them haul it away, I couldn't cope with it."

"I'm sorry, Philip," Lucy said. "I know what that's like. I remember going through that with my mother's stuff."

He smiled at her. "It's not so bad for you. You're still young. When you're my age all you can think is mortality. And not your parents'. Your own."

Lucy had a sudden panicky vision of the junk in her desk, the drawers finically neat but full of bombshells nonetheless: a couple of letters from Jerome, a photograph, ticket stubs, a fortune from a Chinese cookie that said, "Make this moment last a lifetime." She remembered the note in her mother's underwear drawer. She had never forgiven her for it, and she had no desire to do so—to talk it over with a therapist, for instance, or with Mark or Jerome or her mother's sister Nell. She felt it was important to keep that small nugget of resentment.

"Did you go through all this alone?" she asked Philip.

He shrugged. "My sister lives in Saint Paul. My son and daughter are busy with their own lives. Who was I going to rope into such a distasteful task?"

"You could have asked me," she said. "I would have gone with you."

He put his hand on hers and said, "Ah, Lucy." They looked at each other for a moment, and then he released her hand and picked up the menu again, smiling slightly. She studied his face, the bushy eyebrows, beaked nose, thin-lipped humorous mouth. It was a face she would have loved to photograph, but she didn't dare ask, and she couldn't imagine showing him the result.

He looked up from the menu and said, "Why don't we have lunch and then take your portfolio over to my apartment so we can really look at it?"

She said, "Fine," and knew she would end up going to bed with him, not because she loved him or even wanted him, specifically, but because she knew he needed her and because she owed him so much and missed Jerome and was unhappy with Mark. She had known it when she walked into the restaurant—before that, when she ate pizza with Teddy—and maybe even before that: that last night with Jerome, when she told him good-bye, she had known—cynically or not—that there would have to be another Jerome.

. . . . .

ON THE day Mark took Margaret to the Red Sox opener, Lucy went to Providence to have lunch with Teddy. They ate at his apartment; Teddy had a jug of Gallo burgundy and frozen cheese ravioli in little foil trays. He had seen Marie twice. He was seeing her the next night, in fact; she was going to watch a *Mikado* rehearsal, and then he was taking her out to dinner.

"It can't last," he said. "Marie's a sensible woman."

"Don't be so pessimistic, Teddy."

He shrugged and refilled his glass with wine. "A woman is only a woman, but a slug of Gallo is a drink."

"I don't know how you can start drinking so early in the afternoon."

"I don't. I start in the morning."

"Oh, Teddy." She ate a bite of ravioli and looked with revulsion at the glass of wine in front of her; if she didn't drink at least part of it, she would look prissy and disapproving. She took another forkful and then picked up her glass and sipped.

"Well?" Teddy asked. "Truly an extraordinary vintage, don't you think?"

"Yeah, it's great."

He looked at her with concern. "Hey, Luce? Is something bothering you?"

"No."

"No? Really?"

"Really." She wanted to tell him she was sleeping with Philip; she always wanted to tell Teddy things. But all the ways she could think of to say it made it sound sordid or hypocritical or pathetic. There was no plausible way she could say how unexpectedly happy she and Philip were together. She said, "Mark and Margaret and I are going to England for the last two weeks in June."

"Oh God, poor you. Two weeks trapped on that tiny island with the Duke of Boredom."

She smiled. "It won't be so bad. We'll be sightseeing, moving around. I'll be taking photographs. We're going to Stonehenge, and we'll probably see some plays in London." *Call me,* Philip had said. *Call me collect from the Tower of London.* "And of course Margaret wants to do all the Royal Family stuff. You know how she is." She took a sip of wine. "We're leaving on the nineteenth."

"Of June? That's the day Mom died."

"I know. Five years."

"Christ."

Teddy poured himself more wine. Lucy thought as she often did about how Teddy's reckless lonely life seemed suicidal at times. Every time she climbed the steps to his place, she had half a fear that she would find him dead—an overdose of something, or his wrists slit with the shard of a broken bottle—leaving her to clean out his junk, give it to Goodwill, explain his death to Heather and Peter and Ann. She had a horror of suicide because she had no understanding of it. She was well acquainted with the various degrees of depression that stopped short of sheer despair; she was just coming out of one. But as she told Marie, she always, for whatever reason, got out of bed in the morning. She was unable to imagine the particular madness that led to self-destruction.

And yet their mother—the most hardheaded of women, the most self-absorbed and self-sufficient—had killed herself, a fact no one knew but Lucy. Not knew: just strongly suspected. That was how she would put it to anyone she told. But she had never told anyone, not even Teddy. Least of all Teddy.

Not that there was much to tell. An enigmatic remark her mother had made when she was seeing that doctor: one of Caroline's unsuitable suitors, as Aunt Nell used to call the men who flocked around when Stewart finally died—as if they had been waiting in the wings while he coughed himself to death. The doctor was perhaps the worst of the lot; Lucy and Mark had met him once and thought him merely tedious, a foul-mouthed compulsive joke teller. "Good old Mort," Caroline used to call him, and once she had added, "Thanks to him I'll never have to get old and sick." There was that, and there was the note Lucy found under a pile of Caroline's silk underpants.

"I miss that crazy old broad," Teddy said. "In spite of the fact that she claimed that having kids wrecked her life. Do you remember that?"

"She probably didn't mean it."

"Oh, no?"

"Well, maybe she did. But it didn't matter in the end."

"When all she wanted was Dad."

Lucy nodded, and then said, impulsively, "Teddy, I really wish you'd try with Marie. I think you'd be so good for each other."

"Like beets." He poured the last of the wine into his glass. "Like tofu burgers."

"It's time you settled down and lived like a normal person."

"What? Like you and the King of Ennui?"

"Sure. Why not? It's something, Teddy."

He picked the wine bottle up by the neck and held it poised above the table. "You're trying to say my life is empty?"

"No!"

Laughing, she reached for the bottle. Teddy set it down and said,

"Good." He leaned back and folded his arms, staring at her. He looked older lately. The moustache he considered essential for the part of Koko didn't help. Lucy had photographed her brother dozens of times. He was always a willing subject, he'd pose under any conditions, any time, for as long as necessary. But none of the photographs were a success; she had never captured what she considered the real Teddy, the one she saw now, sitting in the white sunlight by the kitchen window, who looked as if nothing mattered to him, nothing ever had or ever could except the present moment: now.

She wondered if she would ever love anyone the way she loved her brother.

"You're a pain," she said. "You know that?"

"I certainly do." He picked up his wineglass and drained it, looking at her steadily with his ironic smile.

Margaret
1974

HE YEAR Margaret was six, there were twelve people at Aunt Nell's for Thanksgiving dinner. Even Aunt Kay showed up, after three years of refusing to associate with her husband's family. Aunt Kay with her diamonds and her French cigarettes. Margaret liked to look at her and Uncle Teddy together. They were like no one else: Teddy tall and curly-haired and elegant, wearing a cashmere jacket and, sometimes, a silk ascot; and plump, beautiful Kay, wearing something long and silky and smelling of Chanel No. 22. Margaret knew they fought a lot when they were at home, but that year at Aunt Nell's they always sat near each other, and sometimes he would reach over and touch her shoulder or link his pinky finger with hers, and she would smile at him. When she put her head back to blow smoke at the ceiling you could see her silver eyelids, and her long eyelashes stuck together with mascara.

Margaret liked Aunt Kay because she paid no attention to children. She neither made a fuss over them nor scolded them; she simply ignored them, her own included. When Margaret threw a tantrum or Heather started showing off, Aunt Kay went into her own world—lit a cigarette and made herself a drink, crossed her legs and hummed an old song and blew smoke at the ceiling. Uncle Teddy was the kind of adult who made a fuss, but he was always fun, so nobody minded. He couldn't yell at the kids without making it into a joke. He used to ride Margaret around on his shoulders, and he was so tall that her head would have hit the light fixtures if he hadn't walked hunched over with his knees bent—his ape walk, he called it, and when he did it he talked the way he pretended apes talked. "Me—want—food," he would growl in a deep voice as he slouched into the kitchen, carrying his glass in one hand, and Margaret would have to reach into the cookie jar on the refrigerator and cram a cookie into his mouth. "Thanks, human," he would mutter, and when he finished the cookie he always said, "Me—want—more." He could eat gingersnaps forever. Sometimes Aunt Nell told him to stop, for heaven's sake—as if he were a little kid. Sometimes, when he came into a room, Margaret's father left it.

Margaret's mother was going to have a baby, and she had to be careful. They all said that: "Lucy has to be careful." More careful, they meant, than ordinary people who had to be careful crossing streets and not spilling their milk and running with scissors. She sat down a lot; some days she stayed in bed. They weren't letting her help with the Thanksgiving dinner. She just sat in the living room with Dinah on her lap and talked to Mr. Fahey while Aunt Nell and her friend Thea cooked dinner. Her mother didn't even bring the two pumpkin pies she usually did. Aunt Kay had brought pies—her own creation: apple-pumpkin tarts, plus a gadget she had bought for the occasion that you filled with cream and it squirted it out whipped.

"Don't let Peter get his hands on *that*," Uncle Teddy said, ruffling his son's hair. Peter danced around Heather and Ann and made squirting motions.

"Will someone please control that child," Heather said, and Ann began to cry. Aunt Kay left the room, trailing smoke.

"Why don't you kids go up and play in the attic?" Uncle Teddy suggested. He picked Ann up and hefted her over his shoulder like a sack of something. She stopped crying and began to giggle. "Come on, I'll escort you up. Let's go, Annie. Margaret and Heather will protect you from that wild animal."

Peter made wild animal noises all the way to the attic. He was twelve, and out of control. All the grown-ups said he was, except Mr. Fahey, who was too polite, and Aunt Kay, who ignored her son. Uncle Teddy said it fondly, but Margaret's parents said it sternly, and Aunt Nell always said it with exasperation, looking like she wanted to tear her hair at the thought of him. Every once in a while a grown-up would say, "Is someone keeping an eye on Peter?" and they'd send Heather to go and find him. The Thanksgiving before, he had gone into the garage and smoked cigarettes in Uncle Jamie's new Chevy, burning a hole in the upholstery. He had also decorated the dining room with a roll of toilet paper, but that wasn't as bad, and he had meant well, Uncle Teddy said; he had really meant it to look nice, the pink paper draped over the chairs, the china, the wineglasses, and hanging from the chandelier in streamers. "I doubt that," Heather had said, and Uncle Teddy got mad at her, and Aunt Nell got mad at Uncle Teddy.

Aunt Nell hated Peter, Margaret knew. She always stuck up for the girls, except for Aunt Kay, whom she detested and who detested her back. When Margaret's grandmother Caroline died, Aunt Kay had gone upstairs after the funeral and tried to walk out with Grandma's leopard coat. Aunt Nell tried to stop her, and Kay said, "Caroline told me she wanted me to have it," and Aunt Nell said, "Oh, my God, the woman is pathological." They got into a fight, ending with slapping, Uncle Jamie holding them apart. Margaret had watched it all, on the front steps, holding the coat after they dropped it, rubbing her cheek against the soft spotted fur.

The attic was enormous, obsessively neat, and nearly empty, full of dusty beige light from the windows and the attic dormer. Two bare lightbulbs with pull chains hung from the ceiling, one on each side of the chimney. At the end of each chain was a miniature red plastic fire hydrant.

There was plenty of space to run around in the attic, even though one whole side of it was walled off to make a bedroom. It had been Uncle Jamie's room when he was a boy, when there were five children and two parents living in a four-bedroom house. Margaret and her cousins loved that room. It still had Uncle Jamie's bed in it, a high, narrow bed like an old-fashioned sleigh. The bedspread was black with cat hair: Dinah liked to sleep up there, away from it all. On the dresser was a collection of jointed wooden animals—giraffe, monkey, tiger, a dozen others—which the children were forbidden to play with, but Peter did anyway. One drawer of the dresser held odd bits of Uncle Jamie's drawing equipment, pieces of charcoal, chalks that crumbled when you tried to use them, pristine pads of yellowing paper, a wooden ruler that said BYRNE DAIRY MILK IS MIGHTY FINE, and a pencil box with a sliding top. They were allowed to use the drawing materials if they were careful with them, and there was a box under the bed full of drawings made by Heather and Peter and Margaret over the years, and some scribbles by Ann from last Thanksgiving.

In the closet Great-Grandpa Kerwin's clothes were hanging. They had a concentrated dust smell, the essence of the attic. Heather had discovered that when you jumped on the bed, dust and cat hair rose from it in clouds, and the cousins used to put on the big old jackets and tie the silk ties around their necks and jump on the bed to make themselves sneeze.

That Thanksgiving, Heather wouldn't play in the attic with the others. She got mad at Peter for something and clumped down the stairs with Dinah. Margaret knew it was only an excuse. The real reason was that Heather was eleven and thought she was too old to play with little kids. Ann cried when she left. Margaret felt like crying herself—Heather was the only cousin she wanted to play with—but she said, "Come on, Annie, let's look in the boxes," to calm her down. Ann was two years younger than Margaret, and a crybaby, but she and Margaret had discovered the boxes the year before, stacked in a niche by the chimney, and they had both been fascinated.

The boxes were labeled in Great-Grandma Kerwin's handwriting. A box for each of her children. Of herself there wasn't a trace. Six years after Aunt Peggy froze to death and three months after Uncle John was killed in the war, she had thrown everything she owned except her nightgowns into the furnace, and a month later she was dead of a brain tumor. She had never been to a doctor, but she knew, and she was famous in the family for foreseeing her own death. When they asked her why she had burned everything, she said, "I didn't want to make trouble," and refused to discuss it further. After she died Great-Grandpa Kerwin got sick, and Margaret had heard Aunt Nell say, "He just got smaller and thinner and sicker until finally he was gone." Margaret tried to imagine this, her disappearing great-grandpa. By the time she was born he had disappeared for good.

There was a box for each aunt and uncle. They were really great-aunts and great-uncles—the old people, most of them dead now. The box Margaret and Ann liked best was Aunt Peggy's, even though it was the smallest. Aunt Nell's had mostly old mittens and woolen scarves and flattened purses in it, and Uncle Jamie's was full of dog-eared science books. The box labeled CAROLINE was empty except for some handkerchiefs and stiff, stinky shoes. Uncle John's box was filled with his soldier suit and letters from France tied with white ribbon. Everyone had loved John, Aunt Nell had told Margaret. When he died, Great-Grandma went crazy. Talking about it, Aunt Nell had cried and smiled at the same time, and then laughed and hugged Margaret. Oh how time flies, she had said. How time does fly.

.   .   .   .   .

PETER HUNG around, dancing and imitating animals and trying to get Margaret and Ann to pay attention to him, and when they decided to play with the boxes, he came over and wanted to see. Margaret had hated Peter for so long that she no longer knew who he was or what he was like. She had seen with surprise when they arrived that morning that he was getting big. He's going to be tall like Teddy, her mother had said. Beanpole, Aunt Kay said. He's a little shit, Heather had said once.

He put his fingers around Margaret's neck and pretended to strangle her. His fingers felt grubby, but he didn't really press hard, so she ignored him and read what it said on each box. She could read and Ann couldn't. Mrs. Morelli, her teacher, said she read at sixth-grade level. She read not only the names—NELL, JAMIE, CAROLINE, PEGGY, JOHN, written in black crayon—but also Hunt's Baked Beans, Six O'Clock Coffee, Crosse & Blackwell's Fine Jams Jellies & Preserves, printed in fading red and blue letters on the sides.

"Come on, let's open one," Ann said, unimpressed, and Peter let go Margaret's neck and dragged the box labeled PEGGY out into the middle of the floor. Ann pulled away the flaps.

Mementos, Margaret's mother called the things in the boxes. *Mementos* was a beautiful word, and all Aunt Peggy's mementos were beautiful. There were silky scarves and a black shawl and a Chinese hat and an empty glass bottle with a glass stopper that still smelled like roses. There was a doll whose eyes would no longer open but who had real leather shoes and a brown wool bonnet trimmed with pink ribbon rosettes that matched her dress. There was a book called *A Girl of the Limberlost* with a picture of a butterfly on the cover. There were more old letters, tied up and stuffed in a tin box with PICKWICK INN CANDY SHOP, SAN FRANCISCO written on the top, and around the sides scenes of long-ago people in top hats and hoopskirts with horses and carriages. Under the letters was Aunt Peggy's old jewelry.

"You can play with it, but don't wreck anything and put every bit of it back," Margaret's mother had told them last year. Ann draped the shawl over her shoulders, and Margaret looked at the book, and they passed the doll back and forth. Peter wasn't very interested in the box once it was opened. He wanted the Chinese hat, but Margaret wouldn't give it to him, so he went into Uncle Jamie's old room to draw pictures of tigers.

"Let's put on all the jewelry," Margaret said. There was a necklace and bracelets for each of them, a gold chain with a half-moon pendant that Ann draped around her ear to make Margaret laugh, a ring that Margaret claimed because it was blue, her favorite color, and a pin in the shape of a cat with emerald eyes that she fastened with difficulty to the front of Ann's sweater. "These are real jewels," she said, fingering her pearls. She picked up a bracelet that looked like it was made of dead beetles and quickly put it down again. "These are worth a lot of money. Aunt Peggy must have been rich before she froze."

"It would be so cold," Ann said, making a face. They both knew that Aunt Peggy had frozen to death ice fishing on Onondaga Lake, long before they were born, even before their parents were born.

"No, it isn't," Margaret said. "You just fall asleep. My father told me."

"I couldn't go to sleep if it was that cold."

"You would if it was cold enough."

Ann wanted to pretend she was Aunt Peggy freezing to death, but Margaret didn't think it sounded like much fun—just going to sleep—and also it didn't seem right, it was so sad about Aunt Peggy, limberlost forever. Frozen as hard as the beetles. There was a picture of her on the piano downstairs with the other family faces, starting with Great-Grandpa Kerwin's mother in a long dress with a train, and ending with Margaret, Heather, Ann, and Peter posed on the front porch, all smiling for once. Aunt Peggy had dark hair pulled back from her face, and thin, straight eyebrows and a rosebud mouth.

She looked sad, as if she had, like her mother, foreseen her own death. Uncle Jamie had once said, "Margaret's the picture of Peggy, isn't she?" and Aunt Nell had replied, "Let's hope the child has a better chance in life."

When Peter called them from the bedroom they put away the jewelry. Margaret didn't want to, but she knew Ann was tired of it, and when Ann got tired of things she started fooling around. Margaret imagined her breaking the strand of blue beads and thinking up a game to play with them—Ann and Peter racing around the attic trying to hit each other with beads. She put everything carefully back in the box. She could come back after the others left. She and her parents always stayed overnight at Aunt Nell's because it was too far to drive back to Boston: her cousins and their parents lived in Albany, so they had to drive home. Margaret slept in the room that had been Aunt Peggy's, which had a bed with pineapple posts. The pineapple on each post was removable, and there was space inside to put something tiny. Last year she had hidden a silk flower from the bouquet in the hall, the year before a tiny tube of lip gloss that belonged to Thea.

The blue ring said SOUVENIR OF COLD SPRINGS in gold letters on the blue; Margaret wanted, desperately, to hide it in one of the bedposts, to keep it safe and private where she could always find it. But she would do that later, and she would snap the tiny snaps on the doll's leather shoes and take the bonnet off and stroke its golden hair, and look at *A Girl of the Limberlost* to see if she could read it. She was just beginning to read real books, with chapters.

Peter had drawn a picture of the two of them as animals. Margaret was just a tiger—well drawn, leaping through a hoop of fire and labeled with her name—but he had drawn Ann as a monkey with long brown hair all over her face and grinning gap-toothed mouth. "Look," he said. "I made you almost as ugly as you really are."

Ann grabbed the picture and ran out of the bedroom, crying. She said, "I'm going to tell Daddy," and Peter said, "Who cares." When she was gone, he looked at Margaret and laughed. "Aren't you going to cry, too? Or don't you mind being a tiger?"

She said, "It's a good drawing."

He looked surprised and said, "Thanks." He went over to the dresser and picked up the pencil box. "Come here," he said. He and Margaret sat on the bed. "Look at this."

"What?"

"This."

From the pencil box he took an eraser and handed it to Margaret. It was pink, and said Eberhard-Faber in faint gray letters. It looked unused.

"So what?"

"What does it remind you of?"

"It doesn't remind me of anything," she said. "It's an eraser."

He snickered. "It doesn't remind you of anything else?"

"No."

"That's because you're a girl. It reminds *me* of—" He took it from her and held it up. "See? You know." She shook her head.

He sighed. "What do boys have that girls don't have?"

She stood up, "Oh, I don't know, Peter, you're such a dope."

He took her hand and tried to pull her back down beside him. She twisted out of his grasp and ran to the bedroom door, but he was quicker than she was, and he slammed it shut. "Don't be a baby," he said. "A big dumb baby like Ann."

"I'm going." She knew she wasn't a baby. She wanted to cry, but she wouldn't let herself. "Let me go."

"Not yet."

The room was darker with the door shut. It was getting late. Dinner, she knew, was at four o'clock. She wondered what time it was.

He said, "You want to see my thing?"

"No." What thing? She didn't care. "I'm going down. I'm going to tell if you don't let me go."

He stood against the door, smiling at her. "Just look at this."

He unzipped his brown pants and pulled it out. She had never seen one before, except on babies. It was bigger than she expected, much bigger than the eraser. He held it in his hand, like a hose. It was deadly white, whiter than his hand in the dim light, and there was scraggly hair around it, like the hair he drew on Ann's monkey face.

Peter waggled it and said, "See? Want to touch it?"

She put her weight against him and pushed with her shoulder. Still smiling, he let her push him, he fell back with an exaggerated stumble, still holding his thing. He was laughing softly, a horrible, artificial laugh that had nothing to do with her, it shut her out, it was all Peter's, but at the same time she knew she was the one he was laughing at.

She opened the door and ran out, across the brown darkness of the attic. "If you tell, I'll kill you," she heard him say. Her own footsteps scared her, heavy and thumping. She ran down the wooden stairs, almost falling, fearing he would come after her. At the bottom, in the safety of the upstairs hall, she slammed the attic door and listened. She heard nothing except the thud of her heart and the conversation from down in the kitchen, but she imagined him creeping down the attic stairs, suppressing his laughter, and bursting out to frighten her. She ran into the room where she slept and shut the door.

Dinah was curled on the pineapple bed, sleeping. Even when Margaret lay down beside her she didn't stir: a round ball like a doughnut, her black tail trapped under her paws, her black wedge of a face scrunched quiet. There was white under her chin, one V-shaped patch where she liked to be stroked, but you couldn't see it when she was all curled up. Margaret whispered, "Wake up, Dinah, Dinah, Dinah," and the cat lifted her head up sleepily and blinked, then yawned and began to purr.

Margaret lay petting her, listening for noises from the attic. She had slept in this bed on Thanksgiving for as long as she could remember. The bedspread was pale blue chenille striped with fluffy ridges, with a flower design in the middle. Her great-grandpa Kerwin had slept in the room across the hall until he got so small he died. Then Grandma Caroline had lived in it, and now her parents slept there when they visited. But this room had never belonged to anyone but Aunt Peggy, as far as Margaret knew. She imagined living in this house herself, when she was old, old as Aunt Nell. This was where old people lived, a house that was full of old people's things, dead people's things. She sniffed in the smell of the bedspread: a good smell of cat and clean cotton. This would be her room, this bed, this bedspread, the blue blankets and cold white sheets, the blue flowers on the wallpaper, the dressing table with the ivory mirror that was always face down.

She wondered how long until dinner. She hoped her mother wouldn't come looking for her; there was a key stuck in the lock of the bedroom door, but she was forbidden to turn it. She hadn't run right to her mother from the attic: that proved she wasn't a baby. A picture of Peter, his big white teeth laughing, hovered just outside her mind; she wouldn't let it in, but she knew it was there, waiting. Sometime it would come to her. The window shade was pulled up. Outside it wasn't quite dark, and everything was cold and black and gray, the treetops crisscrossed lines. She saw a bird fly past, then another, then one stopped in a tree and was lost in the branches. A tear slipped down her cheek, and she wiped it on her sleeve.

She picked up the cat and held her in her arms, and Dinah settled against her, her paws kneading Margaret's shoulder. "You're my Dinah, my baby Dinah," Margaret crooned. Dinah sighed, stopped purring, and went to sleep again, curled against Margaret's stomach. The room grew darker. Margaret dozed, safe, the cat warm against her, until she was awakened by someone screaming.

.   .   .   .   .

"WELL, SHE lost another one," her father said after dinner when he got back. His face was red and frowning, as if he were mad at everyone. He had gone in the ambulance with her mother. Her mother's skirt had been all covered with blood. There was blood on the hall carpet. Thea and Aunt Nell scrubbed it hard with a brush, but it wouldn't come out. They put a yellow bath mat over it.

The rest of them had sat down to dinner. Aunt Nell took Margaret out of the dining room and talked to her in the kitchen because she couldn't stop crying. "The blood wasn't because she was hurt," Aunt Nell said. She knelt down and wrapped her two hands around Margaret's. "There might be a problem with the baby, but your mother will be all right. Don't be scared, Margaret. Come and eat your dinner. That's what Mommy would want you to do. Just calm down and eat some turkey."

Margaret calmed down. She tried to eat some turkey, though she didn't like it, and she drank a big glass of Mr. Fahey's Pepsi when Uncle Teddy brought it for her. She couldn't stop thinking of the blood. In the back of her mind was still the bedroom, Peter's laugh. Across the table Peter looked as subdued as everyone else. He didn't look like Peter anymore—the cousin she hated. She still hated him, but he looked different. The grown-ups talked about the new president, and then about the old one who resigned. Aunt Nell called Nixon Tricky Dick, and Thea said, "That man makes me ashamed to be an American." Uncle Jamie said he didn't like that kind of talk, and Mr. Fahey snickered uneasily, showing his snaggly old yellow teeth. Uncle Jamie said there was such a thing as loyalty. When Margaret looked at him, she thought of his old eraser in the attic.

Margaret's father didn't return until after the dishes were done. Aunt Nell made him a turkey sandwich, and he let Uncle Teddy give him a drink, for once. The grown-ups talked for a while in the kitchen. Margaret went to look at the blood spot in the hall—still there, under the bath mat—and then lay on the floor in the living room, looking at the coals glowing in the fireplace. She could hear Peter and Heather fighting upstairs. Aunt Kay came in and sat at the piano smoking and drinking brandy and picking out tunes. Margaret wished Aunt Nell would come in and talk to her again, or let her sit on her lap. Aunt Nell, who looked so tall and sharp, was the softest and nicest one of all when you sat on her lap. But Ann came in and plopped down on the rug next to Margaret.

"We could look in the attic," she said.

"No," Margaret said. "I'm sick of the attic."

"But we could look. Somebody might have hid it there."

Margaret stared at her. What did she know about the attic? She remembered the blue ring with the yellow letters. "Hid what?"

Ann leaned close and whispered in her ear. "The baby. Maybe we should look in the attic."

Margaret pushed her away. "That's not what it means when you lose a baby, you dummy," she said. Ann began to cry. Aunt Kay's piano playing got louder—big, harsh chords, then "Happy Birthday to You," then "Frère Jacques." Margaret rolled over on her stomach and put her hands over her ears.

Uncle Teddy came in and said, "What's this? What's this? We're going in a few minutes, Annie, so stop crying and go find your jacket. Kay? You about ready?"

Aunt Kay crashed her hands down on the keys with an ugly sound. "I suppose so," she said. "Why not? Assuming you're in a condition to drive."

"Don't give me a hard time, Kay," Uncle Teddy said. "Just this once."

Margaret stayed face down on the rug. She heard Ann and Uncle Teddy leave the room, and then someone knelt beside her and put a hand on her shoulder. She tensed, but it was Aunt Kay. She patted Margaret's back and said, "Don't feel too bad, honey. It's more fun to be an only child."

Margaret's mother stayed at the hospital that night. After the *Charlie Brown Thanksgiving Special* on TV, Aunt Nell tucked Margaret into bed; her father had gone to bed early. Aunt Nell talked to Margaret about the baby, kept saying she was sorry, and her Mommy and her Daddy were sorry, everyone was sorry—as if the baby was Margaret's treat, a toy for her that the store was sold out of.

Aunt Nell helped her take off her sweater and tights, and shook her nightgown out like a flag before she hung it over the radiator to warm. Then she said, "Would you like a massage, little one?"

It sounded like something to eat: something sweet and wobbly, she imagined, like Jell-O. She hated Jell-O. She stood shivering in her underpants, looking dubiously at her aunt. "I don't know."

Aunt Nell laughed and said, "Here—I'll show you. Hop up on the bed."

She lay down and her aunt began to rub her back. Aunt Nell's hands were warm and soft, and they pressed hard but not too hard, cupping around her shoulders and then moving down to the sides where it almost tickled and then down to where her underpants began.

"Feel good?"

"Mmm."

Aunt Nell rubbed the tops of her legs and the backs of her arms and then her back and shoulders again, kneading like a cat. She leaned over close, humming slightly, and when she stopped humming Margaret could feel her breath on her skin. The house was completely quiet. Thea had gone home, and Mr. Fahey. Uncle Jamie was out in his studio over the garage. Her father was asleep. Margaret began to feel drowsy. The massage felt good, but she wished Aunt Nell would stop. She moved restlessly, and Aunt Nell stilled her hands.

"Enough, little bunny?"

"Mmm."

"You're half-asleep." She turned Margaret over as if she were a doll, and put the nightgown over her head, then hugged her close for a minute. "You're a dear girl," she said. "You're my favorite little bunny, do you know that?"

She tucked Margaret's old, flattened-out teddy bear in bed with her; after she left Margaret would set the bear gently on the floor by the bed because she was too old to sleep with a stuffed animal. Aunt Nell smoothed back her hair and kissed her square in the middle of her forehead. With a flash of pain, Margaret missed her mother. Aunt Nell stood up and she clung to her. "What's a souvenir?" she asked, to keep her there.

She pronounced it soo–venner, and it took her aunt a while to catch on. "Souvenir," she said. "Oh—it's a French word. It means something to remind you of something else—a sort of memento."

Of course: a memento. Aunt Nell kissed her forehead again and went out, closing the door softly as if Margaret were already asleep. But she wasn't asleep, not quite. She thought about the ring, but she was afraid to go up to the attic alone. She thought about the baby. What Ann said was stupid. Of course, the baby wasn't lost. But she wondered where it was. It had been in her mother's stomach, and now it wasn't. She wondered how it got out and where it had gone. She wondered why there was blood.

She didn't put the bear on the floor. She hugged it tight. When she closed her eyes, she imagined something coming to the door, opening it, crawling up to the bed: something crying and covered with blood. It was then that Peter's face came back to her, his big teeth, and his mocking laugh that followed her down the stairs and wouldn't let her go.

Caroline
1973

"I WISH I'd known you when you were a nun," Mort said.

"I was never a nun, Morty."

It was nearly noon. Caroline and Mort were having breakfast alone. Nell's summer vacation had just started, and she had gone over to the high school to drop off final grades. Jamie, of course, was out in his loft over the garage—presumably transferring endless tubes of paint to endless yards of canvas.

"Half a nun, then," he said. "Which half, I wonder?"

He reached under the table and put his hand on her thigh, squeezing it through the silk nightgown. She slapped his hand, not hard. "None of that," she said. "You've had more than you deserve."

She poured him more coffee and he dropped in a saccharine tablet. "Damn it, Caroline, I wish you weren't so set on going. I don't see the point."

"I'm homesick," she said. "I really miss the desert, the mountains. And I have friends there."

"You have friends here."

She smiled at him. "I know. And don't think I won't miss you. It's just—" She shrugged. "I can't explain."

She had told him the night before that she was thinking of moving back to New Mexico in the fall. She was negotiating for a little house there, she said, a hacienda overlooking the river, with a view of the blood-red mountains, and she'd be flying out in a couple of weeks to look at it. None of this was true. She wanted to plant in his brain the idea of losing her. She wanted to make it easier.

"You must know what I mean," she said. "How you can feel you belong to a place."

He looked at her—studying her, she felt, as if she were a patient with an elusive symptom. She didn't turn away. "I'll come out and see you at Christmas," he said. "If you're really going."

"I'm going, all right." She let her smile intensify. "You'll love it at Christmas," she said. "Santa Fe is beautiful, so cold and clear, and all the lights."

"You can teach me to ski."

"I never did any skiing."

It was in Santa Fe that she had been half a nun. She had spent years there, listening to God talk to her, trying to find a purpose for her life. Then the purpose had been revealed to her, and she had come home.

"That's right," he said. "Nuns don't ski. Well, you can teach me to pray."

"I've forgotten how, I'm afraid." She smiled at him. "That was in another life, Morty. I do other things now."

They had leisurely third cups of coffee, and then she kissed him good-bye at the front door. He didn't keep office hours on Mondays, but he was due at the hospital. "I'll call you tonight," he said, keeping his arms around her.

"Make it tomorrow, sweetie. I'm really pooped. I think I'll go to bed early." He rubbed his cheek against hers; he was freshly shaved and smelled of Brut. What a nice man he was—still sexy, barely gray, not even a potbelly, just that sweet softness around the middle. And a heart of gold. "I'm awfully fond of you, Morty," she said. "You know that, don't you?"

When he was gone she rinsed their dishes and loaded the dishwasher for Nell. She considered another cup of coffee and decided against it. She went into the living room where Nell kept the liquor, screwed the top off a bottle of Chivas Regal, thought for a minute, and put it back. Then she went slowly upstairs.

She took a shower, being careful to keep her hair dry. She squirted her underarms with Arrid and puffed on the White Shoulders Dusting Powder Mort had given her for her birthday. How could Mort call her beautiful? Her face in the mirror looked ancient, full of strange hollows and creases, her eyes sunk in their sockets. But she looked at it with satisfaction: it was fine, it was the face she wanted.

She went back to her room and put on clean underwear and stockings and finally the bathrobe that had been Stewart's last gift to her. He had made Nell take him downtown to the Addis Company, where he had picked it out himself: red silk lined in hot pink, with kimono sleeves.

"I saw it, and I said to myself: this is what Caro means to me," he told her. "This is what you've done for my life. This is the way I feel about you." She had lain beside him wearing the robe, and he had pulled back the brilliant red and pressed his face between her breasts. He didn't have the strength to do anything else. A week later he was dead.

She had never worn the robe with any other man. With Mort and the rest of them, she wore frilly nylon things, pastels. From Paris, when he was at a medical conference there, Mort had brought her silk stockings and a black garter belt with pink rosettes, and a man named Forrest gave her a quilted calico housecoat that she had passed on to Nell when she and Forrest split up. She saved the red silk for

the evenings when she was alone in her room with Stewart's photograph—when, sitting absolutely still in the old leather reclining chair
she'd brought with her to Nell's, she pulled the robe tightly around
her and looked into his eyes and felt his presence: *really* felt it, as a living entity, the way she used to be conscious of the presence of God.
Sometimes she could hear his voice, as once she used to hear God's
voice. *I don't deserve you,* Stewart had said. God never said that. *I don't
deserve you,* clutching at her hand. His coughing, the oxygen, the
wild flailing of his hands, the look in his eyes. And then nothing but
the smell of his fear lingering in the room. No God at all.

When she heard Nell come back, Caroline called downstairs.
"Nellie? Come up here for a minute?"

When Nell appeared in the doorway, Caroline was back in bed,
propped on pillows with an old *Time* magazine. Nell asked, "Are
you sick?"

"Not really. I think Mort and I had too much breakfast. One fried
egg too many. A touch of indigestion." She laid her hand over her
heart. "Here."

Nell had put on her gardening apron and sneakers and pinned up
her hair. She came over to the bed and laid the back of one hand
against Caroline's forehead. "Not feverish."

"Of course, I'm not feverish," Caroline said. "High cholesterol
doesn't make you feverish, it just clogs up your arteries or some
damn thing."

"Oh come on," Nell said. "Don't tell me we've got to start worrying about that stuff already."

"Not you, child. You're a spring chicken. Mort told me I should
go easy."

Nell smiled. "I like old Mort."

"He's not that old. He's sixty-two."

"He seems younger than that."

"Don't I know it," Caroline said. "I'm glad I didn't know him
when he was fifty." She laid her hand on her chest again and groaned.

"I'll tell you, Nell, I don't know if it was breakfast or what, but I've definitely overdone something. I think I'll just sack out here all day. This hard living is getting to me."

Nell shook her head and pretended to look shocked. "You're certainly a terrible example to your baby sister."

"I try to be."

Nell brought her some more magazines from downstairs and said she was going outside to weed the rose bed, and then to Thea's to cook Chinese and drink champagne and celebrate the school year being over. The mail was here, the usual junk. Dinah had plenty of food and was asleep outside in the sun. And Jamie could eat the leftover stew in the fridge for supper.

Jamie. "Would you tell him not to bother me, Nell?" she asked. "Not that the charming boy is speaking to me, anyway."

Nell laughed. "Did you hear him last night? When Mort was downstairs in the kitchen with me? Jamie came in, saw Mort, got that look on his face and said, *Oh—good evening*. No *Hi, Mort,* no *Hey, Mort, how are you,* or anything, God forbid, just this very pompous little nod and—*Good evening*."

Caroline said, "One of these day's somebody's going to mistake him for the butler."

Jamie: the hell with Jamie. He would be out there painting until the light failed, unless he had a student to worship at the shrine. She couldn't keep track of his students—mostly earnest, dowdy young women who thought Jamie was *interesting*. God: if there was one thing her brother wasn't, it was interesting. He had begun sleeping out in the loft. Every morning he came in for breakfast, then he packed his lunch and carried it back out in an absurd tin lunch box, with a thermos of coffee, as if he were a laborer going off to a hard day's work. The chances of his coming in to eat Nell's stew were very small. He hardly ever came in at all. Nell told her she'd caught him peeing out the garage window.

"Why doesn't he just *move?*" Caroline asked Nell. "Get himself an apartment somewhere away from his degenerate sister."

"Too tight with the buck," Nell said. Also, Caroline knew perfectly well that Jamie thought it was she who should move. He had told her to her face that he wouldn't have agreed to her moving in with them if he'd known she was going to spend her widowhood behaving like a slut. Jamie: what would he say when she was gone? She hoped he would feel so guilty and remorseful he wouldn't be able to paint again. She hated his paintings, which seemed to her drab, formless blobs or—his new thing—soulless and conventional portraits of people she was glad she didn't know. When she looked at Jamie's work, she really did get homesick for New Mexico: the pottery, the vibrant *santos* paintings in the chapel, the woven Rio Grande tapestries in her office at the convent.

Caroline leafed through magazines until she heard Nell's car pull out of the driveway and head down Hillside Street. Then she went to her dresser and removed two things from her underwear drawer: a tiny envelope and an index card. She put the envelope in the pocket of her robe. On the index card was a scrap of poetry copied out in her neatest handwriting:

He first deceased, she for a little tried
To live without him, liked it not and died.

Some seventeenth-century woman's epitaph, she forgot whose. Under it she had written the date of Stewart's death in 1972. Caroline got her pen out of the desk to write another date beneath it: June 19, 1973. Then she put the paper back under a stack of panties and closed the drawer.

Who would find it? Lucy? Nell? Mort? Anyone? It didn't matter. It was her private code, her silly scholarly footnote to her own life. Really: it didn't matter. No one, least of all her own sister, her own children, would have suspected her capable of such a thing. It was important only to her to leave this oblique record: it satisfied her love of order and completeness, the tying up of details.

Not that she was being very scientific about it. She had not made a will, for example. But she knew Lucy and Teddy could be trusted to split things amicably. The jewelry was Lucy's, of course. Caroline had told Kay she could have the leopard coat—poor Kay, who had come to her after Stewart's funeral for a loan, with stories about Teddy's boozing and chubby little Ann's problems at some expensive nursery school. She'd been selling her antiques—the furniture, and the French art glass she'd inherited from her first husband's family. And Teddy had been playing the stock market, losing most of Kay's money, and a real estate deal somewhere had gone wrong. . . . Kay got the loan, and when she admired the coat, Caroline said, "Take it." Kay said she couldn't, and Caroline said, "Take it when I'm dead, then." The other coats would go God knows where. Lucy would never wear them. No fur for Lucy—or Nell either, probably. Caroline couldn't see them on her daughter or her sister. Glamorous Kay could take them all, as far as she was concerned. Give them to the Salvation Army. Put them out with the trash. As if it mattered.

The house was very quiet. When she listened, all she could hear was a crow squawking in the fir trees out back. It made her smile: those damned crows. The whole neighborhood complained about them and their horrible noise. What bad-tempered birds. Or maybe their noise was a sign of happiness? Rapture? Maybe when a crow was in love, its first impulse was to let out an ear-splitting *skrawwk!* Well, why not?

She would miss the crows, she decided. The crows, Mort, Nell, and her children. Was that all? She thought fleetingly of her years at the convent, the long hours she used to spend in prayer, the way her heart yearned for God, for certainty. For something that would open and enfold her. She looked at Stewart's photograph, and her eyes filled with tears. Lucy had taken it years ago, a ridiculous picture of him in a train station wearing a suit and tie—very proper, very much the lawyer, the pillar of the community. But he looked so healthy and robust, and he had that look on his face that she loved, and after long consideration Caroline had decided on it as her favorite and had it framed in silver.

Stewart. *Timor mortis conturbat me*—a line she always remembered from one of the medieval lyrics she was so hung up on when she was young. A million years ago, before everything. *Timor mortis:* fear of death. Imagine the poet back in those pious days, God and His works all around him, and the fear of death as urgent as hunger or love, as much a part of his life. Fear of hell, of course, was what it was. Fear of the loss of God forever and ever was what made him sweat and tremble. What a strange notion, she couldn't help thinking. She had abandoned God for Stewart, and she had lost God completely on the day Stewart died. Loss of God seemed very natural: no sweat, no trembling. Loss of Stewart, whom she had traveled home from the desert to care for, was something else.

God, death, hell—no, those weren't the things she feared.

She would miss the crows, Mort, Nell, Lucy, and Teddy. She considered calling Lucy in Boston and complaining about her indigestion. She imagined Lucy, afterward, saying, "I talked to her just a couple of hours before it happened—she thought she had indigestion." Her dear daughter, whom she had failed so often. She would have liked to hear Lucy's voice once more, say one last thing to her, or to little Margaret—what, she couldn't imagine. Or Teddy—call Teddy? No. Phone calls were like a slug of Scotch: needless complications. It was kinder and easier to leave it as it was. Let them be.

She went down the hall to the bathroom. She brushed her hair and brushed her teeth. She looked in the mirror one last time: all right, yes, she supposed she had been beautiful once, was still. Would be no more. What did it matter now?

She took the tiny envelope from her pocket and shook its contents into the palm of her hand: four white pills. She ran water into her tooth glass and, without thinking about it, swallowed them all at once. Mort's gift: he could be prosecuted, if anyone guessed. No one would. *It's everyone's right,* he said, and yes, it was—though she knew he had meant years and years from now, he meant old age and sickness instead of fifty-four. She stuffed the envelope deep into the bathroom wastebasket, under the tissues and wads of hair.

Back in her room, she stood at the window. Blue sky, green trees,

Nell's roses by the fence. The crows were still at it: *skrawwk!* She stood there a long time. Then she drew the curtains. She got into bed, leaning back comfortably against the pillows. She smiled across the room at Stewart. She never thought of him as a young man: it wasn't as a young man that she had loved him. She had fallen in love with him while he coughed himself to death. Tears came to her eyes, thinking of his suffering. His goodness. The night he died in her arms.

This day, she thought, quoting again—from a source that as the minutes went by she was too drowsy to remember: *this day, thou shalt be with me in Paradise.*

Nell

1968

O N WEDNESDAYS after school, she sat at a card table at the Syracuse Peace Council and addressed envelopes. On Saturdays, she stood on street corners passing out antiwar leaflets. She went to a rally at the university where Eugene McCarthy spoke over closed-circuit television deploring the Tet Offensive. The night Johnson announced he wouldn't seek a second term, she joined a horn-blowing motorcade down Westcott Street and got drunk on cheap beer.

At school she wore her usual dull sweaters and skirts, but sometimes she put on jeans and an embroidered shirt and went to parties in noisy, grungy apartments where she smoked pot with people in their twenties. They were fond of her. They said, "I wish I had your energy." They said she looked like Katharine Hepburn in *Guess Who's*

Coming to Dinner—which Nell knew they meant as a compliment, though Katharine Hepburn was at least ten years older than she.

Nell was in love with a young woman she often went leafletting with, a graduate student in history named Jessie Rose. Jessie didn't know this, of course; no one knew it. The way Jessie's mere existence enriched her life—that was Nell's secret, like a hoard of money in a Swiss bank account: she didn't need to *have* the money, just know that it was there.

Jessie had a sullen, hairy boyfriend named Michael, who looked to Nell like a throwback to a less attractive evolutionary stage in the sublime history of humankind, but even Michael couldn't disturb Nell's contentment. Michael couldn't be taken seriously; he was an absurdity, a nothing. The important things were Jessie's long shining hair, her wonderful smile, the time she touched Nell's hand and said, "You are an absolutely amazing woman, do you know that?"

Nell was also half in love with Eugene McCarthy. She said to Pat Garvey that if all men were like McCarthy she just might be able to imagine herself marrying one. Imagine a poet in the Senate! She liked his elegant wit and his short, crisp hair: the one thing she couldn't approve of in the younger generation was long hair on men, which (no matter how bearded and moustached they were) made them look effeminate. Long hair with a headband was the worst. She also liked McCarthy's cool, stony, reasoned opposition to Johnson's war.

"Even though my brother John was killed in it, I can see that World War II was a necessary war," she used to say. "This one is madness."

She said things like that regularly to Jamie, to get him angry. She also cut out "Fat Freddie's Cat," four-letter words and all, from the *Syracuse New Times* and left it in the kitchen for him to see. The first time she went out in her denim shirt he said, "You look like a pathetic old hag," which didn't bother her at all. She knew she didn't look like any such thing.

"You seem like one of us," Jessie had said once, after a morning tramping the streets for McCarthy. They were sitting in The Orange having coffee. "I wish my mother had half your guts," Jessie said. "She lives for her garden club. When Johnson abdicated, she said what a shame it was, Lady Bird had done so much to beautify Washington."

"So she has, the old bitch," Nell said, and they both laughed. That was the day Jessie told Nell that Michael was getting really weird, he was dropping acid, he was talking about heading for the coast and joining a fringe group called the Diggers. He was beginning to scare her. Nell said, her heart jumping, "He does seem like a rather difficult, hostile young man."

"To say the least," Jessie said. "But damn it, he's so sexy!"

That night Nell lay awake until dawn. She thought not so much of Jessie as of Gillian in England, and the hairdresser Marietta, and the stocky, short-haired woman who had accosted her in the women's room of the Waldorf Cafeteria, and one scary, thrilling night in New York with a woman she met at the Museum of Modern Art.

Jessie wasn't the first young woman she had had a crush on. Her life as a teacher of teenagers was filled with terror and ecstasy. But what she dreamed of, when she designed her personal Utopia, was not a bouncy, nubile young thing in denims and eye makeup, but what she thought of as a counterpart, someone near her age, someone she could talk to. The perfect Friend she had craved all her life.

Sometimes when Nell lay awake, it seemed that all she really wanted was someone to love. Anyone. That even if Jamie were more friendly, less distant—less *Jamie*—she could be content to live in celibate happiness, devoting herself to her brother, like Dorothy Wordsworth. Or if she and Caroline were better friends. Or if life could be as simple for her as it apparently was for Jessie, who found love in the stoned, antisocial, and repulsive person of Michael Spengler.

"Well—lonely, frankly," she responded to Caroline's how-are-you when she went to their place for Sunday dinner—the new house Caroline and Stewart had bought when they moved back to Syracuse after Stewart's emphysema had made it necessary for him to give up his law practice in Albany. "I keep thinking I should rent out a couple of the bedrooms. God knows there's plenty of room in that house. Jamie practically lives out at his studio, anyway."

"Why don't you?" Caroline asked. She was putting dinner on the table—not much of a dinner. Macaroni with butter on it, frozen peas, a wizened little ham. In a crystal pitcher, ice water to drink. On the counter Nell saw a Sara Lee cake thawing in its aluminum pan, a jar of Sanka. "Rent out Jamie's old bedroom in the attic," Caroline said. "You could put an air conditioner up there. Or you could take the attic for yourself, that way you'd have more privacy." She sliced three pieces off the ham and went to the refrigerator for a jar of mustard, which she stuck in the middle of the table with a silver knife in it. "You should, Nell. I'm sure you could use the income, too."

"Oh, I don't know," Nell said. "I don't really need the money, and in a way I must admit I do like having things my own way around the house."

Caroline smiled. Nell had a genetic inability to agree with Caroline, and Caroline knew it. "Well, it's a thought. Maybe you just need some new friends."

"I do have my Peace Council people."

"Kids!"

"I like young people," Nell said. "I enjoy their company. They're teaching me a lot. I've become quite friendly with several of them. There's this graduate student named Jessie that I go canvassing with."

"Jessie, Jessie, Jessie. You've told me all about Jessie. She's the pretty blonde with the awful boyfriend. Right?"

Nell flushed. "Sorry."

Caroline said, "Oh Nellie, forgive me." She kept bustling around the kitchen. Another kind of person, Nell thought, would come and sit down when she apologized—look you in the eye, at least. Caroline was draining the peas, plopping them into a serving dish. She said, "But you know, it's a damned shame you never got married. You could have children of your own instead of getting these hang-ups on other people's kids."

"They're not hang-ups, Caroline. God."

"Well. Whatever they are." Caroline put the peas on the table and went to the door to the hallway. "Stewart? Dinner."

They were both silent, listening. First Stewart's cough. Then the creaking of the bed. Then his slippered feet shuffling down the hall. Caroline had put his bed in the back room on the first floor, plus a big color Sony, a reclining chair for herself, and a shelf unit that held family pictures and library books and copies of *TV Guide* and Caroline's New Mexican Madonna. They sat there in the evenings watching the public television station. They'd watch anything: *Masterpiece Theater, Agronsky & Co.,* nature programs, opera, *Monty Python.* Thinking of Caroline and Stewart, Nell told herself that there were worse things in life than a big silent house with no one but a cat and a reclusive brother for roommates.

Stewart shuffled in. "Hi there, Nell."

She stood up to kiss him on the cheek. He needed a shave, and he smelled musty, like an attic. Unused, she thought. Dead already. "How are you, Stewart?"

It was the wrong question, of course, but all he said was, "Can't complain. How have you been keeping yourself?"

"Nell's thinking of renting out a room," Caroline said. She was watching him and pretending not to, as he lowered himself into his chair, picked up his napkin, and tucked it in the top of his robe. When she saw that he was settled, she sat beside him and began filling his plate.

"Is that so? Go easy on that ham, Caro."

"Not really," Nell said. "It was just an idle thought."

"You want to watch out, bringing strangers into the house. Remember what happened to Janet Murphy." A fit of coughing overcame him, and Nell sat looking down at her peas trying not to listen. Stewart's coughing was dry and desperate. It could escalate into wheezing gasps and Caroline would have to get the respirator.

This time it was brief, but it left him shaken and panting. As if nothing had happened, Caroline said, "Janet Murphy didn't have the sense of a cocker spaniel." To Nell she said, "Remember her? She was the secretary in Jack Wentworth's office who was strangled by—oh, who was it, Stewart? The man who came to read the meter?"

"Plumber," Stewart said, recovered. He raised his head and picked up his fork. His voice was hoarse, and he cleared his throat, grimacing and putting his hand to his Adam's apple. "Told her he was the plumber."

"That's rather different from renting out a room," Nell said.

"Granted," Stewart said. "And you're no Janet Murphy, God knows, Nell. But it always amazes me that she let him in. It makes you wonder."

"I believe that it's better to trust people," Nell said.

"Hmm. Is that true, I wonder." Stewart looked at her soberly, frowning hard, thinking it over. Nell wondered what he had been like in the courtroom. He was a completely transparent person: she imagined that defending a client he despised, he would have doubt and revulsion written all over his face. He said, "Actually, I believe you're right. Seriously. You don't want to go through life expecting the worst. And, when you think about it, most bad things don't happen." He smiled, then sobered again. "Still, you want to check these people out."

"What people?"

"Anybody you're considering renting to."

She laughed. "I'm not considering that at all, Stewart. It was just an idea."

"Not a bad one," Caroline said.

"Caro can rent a room from you when I'm gone," said Stewart. "How would you like that, honey? Rent your old room from your sister until a second husband shows up."

There was a chilled silence while Stewart stabbed his fork in a piece of ham, smiling slightly to himself. He said things like that every once in a while, whether to garner sympathy or to shock people or just because they were true, Nell couldn't figure out.

"You're not going anywhere," Caroline said firmly. "Does anyone want some of this mustard?"

"You never know," Stewart said, still smiling at his food.

"How's Lucy?" Nell asked.

"You mean, how's my baby," Caroline said, and jumped up. "Wait. I've got some new pictures."

"And Kay and Teddy are thinking of producing one of their own," said Stewart. "Wouldn't that be something?"

"That would be wonderful." Knowing Kay, Nell wondered if it would.

"Here. Isn't she adorable?" Caroline had color shots of Margaret, their first grandchild: a hairless, grinning little thing propped up on a sofa with pillows. Some of Lucy pushing her in a stroller down a Boston street, Lucy looking unexpectedly matronly and contented. Caroline said, "See what you're missing, Nell? If only you'd said yes to old what's-his-name. Henry Tillman."

Nell said, "Caroline—please."

"Look at those eyelashes." Stewart gave another weak cough but subdued it with a sip of water. "And that rosebud mouth. What a little beauty."

"He wasn't so bad, if I recall. And he was certainly crazy about you. And what about that other one?" Caroline closed her eyes and raised her head, searching her memory. "The one who always wore a hat. Good-looking guy. What was his name?"

"This is not something I particularly want to talk about," said Nell.

"It's not too late." Stewart put down the chunk of ham he had raised to his lips. "Speaking of Jack Wentworth, Nell, he always asks about you. I mean it. He stopped in just the other day and the first thing he said, practically, was what's Nell up to. Wanted to know if you were still up on the barricades. Still out there marching."

"He's a real card."

"Don't knock Jack," Caroline said. "He's not a bad catch. And nice-looking. He can't be more than—what, Stewart? Fifty-four? Fifty-five?"

"Caroline. Stewart." Nell put down her fork and raised her hands, palms out, in front of her chest. "Please. I think it's very nice that you two got back together." In truth, she found it incomprehensible— that Caroline, who had scorned and despised Stewart when he was a healthy man, adored him as a dying one, and had given up every-thing to come back east and see him through it. She said, "But just because you've found connubial bliss and all that, don't keep trying to inflict it on me. I'm sick of it."

Stewart shook his head back and forth and said, "Oh, Nellie Nel-lie Nellie."

"I mean it." She lowered her hands and clasped them, her knuckles white. "I'm not interested in marrying anyone, least of all a pompous Republican capitalist pig like Jack Wentworth. Please. This may sound crazy to you, but I'm quite content to be a dried-up old spinster with no life. Okay? Will you take my word for it? I like it that way."

Caroline, annoyed, pursed her lips to one side; Stewart looked sad-eyed and chagrined. Neither of them spoke. Nell sliced into her ham. "And another thing. My political activities are not a joke. You can think what you want, you can say what you want, but just don't make fun of what I believe in. Don't treat me like a nutcase because I go out and try to do something about the state of this rotten world." Caroline took a breath and opened her mouth to speak. Nell said, "And don't tell me I wouldn't think the world was so rotten if I had grandchildren, Caroline. Or religion."

"That's not what I was going to say at all."

Stewart looked at his wife with concern. "What were you going to say, honey?"

"I was going to get all humble and apologetic," she said, and stood up to put on water for coffee. "I was going to tell Nell that sometimes I envy her to death."

. . . . .

JESSIE DROVE Nell home from the Peace Council, and Nell invited her in for a cup of coffee. Her house, as they went up the steps, embarrassed her: the pretentious white pillars holding up the roof of the tiny porch, the prissy middle-class lawn, the mailbox with KERWIN painstakingly picked out in stick-on letters. She could imagine Jessie thinking the place was a crime, it ought to be torched or turned into a commune. The scheme for renting out rooms made perfect sense when she was with someone like Jessie—it was so clear to her, the absurdity of two people occupying so much space. She and Jamie could easily put up a couple of grad students, or a welfare mother with her children—or someone like Michael Spengler, who lived wherever he could find a bed and who was chronically short of money because of his efforts on behalf of the peace movement. It would be the ultimate heroic act to take Michael into her house out of the kindness of her heart and her belief in the principles of democracy.

"What a marvelous house," Jessie said.

"My parents bought it in the twenties," Nell said. "They paid four thousand dollars for this place—can you believe it? I've lived here all my life."

Jessie said, "Really," as if that were a truly amazing, even admirable fact. With Jessie at her side, Nell was struck by how little the place had changed since her childhood. It wasn't something she thought about much, but when you looked, there were the same kind of genteel slipcovers her mother had favored, the family photographs on the piano, the worn Persian carpets, the silver urn on the sideboard where it had sat, bright and untouched, since her parents received it as a gift on their tenth wedding anniversary. Even the heavy old black phone on the hall desk had been there as long as she could remember. And the gilt-framed mirror in which she had looked at her face nearly every day of her life.

Amazing it was, but it didn't seem admirable: it seemed to her, all of a sudden, crazy. She thought: someday I'll sell this place, I'll get right the hell out of here, I'll leave this all behind.

"I love the idea of that kind of stability," Jessie said. "It must make you feel like you've got some roots in this world. My parents have moved all over the country. I mean, I went to three separate junior high schools. And now they're selling the house in White Plains and planning to move to Florida. It would be really comforting to have a house like this, I should think."

Comforting? Nell couldn't recall that the house had ever given her comfort. Comfort: that was what happened after her Skiddaw adventure. The image came irresistibly into her mind of Gillian Welsh's naked breasts and her brown plaid housedress in a heap on the floor.

She said, "I suppose it does. But of course it's a ridiculously huge old place."

Jamie started down the stairs, saw Jessie, and ducked back up again without a word. "Hello, Jamie," Nell called after him.

His voice floated down the stairs, an unintelligible syllable followed by the sound of a door closing.

"My brother," Nell said to Jessie, grinning to show that she wasn't blind to his strangeness, and that it wasn't important, it wasn't something that bothered her.

"He lives here too?"

"Sort of. He spends most of his time in his studio over the garage. He's a painter."

"Really? Is he well known?"

Nell pointed to one of Jamie's oils on the wall by the stairs, an enigmatic study he called *Blue Number Eleven* that was mostly white space with an off-center cluster of deep-blue forms that suggested a woman bent forward in an act of either giving or supplication. Nell loved the painting. She had never understood how Jamie could paint like that and be so enclosed in himself.

"James Paul Kerwin—you may have heard of him. He had a show in New York last winter. But he's getting into something new lately. Portraiture. Realism. Commissions." Nell grinned. "Making some money, at last."

"I suppose you have to sell out to make it in art just like you do in everything else," Jessie said. "Not that I know beans about art. I've barely heard of Andy Warhol."

"Well, Jamie's no Andy Warhol, I'm afraid."

Nell made coffee while Jessie sat at the kitchen table and talked about Michael. She told Nell that Michael might leave for California any minute. He was trying to set something up with people he knew at Berkeley.

"And how do you feel about that?" Nell asked her dutifully. She had no real wish to hear the answer. She looked at Jessie's hair, which fanned out over her shoulders, slightly crinkled, as if it had just come out of braids. Sometimes she thought that if she could just touch Jessie's hair—put her hand lightly on her head—she would ask nothing else.

"Lousy. I wish he could just settle down. And he's so scornful of everyone around here. You know? He just dismisses everyone as a bunch of Clean-for-Gene types. I'm sure he'd be the first to criticize anyone who judged people by appearances, but that's exactly what he does. God." She sipped her coffee, frowning. "He really bugs me, Nell. He always thinks someplace else is going to be better than where he is. What does he think he's going to find in California?"

"Well, it does seem that there might be more of Michael's kind of people out there," Nell said, hating the way her voice sounded: prim and disapproving. "More of the radical element."

Jessie snorted. "He doesn't even know what kind of person he is. He thinks he's Abbie Hoffman or somebody, but when it comes right down to it I don't think he's got the commitment for that scene." She sat drinking her coffee in quick little sips, staring out the window. Nell stared out with her, to see what Jessie saw: the untended backyard, just beginning to be touched by spring. Dinah stalking Mr. Fahey's old tabby. The bench Nell was sitting on when she heard her mother screaming that John was dead. Jessie turned away from it. "Sometimes I think he just wants to screw a lot of California women."

"Michael's not good enough for you," Nell said shortly.

Jessie raised her head, her brow cleared, her eyes softened. *She knows,* Nell thought in a flash. Jessie said, "You're a good friend, Nell. And it's nice of you to listen to me rant and rave like this. I know you think I should just ditch him. You and a lot of other people. And I'm sure you're right." She leaned forward suddenly with her hands outstretched, like the woman in Jamie's painting. "The hell with Michael," she said. "Tell me about yourself. It's always so amazing to see people in their own space. You know?" She smiled, showing her tiny, even teeth and a dimple in one cheek. "Come on, Nell. Tell me the story of your life."

Nell shrugged. It was what she had longed for: a moment of intimacy, a real talk. Jessie's eager smile. Her hands reaching out. Not much, but enough to keep a pathetic old hag going. Her soul opened up: oh, the things she could say to this sensitive young person. And yet she could see the moment was false, a gift Jessie was offering because of what she understood.

"There's nothing to tell," Nell said. "Really. I've had the most completely boring, nondescript life you could ever imagine in your wildest dreams."

. . . . .

JACK WENTWORTH called to ask her out to dinner. When she heard his voice on the phone, she thought of Caro and Stewart plotting her fate in their stuffy little TV room, and she saw Jack Wentworth in his swanky James Street penthouse, slavering into the phone like some rank animal, an AMERICA: LOVE IT OR LEAVE IT button in his lapel. But she couldn't think of a plausible excuse, and so she agreed to have dinner with him.

He drove up in a midnight-blue Lincoln, and, from her bedroom window, she watched him get out and come up the walk. Immediately she thought more kindly of him. Was this gray-haired businessman in his absurd car the twisted lecher she had dreaded? This paunchy, aging version of the amiable old Jack she'd known all her life? She ran down to let him in, with the thought that this was the first time a man had come to the house to call for her.

She opened the front door, and he shook her hand energetically and said, "Gee, it's great to see you, Nell."

Jack Wentworth had been her brother John's friend, as much a part of the scenery of Nell's childhood and adolescence as her father's hardware store or the old black phone in the hall. He used to tease her and pull her ponytail and play baseball in the street in front of their house and go skating with them in the winter. She had seen him around, she knew he was a friend of Caro and Stewart's, but she couldn't remember actually talking to him in years—not since that time he came to see them toward the end of the war wearing his army uniform. He had explained to her what all his stripes and stars meant. She could remember his shy pride in them, masked with fussy details about Army regulations, and the way when he had said John's name his mouth still twisted with grief.

Sitting beside him in the air-conditioned Lincoln, Nell realized that aside from his politics she was fond of Jack Wentworth, she was glad to be spending an evening with him. She even felt a benign gratitude toward Caroline's machinations, and a distant approval of

Jack's wavy iron-gray hair, his tan, his white summer suit. The evening might even do him good; let him see there were people around his age who thought about something besides stocks and bonds and expensive cars. She might even get a contribution out of him for the Peace Council.

And then, seated across from him at a tiny table for two in the Rainbow Lounge at the Hotel Syracuse, hearing him say to the waiter, "I think we'll start with a bottle of Veuve Clicquot," her heart sank. His knees were distressingly near hers under the table-cloth, there was a new, calculating look in his eyes that struck her as transparently sensual, and she knew she had been a fool. The champagne came in a bucket of ice, like something in a Cary Grant movie: the grinning waiter with a white towel over his arm, the cork popping, people turning to look, Jack taking a suave sip and nodding approval. She thought of excusing herself to go to the women's room and cutting out through the back door. Or pulling a Michael Spengler: attacking Jack with the champagne bottle, shouting UP AGAINST THE WALL, MOTHERFUCKERS! and singing "We Shall Overcome" until they carted her away.

Jack raised his glass and said, "Here's to you, Nell. You know, you haven't changed in twenty years." He clanked his glass against hers—gently, but it seemed to her an aggressive act, like ordering the champagne in the first place without consulting her. "Not since you used to run around in that striped bathing suit at Sylvan Beach," he said. "God—you and those long legs. I don't know about you, but I'd give a lot to be back there. Be twenty-five years younger and know what I know now." He drank, set down his glass, and leaned forward with his arms folded on the table. "What about it? Do you ever wish for the good old days?"

Nell shook her head. "I believe in moving with the times."

"Really?"

"I certainly do." She took a deep breath. "When you say the good old days, you're talking about a lot more than just your youth. The good old days involved a lot of injustice. They weren't so great for most people, when you think about it."

He looked at her blankly for a minute, and then said, "I take it you approve of what's going on in this country, then. The chaos and the rioting and the filth."

"Call it what you like," Nell said. She thought of Jessie Rose marching down University Avenue, carrying a lighted candle that illuminated her pure young face and her halo of hair. "You have to admit there's a lot wrong with our society."

Jack said, "Well, I'm no Humphrey fan, but I have a lot of sympathy with old Hubert when he says the only thing to do is work from within—not to tear things down but to try to build things up."

"Humphrey," she said. "That lukewarm yes-man."

Jack raised one silver eyebrow and said, "All I can say is if I was taking a bath I'd rather have the water lukewarm than boiling hot."

"It depends how dirty you are, I suppose."

He threw back his head and laughed. Nell noted that his teeth were either excellent or false. He had a shaving cut on his neck. She remembered him at John's funeral, slumped in a pew with his head in his hands. She wondered if John would have grown older to be like this, a fat-cat seducer who ordered champagne in restaurants and laughed at what was serious. It was impossible to imagine John over thirty. She missed her brother, suddenly, so much her eyes stung with tears. If John were alive Jamie wouldn't be so weird. If John were alive there would be his family, his wife, children, people to love.

She stared coldly across the table at Jack Wentworth. He gave one last chuckle and said, "You're something, Nellie." He reached over to lay his hand on hers. "But forgive me for saying so, if there's one thing I don't want to talk about with you tonight, it's politics. Please."

"Oh." With her free hand, she picked up her glass. "I'm sorry."

"That's all right. It's just that when I go out to dinner I like to have a good time."

A good time: what did that mean to a man like Jack Wentworth? Playing footsie under the table. Blowing money on expensive food and wine. Going out on the town with some bimbo who would flatter him to death. Unfortunately, the champagne was glorious. Unfortunately, she was no Michael Spengler. She drained her glass and held it out for a refill.

"I guess I don't see why serious conversations aren't considered a good time," she said.

"Oh, come on, Nell, you know what I mean."

The waiter brought shrimp cocktail. Jack let go her hand to pick up his fork. She dipped a shrimp in red sauce and said, "So what do you want to talk about, Jack?"

He shrugged. "Something pleasant. Something that goes with champagne."

They had a stilted conversation about Jack's skiing trip to Colorado and about Nell's last vacation in England. They skimmed lightly over his law firm and her teaching, and she told him about Jamie's show at his New York gallery. Then finally, inevitably, they got talking about the good old days, after all. What other ground did they have in common, she thought, besides middle age and a taste for champagne?

Jack reminisced about John, some of the wild times they'd had, the girls they'd known, did she remember Peggy's friend Ruth Sawyer, and that time she got so drunk at the Club Dewitt—no, Nell was too young to remember that. But the time John, on a bet, drank a pint of scotch and skated around the lake blindfolded. And Peggy and that snake-in-the-grass Ray Ridley, and the marriage of Caroline and Stewart, which Jack always knew was a mistake, who didn't, and Christ it was a shame about Stewart and the emphysema, though it was great the way things turned out with him and Caroline—not like Jack's own marriage to Penny Horgan, which had gone sour right away and stayed that way through the divorce and even now they didn't speak, they had met at Jack Jr.'s wedding and didn't exchange a word, not that that was a problem, he was better off without her, that was for goddam sure.

Jack ordered more champagne to go with the filet mignon. Another ice bucket, another ostentatious pop, more heads turning. What would they think—Miss Kerwin from the high school out with Jack Wentworth, everyone knew who Jack Wentworth was and what he stood for. Two bottles of champagne.

Nell went to the women's room, where she looked in the mirror and saw that her cheeks were as pink as a teenager's. She combed her hair and peed, and when she got back Jack filled her glass and said, "Tell me frankly. Is all this boring you?"

She was, in fact, surprised at how much she had begun to enjoy herself. She liked the way things were coming back to her as she sat there with Jack eating shrimp and steak and drinking movie-star champagne. She had forgotten those huge picnics at Sylvan Beach, and forgotten that her brother John was such a hell-raiser; his death in the war had erased all that—all his funniness, his love of practical jokes. In spite of everything, how innocent those days seemed. How sunny and perfect and good: if she closed her eyes she was there, that laughing girl in the striped bathing suit. She did close her eyes, briefly, and thought how easy it was, really, to stop time, to retrieve it: surely the girl in the bathing suit, the boy skating blindfolded, Peggy dancing in her black dress, were still alive—more alive, maybe, than a middle-aged woman in a blue dress and a gray-haired man pouring champagne.

"I'm not bored in the least," she said. "Though I must admit I wasn't at all sure I wanted to have dinner with you."

"Oh, really?" He leaned toward her. The table was so small his face nearly touched hers. She pulled back. "May I ask why?"

"I just wondered what we could possibly talk about after all these years." He looked hurt, tightening his lips like Caroline did, and she felt bad for drawing away from him. She said gently, "But I'm enjoying this, Jack. I really am."

She would have liked to elaborate, to tell him she believed that to talk about the dead, the past—what he insisted on calling the good old days—was important, and that the living—this was a confused thought, but—that the living were a sort of repository for what remained of the dead, who could do nothing for themselves, who depended on the living to keep them alive somehow. To stop time by remembering. She wanted to say all that, and she had a feeling Jack would understand her, but before she could speak he leaned toward her again, took her hand, and said, "How come you never married, Nell?"

At the touch of his hand she became aware, suddenly, of how drunk she was. She put down her fork—she couldn't eat another bite—and her eyes closed. She could have gone to sleep right there in her gilded chair. "A good-looking girl like you," Jack said. The inside of her head whirled, and she opened her eyes and looked down at their two hands linked warmly together, palm to palm across the table. His fingernails, she noticed, were clean. His hand was tanned an even beige. There were three pearly buttons on the sleeve of his white jacket. "That's something I could never under-stand," Jack went on, and from the slow carefulness of his voice she knew that he was drunk, too. He said, "Unless you just don't like men. There was some speculation about that, years back. Nothing serious, but—" She looked up at him, into his eyes. His were bright blue, a little sad, crinkled at the corners. "What's the story, Nellie?"

It was partly the champagne, partly the intimacy of their talk, partly his warm sympathy, his concerned steady gaze that didn't fal-ter though she knew he must be shocked, disgusted, repelled to the core. She clutched his hand, and told him the truth.

. . . . .

AND THEN later, in the car in the parking lot, he tried to kiss her. "You intrigue me," he whispered. "God, Nell, women like you, you're so innocent." She pushed him away, but he wouldn't let her go. He said, "Maybe you just need a real man." He slid her dress off her shoulder and put his lips to her skin, and his hands moved down the blue silk over her breasts. She was horrified by a wild urge to give in to him. She hadn't been this close to anyone in years. How long since she had felt someone else's warm breath against her cheek? She closed her eyes with a little sob, and let him kiss her, kiss her again. Then he pushed her down on the seat, put his bulky weight on her, and reached under her skirt.

She gasped and recoiled, twisting away. She was overcome with the need to get out of the car and throw up. She pushed at him, and he let her go, and she sat up and leaned her forehead against the window. The nausea passed. She heard her pulse beating against her temples.

He said, "That's not something you should do to a guy."

"I'm sorry."

He was sitting behind the wheel, breathing hard, running his fingers back through his hair. "You ought to give it a chance, Nellie. You might be surprised."

She shook her head, and after a minute he started the car and backed quickly out of the parking lot. After a minute she said, "I do apologize. It's been a lovely evening. The dinner. The champagne. I enjoyed it very much."

He said, "Well, good, I'm glad," and they were silent the rest of the way to her house.

She woke the next morning feeling sick and panicky. The hangover passed, but the panic stayed with her. She couldn't talk herself out of the cold fear that her life would become at any moment grotesque—shameful and melodramatic and ruined. She waited for Caroline to say something to her, for Stewart to make a joke, and she stopped going leafletting with Jessie, imagining anonymous letters to the Peace Council office. When Jessie phoned, she made excuses to hang up in a hurry, and when they called from the Peace Council and asked her to work she said she was busy. For the rest of the school year she froze whenever Joe Carlucci, the principal at North-side High, spoke to her. He called her to his office one morning, summoned her out of class on the loudspeaker, and she sat down opposite him in a cold sweat, but he wanted her to see the mother of one of her students who had come in about her daughter's problems with the poetry of T. S. Eliot. Nell talked to the woman for ten minutes, and afterward had no idea what she had said. She went to Maine in the summer for two solitary weeks, and was afraid of what she would find when she got back. A notification from the Board of Education, maybe, or a call from Pat Garvey about the astonishing rumors that were sweeping the city.

But nothing happened. She never heard from Jack Wentworth. Eventually, Caroline mentioned that he was going to get married again, to the widow of an old friend. "You missed your chance, sweetie," Caro said, and Nell said, "That old fascist," and they laughed, but she felt the blood rise to her face and her heart thump in her chest. She would never think of Jack Wentworth again without an anguished prayer of thanks. In the fall, when she had a post-card from Jessie and Michael in California, she felt almost nothing but relief, and in the November election she voted for Hubert Humphrey.

Kay
1964

AT HER FIRST wedding, Kay wore a long white satin dress that was a gift from the family of her husband-to-be. At her second, to Teddy Quinn, she wore black silk and a diamond choker that she paid for herself. She also paid for the reception, which was held in the walled back garden of her house on Beacon Hill: flowers everywhere, an open bar and a jazz band, a Japanese chef who cooked steak over an open flame. The wedding cake was flown in from a Viennese bakery in New York City. Kay gave Mrs. Hickey the afternoon off and hired two young nannies—a blonde for Peter, a brunette for Heather—dressed in rented uniforms with frilly white aprons and Mary Poppins straw hats trimmed with cherries.

Heather, who had just had her first birthday, sat placidly in her English pram while the brunette nanny wheeled her around the brick paths showing her off; when she got tired of the pram, she took a few charming, tottering steps hanging on to the garden furniture and grinning at the guests. She had a long nap, and when she woke up she ate a piece of wedding cake and had her picture taken with a mouthful of crumbs, waving her filthy little hands and looking ecstatic.

Peter began screaming shortly after the reception began and had to be taken by the blonde nanny up to his room, where he yelled for at least an hour and then fell asleep. His noise penetrated quite easily to the garden. Kay paid no attention to it, but Teddy kept apologizing and saying, "The terrible twos." When the nanny returned, her Mary Poppins hat had disappeared. Kay made her go back inside and find it and comb her hair; when she came out again, Kay said, "Everything okay?" and the nanny nodded curtly and headed for the bar.

Kay didn't invite any of her family, the Bakers, to her second wedding. The first time, her parents—Carl and Faye—had driven straight through to Boston from Chicago in their broken-down Dodge and showed up at the church half an hour late, her father in a shiny brown suit, her mother squeezed into a turquoise chiffon dress with stains around the armholes. They drank too much at the reception. Carl filled Mr. Hamlin in on his lifetime of bad breaks. Faye kept telling Mrs. Hamlin what a nice-looking young fellow Richard was, you wouldn't think there would be such nice-looking young men at a place like Harvard, she always thought the boys at places like Harvard were—you know. When the dancing began they did the flamboyant dips and spins they'd learned from Arthur Murray's TV show and, finally, when Kay and Richard had changed into their traveling clothes and were about to leave, Kay's parents enveloped her in weepy hugs and wouldn't let her go.

After that, Kay told them news only when it was safely stale: the babies' births, Richard's death, her engagement to Teddy—all of it was relayed in polite belated notes on her engraved stationery. Her parents sent presents to the children that Kay gave to Mrs. Hickey for her grandchildren. They sent a huge sympathy card with a picture of Jesus on the front, and, inside, the words GATHERED TO HIS LOVING ARMS in Gothic script.

Kay planned to let a couple of weeks pass, and then write a letter announcing that she and Teddy had eloped on the spur of the moment and were married by a J.P. somewhere. Or maybe she'd just skip the whole thing. Teddy's mother, Caroline, wasn't at the wedding. Caroline, as Kay understood it, looked like a movie star and was living in a convent in New Mexico. His father, Stewart, was a lawyer in Albany; he drove to Boston on the morning of the wedding and took Teddy and Kay out for a late breakfast at the Ritz-Carlton.

Kay immediately loved Stewart. He was everything she wished her own father was: quiet and courteous and well dressed. At the reception, he made the rounds, introducing himself to all Kay's young friends and playing peek-a-boo with Heather. He didn't talk much, but he knew how to listen, and he had a wonderful smile, like Teddy's. And though he drank a lot he could hold it—which was the main thing, Teddy said: not how much you drank but how well.

She had been lucky in her fathers-in-law. She had adored Mr. Hamlin; she had called him Daddy just as Richard did. After the accident, her grief was divided equally between Richard and his father. The death of her mother-in-law, whom she called Irene and who left Kay a string of pearls in her will, barely touched her.

The three of them had been killed in a head-on collision on Route 1. Richard had just picked up his parents at the airport; they were returning from Paris. It was pouring rain, and foggy. A truck swerved into their lane and demolished the Saab, its inhabitants, and the Hamlins' custom-made leather suitcases, which contained not only some exquisite Parisian baby clothes for the children but a signed Emile Calle vase they had picked up in a shop on the Left Bank. Most of Daddy's money was invested in Boston real estate and

European antiques, particularly French art glass. He had written them about the vase, which he was giving them for a fifth anniversary present. He said it was a very rare specimen, worth ten times what he paid for it. Kay tried hard not to think about the vase, but the image of it smashed to bits on Route 1 outside of Boston haunted her, and she always wondered if there wasn't some way the pieces could have been retrieved from the wreck, just so she could see the colors of it, the delicate browns and mauves, and the blue dragonfly Daddy had described in his letter.

She still missed Richard and his father, even after a year, even after the money, even after the marriage to Teddy Quinn. She missed Richard in an intense, intimate way—missed his body, his smell, his voice. She missed him in a way that she knew would eventually pass. But when she thought of Daddy, she saw him in the shop on the Left Bank, imagining a nondescript little place full of clutter and a shrewd, stout Frenchwoman in an old cardigan and shapeless shoes, her hair in a bun. The vase would be sitting dustily on the bottom shelf of an étagère that was partially blocked by a fake Empire bureau and a couple of authentic but battered Louis XVI chairs. Daddy would spot it. His face would reveal nothing; he wouldn't even lift an eyebrow at Irene, who would be examining some old Marseilles linens, for which she had a passion. Daddy would take his time. Eventually, in his fluent but badly pronounced French, he would ask the woman about the vase. She would shrug and quote a price, Daddy would look skeptical and argue, the woman would protest a bit and then come down, come down again, and the deal would be made. Daddy would take Irene to Chez Gaston for dinner.

His letter to Kay and Richard said, "If you think a piece of glass can't be full of elegance and wit, you are wrong," and went on to describe the blues and mauves. He was the kindest man Kay had ever known, as well as the richest.

She married Teddy because he was unusual. She could afford to marry a poor man (an unemployed struggling writer five years younger than she) because she had money of her own—all the Hamlin money, which came to the ghost of Richard through his parents' death and to her through Richard's.

The money was a shock she got over quickly. She found that having money of her own suited her—something she couldn't have foreseen. She had grown up in poverty on Chicago's northwest side, had waitressed her way through Boston University and then worked at Gottlieb/Bayard writing ad copy for three hundred dollars a month, and even after she met Richard they lived mostly on her salary plus his stipend at Harvard, where he was a graduate teaching assistant in art history. There were gifts from his parents, of course, but the Hamlins believed their only son should learn to get along on his own. They did pay for Mrs. Hickey, and for the 1962 Saab in which they had eventually died; they took Richard and Kay out to dinner every Friday night; they bought them extravagant birthday and anniversary gifts; and when he was killed Daddy was pondering the wisest way to set up trust funds for Heather and Peter.

But daily life in Richard and Kay's Dartmouth Street apartment was Spartan; they lived on hamburger, Kay carried her lunch to work, and twenty cents for Richard's MTA ride to Cambridge the last couple of mornings before payday sometimes had to be borrowed from Mrs. Hickey. When Kay went from all that to sudden wealth in one rainy afternoon, she was surprised at the ease with which she made the transition.

The first thing she did was get her own lawyer. Mr. Hensley, from Daddy's firm, tended to look at her with disapproval no matter how polite she was to him, no matter how much black she wore to conferences in his office—as if she had personally engineered the accident for the purpose of becoming an absurdly young, obscenely wealthy widow. He also thought it was somehow improper of her to keep her job; now, he seemed to feel, she was free to stay home with her children.

Her new lawyer was a man named Mel Katzmeyer; she hired him

because his office was on Newbury Street, down the block from Gottlieb/Bayard, and she could pop in on her lunch hour. He introduced her to Gauloise cigarettes in their classy blue packets, and to the Merry-Go-Round Room at the Copley Plaza. He also handled her investments, and he recommended that she buy the Joy Street house, which Mr. Hensley had cautioned her to wait on, and the diamond choker, which Mel said would cheer her up.

It did cheer her up. The whole process of going from rags to riches cheered her up. Teddy came along in the course of it. She met him at Gottlieb/Bayard, where he had come in to apply for a job. Kay talked to him because both Sam Gottlieb and Tom Bayard were in a conference that Teddy didn't seem worth leaving to interview. He was twenty-three, not long out of college, and he had just come to Boston from Binghamton, New York. His only working experience was a brief stint on the *Binghamton Record* and two months as a stock boy at the IBM Corporation over on Boylston Street where his sister Lucy worked in the office. He had been fired for inattention, he told Kay, and, smiling his wide, beautiful smile, he told her that he wanted to be a writer. He had a room on Marlborough Street. He was writing a novel about a reclusive painter who lived in Monterey and was, he said, based on his uncle Jamie. He had never been to Monterey, and neither had his uncle. He didn't think it was a good idea to get too close to your material. Did she?

Kay said she thought you were supposed to write about what you know; Teddy said in his opinion that was one of the most shortsighted and destructive literary clichés going; Kay said he was certainly an original thinker. They sat smiling at each other across Kay's desk. She liked his sandy-colored curly hair and his ears, which had no lobes—like the ears of royalty. Then Kay said she was really sorry, she could see he was very gifted, but it was hopeless, they needed someone with extensive copywriting experience. He asked her out to lunch, and when she accepted he told her it would have to be down the street at the Raleigh Cafeteria: they had great hot roastbeef sandwiches, he said. Kay picked up the phone and made a reservation at the Merry-Go-Round Room.

They drank martinis at the revolving bar and forgot to eat lunch. They ended up at her house on Joy Street. The babies were napping, and Mrs. Hickey was in the kitchen knitting and watching the soaps. Kay introduced Teddy as Theodore Vanderhagen because she'd forgotten his last name. Mrs. Hickey said please be nice and quiet and don't wake the babies. Kay and Teddy went upstairs to the bedroom and locked the door. While Kay called the office and said she must have gotten food poisoning at lunch, Teddy slowly, tenderly removed her stockings and her half-slip and her underpants and gently eased himself down on top of her.

"Why Vanderhagen?" he asked her eventually. "And my name isn't Theodore, anyway, it's Edward."

"But didn't it just sound marvelous?" Kay asked him. "All those syllables?"

When they got married, she became monosyllabic: Kay Quinn, which she also thought sounded marvelous, and was quick and efficient for signing checks. "I'll give you one piece of advice," Mrs. Hickey said. "Make sure he's a good father to those children." Mel Katzmeyer also gave her one piece of advice: "Don't lose control of your own money."

The marriage was a success for a long time. The only mistake she made (and it took her years to realize it) was in not keeping control of her money. By the time they were divorced, they were broke; all that was left was the French art glass. On the other hand, Teddy was a good father.

.   .   .   .   .

THEY SAW a lot of the Neals—Teddy's sister Lucy and her husband. Mark was a postdoc at MIT. Lucy was a painter and photographer but she was working at IBM because they needed the money. Kay never understood what it was exactly that either of them did: Mark was part of some big-shot physics professor's grant to study some sort of particles, and Lucy had a cretinous office job that involved punched cards being put into computers to do something or other. Kay offered to get her into the graphics department at Gottlieb / Bayard, but Lucy said she didn't mind her job because it left her brain free to think.

The Neals lived in a first-floor apartment on Commonwealth Avenue in Allston. The MTA rattled by their front windows. Their back windows looked out on an alley full of trash cans. They had two white cats, Peachy and Bingo; Kay learned never to wear black to their apartment. What Lucy really wanted was a baby; they were "trying," but it was going to be a problem because of a botched abortion Lucy had when she was in college. Kay tried not to think about Lucy and Mark trying to make a baby: she imagined grunting and prayer.

The two women met for lunch sometimes, usually at the Raleigh because Lucy couldn't afford anything else and wouldn't let Kay pick up the check.

"I don't understand that kind of pride," Kay said. "It's not like real money, Lucy. Nobody earned it. It's just there, to be spent. Think of it as pennies from heaven."

"You don't know what it is to be poor," Lucy said.

"Richard and I weren't exactly rolling in it. We ate plenty of peanut butter."

"That doesn't count. You had the Hamlins."

"You've got Stewart."

"Oh, come *on*—there's no comparison," Lucy said. "My God, Kay, you were driving a Saab, you had a nanny for the kids, you had leather boots from Bonwit's."

Kay shrugged. She had no intention of telling Lucy about her life before she met Richard. But she thought about it. Back when she was living at home on the canned spaghetti and soda her mother served for dinner, or when she was struggling to keep herself alive

and independent all through college—or even when she and Richard were flat broke by midweek: would she have accepted free
lunches from a wealthy relative? The question was absurd.

"If you're so poor, should you be thinking about having children?" she asked Lucy.

"That's a whole other thing," Lucy said, and bit savagely into her
egg salad sandwich.

Kay told Teddy his sister was a self-righteous wet blanket, and
Teddy said, "You're always judging. Lucy's been through a lot."

"Who hasn't?" asked Kay. "So she had an abortion. Big deal." Kay
had had two abortions when she was in college. She hadn't told
Teddy about them, and she hadn't told anyone that she would never
have given birth to Heather if Richard hadn't been so thrilled at the
prospect of a second child so soon after the first. When she told
Richard she'd missed her period—Peter was only six months old—
he went out and bought her a dozen red roses and a satin negligee.
It was almost the only grudge she had against him.

Kay said, "Maybe it's being brought up Catholic."

"We weren't exactly brought up Catholic. Except for my mother,
the family's about as lapsed as you can get."

"Maybe it passes through the maternal line, like Judaism."

Teddy said, "It's not religion, Kay. It's not anything. Lucy just
wants a kid. Why is that so hard for you to understand?"

Kay would have been happier if her children didn't exist; that was
another truth she never told anyone. It wasn't that she didn't love
them. It was just that children were so difficult and so time-
consuming. Mrs. Hickey arrived at seven-thirty in the morning and
left at six, except for Saturday nights, when she stayed late. She had
Sundays off. On Saturdays, Kay and Teddy almost always went out
for the day—shopping, or to the museum, or for drives to the north
shore in the new Saab, which was just like the old one but a later
model, and red instead of blue. They often went right from their
outing to dinner with friends. If they ate with Mark and Lucy, it

was in the Allston apartment or at a pizza place because the Neals wouldn't let the Quinns pay for a good dinner out and Kay refused to cook. On Sundays, after a chaotic family breakfast, Teddy took the children out to the park or the zoo or just for walks around the neighborhood—things parents were supposed to love doing with their kids but that Kay hated. Peter would get whiny; Heather would want to climb out of her stroller and be carried; Peter would ask for everything he saw, from the giant panda in the window of F. A.O. Schwartz to the ducks on the pond in the Public Garden; Heather would scream if she saw a dog. They would have to stop and carry on inane conversations with perfect strangers about Peter's bear and Heather's pretty pink dress.

Teddy bore all this with amused patience. Kay was touched by his affection for her children. They had adapted to their new daddy without a fuss. They still preferred Kay or Mrs. Hickey, but there were times when they clung to Teddy and wouldn't let him go, and he would look helplessly at Kay and pretend to scream, "Eek! I'm being attacked by little people from outer space." This never failed to crack Peter up, and he would run around the house yelling, "I'm from outer space!" which made Heather cry and drove Kay crazy.

When she was alone in the silent house, Kay was perfectly happy. The house, she sometimes thought, was her one true friend. It also occurred to her that between the day that Richard died and the day she married Teddy, she had been most vehemently herself—maybe not happy, but herself, the self that had lurked all those years, constrained by parents and poverty and hard work and trying to please. The self that really wanted, underneath everything, most desperately to be left alone.

On Sundays, while Teddy was out with the children, Kay filled up the coffeemaker and spent the day drinking coffee and eating pastry and reading the newspaper and sitting in the garden and taking long hot baths and prowling around the house thinking of further improvements she could make. The house was, as Mel Katzmeyer had said, a real bijou, a gem, with its walled-in backyard and the herb garden and the vaulted entrance hall and the Adam mantel her decorator had found in a junkyard and rehabilitated. Kay was thinking of installing shelves in the living room for the Hamlins' art glass, which was presently in storage; on the other hand, she could sell the collection; or she could donate it to a museum and get a tax break. She and Mel often spent her lunch hour discussing the pros and cons.

She was also thinking of making the third floor into what the decorator called the children's suite: two bedrooms, a playroom, a kitchenette, and a tiny sitting room for Mrs. Hickey.

"They'll love it," Kay imagined herself saying to Teddy. "Their own little apartment, their own little table for meals, a place to play where they can be as messy as they want. And think of when they're teenagers."

What she couldn't imagine was Teddy responding with, "That's a great idea, honey." She imagined him looking at her oddly and saying, "Kay, I think we should have a talk."

She did love them. She expected to love them even more when they were ten, eleven, fourteen, when their diapers didn't need changing and they didn't scream when they wanted something. What scared her was Teddy's desire for a child of his own. No rush, he said. He knew Kay wasn't ready for another pregnancy, and that Mrs. Hickey wouldn't be up to handling three little ones. And he also knew that Kay liked her job and wasn't ready to quit and stay home with the kids. He understood that.

They talked about it sometimes on their Saturdays out, and when Teddy made this reasonable speech Kay always felt chilled. She did like her job, but that wasn't why she worked; she worked precisely so that she wouldn't have to stay home with the kids. This wasn't something she could tell Teddy, but his failure to see it was like a pit opening before her feet. She would fall into the pit and be caught by screaming children lifting up their hands and wanting, wanting.

There was something else that bothered her. Teddy had given up his novel soon after they were married, and gotten a job as a reporter at the *Boston Globe.* He had gone to the interview on a whim, and neither of them could imagine why he had been hired. Kay thought it was his charm, his smile. Teddy said it was the new Brooks Brothers suit Kay had bought him. Neither of them considered that, in spite of his inexperience, he had demonstrated talent and intelligence, and so an even bigger surprise was that he was good at his job. He had been sent to cover a race riot in Roxbury because another reporter was sick, and the story made the front page and resulted in a three-part series on the problem and eventually a small promotion after only four months on the paper.

Kay had married Teddy because he was unusual, and part of his interesting uniqueness was his lack of a job, his loony devotion to his writing, his incompetence in the real world. Now he was a reporter for the *Globe.* Of course, she was proud of him, but his new career changed him, gave him harder edges. He even talked differently; he knew a lot about things that were mysteries to Kay. He had new friends, new hours, a new vocabulary. He even had a new name: his byline was Edward S. Quinn.

Teddy's job also changed her life. He sometimes had to work nights, leaving Kay to give the kids their baths and put them to bed without help. She couldn't control them the way he could, she couldn't laugh them out of sullenness and tears, and by the time they were in their pajamas she was exhausted. Getting them to sleep was something else. Peter wanted her to read to him, and Heather was afraid of the dark. Once they were in bed, she would sit downstairs with a glass of wine, tensed for a cry from above, too tired to eat her solitary dinner.

Kay tried to get Mrs. Hickey to stay until eight, as she used to before Teddy moved in, but even a major salary increase—even tears and pleading—didn't persuade her. Bedtimes would get better, Teddy said. She knew that, of course, but she also knew Teddy wouldn't want to put off a new baby for more than a couple of years. "We're not getting any younger," he sometimes reminded her in the midst of his no-rush speech—by which he meant that she was nearly thirty. Worse yet, one of Stewart's friends was editor of the *Albany Times-Union;* he had seen the Roxbury series and was interested in talking to Teddy about a job.

"You wouldn't seriously want to move to Albany, would you?" Kay asked him.

"Albany's not a bad city," Teddy said. "There's a lot going on in Albany. You'd be surprised."

. . . . .

IN LATE summer, over lunch at the Raleigh, Lucy announced that she was pregnant. Kay jumped up and hugged her and said how wonderful it was, imagining the grungy apartment full of cat hair and dirty diapers and cheap toys like the ones she gave away to Mrs. Hickey.

She and Teddy went shopping and sent the Neals a furnished dollhouse from Schwartz, complete with towel racks and china and needlepoint cushions and a tiny Franklin stove with a bucket of coal. Lucy called up when it was delivered and said, "Really, Kay, you shouldn't have, my God, we're overwhelmed," and the next time they all got together Mark said he hated to think what that thing cost, and he sure hoped they had a girl, he couldn't really imagine a little boy playing with all that furniture.

They were at Ernie's Pizza on Harvard Street. They all stayed silent, chewing, after Mark spoke. The Beatles were on the jukebox. *Help! I need somebody. Help!* Kay listened absently, leaning back in the booth, nibbling on a crust, and thinking how much Mark's looks repelled her—his handsome jutting chin and his thick neck and his blue-black five o'clock shadow. He was like the slow-witted, beefy football players she had gone to school with at Irving Park High, except that Mark was supposed to be brilliant. It was true that he could be good company, in a witty, mean-spirited sort of way. And he wasn't entirely insensitive, a fact that astonished her every time she saw evidence of it. And he apparently adored Lucy, and vice versa. He and Teddy, however, were beginning to dislike each other, and sitting across from him at the table, digesting his remark about her gift, Kay decided she hated him.

Teddy washed down his pizza with a swig of beer and said, "Well, personally, I don't think there's kid alive who wouldn't get a kick out of that house."

"You and I would have both loved it," Lucy said quickly. "It would have been perfect for The Poor Servant Girl."

Kay and Mark were both well educated in the intricacies of The Poor Servant Girl, a game Lucy and Teddy had played as children that sounded creepy to Kay—like the Brontës and their mad kingdoms—but Teddy remembered it fondly. He claimed it had kept him and Lucy sane through their parents' troubled marriage.

"I would have freaked out over a dollhouse like that," Teddy said.

"Oh, I'm sure," Mark said with a snicker.

There was a silence. Lucy looked nervously at Teddy and Kay. Mark was hunched over his pizza, chewing noisily. Teddy drained his glass and put it down on the table very gently. Lucy laughed shortly and said, "God! This song! I just don't get what's so great about the Beatles. Don't you think they're overrated?"

Kay stared back at Lucy—that desperate little smile, her hair pulled back with barrettes into a tangled mess, the collection of cheap rings on her fingers. She had another of her visions of the two of them in bed: Mark would be swift and silent and masculine while Lucy emitted ovine cries. *These people should not be allowed to produce children,* she thought to herself. Under the table, she touched Teddy's knee.

"As a matter of fact, I don't," she said. "I think the Beatles are the Shakespeare of our age."

In October, when Lucy had the miscarriage, Kay felt like a shit. It happened at Peck and Peck, where the two of them stopped after lunch to pick up a dress Kay was having altered. Lucy suddenly doubled over in pain, and then Kay noticed a puddle of blood on the carpet. Lucy saw the blood and began to scream. It was Kay who took over, got someone to call an ambulance, made Lucy sit down and stay calm. She rode with her to the hospital, and she called Mark and Teddy when it was over, glad she could do something, at least. Not that Mark had a word of thanks.

Lucy stayed overnight at Beth Israel, crying in a room with two other women who had just given birth—massive tactlessness that Kay tried to buy Lucy out of. But there was a shortage of beds. The baby had been a girl. Lucy's doctor said it wasn't impossible that she could have another, just highly unlikely.

"It was probably my fault," Teddy said that night when the children were in bed.

"How on earth could it be your fault?"

"The abortion she had in college. It was horrible. I arranged for this quack doctor to do it. He was a butcher. She was all cut up."

"Oh Teddy." Kay lit a Gauloise and held it to Teddy's lips. He took a puff, then waved it away. She watched him exhale, frowning. "Don't exaggerate."

"You should have seen the blood, Kay."

"Oh—blood," she said. "Big deal—blood."

Kay's first abortion had been done in Puerto Rico, in a hospital. Derek Wayne had paid for it—that frat-boy jerk. She could still remember the outrageously handsome doctor. He spoke a little English, she spoke a little Spanish. She had never seen eyes like his again— a sort of topaz darkening to brown. For the second abortion, she had gone to New York, to a shabby walkup office on Ninth Avenue that smelled of Raid. She remembered nothing else about it but crying in a taxi.

She said, "Teddy, millions of women have had abortions. In the

offices of quack doctors. On kitchen tables. Whatever. That doesn't
mean they all have miscarriages afterward."

"She's my sister. I'm supposed to take care of her."

"Oh Christ, Teddy, she's not a little kid any more."

"I've probably ruined her life."

"Don't overdramatize. These things happen. God, honey, even if
the abortion did screw up her insides, you didn't do it on purpose.
You obviously meant well. It certainly would have been worse if
she'd had a baby then. Right?"

He just shook his head, staring at the fireplace. The nights were
cool; they had just started having fires. Kay sat beside him on the sofa
and finished the cigarette. She hated it that Lucy could do this to
him. Maybe they should move away, to some hellhole like Albany,
what did it matter.

She stood up and put another log on the fire and poked the coals.
She wasn't sure what good poking did—she still wasn't used to the
fireplace—but the fire seemed to lick around the new log in a pur-
poseful way. The andirons were owls with green glass eyes; they came
from a forge in Vermont. Kay knelt on the floor looking at the
flames' crazy dance, orange and reddish black, and greenish black in
the owls' eyes. Behind her, Teddy was perfectly silent. She could hear
the noise of the fire and the tick of the grandfather clock on the
landing. She thought: it will kill me to leave this house.

She sat down close to him again and put his hand on her breast.
"Let me cheer you up, lovey. Hmm?"

He took his hand away. "Come on, Kay. Not now. Please. Let me
be for a while."

Mark would be bringing Lucy home from the hospital the next
afternoon. That morning before work, Teddy and Kay drove out to
Allston and loaded the dollhouse with difficulty into the trunk of
the Saab. Kay considered keeping it for Heather and Peter, but in the
end what seemed right was to take it to the dump in Brighton and

set it carefully on a pile of neatly tied plastic garbage bags. Maybe someone would pick it up. Later, on her lunch hour, Kay walked over to Bonwit's and picked out a quilted French silk bed jacket trimmed in marabou and had it sent to Lucy with a bottle of champagne and a card that read: *Deepest sympathy from your loving sister, Kay.*

Lucy

1963

THE FIRST photograph Lucy took of Nick Madziuk showed him playing his guitar. It was taken from slightly above, so that his cast-down eyes could hardly be seen, but the angle of his head conveyed deep absorption in the music and pleasure in what he was doing. His fingers touched the strings with love and attention; the long thumbnail he used for picking was a blur. The look of anguish that sometimes crossed his face when he played wasn't there in this photograph. If anything, he looked as if life was going well for him, as if he asked nothing more from it than to play his guitar and sing. There was absolutely no indication that what he was playing was a version of an old Kokomo Arnold blues number and that the words he was singing at the moment the picture was taken were

Good-bye, Mister Blues, why don't you leave me alone?
You been my best friend ever since my gal been gone.

. . . . .

DURING HER senior year, Lucy spent part of her Christmas vacation in New Mexico. By mid-December, that particular winter in
Ithaca was already cold and blizzard-plagued, and school wasn't
going well. Lucy was an English major, but she had been interested
in art and photography all through college, and she had begun to
wish, desperately and belatedly, that she had majored in art. When
she tried to settle down and wade through the critical works she
needed for a paper on Shakespeare or Chaucer, she felt that her
whole life was in question, that she had wasted twenty-one years,
that the future held nothing for her. She would have liked to stay in
college forever, living in her tiny apartment on Eddy Street and
spending long hours in the photography lab. She had lost interest in
her English courses and was two papers behind in her Chaucer sem-
inar, but the real problem was Photography 315: The Portrait, an
upper-level course she had been allowed into by permission of the
instructor, Mr. Ziedrich, who seemed to regret his magnanimity —
seemed, in fact, to dislike her. Her highest grade from him had been
an A-minus for a self-portrait that was technically more adept than
anything she'd done but that made her look ugly, squinty-eyed, fat,
slightly cretinous. It was hanging prominently in a student exhibit in
Wells Hall.

"I've got to get away," she said to her father, and added, hesitantly,
"What I'd really like to do is go out and see Mom."

Stewart gave her the trip west as a Christmas present. "Just do me
a favor and make it clear to your mother that I'm the one who's
shelling out for this," he said. He spoke in the ironic, distantly affectionate tone he'd developed for dealing with Caroline since the
divorce — a tone that revealed nothing about his true feelings. "And
give her my regards," he said.

Lucy had been out to New Mexico once before, in the summer, with a group of friends from college; they had camped in Apache Canyon, and she had seen her mother only twice, at the beginning and the end of her trip. This time she went alone, stayed in town at a hotel, did some sightseeing in Santa Fe, rode to Taos on a bus, and dragged her Nikon wherever she went, Ziedrich continually on her mind.

She met her mother in the convent parlor each morning and evening for roughly an hour—an apparently arbitrary restriction imposed, as far as Lucy could see, by Caroline herself. They had strangely formal conversations about school, about what Teddy was up to, about what Lucy had seen on her snowy walks around town. They spoke very little about life at the convent; when the subject came up, Caroline tended to veer off on some newsy topic, as if Lucy were an inquisitive stranger she met on an airplane. They talked about the Kennedys and thalidomide babies and *Dr. Strangelove,* which Caroline was dying to see but couldn't, of course.

"Why *of course,* Mom?" Lucy asked. "Is there an actual rule that says you can't go to the movies? Or that you can't go out to a restaurant or someplace with me instead of sitting in this parlor every day? Dad gave me plenty of money, I could take you out for a good Mexican meal."

Caroline frowned and looked down at her hands, which were folded in her lap. She wore a navy blue gabardine skirt and a long-sleeved cotton blouse, with stockings and sensible shoes. Her hair was clipped short. She was thinner than Lucy remembered, and from a distance she looked young and vulnerable: it was hard to think of her as *Mother, Mom.* She could be a girl recovering from a wasting illness. But up close she seemed gaunt, and her scrubbed face was sallow, with dry little wrinkles at the corners of her eyes and new hollows under them. She was beginning to look like old pictures of Lucy's grandmother.

Caroline said, reluctantly, "My position here is so odd, Lucy, that I have to make my own rules."

"In other words, you could go to movies but you won't."

"I feel I shouldn't, really, if I want to be part of the life of the convent."

"Holier than the Pope? So they'll let you take the veil?"

"Something like that. It's going very slowly. I'm starting to think it will never happen."

"Would that be so terrible?"

Caroline shrugged, looking annoyed; she obviously didn't want to continue the conversation.

"Well, would it?" Lucy asked stubbornly, and waited. If her mother was no longer like a mother, what was she like? Not a sister, not a friend. And—to be fair—not really like a stranger on a plane: Caroline was warmer than that, gladder to see her. She had listened to Lucy's recital of her school troubles with sympathy, had even suggested she spend another year at Cornell taking enough courses to get her into graduate school in art.

"Stewart can afford it," she said, and her tone was similar to his, though perhaps marginally less affectionate and more detached.

Like a nice but distant auntie you don't see very often, Lucy thought. Like Aunt Nell.

Her mind wandered. It was very warm in the visitors' parlor. The walls were an interesting shade of aged, dark beige, like walls in an old sepia photograph. The furniture was Anglo and antique, probably valuable. The convent was almost completely silent. Lucy imagined the nuns in their bare cells, down on their bony knees; they taught in the mission school and ran a soup kitchen but spent a good proportion of their time in silent prayer and contemplation. That was the word they used: contemplation. Contemplation of what? God, probably. But how did you contemplate God? What was there to contemplate?

Abruptly, Caroline spoke. "I would like to have some official place in the world," she said. "I would like to belong to something. I would like to have my function in life set before me clearly. I would like to be of use."

The short, impersonal sentences were like part of a legal deposition—as perhaps they were, part of the petition to Rome that had been pending nearly two years.

"I would like to have my position clarified," Caroline went on, as if she were the mistress of a man who refused to marry her. "And I would like to be able to give myself heart and soul to the life I've chosen."

Like a legal deposition. Like Caroline's prim blouse and sturdy shoes. Like the sterilized atmosphere of the parlor, where the windows gleamed and no speck of dust was allowed to exist. Perversely, Lucy thought of Nick Madziuk. She was still, technically, a virgin, but the last time they were together they had wrestled half-naked on his bed, on filthy sheets that smelled of sweat and sex and cigarette smoke, and lying there with him, his semen sticky against her thigh, she had loved the mess of it all, the friendly sordidness of the stinking bed, the cheap disorderly room with their clothes all over and the ashtrays overflowing and empty beer cans on the windowsill and Nick's guitar propped against a chair.

"It doesn't seem to me that life is meant to be that neat," Lucy said. "That clear-cut and easy, all laid out for you."

"I'm not talking about an easy life," Caroline corrected her. "Quite the contrary. And you don't have to agree with me. I'm an adult, Lucy. I've been here four years. I know what I want."

Lucy felt a pang of envy. Do you have to wait until you're past forty, she wondered, to know what you want? About herself, all she knew was what she didn't want: she didn't want to leave college to work at some hateful job, she didn't want a life like her mother's, she didn't want a stormy, disappointed marriage like the one her parents had had. She didn't even know if she wanted Nick, a Cornell drop-out, an itinerant guitar player with the stage name Nicky Magic. To give yourself heart and soul to something: when Lucy tried to imagine what that would be, her mind skittered off and came to rest with the idea that what she'd really like was to get an A in the course from Ziedrich.

"I guess I'll just never understand why you want what you want," Lucy said, and added, "Mom."

"That's all right," Caroline said in her gentle, hesitating voice. "I don't expect you to understand."

From the corner of her eye, Lucy saw the black shape of a nun hurry by the doorway, head down, beads rattling. It was nearly time for evening prayers, which Caroline never missed. Lucy sighed, and they both stood up.

Lucy said, "You might like to know that Dad still spends a lot of time trying to convince me you're crazy."

Caroline narrowed her eyes, and for a moment Lucy imagined that her mother might lash out against her father in anger like she used to do. Lucy remembered those monumental fights almost with pleasure — times when she and Teddy clung to each other upstairs in the hall, unable not to listen, their hearts thudding together.

Caroline rearranged her face into a benign, ironic look. "Has he convinced you, Lucy?"

Lucy said, "Almost," but she smiled so her mother would think she didn't mean it.

. . . . .

SHE PHOTOGRAPHED her mother before she left Santa Fe. It was a clear, sunny day, and Caroline was standing in the courtyard of the convent, wearing her blouse and skirt with a heavy cardigan. In the picture there was no visible snow. Caroline, however, looked chilled; she stood with her shoulders hunched and her arms crossed, a palm cupping each elbow. The shadow from a tree fell across her face and chest, marking her with bolts of shade. (This was, at best, Lucy knew, a C-plus photograph.) From her pose it was obvious that she wished she were elsewhere—indoors, warm, alone—but from the look on her face nothing could be deduced. There was no look on her face: her face was a pale oval half-framed by her cropped hair, her mouth was slightly open, and her eyes were beautiful and dark and perfectly blank.

. . . . .

LUCY HAD met Nick Madziuk through her roommate, Liz, who was dating his friend Tony. Nick was blond and very tall, with an ugly appealing face—big nose, thin lips, pitted cheeks, and narrow eyes of an unusual light blue that when he stood in the sunlight almost disappeared, giving him the white-eyed look of an Alsatian dog. He had dropped out of college to do what he really wanted, which was to practice the guitar and play at places like the Cellar on weekend nights. He sang folk songs and blues in a deep, rough growl, and his face when he sang was preoccupied and sad, as if he felt the words about faithless women and wandering men deep in his soul. He paused frequently for intricate riffs on the guitar that were mean-ingless to Lucy—like something other than music—but that drew whistles and applause from the audience.

She used to sit at a table near the stage and listen to him. During his breaks he came and sat with her, and when the place closed they used to go out with his friends and drink beer or go over to Nick's basement apartment to smoke some pot and listen to records—Dylan, Joan Baez, Pete Seeger, and scratched 78s featuring the old blues musicians that Nick revered: Big Bill Broonzy and Robert Johnson and Kokomo Arnold. Sometimes Nick and his friend Tony would play together—guitar and harmonica—and get so absorbed in what they were doing that the crowd would gradually thin out, people would leave, and only Lucy would be there, half-listening, trying to find a pattern in the music, drinking too much beer, wait-ing—finally dozing off at a table or on someone's sagging couch.

Then she and Nick went into his bedroom and almost, but not quite, made love. He wasn't pressuring her. He kept a package of Trojans in a drawer and occasionally took them out and looked at them: they've got cobwebs all over them, he said, they're turning into fossils—but good-natured, joking. He loved her, he said. He didn't want her to rush into anything.

When she returned from Santa Fe, she decided to go ahead and do it. All the way back on the plane, her mother's pale silences haunted her, and her failure to penetrate them. She thought of her father's decorous, uneventful life. She thought of Liz, her roommate, who had quit dating Tony because he was too weird. The more she thought about Nick Madziuk, the more she missed him, the more she feared that even to leave him for this short time had been a mistake—as if reality were that convent parlor, and Nick might be a mirage.

But when the plane landed at the Syracuse airport, he was waiting for her at the gate wearing his old wool jacket and leather boots, needing a haircut, looking like a cowboy down on his luck. They drove fast back to Ithaca; it was a Friday night, her plane had been late, he was due at the Cellar. She sat there at her table, dazed, talking to people about her trip, listening to Nick play, grateful that she hadn't dreamed it all. She felt as if she had undergone some trial and come through it. When he came to sit with her he held her hand, rubbing his calloused fingertips over the back of it. His other hand, the one with the long yellow thumbnail, was wrapped around a glass of beer: Lowenbrau Dark, his favorite, which always tasted to Lucy of molasses. He was talking about—what? She couldn't have said. Something entirely ordinary—the snow, maybe, or someone they knew, or his puppy. He had just acquired a mongrel mutt, named Peeve. "This is my pet, Peeve," was how Nick introduced him to people, and Lucy's photographs of Nick and Peeve roughhousing in the quad were what finally earned her the A from Ziedrich.

Lucy sat looking at Nick's bony, calloused, used-looking hand holding her pale white one, and it came to her like a flash of light that Nick was the answer to a question she'd hardly even allowed herself to ask.

. . . . . .

IN APRIL, when she realized she was pregnant, her first impulse was to do what her friend Gwen had done: go to New York and have an abortion. "Have it out," was the way Gwen put it, as if it were a tooth. But the abortionist Gwen knew in New York was no longer in business, and another contact she had through a friend of a friend fell through. Liz knew vaguely of a doctor in Syracuse who might do it, but Lucy said she couldn't go to Syracuse, all her relatives lived there, she couldn't risk it. She went to the gym and ran laps until her side hurt. She jumped down three steps, then four, then five in the front hall of her apartment building, feeling as if her teeth would jar loose from her head. Liz bought her a bottle of brandy, and Lucy sat in a tub of scalding water all one night getting drunk and then puking her guts out—a remedy Liz had read about in a novel—but nothing happened.

Finally she called Teddy. "For Christ's sake," he said. "Weren't you assholes using anything?"

"Rubbers," she told him. She was beyond embarrassment.

"Eighty-five percent effective," Teddy said. "Great. Why didn't you get yourself a diaphragm?"

"It's not that easy, Teddy. What am I supposed to do—go to Student Health and say I'm sleeping with my boyfriend?"

"Why don't you ask me these things, Lucy? What do you think brothers are for?"

"Well, I'm asking you now. Do you know anybody?"

He called her back. He had found a doctor in Binghamton who would do it. He'd pick her up Friday after her last class. She'd have to bring a box of sanitary napkins and a hundred dollars in unmarked bills—tens and fives. She could stay with him over the weekend, and she'd be back in school Monday morning. He asked her, "Is Nick going to pay?"

"Nick doesn't know," she said.

"When are you going to tell him?"

"I'm not going to tell him."

"Am I allowed to ask you why the hell not?"

She thought of Nick's face, the way he looked at her after they made love: how serene he was, how content with his life, with her. Gwen had said that when she told her boyfriend she was pregnant, he'd given her the money for Puerto Rico and then dropped her like a hot potato.

"No," she said.

Teddy picked her up, and she arrived in Binghamton in good spirits. She had her camera with her, and she took photographs of Teddy and his girlfriend, Deanna, who went part-time to the state college, in front of the pizza parlor where Deanna worked, and then they all went inside and had pizza. Afterward the three of them drove to the doctor's office—a shabby frame building on Watson Boulevard. The building was dark. There was a sign in the front window, but Lucy couldn't read what it said. Teddy parked the car and said, "Wait here, count to a hundred, and then follow me around to the back and walk in the door fast—don't waste any time."

It was like buying pot—there was a place in Ithaca where Nick ran in while she kept the motor running: the same secrecy, the same haste, the same elaborate planning. Deanna counted soberly to a hundred while Lucy fought the urge to either laugh or drive away, and then they groped their way through the dark to the back door.

Teddy was there to let them in. He locked the door behind them and led them down an unlit corridor. Lucy wondered if he'd been there before, if Deanna had. Teddy always bragged about his wild life in Binghamton, where he worked as a newspaper reporter and spent his weekends drunk in bars picking up girls from the college. Did that life involve arranging abortions?

At the end of the hall, Teddy stopped outside a closed door and flicked a light switch. The corridor sprang to life; it smelled bad—of what? Lucy couldn't place it—and looked as if it hadn't been swept in a year. There was a piece gouged out of the wall, as if someone had struck it with an axe. The closed door had a filthy glass panel. "Maybe we should just forget it," she whispered, but so softly that no one heard her.

Then the doctor opened the door, and he looked all right. He was dressed in spotless white; even his shoes were white, and a surgical mask hung at his chin. The room contained an old oak desk, a kitchen sink, a folding screen, and a table with stirrups that was both ominous and reassuring—it was just like the one a regular doctor might have. There was one window, covered with a piece of plywood painted the same color as the walls, the ancient sepia of Caroline's convent parlor. Teddy counted out the money while the doctor watched; he made Teddy turn over each bill to show that it wasn't marked, and then he instructed Teddy to put the bills back in their envelope and the envelope in the drawer of the desk at the end of the room. His voice was both matter-of-fact and soothing: he seemed like any doctor, any ordinary gray-haired G.P. that you'd go to for a shot of penicillin or a throat culture.

He told Teddy to wait outside, but Deanna could stay. Lucy went behind the screen and took off her skirt and underpants. She draped herself in a white sheet and climbed up on the table. Deanna wandered around the room until the doctor said, "Please—stay with the patient if you don't mind," and Deanna came over and stood next to Lucy, holding her hand, looking away while the doctor performed his examination.

He confirmed that she was three months gone. Lucky she hadn't waited much longer. And she should really get fitted for a diaphragm when this was all over. He said he'd be glad to do it himself if she came back after her next menstrual period. Lucy said that she would. The doctor smiled briefly at her, and then he asked Deanna to go over to the desk where Teddy had put the money, and turn on the radio, volume high. While something by the Beatles blared into the room, the doctor pulled up his mask. "You're going to feel just a little discomfort," he said, and began to scrape.

The pain was immediately unbearable, a violent cramping that twisted inside her like death. She hadn't known there was pain like that: was it worse than childbirth, some distant part of her brain wondered. The doctor paused, changed instruments, and the pain ebbed, lapped at her from a distance. Deanna asked, "Are you all right?" and Lucy nodded. She was all right, she would be sensible, it would be over soon, it couldn't take long, it must be over soon.

She saw the doctor's gray head again between her knees. The pain resumed, familiar now, expected. Lucy gripped Deanna's hand and tried to concentrate on the music. That was why the radio was on, of course: to give you something to think about besides the pain, the red pain. She couldn't see what was so special about the Beatles; they sounded like every rock-and-roll group she had ever heard: pound, pound, pound, a little falsetto, and very ordinary guitar work compared, say, to Big Bill. It wasn't until Deanna put her hand gently over Lucy's mouth and said, "Shh, Lucy, shh, please," that she realized the music might be on to drown out her screams.

The doctor stopped his scraping and laid his hand on her stomach. The pain subsided to a whine, a shadow, a small crimson center. "You aren't allowed to move," the doctor said. His voice was very calm. "It's important that you not move. Do you understand me?"

"Yes," Lucy said, and when he began again she screamed and felt Deanna's hand over her mouth. The music seemed to fade. She wished, suddenly, that Nick was there: his calm voice, his hands on the guitar, his rough music would cut through all the noise, the pain.

"Hold her."

"Lucy, please," Deanna said. Lucy looked up at Deanna's face and saw it was contorted, her mouth stretched wide, teeth bared, tears dripping down her cheeks. A primitive mask that said, "Please, Lucy."

The pain struck again, and she screamed for Teddy; from behind the door he said, "Oh Christ, I'm here, baby, I'm here, Luce."

She heard the doctor's quick intake of breath. He muttered, "Goddam it," and then, "*Don't move,* for Christ's sake," and then it was over. The doctor stopped scraping, she heard a metal instrument clink into a pan, and she opened her eyes. "She Loves You" was just finishing up. The doctor stripped off his gloves and dropped them into a plastic-lined wastebasket. The gloves were red. Lucy closed her eyes. Someone snapped off the radio. "Give her aspirin if there's any pain," the doctor said. "If she bleeds for more than a day or two, call me." He took the envelope from the desk drawer and left the room, still in his surgical mask. Deanna helped her down from the table, helped her get dressed. Deanna's right hand, where Lucy had held it, was red and swollen.

Back at Teddy's apartment, the bleeding became worse. The sanitary napkins were no good. Deanna made a contraption with half a box of napkins wrapped in a pillowcase, and it soaked through in a couple of minutes. The pain never completely stopped, and from time to time it intensified, so that it was difficult not to scream. Lucy sat on the toilet, listening to the blood drip from her, sure she was dying. Teddy tried to call the doctor, but there was no answer. Finally she put a wad of bath towels between her legs, and they took her to the emergency room.

The admitting doctor called it a spontaneous abortion. Teddy registered her as Mrs. Nicholas Madziuk. "My sister," he said. "This is their first baby. She comes to visit me for the weekend and this has to happen." In the hospital they gave her something for the pain, and the nurses thought it only natural that she should cry.

. . . . .

ONE OF THE photographs of Teddy and Deanna showed them standing in front of Teddy's car, which was parked at the curb of Angelo's Pizza House. The car was a 1958 Chevy, a model strangely

curvy and finless for its period. Teddy was wearing chinos, a plaid
shirt, and a short jacket from the pocket of which protruded what
looked like a paper bag with a bottle in it. Deanna wore a miniskirt
with tights and had a leather drawstring bag slung over her shoulder.
In the preceding shots, they had been mugging for the camera—
grinning widely, heads together, Teddy making a V of horns behind
Deanna's head, Deanna kicking up one leg like a pinup girl. In this
picture, no one was smiling. Deanna was frowning off to one side;
Teddy was staring straight ahead at the camera and he looked, for
some reason, angry.

.   .   .   .   .

ALL HER dreams ended in blood. She entered a cafeteria; she was
working in the art library; she sat at the front table at the Cellar,
listening to Nicky Magic play his guitar; but always, eventually, there
was the blood oozing from her like a red scarf.

She was at her father's house, resting. He had picked her up at
Teddy's in his new white Bonneville, and had made her lie in the
backseat all the way to Albany. Teddy had told him about the abortion, a fact Lucy still couldn't take in. She kept trying to imagine
Teddy and her father having this conversation, Teddy saying the
words "pregnant" and "abortion," her father apparently taking it all
calmly, saying Lucy needed to rest, arranging to drive down and pick
her up.

He put her to bed in her old room and went downstairs to make
her some lunch. She dozed: she was in the library, the pain was like a
knife in her belly, and the blood pursued her down the stairs. When
her father came in with soup and an English muffin on a tray, she
woke and began to cry. Stewart stood there with the tray for a
moment. Then he came over to the bed and patted her arm while
she cried. She heard him take a cigarette from the pack in his shirt
pocket and light it with his ancient Zippo. She stopped crying and
kept her eyes closed, listening to him smoke—the small breathy

sound on an inhale, pause, the cigarette tapped against the side of an ashtray, then a noisy exhale which meant that he had something on his mind. She tried to guess, out of all the possibilities, what it could be.

"What is it, Dad?" she asked finally, and turned her head to look at him. Nice sad old Daddy, gray hair falling over his forehead, his thin old lips pursed around his cigarette. She and Teddy speculated endlessly about whether Stewart had women. There had never been a shred of evidence. As far as they could tell—even though she had walked out on him, divorced him against his will, refused to communicate with him, and now was trying to get Rome to declare their marriage null and void so she could enter the convent—he was still faithful to Caroline. One of her glamorous 1940s photographs was in his bedroom, framed, on the wall. "Your mother and I are still married, as far as I'm concerned," he had said once when Teddy hinted.

The tray was on the dresser. She could smell the soup, and she realized she was hungry. Stewart exhaled a stream of smoke and said, "I guess I just wonder about the boy involved, Lucy."

There was a silence, and then a cough caught him by surprise— the fierce, painful smoker's cough that could jerk his body back like a gunshot and leave him red-faced and breathless. But it didn't last long this time, and when he finished Lucy said, "What about him?"

"I just wonder why you chose this route. Why marriage wasn't an option."

"I just didn't think it was."

"You mean you don't want to marry him?"

"I mean I didn't think he'd want to marry me."

He stared at her. "He wasn't consulted about this at all?"

"I might tell him eventually."

"It's this boy Nick you talked about at Christmas?"

Boy. She turned her head away. "Yes."

"You made him sound like a reasonable young man, Lucy. I don't understand why you wouldn't tell him a thing like this." She didn't speak. "Lucy? It does seem to me that it's his business, as well as yours. Not that I don't think you should make the final decision, but it seems unfair that this should be a secret from him. I can't believe he wouldn't want to take some responsibility."

The pain came again—not a bad one, just a cramp—and she could feel blood gush out onto the sanitary napkin. She might bleed slightly for several days, they had told her at the hospital. "But nothing to worry about," the nurse said. "Just treat it like a normal period." Then the doctor came in and said, "You may have trouble getting pregnant again, Mrs. Madziuk. We may have to get you in here for some repairs." He had refused to look her in the eye: he knew everything, of course, and he had pronounced the name wrong, three syllables. *Magic,* she thought. It's pronounced *magic.* "These old magic fingers," Nick had said, touching her. One of the blues songs he liked to sing contained the line, *You gave me seven children, and now I'm givin' them back to you.*

"Lucy?"

She pushed herself up, bunching the pillow behind her, and smiled at him. "Could I have my soup now, please, Dad?"

He sighed and went across the room for the tray. When he set it in front of her, she was already crying again.

. . . . . .

THERE WAS still film in her camera, and she photographed Stewart that Monday morning before she got on the train for Ithaca. He was dressed for the office: suit, tie, white shirt, overcoat, shiny black shoes. The photograph was taken at the train station, and he was flanked by posters advertising *Who's Afraid of Virginia Woolf?* and Dewar's scotch. Stewart was smiling. He looked like what he was: a successful lawyer posing patiently for his daughter the photographer because he loved her. He didn't look at all like what he also was: a sad wreck of a man, whose life had let him down at every turn.

. . . . .

BACK IN Ithaca, Lucy threw herself into her new photography course: Photographic Abstraction, it was called. They were supposed to take something ordinary and distort it, make it into something unidentifiable and striking. They dabbled in macro-photography; Lucy turned a scrap of Kleenex into a desolate lunar landscape. They practiced unorthodox darkroom techniques; they slashed the film and painted on it; they studied Aaron Siskind and Minor White, and Edward Weston's fruitlike nudes and animal-like vegetables. "What you are photographing here, always, is yourself," Ziedrich said.

Lucy told Nick, finally, about the abortion, mainly to explain why she was too sore for sex. He didn't have much to say. When he asked her why he hadn't been informed, she told him about Gwen's boyfriend. "You think I'm like that asshole?" he asked. "Thanks a lot."

Things didn't go well between them. They lost the knack of talking to each other, of telling every little thing that was on their minds. When they were together they went on long walks so the puppy could get some exercise and Lucy could take photographs. After a while they gave up on the idea of sex; Lucy stopped going to the Cellar; she began dating a graduate student in physics named Mark Neal. Just before final exams Nick told her that he and Tony were driving out to the coast, where they had a lead on a job in a club in L.A. At the end of the summer, Lucy and Mark were married at Stewart's church in Albany; Mark was going into the postdoctoral program at M.I.T., and they would be moving to Boston. Caroline didn't come to the wedding, but she sent a Hopi kachina that she said was a symbol of fertility.

. . . . .

THE LAST photograph Lucy took of Nick showed him in front of the apartment house, leaning against an iron fence. The building, of dark brick, was on a nondescript street north of the Cornell campus. The season was early spring; there was a small tree behind him

to the left, just budding. His hands were in his pockets. He was wearing baggy camouflage pants, his tattered wool jacket, and leather
boots that showed beneath his cuffs where one foot crossed the
other. There was something in his pose, in his light-colored eyes,
even in the gentle gleam of the sun on his blond hair, that suggested
he would be perfectly happy to stand there forever, leaning against
the fence and smiling at the photographer.

Caroline
1959

THE SUN in Santa Fe was different from the sun back home. Not just hotter: she thought of it as more aggressive, more intimate, the way it entered your body and became a part of it, the way it penetrated your bones and your blood. Even at night, when the sun retreated and the cool, black mountain air made it necessary to wear a sweater and put blankets on the bed, she was aware of the sun banked behind the mountains, waiting.

I will never go back, she thought.

She got the job at the convent almost immediately, through an employment agency. Mother Rosaria interviewed her and pronounced her skills superb. The Sisters of Mary had never had a real secretary before; Sister Marguerite had done the job for thirty years, until she got too old, and none of the other sisters could type. They were a semicontemplative order connected with the mission church of Saint Grazia; they ran a small school and a soup kitchen for the poor, but they spent most of their time in prayer. Caroline did the same things for the nuns that she had done for Mr. Fahey at Pepsi-Cola the past six years: took dictation, typed letters, and answered the phone. The salary was exactly half what Mr. Fahey was paying her when she left, but her expenses were light.

She lived in three rooms on Camino del Monte Sol not far from the river, on the top floor of an apartment house built in the twenties. Her place was sparsely furnished, with thick stucco walls that kept out sound. There were niches in the walls for statues of saints, which Caroline left empty. The apartment suggested a stage set—it had that same hushed, expectant, alien quality. When she came home from work and entered the apartment, the quiet leapt out at her. The phone ringing or the noise of the radio was like a violation— even dishes left undone or her coat thrown across a chair. She became very neat.

Her living-room windows looked down on the street and across to a taller building that blocked the view, but the bedroom ones faced east, with a view of the Sangre de Christo Mountains. She had never seen mountains before—just one trip to the Adirondacks long ago, with Stewart and the children. She'd barely noticed the mountains then: all she remembered from that vacation was exhaustion and arguing. But she was sure the Adirondacks were nothing like this.

The winters were going to be cold, people told her. There would be snow—as much, maybe, as back home in the Snow Belt of upstate New York. Even now, in September, October, there was snow in the mountains. And Santa Fe could be very dull in the winter, her friend Lee said. "You'll want to go out and meet people, do things, but there's nothing. Not even tourists. Just a bunch of ski bums and freezing Indians on the Plaza. The isolation can get to you."

"I don't care," Caroline said. "That's exactly what I'm looking for."

Lee laughed at her. "What? Ski bums or freezing Indians?"

"Isolation," Caroline said. "Nothing." Sometimes she had trouble seeing a joke.

She met Lee at Mass. A tall woman in a black lace mantilla and suede jacket slipped into a pew next to her one Sunday at the Cathedral—ten minutes late, they had already reached the Epistle. All through the service, Caroline admired the woman's rings, two of them on the skinny fingers of her left hand, one on her right: hammered silver set with small turquoises. On the way out they got talking. Caroline told her she was new in town; Lee said she was a jewelry maker and managed an art gallery on San Francisco Street. When they saw each other again the next Sunday, Lee asked Caroline over to her place for lunch. She lived upstairs from the gallery in a bright, chaotic, art-filled apartment that overlooked a *plazuela*. She was a native of Santa Fe, part Navajo, a widow. Her husband had been a climber and tour guide who became lost in the mountains three years before; a blizzard had come up and stranded him somewhere near the summit of Truchas Peak. The rest of the party had been rescued, but he had been out scouting and his body was never found.

Caroline thought immediately of Ray and Peggy, whose deaths on the ice had seemed not only horrible but strange and singular. And yet here was a woman she'd met by chance, telling the same story. Did that mean life was more strange, or less strange, than she had thought?

Lee told Caroline about her lost husband that first day, over lunch. "I can't marry again," Lee said. "I'll never know what happened to him."

"But after a certain number of years—"

"Oh yes, legally there's no problem, but how do I know he didn't just take the opportunity to run off? Maybe he's living in Chimayo right this minute. Or up in the mountains, a hermit, biding his time. He had a strange sense of humor. Maybe he's living right here in

Santa Fe." She laughed. "While I light a candle for him every Friday at the Cathedral."

Lee was exactly Caroline's age: forty. She was bony and flat-chested, her graying hair was cropped short, she had a tooth missing near the front, her skin was pitted and tanned to leather. But men liked her. "I don't know what it is," she said to Caroline. "They won't leave me alone. I guess they know I like them. I give off vibes, some-body told me."

"I hope I don't give off vibes," Caroline said.

"You don't need vibes. You're gorgeous."

"Thank you," Caroline said. "But I've had it with men."

Lee made a face. "Bad divorce?"

"You could say that." She laughed. "Bad life."

"You'll get over it. You're too pretty to be alone for long."

Caroline had chosen Santa Fe because Mr. Fahey's son Jerry had gone to New Mexico to see the Pepsi bottling plant in Albuquerque. They were experimenting with a new capping device there, and Mr. Fahey wanted it checked out. Jerry and his wife had turned the trip into a vacation—had rented a car and driven to Santa Fe and Taos and up as far as Denver before they flew home. They sent back post-cards to the office, and Caroline took one look at the austere lines of the adobe church against a pure blue sky and thought: *why not?* She was ready to do something extravagant, something as unlike the rest of her life as possible. She squinted at the postcard, imagining that one of the tiny people in front of the chapel was herself.

That was in the spring. By September, when Teddy and Lucy were ready to leave for Colgate and Cornell, she had sold every-thing, packed her bags, and blown most of her savings on a plane ticket. Teddy and Lucy didn't take it well.

"So where do I go on vacations?" Lucy demanded.

"You go to Daddy in Albany, of course. I'll come back at Christ-mas. At Thanksgiving, you can go to Aunt Nell and Uncle Jamie's. Then next summer you can decide what you want to do."

"This is my first year away. I'd like to be able to come home sometimes. Just on the spur of the moment, if I want to."

"Your father would be very hurt to hear you say that his place isn't home. Especially since he's paying the bills."

Lucy said, with tears in her eyes, "You always do something like this."

"Like what? Something like what? What are you talking about?" Caroline heard her voice get shrill and unconvincing, the way it used to during arguments with Stewart when she suspected he was right.

Teddy took his mother aside and told her she was being unfair to them, especially Lucy. Teddy was seldom entirely serious, but when he was he took on some of Stewart's mannerisms—squinting up his eyes and stuttering slightly, his whole body tight with earnestness. Caroline blew up at Teddy's solemn little speech. She said he and Lucy were grown up, they were in college, and if he could manage to join a fraternity and stay drunk all weekend he could certainly manage to take care of himself. As for Lucy, she had her brother and her father and a will of iron, and it was time she learned to get along in the world.

She also said something she immediately regretted: that it was the simple truth that having children so young and so close together had screwed up her life and now she was getting it back. Teddy's face was stricken, and she apologized, tried to hug him. Teddy pushed away, said, "The hell with it," and slammed out of the house.

. . . . .

SHE WALKED a mile to work every morning. The names of the streets were like incantations. Camino del Monte Sol, Acequia Madre, Alameda, Paseo de Peralta. She had lunch at a little place called Tomasita's and ate the hot, unfamiliar foods happily, though she had to wash them down with cold milk, which amused the waiters. It also amused them that she showed up every day promptly at noon. Even Tomasita advised her once, "You should try another place. Make a change. Eat some other kind of food." But she knew Tomasita's; the menu was familiar, and the corner table, where she could turn her back on the room and read while she ate, was almost always available.

She was hurt that she wasn't asked to have lunch with the nuns. She had confided to Mother Rosaria that she had been away from the Church for years and had just had a change of heart; she had expected that fact to make the nuns befriend her—the prodigal daughter, the lost lamb returned to the fold. Mother Rosaria had asked, almost absently, "What brought you back to the Church, then?"

The honest answer would have sounded peculiar: to say that one day last spring in Syracuse, walking home from the Italian bakery where she bought bread, she had stopped in at Assumption Church to get out of the rain. She had sat in the back pew and looked around her as if she had never seen it before, marveling at how really beautiful it all was, how abundant and welcoming: gold everywhere, red carpeting, statues smiling down on her, masses of Paschal lilies on the elaborate carved altar with its three arches. Even on a rainy day, the stained glass windows glowed with a secret light. She had thought to herself: *maybe I'll stop in at Mass on Sunday,* the way she might think: *maybe I'll pick up a loaf of semolina bread at the bakery;* and at that moment she had heard, very distinctly, a voice say; *yes.* She was Saint Paul, felled from his horse and blinded. She had whirled around, searching the church for someone, some mumbling sacristan whose voice she had mistaken for the Voice, but there was nothing, no one in the church but herself and the statues and the presence, the Real Presence, the presence that was always there, always watching, always reaching out, always wanting . . .

She had flung herself down on her knees and put her head in her hands. Long after the rain had stopped and the setting sun blazed like fire through the stained glass, she was still there.

To Mother Rosaria, she said, "I guess I just felt something was missing from my life"—which was true enough but had nothing to do with the Church.

Mother Rosaria smiled and patted her arm. "Well, I'm glad you found it," she said, and gave Caroline the bulletin for next Sunday to type and run off on the hectograph machine.

Lee was her only real friend. She liked Lee, but she didn't know what to make of her, and she had no idea how Lee reconciled her sex life with Holy Communion every Sunday. She did stop in at the Santuaria on Guadaloupe Street to light a candle every Friday on her way home from work. But Caroline knew she didn't go regularly to Confession, because during the hours of Confession on Saturday afternoons, she and Lee were often together, browsing the art galleries or sitting in cafes eating pastry.

Lee's only real interests were art and sex. The jewelry she made was magnificent. She worked in silver, using Zuni and Navajo techniques, which she explained to Caroline in meticulous detail. She offered to make Caroline her apprentice. She offered to teach her Spanish. For her birthday, she gave her a cast silver-and-turquoise bracelet. She offered to introduce her to men. She told her the nuns were exploiting her, and advised her to take a hatcheck job at some night spot like Juanita's, where with her looks she could make on tips alone what she was making at the convent.

Every Saturday around five o'clock, Lee looked at her watch and said, "Oh my God, what am I thinking of, I've got to get going." She always had a date, with a variety of men that bewildered Caroline. Caroline never met any of them. Lee would say, "Sure you don't want to come? I could fix you up like that," and snap her fingers. Caroline always said no, feeling like a child—the way she used to feel when she was twelve and Peggy was thirteen, watching Peggy put on forbidden lipstick to sneak out and meet a forbidden boyfriend. Lee would laugh at her, tell her she was missing a good time, and the next morning, there she would be—black-mantillaed and late—in the back row at the eleven o'clock High Mass, rolling her eyes and saying, "Am I exhausted! What a night!" Then going to Communion.

Caroline was grateful for Lee. It took her months to admit to herself that her new life was more difficult than she had expected. Once she got used to the charm of the Spanish names and the food and the warmth and the old adobe convent where she worked, it was a lonely life. Her footsteps in the spare white apartment still echoed. The empty niches in the walls were a constant reproach, but when she tried to fill them—with a vase of flowers, a plant, a cheap carved statue of the Virgin she bought in a shop on Cerrillos Road—they still looked wrong. Everything she did seemed silly and arbitrary and irrelevant. She began to think there was some secret to living in the West that she hadn't divined—some secret, perhaps, of living comfortably in her own skin.

She spoke only to Lee, to the nuns, to people who came to the convent, to waiters, to Mrs. Rivera across the hall. Father Grady, who was originally from Brooklyn, stopped in the office to talk and bring her an occasional *New York Times* because he knew she liked the crossword.

On her way to and from work, men looked at her, men spoke to her, once a man stopped her and begged her to have coffee with him—a nice-looking man dressed in a suit. He walked along beside her down Alameda, told her he saw her every morning, his intentions were purely honorable, if he could only buy her a cup of coffee so they could get to know each other a little. She walked quickly, shaking her head, looking down at the sidewalk, and eventually he stopped and let her go.

"But don't you like being pretty?" Lee asked her.

"I've never really thought about it," Caroline said, vaguely aware that this was a lie—that in some other life she had thought about it plenty.

"Think about it now," Lee said. "If you could trade the way you look for the way I look, would you?" Lee grinned at her, showing her missing tooth.

"Oh, Lee, you keep saying you're so ugly, but you're not."

Lee didn't stop grinning. "That's not the point at issue here."

Caroline thought about it. Lee waited, sipping her coffee. They were sitting on the floor in Caroline's living room. It was late on a Saturday afternoon. Not much sun came in through the tall windows on this side, only a colorless slice of light that moved across the bare wood floor. Caroline put her hand on it. Even her hand—cool and white and long-fingered—was prettier than Lee's skinny brown one. She didn't really have to think: of course she liked being pretty. she loved her hand. She loved her whole body. She wanted to say to Lee that her body was like her wedding dress, something beautiful and useless, to be treasured but not put into circulation, but it made her sound nutty, like a Faulkner heroine undone by years of inbreeding and degeneracy. And, in fact, it occurred to her that her wedding dress was one of the things her mother had burned in the furnace before she died.

She shrugged and said, "I'm used to the way I look."

Lee asked, "It's not that you prefer women, is it?"

That was something she used to think about, back in the days when men had begun to touch her and she had shrunk from them. But sex with a woman was not the solution: to imagine being in bed with a man gave her a sick, anxious feeling, but going to bed with some version of herself seemed merely silly and pointless.

She shook her head. "No. My sister Nell does, I think. Not that she's ever done anything. But I suspect she's—you know."

"You suspect? You don't know?"

"We're not very close."

"Really? God, my sister and I tell each other everything."

"I'm not that close to anyone in my family." Or to anyone anywhere, at least since Mother died. That was something, at least. *I did love my mother,* she thought, and for a moment she had an irrational impulse to tell Lee all about her mother's last days: *she wasn't herself, she burned things, she burned everything that belonged to me.* She wanted to say: *I was there when she died, I leaned over the bed, I held her hand, I said Mother, don't go, what will I do?* She frowned, picked up her coffee and sipped.

Lee said, "Gee, that's too bad, honey—that must make it rough. I don't know what I'd do without my family."

For a moment, she did wish she were Lee, not for her looks but for her ability to chat, to take life easily, to sympathize with everyone and fit in anywhere—even to impose her personality on her apartment and fill it unself-consciously with the interesting clutter of her life.

"So why don't you want a man?" Lee refused to let the subject be dropped.

"It's complicated." It was complicated by the fact that sometimes she lay awake, especially on Saturday nights, touching her body, thinking she would die if no one, ever again, loved her. It was only when she tried to match up that feeling with the man in the suit, or Stewart, or anyone she had ever known, that she could dismiss it and go to sleep.

She would have liked to tell these things to Lee, but she suspected that Lee would wink at her and say she knew just the cure. And, in a way, she was tempted to have Lee fix her up; at least, with a date on Saturday nights, she would feel less lonely, she would have something to think about, she might not feel quite so sorry for herself. It seemed to her sometimes that she had felt sorry for herself for twenty years. She had no idea how to stop.

She wrote far too many letters home—to Nell, Jamie, her old friends from work. To Lucy and Teddy she wrote long, regular, guilty letters full of Santa Fe history and descriptions of Lee and the nuns and Father Grady, half of which she didn't even mail and most of which weren't answered. Writing them, she missed her children

badly. Sometimes, writing to them, she thought about their childhood, the days when she could hold their lithe little bodies on her
lap and kiss them. When they were in Albany with Stewart, her house
used to go dead, become full of something like the creepy quiet she
came home to now every day in her apartment. In those days the
quiet had made her feel both grateful and restless.

Lee flew to Texas to have Thanksgiving dinner with her sister's
family, and Tomasita's was closed, so Caroline ate Thanksgiving dinner at home: a piece of leftover chicken and some frozen French
fries. She was unable to decide whether she would rather be at
Nell's. She thought of what she was missing—not just the long, logy
Thanksgiving dinner, but all the rest of it: Jamie being sullen when
he wasn't pontificating about politics or art, Mr. Fahey making his
lame jokes, probably a couple of Nell's schoolmarm friends grilling
Lucy and Teddy about their English courses. Everyone drinking too
much of Nell's cheap wine. Stewart would call, of course, and talk
about her with Teddy and Lucy. How peculiar Mom was getting,
how hostile it was for her to move so far away on a whim—and the
whole thing with her going back to the Church. Well, you know
you're always welcome at my place, kids. We know, Daddy. Be good.
Take care. Don't worry too much about it. She's always been a
strange bird. Everything will work out.

When she was sure they would be done with dinner, she telephoned. Lucy and Teddy no longer sounded resentful. Teddy asked
her to send him a sombrero. Lucy had a boyfriend and was learning
photography. Nell got on the phone and said they were having the
house painted in the spring, Mr. Fahey's new secretary was a disaster, Jack and Penny Wentworth were divorcing, the turkey had been
a bit too dry. When they asked, Caroline told them she loved Santa
Fe, her job was very interesting. She didn't know how long she
would stay. The mountains were beautiful, the city was lovely, especially now that the tourists were gone, there had been snow but the
sun was so strong it melted fast.

When she hung up, she knew she was right not to go home as she had thought of doing. That wasn't what she wanted—that easy descent into the family routines, the conversation of her children, the old quarrels and jokes. The Caroline who could sink into that and lie there drowning was the Caroline she wanted to be rid of.

But the apartment was very silent, and so was the wet street outside her windows. She turned on the radio and heard Christmas carols. When she sang along, her voice was thin and wobbly, and the songs seemed either ludicrous or impossibly sad.

She thought: *you wanted isolation; this is isolation.* She had never expected it to be so empty and so alien. She had thought she could fill it with herself, that her self would be enough. Someone had told her that in 1598 a Spanish missionary in the area had sent home confused reports locating New Mexico somewhere between Newfoundland and China, and that was exactly how it felt to her—like another continent, an alien world of vast and terrifying spaces, where the person she had been was obliterated but nothing had come to take its place.

She washed the dishes and then wandered around the apartment, straightening things that were already neat. She had emptied the wall niches again, and she dusted them all with the hem of her apron. Once, someone rang her bell—a couple of confused Rivera relatives. When Mrs. Rivera opened her door, there was noisy laughter and the smell of cooking and a radio playing Pérez Prado.

She considered getting dressed and going to someplace like Juanita's and picking up a man and bringing him home with her. She imagined telling Lee what she had done, and Lee's delighted, incredulous laugh. She went so far as to change into stockings and high heels and open her closet looking for a dress before she had to run into the bathroom and throw up. She sat for a while on the cold floor, conscious of a run in one of her stockings slowly, with a soft tearing sound, making its way up her leg. Then she rose, cleaned the toilet, washed her face, and sat on her bed in her bathrobe, wondering if she was sick because the chicken she'd eaten had been around too long, or whether her soul-sickness, or whatever it was, had made itself felt as a physical thing, and then decided she was being fanciful.

After a while, she raised the shade and looked out at the mountains, black masses against an ink-blue sky. She thought of Lee's husband, lost somewhere in that space: a heap of bones or a mad mountain man, he was no more than a speck up there, something small and forgotten in a cave. She sat until dawn, dozing off and on, until the mountains began to light up with the bloody red-orange flush that gave them their name, and then she got dressed and went to early Mass at the Cathedral.

. . . . .

THE NEXT week, she saw the man in the suit. He was coming out of a café on Alameda. He looked at her, and she smiled at him.

They had a cup of coffee together. His name was Lloyd Vegara, and he was an anthropologist who worked for the state Conservation Department. It turned out he knew Lee—he collected Pueblo pottery, which she sold in her shop. He asked Caroline if she had seen the cliff dwellings at Bandelier, and offered to take her there—maybe Saturday? But first she had to let him take her out to dinner Friday night.

She agreed. He was really very nice—a big, talkative man with wavy black hair. He was divorced, had three grown children, lived alone in a restored adobe house on the old Santa Fe Trail. It was built in 1765 on the site of a thirteenth-century *rancheria,* and he wanted her to see it. He talked interestingly about his job: his mission in life was to preserve the architecture of the Pueblos. Had she been to Chaco Canyon? He would take her to Chaco Canyon.

"It must be wonderful to have a mission in life," she said.

He smiled at her. "Now I have another one."

She called Lee and asked her about him. "Lloyd? He's great," Lee said. "If I had to pick one guy in Santa Fe for you to go out with, I'd pick him. He's nice and he's loaded and he's not kinky, and I think he's still under fifty."

They ate dinner at La Cantina, and afterward Lloyd showed her his house. It was a cold, clear, windless night. The sky was full of stars and there was a crescent moon. They walked from the restaurant, their shadows cutting through sidewalks made yellow by the street lamps. The house was very beautiful. The *vigas,* he told her, were original. He had rebuilt the walls with adobe bricks he made himself. In the *sala,* he lit a fire in the fireplace, watched it until it caught, then turned to her and began kissing her.

They made love before the fire. Over his shoulder, Caroline watched the small flames dart between the logs and gain strength. Lloyd kept saying her name. She dug her nails into his back and tasted his salty skin. Lloyd held her face between his hands and said he was in love with her, he had known her only a few days and he loved her already, he loved her so much he wanted to weep—and he did weep a little, laughing at himself, kissing her, telling her she was beautiful, he had never expected this to happen to him again.

She watched him get up awkwardly and put his pants back on. He was soft around the middle; his legs were skinny and covered with rough black hairs. He went barefoot over the stone floor to get them some brandy. Caroline lay on the rug, propped up on one elbow, looking into the flames, remembering Stewart crying in her arms over Peggy, and how his sorrow had turned to lust.

She drank the brandy too quickly and, in the middle of one of Lloyd's stories about his restoration of the house, asked him to take her home. She said she was sorry, she wasn't feeling well, maybe she was coming down with something. He was concerned. He helped her into her clothes, buttoning her dress tenderly, kissing her neck. Yes, he said, she seemed feverish. He offered to stay with her, offered to perform any task, get her anything that would help. She said it was probably just a cold, she'd had a headache and a sort of sore throat all day. He drove her home and kissed her gently at the door.

"Maybe next week we'll have our outing, then," he said. He laid his cheek against her hair; she felt his warm breath. He whispered, "Tonight has changed my life." He told her to take care of herself, he would call her tomorrow.

"I'll probably just sleep most of the day," she said. "Let me call you when I'm feeling better."

She didn't call him. When he phoned her two days later, she said she still didn't feel very well. She called in sick at work and stayed home most of that week, doing crossword puzzles in a book she bought and listening to the radio, turned down very low. When Lloyd called her again, she told him she was sorry, she didn't want to mislead him, she liked him very much, but she wasn't ready to start seeing anyone, she was very very sorry.

She stopped eating at Tomasita's. She walked home on her lunch hour and ate any old thing, sitting on her bed and looking out the window at the mountains. She took a different route to work, so she wouldn't run into Lloyd Vegara. She stopped spending Saturdays with Lee; instead she joined the group that cleaned and tended the altar at the Santuaria on weekends. She got involved with organizing their building fund, and she went to a Bible study group on Sunday afternoons. When she went to get her hair cut short, the hairdresser told her she should keep the pageboy, she looked like Eva Marie Saint, it was a crime to cut that hair, but in the end she snipped it as short as Jean Seberg's in *Saint Joan*.

At night she began to dream of suffering—her own and that of others—sometimes rooms full of hospital beds and people crying out in pain, sometimes her own dull red anguish as she lay in a desolate place, wounded and wanting to die. Once she was making her way through the ruins of a city that had been devastated by an earthquake, climbing over rubble, hearing the screams of the injured. Once she was running through a narrow tunnel full of bodies that pressed against her, oozing blood. Her own cries often woke her up—sweating, with tears in her eyes.

On Saturdays, after she arranged the flowers and polished the carvings at the Santuaria, she went to Confession. After she had confessed to having sex with Lloyd Vegara, she had nothing more to say than, "I have given in to despair because I feel my life is useless." And Father Grady would reply, "The sin of despair is a very great one, my child. You must work hard at your life to make it worthwhile." After a few weeks, he asked her if she wanted an appointment to talk to him, to discuss her problem, and she said, no, thank you, that wouldn't be necessary, and began going to Confession at the Cathedral, where she could confess to a different priest every week.

After work one day just before Christmas, she stayed behind to speak to Mother Rosaria in the convent parlor.

"I want to become a nun," she said.

Mother Rosaria crossed her hands on her breast. "My dear," she said. "This is rather a sudden vocation."

Caroline shook her head. "It isn't. I've wanted to be a nun for years. I used to dream about it, when I was first married."

"But—you have been a married woman, Caroline. What do you mean by this?"

"I mean I want to join the order. I'm divorced. I haven't lived with my husband in six years."

"But you know the Church doesn't recognize divorce," said Mother Rosaria. "If you were married as a Catholic, then you are still married in the eyes of God."

They were sitting together on a small sofa. Caroline slid off the sofa and fell to her knees. She took Mother Rosaria's hand and bowed her head over it. Against her forehead she could feel the coarse wool of the habit. "Please," she said. "I want this so much. There must be some way."

Sister Marie brought them a pot of coffee on a tray, and they sat in the parlor discussing it for the rest of the evening. Mother Rosaria was very kind. She said Caroline's sincerity impressed her, and she had been unable not to notice her piety. She believed that she might have a real vocation. But the divorce could be an insurmountable obstacle. A dispensation from the Pope, perhaps. An annulment. That would take a long time, maybe years.

Caroline wept. She told Mother Rosaria about the sin of despair that lurked in her heart, no matter what she did. She refrained from saying that if she couldn't join the order she wanted to die, because she suspected Mother Rosaria would recommend medical instead of spiritual help.

Finally, Mother Rosaria said she would consult Father Grady. Perhaps Father Grady could talk with the bishop. Caroline should put it out of her mind for now. She should certainly not get her hopes up. They would talk further.

Caroline walked home in the cold, through streets lit with *farolitos,* and wrote letters to Lucy and Teddy explaining that she wouldn't be coming east for Christmas, after all. She was mailing their presents: sombrero for Teddy, turquoise jewelry for Lucy. They must forgive her. She was ill with a cold she couldn't shake.

And, in fact, when she went to bed that night she was hot and feverish, unable to sleep. The pleading litany to Mother Rosaria went on and on in her head: *If I could only make you understand. My life depends on this. If you knew what goes on in my head, in my soul, in my body. I need this. I need something. If you could see inside my soul.*

Please.

She wished for a Voice, a *yes* from the heavens, from the white walls with their empty niches, from the red mountains outside her window, but it wasn't going to be made so easy for her: the only voice she heard was her own.

Christmas passed, Epiphany passed, Lent began. Caroline helped drape the statues in the Santuaria in their purple shrouds. She went daily to Mass. She told Lee the truth: that she hoped to enter the convent, and she watched Lee's eyes fill with tears as if she had admitted she had a terminal illness.

She had a letter from Stewart that surprised her with its passion.

He accused her of alienating the children by her long absence. Lucy was unhappy at college, already thinking of transferring, and she was deeply in need of her mother. Could Caroline come home in the spring? Or at the very least invite Lucy to visit her out there? Just because her children were growing up she had no right to abdicate her responsibility to them. Hadn't he, all those years when Caroline had custody, done his duty by them? And shouldn't the same standards apply to her? Caroline imagined Stewart in his office, biting his lip, wrestling with the stilted phrasing. She didn't answer the letter. She wrote to Lucy and told her she loved her, she was sorry, she knew Lucy was going through a crisis in her life but she was going through one herself.

It was finally agreed that, for the moment, she could become a lay sister. She would continue her secretarial duties, but she would live at the convent and dress in a modified habit and wear a small veil. She would receive a reduced salary. Although the prospects were dim, she could petition to Rome through the Chancery Office for an annulment of her marriage. If grounds were found, and the annulment was granted, she could begin the process of entering the order. The path was long and hard, full of pitfalls. There was no guarantee that she would end as a Sister of Mary. Nor was entering the convent in any form a guarantee of God's grace. As a prospective sister, even more would be asked of her by God: He made great demands on His chosen ones.

After Easter, Caroline closed up the apartment on Camino del Monte Sol. She had few possessions, mostly clothes and books and collections of crossword puzzles. She sent her jewelry home to Lucy and gave her clothes to the mission; she threw out everything else except the carved statue of the Virgin, which she brought with her to her cubicle at the convent.

In some ways, her new room wasn't much different from her old apartment. It was smaller, and the view from her tiny window was of the parking lot instead of the mountains, but it was just as clean and just as still. At night after Vespers, when she was free to go to her room, she listened to the silence, and nearly every night, as soft and as distinct as the wind in the aspen grove beyond the parking light, she thought she could hear the Voice, and she wasn't sure, it was very faint, but she thought it said her name.

ORIS DAY hadn't dried the dishes, and Queen Dragnetta was very, very angry.

"It's not enough to just wash," said Gold, moving toward Doris
threateningly.

"I'm sorry," whimpered Doris Day. "I'm just a poor servant girl."

"And it's not enough to be sorry," said Gold.

"Let's get her," Weasel suggested. He had the broom, and he
lurched forward with it. "Let's make her really, really sorry for this."

"Not yet," said Lucy.

Teddy frowned at her. "Why not?"

"It's too soon. We just started."

"All right, if you want to be the boss, *you* do Weasel."

"You know I don't like doing Weasel. Besides, Weasel's yours."

"Yeah, but Gold is yours, and I did Gold."

Lucy hesitated, considering this. The real reason she wouldn't do Weasel was that she hated him. Teddy had made him in art class from a plaster cast, and he was badly painted and beginning to chip. She didn't think he looked like a weasel at all. In spite of his snarl, he looked more like a plain dog. But Teddy said Mrs. Palmer said he was a weasel.

She looked at Teddy. He was sitting on the rug with his knees hunched up and his chin on them. He wore brown corduroy pants and brown socks with a hole in one. His big toe stuck out. In his right hand he held Weasel, in his left Gold. He was moving his lips and making first Weasel, then Gold, sway back and forth and bow, which was how Teddy showed that they were talking.

"What are they saying?"

"Ssh, just a minute." More bowing and swaying, mostly by Gold. Then Teddy said, "Gold's on your side. He convinced Weasel that they should wait."

"Oh, good." It was what she had suspected. She knew she wasn't allowed to thank him, but she couldn't help smiling. He smiled back. It was a Wednesday morning, and they were both home from school with colds. Lucy said, "So."

"Okay," Teddy said. "Back to that kitchen."

Lucy coughed and cleared her throat. "We can't have this," said Queen Dragnetta. "It may seem like a small thing, Doris, but the kingdom is going to wrack and ruin. Look at this place. It's a pigsty."

"I—I'm so sorry," Doris said. "I didn't know. I'm just a stupid servant girl."

"I'll say," said Gold. "Well, get those dishes dried and put away before I count to ten."

Doris limped over to the sink. She had had polio and then a broken leg. The Queen had magnanimously allowed her to be cured, but she was left with a limp. The kitchen was the area next to Teddy's bed, and the sink was a cigar box filled with Lucy's tin doll dishes. The cupboard was an egg carton. The dish towel was one of their mother's old embroidered hankies. The dishes were too big for Doris to manipulate, but Lucy helped and got them all dried and stacked in the cupboard. Then the Queen said, "And now I want you to scrub this floor. On your hands and knees. And if I see one spot, you will be severely punished."

"And when the Queen says severely, she means it," said Weasel.

"I mean everything I say," shouted Queen Dragnetta, jumping up and down. Her crown fell off, and Lucy replaced it. "Everything!"

"Y-yes, your majesty," whimpered Doris. "I'm so tired, and my hands are red and raw from all the work I've done all day. I-I don't think I can scrub the floor. I think I'm going to faint."

She bounced around and swayed for a few seconds, and fell to the rug in a dead faint, her red felt dress above her knees. Underneath she wore panties made from a white sock.

"Water!" shouted the Queen. "Awaken her! We can't have this!"

"Water!" cried Gold. "The show must go on!"

Lucy giggled. "It's not a show, dummy."

Gold began to bounce across the rug. "The show must go on! The show must go on! Where is that stupid Renard? Renard! Get in here with a bucket of water."

Teddy dropped Gold and brought in Renard with a thimble that had belonged to their grandmother. Renard dumped the water on Doris Day while Teddy said, "Pssssshh!" Doris groaned and stood up, wobbling dangerously. "Oh oh oh, this is terrible. I feel awful, oh poor me, what am I going to do?"

"Get to work, that's what!"

"I can't, I can't," sobbed Doris Day. Lucy had perfected sobbing; she loved any part where she could do it. Doris swayed desperately back and forth, her long golden hair fanning out. "I'm tired, I'm sick, I haven't eaten in over a week."

Teddy looked at Lucy; Lucy nodded. Queen Dragnetta bowed. "Let's get her," said Weasel. Renard went out and Gold came in. "Gold. Are you ready?"

"I'm ready."

"Wh-what are you going to do to me this time?" whimpered Doris.

"You'll see," said Gold. He approached her with the broom and whacked her over the head. "Take that! Take that! And that!"

Doris Day screamed. "No no no! I'm only a poor servant girl. Help me, someone!"

Caroline stuck her head in the door of the bedroom. "Could you be just a *little* quieter? I'm trying to read. I can hear you all the way downstairs."

"Sorry."

"What do you want for lunch?"

"Peanut butter."

"Chicken noodle. Do we have any cookies?"

"I'll see. Be careful with those pebbles. Don't leave any on the rug when you're done."

"We won't."

"What on earth are you doing with them?"

"Stoning Doris Day," said Teddy.

"We're *about* to stone Doris Day," Lucy corrected him.

"Good Lord."

"Don't worry, Mom."

"I'm not sure you should be playing on the floor with those colds. How do you feel?"

"Okay," they chorused. "Fine," Lucy added.

Caroline stood in the doorway looking at them. She wore her blue checked dress with an old sweater over it. She was holding a book in one hand, her pinky finger marking the place.

"You both need your hair washed."

"We're sick."

"If you're so sick, play more quietly."

"We will."

She went downstairs, and they heard her in the kitchen opening a can with the squeaky can opener and lighting the stove with a match. The radio came on, a woman's voice singing the shrimp boat song that Lucy hated and Teddy loved.

Teddy said, "Okay," and Doris Day began to sob.

"Shut up," said the Queen. "You've ruined my life. How do you expect me to go on like this? I'm nothing but a slave to this family."

Teddy looked at her and said, "Lucy."

"Well, it's true." Lucy put Queen Dragnetta in front of her face and spoke in her haughty Queen voice. "We've got to come to some decision, Stewart. This is not the life I planned for myself."

Teddy began to laugh.

"Come on," said Lucy.

"No! No! It's too crazy."

"Come on," Lucy said. "Be Gold."

Teddy got control of himself and picked up Gold. "What do I say?"

"Come on. You know."

Teddy snickered, then sobered up. "All right." He put on his Gold voice, which was deep and slow. "Well, what do you suggest?" he asked. "What's your latest brilliant idea?"

"You know perfectly well," said the Queen.

"Then do it," said Gold. "Do you think I'm going to cry myself to sleep over it? Go ahead and do it."

"I just might. You just might get home one of these days and find me gone."

"Oh, really?"

"Yes, really."

"Well, get one thing straight. Don't count on me for a dime."

"We'll see about that."

Teddy began to cough. Lucy adjusted Queen Dragnetta's robe and retied her sash. Teddy hacked and spit into the linen handkerchief, then looked at the result.

"That's disgusting," Lucy said.

"It's sort of greenish."

"Ugh." She picked up Doris Day. "This is getting boring. Let's do the poor servant girl."

"Okay."

Gold said, "It's time for the rough stuff."

Doris Day gave a quiet, resigned scream. "No no no!"

"Yes yes yes!" said Weasel triumphantly. He picked up a stone and threw it at her. Lucy dropped Doris and jumped back just in time. The stone hit Doris on the chest. She screamed: "Ah ah ah!" Then Gold threw one and missed. He threw another and got her in the leg. She lay on her face without moving, but they could hear her whimper.

Gold picked up more stones. "Take that," said Gold. "And that."

"Let me throw one," said the Queen in her most imperious voice.

"No no! Please don't hurt me any more! I'll do whatever you wish."

"It's too late for that," said the Queen, and tossed her stone. It hit Doris square in the back of the head. Doris gasped once and was silent.

"She's done for," said Weasel, and laughed his maniacal laugh.

"You mean she's dead?"

"Yes, your majesty."

Lucy and Teddy looked at each other. "You mean, really dead?"

"Yeah. Sure. Why not?"

Lucy said, "Why not?" and sat looking down at the still body of Doris in her red dress. Then the Queen said, "Good." She turned to Weasel and Gold, who bowed in unison. "A fine day's work, my faithful ones."

"A privilege, your majesty."

"And now—remove the body," said Queen Dragnetta. "We will have to find a new servant girl."

From downstairs, Caroline called. "Wash up! Lunch in five minutes!"

"You go first," said Lucy.

"Pick up the stones, or she'll murdalize us."

Teddy went down the hall to the bathroom, and Lucy gathered up the stones and put them in the box that had been Doris Day's iron lung when she had polio. Now she was dead: what next? She straightened Doris Day's dress again, and stowed her away in another box with Gold and Weasel and the Queen and Renard. Then she lay down on Teddy's bed and looked straight up at the ceiling. Teddy had put a piece of bubble gum on the end of a baseball bat, stood on the bed, and attached the gum to the ceiling. Then he pressed a piece of newspaper to the gum, a headline from the *Syracuse Herald-Journal:* YANKS SLAM PHILLY IN FOUR. It was dated October 10, 1950, and it had turned a brownish yellow, darker in the center where the wad of gum held it. You could barely read the words, but after a year and a half Lucy knew them by heart. Teddy wanted to see how long the gum would stick. He was betting on ten years, but Lucy gave it five at the most.

Teddy came out of the bathroom and clomped downstairs. Caroline said, "Must you always, always make so much noise? Even in stocking feet?" and there was an argument about milk versus Pepsi, which Teddy won. On the radio, an announcer began to give the news. From outside came the noon whistle from the candle factory. Lucy could smell chicken-noodle soup. Any minute, her mother would call her in that high voice she used when she was impatient, and she would have to go down and eat her lunch and listen to Teddy's singing along with the radio. But she lay for one more peaceful moment on her back, looking up at YANKS SLAM PHILLY, feeling her nose stuff up again. *I must have been crazy to marry you,* she said softly. *Oh really. Yes really. Oh really.* Then her mother called her, and she went downstairs.

Nell

1950

*J*UNE WAS an endless month. The students were sleepy and sweating in the hot classrooms, oblivious to the delights of Browning and Tennyson and adverbial clauses.

Nell wrote on the blackboard: *Though much is taken, much abides.*

"These are just possibly my favorite lines of poetry," she said. "What do they mean to you?"

The students, even the good ones, yawned and looked out the window at green trees, hot sun.

In the teachers' lounge, where Nell spent her fourth-period break, the conversations were bleak and irritable, mainly about the attitude problem of various students and about the difficulty of planning anything decent for the summer on a schoolteacher's salary. In central New York, they desperately needed rain; the governor asked people to cut back on water use. All through final exam week, the temperature was in the high eighties, and the air in the classrooms of Northside High was yellow with heat, dank with humidity.

At the end of that week, Nell graded the last set of senior Regents English papers and figured out averages. Wearing her new blue shirt-waist dress, she attended graduation and presented the English award to Barbara Swain, who didn't deserve it but who, undeniably, had the highest average. She took Ruth Ann Grundberg, who missed out on the English award because of her inventive spelling, out to lunch at Edwards Tea Room and gave her *Ten Steps to Spelling Power* and the Modern Library edition of *To the Lighthouse* as a consolation prize, and basked in Ruth Ann's green-eyed smile.

She went to a barbecue at Florence Weiss's, where one group of her colleagues sat out on the lawn drinking gin and talking about Senator McCarthy, and another group drank beer and danced, and where Henry Tillman, who had been with the gin group, waylaid her when she came out of the bathroom and tried, and failed, to kiss her.

She bought groceries, including enough cornflakes and spaghetti and Jell-O and canned peas and Puss-in-Boots cat food to last Jamie and Dinah for a month.

She had a farewell dinner with Caroline and Stewart and the children.

She went to the bank to trade what was left of her savings for traveler's checks, and she stopped at Walgreen's to pick up a hot-water bottle and some motion-sickness pills. She packed her two matching blue suitcases with summer clothes, not forgetting to include a heavy sweater, a raincoat, and a pair of lightweight boots that folded into a canvas pouch. She put her tickets and her passport in a leather folder she had bought for the purpose and tucked that firmly down in the recesses of her shoulder bag. She took the train to New York.

On the first of July she boarded the *Queen Mary*.

She was a tall, spare, freckled woman with light-brown hair worn in a ponytail. She had good legs which, even on hot days, she covered with nylon stockings. Ever since her friend Pat Garvey told her she looked like an angel in blue, she thought of it as her trademark. She wore no makeup but pink lipstick, like a teenager with strict parents—though she was twenty-seven that summer and her last remaining parent had died in March. She owned a compact with powder in a shade called Dresden Cream, two cakes of eye shadow (Blue Heaven and Lavender Blue), and a pot of rose-colored rouge. The cosmetic saleswoman at Dey Brothers had helped her choose them, and showed her how to apply them to bring out her hidden beauty. Nell didn't like the way the makeup felt on her skin, and she felt conspicuous and Carolinish in it, but she packed it all anyway in the zipped cosmetic case that matched her luggage, thinking she might have the urge, in England if not in America, to reveal her hidden beauty.

The trip to England was something she had wanted since, when she was sixteen, Sister Constance had read "Tintern Abbey" aloud in English class and passed around pictures of a romantic ruin surrounded by wooded hills.

> . . . *Therefore let the moon*
> *Shine on thee in thy solitary walk;*
> *And let the misty mountain winds be free*
> *To blow against thee.*

Even now, she couldn't read the poem without feeling her soul yearn for something she fancied could be found only in England. And, of course, her trip would enrich her own teaching; she would bring back photographs to show her students, and would be able to convey to them exactly what it was like to walk the London streets where Pope and Swift once walked, to hike the landscape that inspired "Tintern Abbey," to view the parsonage where Emily Brontë baked bread and wrote *Wuthering Heights*.

Going to England was also a means of getting away from Jamie,

who refused to find a job after he graduated from art school—
refused to do anything but paint, it seemed, out in his studio over the
garage, coming in for meals if he felt like it, and, if he didn't, refusing to show his face, living on the smell of turpentine and oils, leaving Nell to sit alone with a whole meat loaf or a macaroni-and-
cheese casserole—wishing at least that Dad were still alive so she
could bring him dinner on a tray, sit by his bedside coaxing him to
eat, and then bring her work up to his room, grading papers or reading while he listened to Jack Benny on the radio and sucked the endless striped peppermints that, toward the end, were the only food he
liked. There were times she even wished Caroline and Stewart and
the children would come over more often. Caro and Stewart weren't
the easiest people in the world to be around; their desperate, idiotic
marriage was crumbling, predictably, before everyone's eyes like a
sand castle in the rain. But Lucy was a joy, and Teddy was cheerful
and lively—two little beams of sunshine, Caroline always said in that
listless way that could mean perfect sincerity or heavy sarcasm,
depending on how much you knew about Caroline.

Sometimes Nell had dinner with Florence Weiss and her husband,
or with Pat Garvey or Marian Gelbert. But most of her dinners were
eaten alone, and that spring after Dad died, she began to find it boring and oppressive to come home each evening—after an exhaust-
ing day cramming English literature into minds that longed only for
release—to an empty house, a lonely dinner, a solitary evening, no
one but the cat for company.

She told people she was taking the trip to enrich her teaching and
to get some good clean exercise walking through the English coun-
tryside. To no one did she admit that she was going to England in
the hope of having some fun—partly because she wasn't sure what
she meant. She could imagine vague scenarios in which she capti-
vated the English: encounters in hotels and cathedrals and teashops,
on Salisbury Plain, on the shores of Derwentwater, in front of the
Elgin Marbles in the British Museum. *That delightful American school-*

teacher, that wonderful Miss Kerwin, have you met Nell, isn't she mar-velous—and there she would be, at dinner tables all over England, her conversation sparkling like champagne, her wit as legendary as the wit of Samuel Johnson.

She knew, of course, that her daydreams were absurd, that she would plow through England on her own, a solitary nondescript spinster like someone in an E. M. Forster novel or a Katherine Mans-field story. But in spite of herself, she thought of England as a land of limitless prospects—for what, she wasn't sure. *Fun,* yes—that and something else she couldn't name, couldn't even imagine: whatever it was that she felt when she read Wordsworth, and that certainly wasn't available to her in Syracuse, New York, in the silent, empty house on Hillside Street.

. . . . .

ON THE ship, she shared a cabin with a middle-aged Englishwoman named Lenore Massingham, who saw it as her duty to instruct Nell in the ways of the English by telling her in detail about everyone she knew, from the accountant son living in Leeds to the alcoholic son-in-law tormenting her daughter in Exeter to the expatriate nephew she had been visiting in Buffalo to the London doctor who had botched her hysterectomy. This was amusing for a day or two, and by the time Nell began to find it tedious she and Mrs. Massingham were fast friends who ate their meals together, took bracing walks arm in arm around the deck, and had long cozy talks in their bunks before falling asleep. The only other people Nell met on the ship were the respectable ladies in pearls and sensible shoes that Mrs. Massingham gravitated toward. Nell learned a great deal about hys-terectomies and sons-in-law. When they parted at Southampton, Nell gave her friend a hug, told her quite truthfully that she was happy to have met her, and promised—quite untruthfully—to get in touch when she passed through Leeds on her way north.

In London, at her hotel, she met a group of Canadians—two

married couples with a widowed friend and a young niece—who took a fancy to her and with whom she saw the sights. She and the niece, a college girl named Amy, went together to Westminster Abbey, where they had a guided tour (Nell's treat) by a gaunt, aged sexton whose mumbling English accent was almost impenetrable, and where Amy wept over the memorial to Blake. (*Real and very pretty tears—fake emotion,* Nell wrote in her diary.)

On the train to Oxford she met a don who bought her a sherry and wanted to show her the inn where Pope got drunk and the room at Christ Church where Lewis Carroll wrote *Alice in Wonderland*—an invitation which, after some thought, she declined. Something about his gray moustache made her think of Mr. Fahey's hands cupped over her breasts, the horrifying shock of his hard penis pressed against her, his voice in her ear begging her not to tell.

In Stratford, she attended a performance of *Much Ado About Nothing* with a touring group of librarians from Iowa, and she spent two lonely, overcast days in Shrewsbury, strolling along the banks of the Severn feeling sorry for herself.

The Brontë parsonage in Haworth was closed, and the Yorkshire moors were awash in rain. She took refuge in the Black Bull Inn ("one of the scenes of the unfortunate Branwell Brontë's humiliation," she would say to her students, without elaborating, when she showed them her snapshot) and discussed growing roses with a bus driver and his wife on holiday from Manchester, getting quietly tipsy on Worthington's Pale Ale while the rain thudded against the windows.

In York she toured the cathedral alone, but she met some nice people in a pub, and ended up going out to dinner at the Maid's Head with an art historian from York University who was writing a book on medieval glazing. He talked about the glasswork in the Chapter House at York Minster. They shared a bottle of wine and then had a nightcap. When he took her back to her hotel he kissed her several times, with increasing insistence and passion, in the hallway outside her door. Finally, his lips on her neck, he asked her if he could come into her room. She enjoyed kissing him, and she liked his hair, which was thick and thatchy, and his full lower lip, and his tweed jacket. Also, she looked forward to telling Pat Garvey about the encounter, so she opened the door with her key, took his hand, and, smiling, led him inside.

"I like you independent American girls," he said as he unbuttoned her blouse. He wasn't her first; he was, in fact, her third. His name was Colin; when he asked her if she had a steady boyfriend, she told him that she was engaged to a man back home named Oscar, who ran a butcher shop. They struggled on her bed for what seemed to Nell a very long time—he had trouble, it turned out, staying hard—until finally, when she thought she was surely going to fall asleep, he achieved an orgasm and collapsed on her, by which time they were both hot, sweaty, and exhausted, and heartily disliked each other.

After he left, she was wide awake and depressed. She wrote in her diary: *sex with an Englishman named Colin. The usual combination of disgust and amusement, in about equal amounts.*

. . . . .

IN THE Lake District, which she had longed to see more than any part of England, she was unhappier than she had been in years. The weather was perfect: Nell stayed for a week in Keswick and it didn't rain once—most unusual, she was constantly told by Mrs. Welsh, the widowed ex-schoolteacher from London who ran the hotel. *You've brought the good weather,* Mrs. Welsh said, beaming at her.

Every morning, awakened in her sunny room by birdsong and the voices of her fellow guests on their way down to breakfast, Nell became more and more reluctant to get up and spend the day in her own company. She bought a guidebook and went sightseeing, always feeling she was missing the best things. The village of Grasmere was crowded with people who had come to see the wrestling matches and sheepdog trials. Dove Cottage was closed, and the Wordsworth Museum seemed expensive for what it contained. On the day she took the steamer around Lake Windermere, the sun was so bright she developed a headache and missed most of the trip because she was lying on a bench belowdecks waiting for the aspirin to work and counting up mentally how much money she had left. She worried constantly about running out of money or losing her traveler's checks. Everywhere she went, the mountains bulked blackish-green against the blue sky, menacing the tiny perfect villages: the terrifying monsters Wordsworth had bad dreams about and called "huge and mighty forms that do not live like living men."

The Keswick Hotel seemed to be full of the members of a climbing club who debated endlessly the merits of Pillar Rock versus Glimmer Crag, and rowdy salmon fishermen who ate their catch for dinner every evening, washing it down with pitchers of ale. At night after dinner, Nell sat in the hotel parlor waiting for someone to talk to her about something besides fish and mountains. She wrote cheery postcards to Pat and Florence and Marian, composed poetic descriptions of the scenery for the benefit of her diary, and devoured the vast collection of Agatha Christies provided by the hotel. She also found a tattered copy of Wordsworth, read "Tintern Abbey," and wept tears of self-pity when she came to the lines:

> *For thou art with me here upon the banks*
> *Of this fair river; thou my dearest Friend,*
> *My dear, dear Friend . . .*

. . . . .

ON THE last full day of her stay, she joined a climb up Skiddaw organized by the local Fell and Rock Climbing Club. The guidebook called the route "safe and easy, with rewarding views." Her fellow climbers were mostly huge Germans in shorts who gave her a hand when the climbing was difficult but otherwise ignored her.

Nell, with her hair in a braid, wearing trousers and a blue sweater in which she was much too hot, gave up halfway through the climb and started back down on her own. Almost immediately the air turned colder, the clouds thickened, and it began to rain. By the time she reached the railway station at the base of the mountain she was wet and freezing and bedraggled, and covered with mud where she had missed her footing and slipped for several feet down a steep ridge— thinking as she fell of her sister Peggy dying on the ice twelve years before: surprised at seeing Peggy's pale face, laughing under her stocking cap, as clearly as she saw the slide of mud and the grayish bark of the young tree she grabbed to break her fall.

She walked into the back garden of the hotel crying. She had lost her rubber band, and her hair hung dripping around her face. Her hands were filthy. The knees of her trousers were ripped, and her legs showed through bleeding and mud-covered.

Mrs. Welsh was standing at the door looking out into the rain, smoking a cigarette. She came running when she saw Nell.

"You poor lamb, look at you," she said, and sent the vacant-eyed Irish maid to run a bath in the second-floor bathroom. Nell sat dripping on a stool in the kitchen, drinking whiskey and listening to Mrs. Welsh's stories about climbers who were lost on the mountain, including Wordsworth's Charles Gough and a man named Scoursby who had stayed at that very hotel.

The whiskey tasted wonderful to Nell. Her bones warmed. The sun came out and filled the kitchen with dusty light. The flowers in the back garden gleamed like gems. Mrs. Welsh refilled her glass, and by the time her bathwater was ready, the mud, the slide, the silly fear of Skiddaw had moved to a distant part of her mind, and it didn't seem at all odd that Mrs. Welsh came into the bathroom with her, helped her out of her unspeakable clothes, and then scrubbed her all over with a big soft sponge as if she were a child, talking in her quiet London voice about Wordsworth's sister Dorothy who, in her opinion, had more to do with Willie's poems than anyone would admit.

Nell sat happily in the hot water, watching her skin turn red and the suds turn gray. She lowered her head to her bruised knees while Mrs. Welsh soaped her back. She thought of nothing except the perfect comfort she had found. When she stepped out of the tub, Mrs. Welsh wrapped her in an immense terry-cloth robe and took her across the hall to her own room where Nell, much to her own surprise, put her arms around the woman and kissed her. When Mrs. Welsh kissed her back, Nell had to suppress the urge to laugh—to do something crazy, like racing away down the hall, giggling. She had never kissed a woman before—not like that. Mrs. Welsh untied Nell's robe, let her own cotton dress be unzipped. She was tall, not slender, not especially young or beautiful, but her large soft body was as full of knolls and hollows as a kind, welcoming mountain.

They kissed again, and Nell stopped wanting to laugh. "Ah, my dear girl," the woman kept saying, and she had a way of tipping her head back with a gasp of pleasure, exposing her long white throat where a blue vein pulsed.

They spent an hour in her bed with the door locked while the maid coped with the salmon fishermen who came back and wanted their tea. Nell found herself knowing things she hadn't even suspected were there to be known. When Mrs. Welsh left—her name was Gillian, she was forty-four, she had been widowed two months after her wedding, that was all Nell knew about her—she fell asleep with the feeling that she had experienced this before in another existence, or in some vast dark dream world that had been there, all those years, alongside the innocent, meager world of Hillside Street. And, being truly honest with herself for (it seemed to Nell) the first time in her life, she understood why she had taken all her money out of the bank and sailed over three thousand miles away from home: for *this,* this thing for which she had no word, this feeling of perfect peace and well-being slightly tinged with wickedness that she carried with her into sleep and into the years to come.

Alice

1946

O ONE but Nell wanted to talk about Peggy, and Nell seemed satisfied with whatever she was told. Easily pleased, Alice thought. Easily fooled. Still infatuated with her sister. Alice had brought with her the issue of *Art News Today* with the spread about the 1939 San Francisco Art League show—with her sculpture, *The Future,* prominently displayed. Just in case any of them had been told the truth.

But Alice kept the magazine locked up in her dressing case: Mary had taken her daughter's secret to the grave. Caroline told her aunt about Mary's last weeks. A weeping Caroline—not the girl Alice remembered, the pretty little exhibitionist she'd met on her last trip east to see Mary: 1923, Caro must have been four or five. The scene in her mind was of her sister brushing Caroline's curls around her

finger, making them fall in thick, perfect blond sausages, then loop-
ing them back with a white ribbon. And Caroline hanging on Mary,
interrupting by touching Mary's cheek to make her turn her head.
"Mommy, Mommy," and Mary's indulgent smile, Caroline's confid-
ing whispers: she wanted to dance for Auntie Alice. Auntie had not
been impressed.

And now she was this weeping wife, mother, daughter, holding
tight to Alice's hand as she talked. "She burned everything," she said.
"The strangest things, like her clothes, things we'd given her, our old
schoolbooks and toys. It was as if she wanted to wipe us all out. It
was a superhuman act, Aunt Alice, to do what she did. She packed
just one box for each of us, mostly useless odds and ends. Everything
else went into the furnace! And she wasn't strong, she must have
been in pain all that time, Dr. McCarthy said."

Caroline's lower lip trembled, and she caught it in her teeth, looking down at their linked hands while tears gathered on her lower lids.
Lord, the girl was pretty! Alice felt a pang of envy, and was immediately ashamed.

"I just wonder if she ever loved us," Caroline said. She sobbed
once and clutched her aunt's hand tighter. "I wonder if she loved me
at all. How could she just burn everything I ever gave her?"

"Hush, hush, my girl." Alice knew she should put her arms around
her. This was the time to hug her, to cuddle little Caroline against
her breast. She was unable to do it: if she took this pretty young niece
close to her she would begin to weep herself, not for Caroline's sor-
rows but for her own. "Hush now," she said, and pulled a clean handkerchief out of her sleeve with her free hand. "She wasn't herself.
Mary adored you, you know that. You were her favorite. You and
John. Here."

Caroline took the handkerchief and blew her nose. It was Thanksgiving Day. There was dinner to be seen to. The smell of turkey was
already wafting faintly from the kitchen. Nell was there, and Marge
Fahey from next door. Jamie was shoveling the front walk—a steady

metallic *scrape scrape*—his first appearance since Alice's arrival. And
Charles was in the back room, in his easy chair, with the cat on his
lap and the radio on. He was resting, Nell said. He hadn't been well,
apparently—working only two or three days a week at Unger's. The
old Butternut Street store was closed, all those bolts and brooms and
saws Charles had loved so much and Mary had been so proud of.
There was a drugstore there now, Nell said, and they were talking
about tearing the building down and putting up an apartment house.

Alice couldn't imagine how they were managing. Nell's schoolteacher salary couldn't be large, and Jamie had just started at the university. Studying art. She would have loved to see some of his work,
but Nell said he was very secretive. That strange, silent boy: *damaged*
was the word that came to mind. She should get close to him, do her
duty as his artist-aunt, try to help him. But who could get close to
such a sullen young person? He had said hello without looking at
her, his head down, snow shovel cocked like a weapon. From what
she could see of his face, he looked startlingly like Mary—a drabber
version of Mary in her youth, and with Charles's long nose.

She had seen Charles the night before—gone in to say hello to
him. He'd seemed fine at first, turned off Jack Benny to ask her a
million questions, all about money one way or another. Was she selling her sculpture? How much were people willing to pay for things
like that? What kind of commission did those New York galleries
get? And how was Ralph's shipping business doing? Then he got
tired—visibly. His face grayed, sagged. He asked her if she was aware
of the astonishing fact that Mary had died five months to the day
after FDR. This wasn't quite accurate: the president had died on the
twelfth of April, Mary on the ninth of September. But never mind.
Alice kissed his cheek and told him she would leave "a little something" with Nell before she left, and he turned his head aside so that
she saw his sharp profile against the white doily, and whispered,
"You're a lifesaver, Alice. Always have been."

Old Charlie Kerwin. Not so old, really. Younger than Ralph by several years, but wasted, his daughters said, since Mary's death. His hair had gone from graying to white, and he had no more pep than an old dog. He'd been attractive once—light-haired like Caroline, tall and muscular. Alice remembered him at the wedding, how he could hardly keep his hands off Mary. Her little sister, married at nineteen to this tall man of thirty. Alice had liked him herself, but he had never looked at her once he saw her sister. "What a pretty traveling suit," someone said when Mary had changed and come down the steps. A gray suit, hobble-skirted, with a polka-dotted shirtwaist and a straw hat trimmed with red ribbon. Charlie's brother had grinned and said, low-voiced, "Charlie can't wait to get it off her," and Alice had felt thrilled by these words, and by the sight of Mary and Charles in the rumble seat of Larry Laidlaw's Ford, his head bent to hers, Mary's hand up to hold her hat on. Larry was driving them to the train station; they would take a sleeper up to Plattsburgh, to honeymoon at Lake Champlain. Alice imagined them in the narrow berth, naked together. Alice was twenty-six, but she'd never had a serious beau, and wouldn't meet Ralph Steele for three years. Standing there watching them go, thinking of marriage, of being in bed with a man like Charles Kerwin, she could feel her pulse beating hard in her temples.

And now look at him. And Mary dead.

Alice watched Caroline dab at her eyes one last time and stow the handkerchief in her pocket. The children were out playing in the snow with Stewart; she could hear Lucy's shrill cries. Stewart was a better father than Caroline was a mother—or so it seemed to Alice. But what was wrong with that? She had a quick vision of Ralph, when the doctor told him they would never have children—his face stricken as if he had a dozen children and he'd heard that all of them had died, all at once, in that instant.

"I loved her," Caroline said. "Mom."

They stood up. "I know you did, Caroline," Alice said. "And you made her happy, she was always telling me that." She patted her niece's shoulder. "I don't know how to explain what she did at the end. All I can say it was her illness, it was the tumor on her brain, it wasn't lack of love."

They went down to the kitchen, Alice to peel potatoes, Caroline to stand at the door and wave at her boisterous children in the snow. Marge Fahey in a hideous frilled apron was talking to Nell about lipstick shades. "You should try something that's not so pink and girlish," she said. "What do you think, Alice? Isn't she too old for the Tangee look?"

"I think she looks lovely." Poor Nell, the plainest of her nieces, all freckles and angles and flushed from turkey basting, actually looked ugly and miserable, any makeup she might have worn sweated off in the hot kitchen.

"I'm going to get you a tube of Montezuma Red," Marge said with decision. "Elizabeth Arden. Sixty cents plus tax down at Dey Brothers. It'll be my Christmas present to you, Nell. I have a hunch you need some livening up."

Nell said nothing. She shut the oven door and brushed the hair out of her eyes with the back of her hand. Alice smiled at her—a smile meant to be conspiratorial, comforting—and Nell smiled back, closing her eyes to indicate her weariness with good-hearted Marge. She and Alice had had a long talk the night before. Nell, in fact, had met her aunt at the station. The train from New York was late, but when Alice had finally got in, there had been Nell, sitting upright and patient in the waiting room, reading a book of poetry. Alice kissed her cheek and said, "What's this? Byron?" and Nell had blushed and said, "It's my only vice." The two of them had stayed up until midnight, drinking cocoa in the kitchen.

As she peeled each potato, Alice set it in a big pan of water. She hadn't peeled a potato in years, and she was rather enjoying it—trying to get the peel off in one continuous strip. She thought about Mary, who had probably peeled potatoes every day of her life: Mary at the end destroying the evidence that life had been lived. Alice imagined the tumor pressing against her brain, telling her to let go, let go . . .

All those letters must have been burnt, then. The bulletins on Peggy's health and progress. Or maybe they were destroyed as soon as they were received. Too risky: what if Charles read them? Or the children. Dear Mary—so timid and conventional, so Catholic. All those children. And now only three left—two and a half, considering Jamie. Mary had quit the Church after John's death. They all had, Nell said, except her father. The damned war, Nell said, and looked at Alice to see if she was shocked by her profanity, but Alice echoed what she said: *yes, the damned war, it took so many.* Her friend Cora's son, she was thinking of, who left those lovely babies. Ralph's sister's boy, George, who would have gone into the business with him. Her own nephew John, that handsome lad, Mary's pride and joy.

But as they sat there drinking cocoa, Nell didn't want to talk about the war or John or Mary's death—only about Peggy. "She wrote me the most wonderful letters," Nell said. She had showed Alice Peggy's picture, framed, in the place of honor on her bureau: her high-school graduation picture, idealized, with spit curls. "All about Chinatown, and Uncle Ralph's ships, and all the flowers. She made San Francisco, California, sound like heaven on earth."

"Well, it's a very pretty place," Alice said. It occurred to her that she could invite Nell out to visit in the summer, when school was out. But better check with Ralph before she mentioned it. He was getting crotchety as he got older. Set in his ways. Liked his comforts, his routines. And Peggy, after all, had been a bit of a trial. "Every time I come home, there she is, just moping around, Alice. Why doesn't the girl *do* something?" Not that he hadn't come to love her, finally. But a difficult girl. Of course, Nell would be different. She had a lively mind: Byron in the Syracuse train station! A good schoolteacher, Alice had no doubt. The kind that inspires her students, the girls especially—gives them noble and romantic ideas, broadens their lives. Reads poetry aloud, with expression. Puts on little plays, scenes from Shakespeare, costumes whipped up from bedsheets and old curtains. Ralph would like her immediately, even her sharp face and her tall angular body, the hair pulled tight into a ponytail, those bright naïve blue eyes. Not a moper. Of course, Peggy had had some reasons to mope. But another kind of girl would have handled it differently. Alice thought wistfully of the baby, a fat-faced boy—nameless. Peggy had given him up without a second thought, apparently. *Ralph and I should have taken him,* Alice thought as she often did.

"I miss her so much," Nell said. "Even now. After all these long, long years."

"She was a dear girl," Alice said. "I'm glad I got to know her. We loved having her with us."

"She was always such fun," Nell's blue eyes were tearful, her hands clasped together under her chin. "She was always so—I don't know. You never knew what she would say. She didn't care what anyone thought of her. She was such an original."

"Wasn't she?" Alice tried to remember. "We had a lot of laughs," she said, though when she thought back eight years she couldn't remember that many. What she remembered was just Peggy, as lumpish in her pregnancy as the red clay that Alice transformed by her own hands into something beautiful—into *The Future,* whose memorial rested upstairs in her dressing case. What if she told Nell about it? Showed her the pictures? *This is your sister who didn't care what anyone thought of her. This is when she was hiding out in California before she gave her baby away.* And she was shocked at the contempt she felt—even now, as Nell would say, after all these long, long years.

. . . . . .

THANKSGIVING dinner was moderately unpleasant. There were eleven of them, counting the children—Caroline's little Lucy and Teddy, who spent most of the time crying and complaining over one thing or another, plus the Faheys' sixteen-year-old son Jerry, who had pimples and talked football football football, whether anyone listened or not.

Alice knew the Faheys only from Mary's letters. Bill and Marge— they had lived next door forever, and Mary had been close to them. When she met them in person, Alice was surprised that Marge was so empty-headed—Marge's conversation, Alice thought, would drive her over the brink if she lived next door to her—and that no one seemed to notice that Bill, the big Pepsi executive, had a crush on Nell. He had brought cheap pink sparkling wine, and the more he drank of it the worse he got—teasing Nell about her freckles, her long bones, the way she must drive the boys wild, all of which would have been not amusing, not even acceptable, but at least bearable if Nell were fourteen. But she was twenty-three, a grown woman, a university graduate and a teacher at the high school. When Bill Fahey leaned across the table to squeeze her arm, it was Alice's opinion that Nell should have given him a slap instead of a weak giggle.

"This should be an annual event," Charles said when Bill had carved the turkey, and Marge had forced her marshmallow-topped sweet potatoes on everyone, and the glasses were filled, and the gravy was passed, and spilled on the white tablecloth, and passed again, and grace was garbled by Lucy while Teddy sulked because he had wanted to be the one to say it. "The Kerwins and the Faheys, and the Steeles from California," Charles said. He sat at the head of the table smiling, not eating much. On his right, where Mary must have sat every night for the thirty years of their marriage, was Nell, still drooping from the effort of cooking, her wineglass untouched in front of her.

"You should come every year, Aunt Alice," Nell said. "And next time bring Uncle Ralph. I think it's such a shame that he has to stay all alone in San Francisco for Thanksgiving."

"He'll go to his sister's house in Oakland."

"But we want him here," Caroline said, smiling, pretending to pout. "We've never even met Uncle Ralph."

Alice tried to imagine Ralph drinking the sweet fizzy wine and listening to Marge's complaints about the price of meat now that rationing was over. Eating the marshmallow stuff and the dried-out turkey—overcooked because Bill Fahey and his son were late: Northside High was playing Valley, and they'd stayed until the last heartbreaking touchdown.

"When it's your boys out there, you don't give up hope until the clock runs out," Bill said. Jerry was on crutches; a broken ankle was keeping him out of the game. "Of course, Jerry's too modest to say that the score would have been a lot different if his ankle was healed."

"I'm not too modest, Dad," Jerry said, laughing. Bill had poured him a glass of wine, and he drank half of it down right away as if it were Pepsi. "Heck, any fool could see they needed me out there to save their asses. Whoops, excuse me, ladies."

"Jerry," Marge said, blushing.

Charles changed the subject. "Now tell us all about this New York thing, Alice. Marge here has been wanting the inside dope about the gallery that's giving you a show."

Marge dabbled in watercolor, Alice knew, and so she told Marge all about her New York solo show—not her first, but undoubtedly her biggest and most important, in a gallery on Fifty-Seventh Street. As she talked, she could see that Jamie was listening, and she tried to speak directly to him, to say what she thought he might like to know—how hard it was to get started, to get any kind of recognition, and how gradually over the years she had built up a clientele, a sort of fan club, people who were aware of her work and looked for her name.

"Of course, the important thing is to keep at it, keep doing it, don't let anything else get in the way," Alice said.

It was meant as encouragement for Jamie, but Marge took offense. "Unless you have to take time out for child raising," she said. Her voice was so sarcastic, and she cut so savagely into a piece of dark meat, that Alice wondered how often Mary had wounded her neighbor with extravagant tales of her successful artist sister. Marge jammed the turkey in her mouth, chewed it fast, and washed it down with wine. "It certainly would be wonderful to have the luxury to do nothing but paint," she said.

Jamie raised his head and looked at his aunt. "Do you ever paint? Or have you always worked in clay?"

For a moment, Alice wasn't sure who had spoken; until now, she hadn't heard Jamie utter more than two words at a time. She looked at him, and he dropped his eyes quickly to his plate. "No, I've always been a sculptor," she said. "At least since one of my teachers in art school told me I had the most depressingly conventional color sense he'd ever seen."

Jamie didn't look at her again, but the corners of his mouth turned up, just slightly, and Alice felt she had taken the first step toward taming a scared animal. She looked at his bowed head, the long Kerwin nose and gaunt cheeks, the sandy hair that matched his skin, and her heart soared. Somehow, she knew he had the gift: she sensed it. And she would help him. Jamie would be her discovery—her own nephew, the son she had never had, who would follow in her footsteps.

The conversation turned back to football, to the phenomenal growth of Pepsi stock since the war, to Stewart's law firm and Teddy's loose front tooth and the early snow, early even for Syracuse. It was the kind of talk that made Alice confused and unhappy—no real conversation, no subject dwelt on for more than a moment, just noise, and silences filled up. Alice ate too much and began to feel sick to her stomach, and then there were two kinds of pie, and coffee.

When it was time to do the dishes, Bill offered to help Nell in the kitchen, but Alice roused herself to say firmly that Nell had done enough, and offered her own services, which, fortunately, were refused. In the end, the men did the dishes—Bill and Jerry and Stewart—while Caroline took the cranky children upstairs to read them stories, and Charles went back to his easy chair and his radio, and Jamie went out in the dark to shovel more snow, and Alice and Marge and Nell sat dozing and looking at newspapers in the living room.

After a while, Alice went upstairs to the bathroom, and stood for a moment in the hall, listening. From downstairs, the rattle of dishes, a low rumble of male voices, and, very faintly, Charles's radio. Outside, the clink of tire chains as a car labored up Hillside Street in the snow. She heard Nell cough, and Marge's voice saying, "Oh my goodness me, I must have dozed off." Lucy and Teddy were quiet at last; Alice peeked into Nell's room and saw the two of them cuddled together on the bed with Caroline beside them, asleep sitting up with a book in her lap.

Across the hall, the door was closed to the attic where Jamie had his room. On impulse she opened it and flipped the light switch, and then went quietly up the stairs. At the top was another switch, and when the light came on she saw that the attic room was full of paint-ings—a wall-to-wall explosion of canvases that almost made her reel backward. The paintings were startling in themselves, but it was the fact that they were Jamie's that made her gasp and press her hand to her heart. Jamie did this: this was what he did up here alone. Every minute of his spare time, Nell said, was spent in this room. He never showed anyone anything. He had implied once that what he pro-duced in the studio at school was only to make his teachers happy, and that his real work was done here.

Alice took two steps into the room and looked around, over-whelmed. She thought of what she had said at dinner about her defective color sense. No wonder Jamie smiled. The paintings were mostly portraits, mostly of women, slightly abstracted, brilliantly colored, full of reds and yellows and a particular shade of clear, greenish blue that he seemed to favor. The portraits were remark-able, but what she found herself staring at, coming back to again and again, was a work-in-progress on the easel, a still life of apples and a blue bowl in a space filled with pure white light—too simple a subject, undoubtedly. Trite, Lord knew. What more was there to say about apples in a bowl? Maybe a school assignment, the same sort of dreary uninspired thing she'd been assigned thirty-five years ago. And yet all she could think of was a Van Gogh she had once seen in Amsterdam, pears in a basket glowing, trembling, with life and color.

The noise behind her was, of course, Jamie. He stood in the stairway, his eyes stricken, his cheeks bright red from shoveling snow.

"Please," he said in a choked voice. "Please don't look."

"Jamie, your work is marvelous."

"No, it isn't."

"But it is!"

"It isn't." They stood there looking at each other, and then he said, "What does it matter, anyway? I just don't want anyone to see it," and went over to stand by the window under the pointed roof, his back to her, hands clenched at his sides, waiting for her to leave.

She stood there obstinately. "It matters, Jamie," she said. "I assure you it does. It matters more than almost anything." He didn't reply. She went on. "I hope this doesn't sound condescending, because I certainly don't mean it to, but this is amazing work for an eighteen-year-old. I'm in awe of what you've done here. Listen to me, Jamie. If for any reason you aren't satisfied with the teaching at the university, with the art department, and you want to study somewhere else, let me know. Just tell me, and I'll arrange for you to study wherever you like. New York, Paris. Anywhere."

He whirled around to face her, and she saw the fear in his face before he turned back to the window. No one said anything. She stood there a while looking at the apples in the blue bowl.

"All right, Jamie?"

He made an impatient movement with his shoulders. From the hall downstairs, she could hear the Faheys at the front door putting on their overshoes and coats, calling loud good-nights to Charles in his back room. Alice stood there waiting for what seemed like a long time, watching Jamie's back as he gazed out the window into the snowy dark, and then she turned and went quickly down the stairs. Behind her, she could hear Jamie's door close softly, and that was the image she was left with: of something beautiful—of life, joyful and pulsing—shut up in an attic behind a closed door.

All of a sudden she couldn't wait to leave, to get out of this house that was once her sister's and now seemed to belong to no one, a house full of death and memories and lost souls. She wanted to go home to Ralph, to her own place, to her big cold studio with its sweet smell of the red earth.

Mary
1945

AFTER PEGGY died, she was always expecting the worst, so that when the telegram came about John she hadn't really been surprised. One by one, they would all die—Peggy, John, all of them, her children, those babies, those blessed little troubles. But she wouldn't be seeing any more of it, thank God. If any fact was clear to her, it was that one.

The house was too big. Ridiculous, with just the four of them in it now. It was a long way from the attic to the cellar, and it took her days to cart everything down and burn it. She filled a box for each child, and stowed it away neatly in the attic, but everything else went into the furnace: letters, books, old clothes, you name it. Like a witch in a fairy tale. Open the heavy iron door, squeak squeak, see the red coals, and in you go, my pretties.

Ice kills, fire kills: *how strange,* she thought. She didn't watch it burn. Black coal, red flame, gray ash—she didn't stay, just slammed the furnace door shut and went back upstairs to rest before she crammed in another load. It was the dead of winter; the furnace was hot. There was a smell, but no one was home to notice. She sorted and labeled and burned, and went up and down the stairs, cellar to attic, a million times. Once she started, it was hard to stop. She liked the bareness of those attic corners, the empty bureau drawers in the dusty unused bedrooms, the closets freed from their mess. She herself needed nothing, and it wasn't good to leave trouble and secrets behind for the others.

She needed nothing: nothing was enough. There was something wrong with her head. It made it no better to stay in bed, but she preferred that, propped up against the pillows. It was easier, she was left alone more. She wore the rose-colored nightgown John had sent her for Christmas. Rosy silk, lace-trimmed, and by the time the package arrived he was dead.

Charles came in. Nell, Jamie. Did she want dinner on a tray, a cup of tea, would she rather sit downstairs, they would make her comfortable on the couch. No no no. Nothing. Just thinking of John, just tired, just gathering my thoughts. Smile, and they wouldn't stay long. Charles touching her cheek, her neck, then her breast through the rose silk, once, gently, then going away.

It wasn't a headache exactly—nothing so definite. She thought of soldiers marching, men in helmets, men with guns, the sun glinting off cold metal. *Thump thump,* never reaching their destination, marching in circles, marching for the sake of noise and pain. No, not exactly pain: more like *consciousness,* a small separate brain that registered—what? *Here I am, inside this head.* One small soldier, a nice little man, a soldier without a gun, with tiny pink hands, sandy hair, brown boots: *here I am, what's going on, what's this.* And the men in helmets, always increasing, marching in circles, going *thump thump thump.*

John died of his wounds, they said, on the way to the field hospital. Conscious? She had asked the man who came to the house to see them, after the telegram arrived. Yes, conscious to the end, joking even, and not in pain. How could that be? Jokes, eyes open, painless wounds. And Peggy had felt no pain, they said. Dozed off in the cold, while her blood turned to ice. Just slept, like a baby. Except that when Peggy was a baby she screamed herself to sleep as if she didn't want to go wherever it was.

At Peggy's funeral, John didn't cry. Charles had cried, and poor Nell. They made Jamie stay home, Marge Fahey with him. Caroline: did Caro cry? She couldn't remember. Lovely Caroline. Caro wasn't a crier. Stewart, of course. He hadn't even been able to go to the funeral. Ray's mother was there, and fainted. But John hadn't shed a tear. Then afterward, after the church and the cemetery, after the guests back at the house, the food, the dishes, the dark empty rooms, in the silence she had heard him in the cellar, she had found him down there in the old armchair crying himself sick, and had held him—her favorite, her love, her first boy—remembering still his strong young hard body in her arms. And yet at his own death he had joked, had died of wounds that caused no pain.

They lied. They would say anything.

She remembered how when her own mother lay there white and silent, one of her aunts had taken Mary on her knee and said, "Your mother has gone to sleep, Mary. But if you're a very good girl, and if you wait long enough, Mother will wake up."

Even when they took her mother away, she believed it, and she waited. She was a good girl. Alice went away to college, and her father said, "It's just you and me now, little Mary Woodruff."

"And someday Mother," Mary said, and that was when her father told her that Auntie Val had lied to her. Mother wouldn't be coming back. Mother was dead.

Did she want breakfast? It was morning, then. Breakfast: no, not just now. Did she sleep well? Yes, I slept like a tree—no, a log. The children used to ask: *what is sleep.* She smiled to think of all the children crowded around the table in the mornings before they set off for school. Peggy, Caroline, John, Nellie a toddler, and Jamie just a baby. *What did you dream. I dreamed I had a dog. I dreamed I saw Santa Claus. I dreamed my foot fell off.* What did Peggy dream of. Did she dream of the ice, dream of the lost baby, dream her secrets, dream of fire and warmth.

It's a beautiful day, sun on the snow, and Caroline is coming to see you, with Teddy and Lucy. Here's a letter from Alice, she says she and Ralph are going to Mexico. Would it be all right if Bill Fahey stopped in, just for a moment. With chocolates, of all things. Charles brought the paper, with the war news. Burma, they said. Warsaw. Budapest.

John died in France. She had known he would die, it was in his eyes the day he left: death, like a flash of cold light. Every time she got a letter from him, she wondered if he was dead yet, if the letter was from a dead boy. The letters said: *Chère Maman, les petits villages sont très beaux, la vie ici est très étrange, je vais bien.* He'd met a French girl with a funny name: Solange. She had picked out the rose nightgown, was teaching him to talk French. He might have married her. My daughter-in-law Solange. *Elle est belle, Maman. Elle est gentille.*

Il est mort, Solange would cry. *Mon amour, mon soldat, mon américain, il est mort.*

Mary could remember bits of the French she had learned in high school. Remembered how Alice came back from her year in Paris and helped her with the accent. She thought of Alice and Ralph in a Mexican hotel with a courtyard filled with flowers. She remembered when Alice met Ralph—Alice who had hardly ever had a date, who lived only to paint and mold things in clay, who was too tall and too plump, but was always so serene, always happy. So smart! What a surprise when they got married. "Aren't you proud of your sister—imagine Alice marrying money!" She remembered someone saying that at the wedding as a silent reproach to Mary, who was there pregnant with her third, and married not to money but to Charles Kerwin.

Lying in bed, she remembered irregular verbs, whispering the conjugations to herself. She remembered so much, even things she didn't want to. Why couldn't she remember if Caroline had cried at Peggy's funeral? She couldn't remember her even being there. But Caroline must have been there. Only Jamie had stayed at home, with a pill to stop his noise and make him sleep. Was that Caro with her hair tied back under a black velvet hat with a veil? Crying? It was gone, a blur, so many years ago now, there was only Charles with his hand up to his face, John with his stricken eyes, Nell's loud frantic sobbing, the icy wind at the cemetery. Cold Peggy in the ground so hard they used a special machine to dig it. Buried, and took her disgrace down with her into the cold earth.

And now Caro had her babies. She touched their little hands. Lucy's chubby knees. The boy: Teddy, just like John. Caro's boy, and baby Lucy. Death lighting their eyes like winter sunshine.

Please take them away. I'm too—forgive me.

The soldier in the brown boots was getting smaller, but she could hear his voice clearly: *what is this, what's going on here*—a tiny piping, petulant as a child's, somewhere at the back of her head, while the marching never stopped, went up and down, went on and on.

It wasn't exactly a headache. More what waves must be like hitting the shore, a rough sea, hitting a small white shell on the beach over and over, battering, the men in helmets marching out of the sea, over the sand, the Germans in Russia, the Germans in France, John's division in what was the name of that town, the *beau village* where he found Solange, the ruined church, the *boulangerie,* what was the name. The town where he bought the rose nightgown. She had saved John's letters, tied up neatly with one of Peggy's ribbons. She could look up the name. Someone could.

Charles brought the doctor. She refused to have a priest, though

Charles suggested that maybe Father Carmichael could come and talk to her. No, thanks. She had given up priests after Peggy. All those things Jamie said: how awful for a young boy to talk like that, to lose his faith, but of course what he said was true.

"No priests," she said—shouting. She heard herself and subsided. Charles took her hand. She saw him glance at Caroline, Caroline's face with her mouth twisted. Then the doctor came, old what's-his-name: white hair, glasses slipping down his nose, bad breath, his hand on her pulse.

"How's my pulse? Am I alive?"

"Ha ha. Very much alive." He took off the glasses, sat back. "Tired, Mary? You're tired lately? No other symptoms?"

How could she tell him about the little soldier, the waves washing on the shore.

"Well, Mary. These years have been hard on you. Plenty of reason for you to be tired. But we might want to run some tests."

Then he and Charles talked in the hall. She closed her eyes. *Thump thump.* Whatever it was, whatever the tests showed, she knew she was a goner.

Nell came with cocoa and a paper to write for school, and poor young Jamie with his drawing pad. They sat with her in silence, and their presence was a comfort. Charles with his sad face, holding her hand. Then they were gone, into the dark, and wasn't the wind at the cemetery like ice, like fire, wasn't it cold, his body flown in over the cold sea. Not much of a Christmas this year, Mrs. Kerwin. No. She heard the springs squeak as Charles got quietly into the bed, heard him blow his nose in the dark, heard him lie there awake, quiet, and then heard him go to sleep.

Something nagged at her: the store. Harper and Kerwin Hardware, been there on Butternut Street forever. Well, it had fallen on hard times. Never be the same. Hard Times Hardware, Charles called it. Did they get that loan? Or was that just talk, just an idea. No: they were closing the store. Don Harper wanted to retire. Charles said: *hell, Don, we're too young to retire. I'm not sixty.* Don and Florence were going to Texas. Texas! Live in the desert, dry up, become skeletons in the sand. Charles went to work for Unger's. *It's a comedown, Mary. A lifetime's work, gone.* His hand was warm and dry, rough, as familiar as her own. *Hard times,* he said. *Hard times, Mary, my love, my dear.* She remembered his warm insistence in the night, his hands on her, waking up to find his knee parting her thighs, always in silence and darkness, and she gave him the comfort she could. *We had some good years, though. Didn't we?*

She slept, and woke again in the dark. It seemed always dark. She liked the curtains open. Without her glasses, the windows were squares of powdery gray that shifted and pulsed, they were doors that let them in, the soldiers, they grew bigger, they filled the room, the waves battered the shore, the brave little soldier said *no no no.*

Once when she woke up in the dark, she was remembering the first time with Charles, before the wedding, her shock at how big he was—that this was what it was like. How he had kissed her, whispered her name, tears in his eyes: his awful gratitude, as if she had made some monumental sacrifice for him. She wanted to say *please, it was nothing,* but it didn't sound right. She remembered how embarrassed they had both been the next morning. She remembered what Charles told her once when he had too much to drink: that he desired her so much he told it in Confession, even though she was his wife. By then—by then, she had gotten almost to like it, and what he said pained her, that he thought she was a sin.

Another time, she remembered Peggy's birth—her first baby—the long pain, the endless pain like a knife, the exhilarating pain, and the baby coming out: that dark wet head like a swimming dog, like a piglet: her daughter, yelling into her face.

And then—ah, then, she remembered Caroline at the funeral. Cried: of course she had cried, her lovely blue eyes brimmed with tears, the tears ran down her white cheeks and dripped onto the fur collar of her coat. *Mama, what can I do, what am I going to do, oh God, oh God, help me, what can I do.*

The light of death is very cold. They're coming.

Nothing, was what she thought, trying to remember how to say it in French. It wouldn't come to her. *Nothing,* she thought. Did she say it out loud? *Nothing,* hearing Caroline's anguished pleading, seeing Caroline's beautiful tears.

Caroline

1940

CAROLINE was in the library reading about the Middle Ages. She had found a carrel in front of an open window that let in a breeze, and she sat with her feet tucked under her, a book about thirteenth-century monastery life on her lap. Yes: she would be a prioress, like Chaucer's Madame Eglantine with her little dogs, her coral beads, her golden brooch, her tender heart.

The book said that prioresses, for all their sanctity and goodness, lived well. They sometimes had their own cooks, their own personal attendants, their jewels and horses and musicians. They were almost the only medieval women who were taught to read. They spent their days seeing to the business of the convent, keeping the nuns in order. Or embroidering vestments with gold thread, sometimes strolling in the garden composing poetry in French, or entertaining bishops who came to visit. They were revered by their nuns, deferred to by the clergy, admired by everyone for their goodness and refinement . . .

She closed the book and opened another: *The Canterbury Tales.* She turned to Chaucer's prioress:

> *She was so charitable and so pitous*
> *She wolde wepe, if that she saw a mous*
> *Caught in a trap . . .*

In her Medieval Literature course, Mr. Tyler had said that Chaucer's portrait of Madame Eglantine was meant as an attack on materialism and corruption within the Church. She wore jewels, she wept for mice, she fed tidbits to her dogs—worst of all, she exposed her pretty forehead for all to see in days when a woman's forehead was considered sexually provocative. What a strange idea. "It would be like seeing a nun nowadays in a dress slit down to here," Mr. Tyler had said, poking himself in the vague area of his sternum. "Chaucer's satire is subtle, but we can see that the woman was a scandal."

Caroline didn't agree with him, and she went to his office one day to talk about it. It seemed plain to her that Chaucer was fond of Madame Eglantine and considered her a type of the ideal woman— a gentle, loving, trusting soul who did only good and wished no one harm. Worldly, maybe—just a bit. A good-looking woman who still felt herself to be attractive, even after years and years in the convent. Girls became nuns at fourteen in those days.

"You have a point, Miss Kerwin," Mr. Tyler said. "But I'm afraid we do have to conclude that according to the medieval scheme of things her faults outweigh her virtues." He smiled at her: wrinkled-up eyes behind thick glasses. "Of course, Madame Eglantine is indeed very likable. And don't think I'm blaming her for her shortcomings," he went on. "Imagine your little sister, if you have one, giving herself to God before she knew what she was doing. Before she even understood clearly what her other choices were. Just because her father couldn't afford a big dowry to get her a rich husband."

Caroline tried to imagine Nell, and failed. Nell looked like a nun, maybe, with her sharp nose and her piercing eyes—the plain worka-day kind of nun, not a Madame Eglantine. But Nell was too out-going, too crazy about people. If they were a family in the Middle Ages—her father a prosperous merchant, say—Nell was the one who would make the good marriage and have a bunch of children. It was Caroline, the oldest daughter after Peggy's death, who would enter the convent—willingly, no argument—and who would sur-prise them all by rising to the position of prioress. She knew she would be good at it, and she knew the life would suit her: silence and beauty, people leaving her alone, strolls in the garden, intimate talks with bishops who came to call—men who could be relied on to keep their hands to themselves.

"You're probably tired of hearing this," Mr. Tyler said as she stood up to leave. "But you really do have the most extraordinary hair." He pressed his lips tight together as if he were concentrating and, with one finger, lifted a curl from her shoulder. "Just amazing."

"No, I'm not, actually," Caroline had said.

The library was cool and quiet. Caroline loved the serenity of the summer campus. Out the window behind her she could see the deserted path leading up to the library, a neat gray stripe through the green. Beyond the treetops, the university buildings were backed by clear blue sky. She could almost imagine herself in another time, another place. She had settled on medieval England, but almost any other time would do, any other place.

All through June, she had been coming to the campus two or three times a week—early in the afternoon, after she had done the housework, eaten lunch, and baked herself beige in the backyard for exactly half an hour on each side. The big Gothic library welcomed her with its silence and order, and even the grim-faced librarians smiled at her, as if they were genuinely glad to see her there—as if they felt she belonged. She would spend some time browsing through the stacks, deciding what to read—nearly always *The Medieval Village* by G. G. Coulter or the Robinson edition of *The Canterbury Tales* or a volume of thirteenth-century lyrics. Then she sat for a couple of hours, reading, looking out the window, memorizing bits of the General Prologue or one of the beautiful, earthy lyrics written by some troubadour or nobleman or prioress. It was the only thing she had found that could take her mind off what usually preoccupied her: wondering how she had gotten where she was, a housewife at twenty-one, married to Stewart Quinn.

. . . . . .

WHEN SHE left the library that day, going down the cool steps into the heat, she met Louise Stocker coming up. Louise was a girl she knew from her university days, one of John's perennial flames, a sometime friend of Peggy's. Caroline hadn't seen her since that freezing January morning of the funeral, when Louise in a black babushka and no lipstick had embraced John with a cry of sorrow. It was one of the things that meant Peggy's funeral to her: Louise in her scarf, John and the cousins with the coffin on their shoulders as if it weighed nothing, her parents each taking off a glove to hold hands.

She and Louise paused on the steps to chat. After the hours alone in the silence of the library, Caroline somehow couldn't stop talking. Her voice ran on and on, too quickly, saying too much—how well Stewart's firm was doing, what a beautiful apartment they had with its fireplace and sunny kitchen, how he still brought her flowers every Friday, how she had learned to cook all his favorite dishes—even sauerbraten, which she hated.

Louise looked impressed, not just with Stewart's devotion and the posh apartment on Teall Avenue, but with Caroline's involvement in the daily life of marriage, the necessity of getting dinner on the table for her man. "It sounds heavenly," she said—smiling, sighing. "I wouldn't mind being in your shoes. And believe me, I think it's wonderful that you've come through that terrible time so well."

That terrible time. Caroline remembered, the day after Peggy and Ray died, when she and Stewart had turned to each other for comfort, that one of the things he had said was, "I can see that it's going to be worse for you than it is for me."

She hadn't understood. For her, the shock of the tragedy was that she had found so little love for Ray Ridley among the complicated emotions that assailed her. When Stewart used to break down in her arms, she had cried along with him more from sympathy than from grief. "But you loved Peggy more than I ever loved Ray," she had protested.

He said, "No, I mean the humiliation."

To Louise, she said, "What did you think? I was going to kill myself? Crack up or something?"

Louise said, "It's just that I can imagine how hard it must have been, Caro. I felt so bad for you all."

Caroline studied her: yes, she seemed sincere. She had always been a sweet, unaffected person—Louise. The type who would consider it disrespectful to wear makeup to a funeral. She said, "Well, it was hard. It's not easy to lose a sister. I still miss her a lot. Thank God I've got a husband like Stewart."

She looked Louise in the eye, daring her to mention her engagement to Ray, Ray's perfidy. Louise's eyes filled with tears. "I'm so happy for you," she said, which was almost worse.

.   .   .   .   .

STEWART's car was in the driveway. Going up the front steps, Caroline looked at her watch. Almost four o'clock. She held it to her ear: still ticking. Which meant Stewart was home two hours early. Her heart pounded. It occurred to her that never, since they'd been married, had Stewart surprised her or done anything out of character or been where he wasn't supposed to be when he wasn't supposed to be there.

Something was wrong, and what she wanted to do was flee from it, but she hurried up the steps and opened the door. His straw summer hat hung from the stand in the front hall.

"Stewart?" She went into the living room. "Stewart? Are you here?"

She heard nothing, but she sensed he was in the apartment. Ill? Collapsed? Dead? She went down the dark hallway to the end where the kitchen was flooded with light. The afternoon sun entered there in full force, making it, on summer days, almost too hot to cook—but wonderful in winter, just as she had told Louise.

Sounds heavenly.

He was sitting at the kitchen table looking old: that was what she noticed first. He had just turned thirty, and he looked years more than that. In the brilliant sunshine, she could see gray lights in his brown hair.

"Stewart?"

He lifted his head and said, "Sit down, honey."

She sat. "What's wrong?" How odd it was to see him in the kitchen at this time of day, just sitting, in his white shirt and striped tie, the coat of his brown linen suit thrown carelessly on a chair. She had helped him pick it out the Saturday before, at Wells and Coverly. He loved it that she took an interest in his clothes—his hairbrush, even. She had bought him a new one when they got married, his was so old and ratty. She picked up the suit coat and hung it over the back of the chair. There were half-moons of sweat under the arms.

"You don't look good," she said. He had a small heart murmur, a defect from a childhood bout with rheumatic fever that would keep him out of the war if war was ever declared. He looked like a man having a heart attack. "Stewart? Are you all right? Are you sick?"

"Yes, I'm sick," he said. She reached her hand out to feel his forehead, but he shook his head. "No—sick at heart, Caroline. I heard something today that just knocked me out. I had to come home."

She removed her hand. He took a pack of Camels from his shirt pocket and lit one, shaking out the match with a listless motion, as if he cared about nothing. What could he have heard? Something about her. Someone was reading her mind. *Caroline's unhappy, she regrets the marriage, she wants out.* Or that stupid party at the Maloneys' where Chip Maloney cornered her in the kitchen.

"It's about Peggy."

"Peggy. What about Peggy?" She pressed her two hands to her heart, feeling it pound. "Goodness, Stewart, I thought—I don't know what I thought." She stared at his suffering face, the pouches under his eyes. She watched him inhale, exhale, puffing out his cheeks. "Peggy. Everywhere I go I hear about Peggy. Who cares? Peggy's dead."

Her words, coming out like that, shocked her, but he ignored them. "I don't even know if I should tell you this."

"Then don't," she said abruptly, and stood up. There was Pepsi from Mr. Fahey in the icebox. "Whatever it is, I don't want to hear it."

Behind her, she heard him sigh heavily—a shaky sigh that made her suspect he had been crying when she came in. During Stewart's breakdown after Peggy and Ray died—whole days of his helpless weeping, and long, miserable nights—she had felt a kind of affectionate contempt for him, but along with it there had been genuine awe that he cared for her sister so deeply. She imagined Ray, if it had happened to her: how long would he have cried? *No one has ever loved me like this,* she had thought. And also: *I will never love anyone like this.*

What had impressed her especially were Stewart's dreams. They were like the newspaper accounts come to life, made into a nightmare of a movie. He would dream he was out on the ice with Peggy, or with Peggy and Ray both, and the storm would begin, first just scattered snowflakes, then a serious blizzard, and they would laugh at first, say how beautiful it was, everything white, Peggy would throw her head back and catch the flakes on her tongue, and then it would get worse, and they would decide to head back to shore, and that was when the snow got so thick, the wind came up, and there was only white air, white ground, white horizon, and then nothing, nothing, so that Stewart woke up screaming, shaking with cold no matter how many blankets he slept under.

Sometimes in the dream he became separated from Peggy, and knew that if he could reach her he could save her, but he never made it. Sometimes he was on shore, and could catch glimpses of Peggy and Ray out in the middle of the lake—Peggy's striped stocking cap, or her red boots. He would call and they wouldn't hear. Or he would see nothing, just hear Peggy calling his name.

People said: what happens is that you get drowsy and fall asleep. It's a very peaceful death. They were found almost halfway across the lake, far from shore, far from Ray's ice-fishing hut. They were huddled together, his coat tucked around her, his gloves on her frozen hands, his scarf wound around her head. His body over hers. In the hut were four lake trout, a half-empty flask of rye, and a used condom frozen solid.

Caroline's dreams, when she remembered them, were never about Ray, much less Peggy. They were full of people she'd never seen before and mysterious events. The night Stewart had his first freezing dream she had dreamed she was shelling peas in the kitchen of her grandmother's house on Fernwood Avenue, and a strange fat man was looking for something—a book? a pen? And while the peas plopped into Grandma Woodruff's old tin pan, Stewart had been shivering and screaming, dreaming of ice.

But that was a year and a half ago. She stood at the sink, drinking Pepsi from the bottle—long cold swallows that numbed her throat. Her lunch leavings were still on the counter: coffee cup, plate, the crusts from her sandwich. She read what it said on the Duz box: DUZ DOES EVERYTHING. The hell it does. And the Dutch Cleanser with its inane grinning Dutch girl, stupid fake windmill. *Deliver me,* she thought. *Deliver me, God, from all evils, past, present, and to come.* A line from the Mass. Why should she remember it? She hadn't been to church in all that time, not since Peggy's funeral.

"I think you should know," he said. "She had a baby not long before she died. It must have been in California, she must have had it out there. Tom Wilhelm told me. He heard it from a guy he knows at the—you know. Bogan and McKay."

She whirled around to face him. "The funeral home? Some ghoul who embalmed her? They *looked* at her? That's disgusting. That makes me sick."

"I know," he said, but from the look on his face—wary, hesitating, the eyes hooded—she could tell he was titillated by it, just a little. Liked imagining it. Got a kick out of telling it to her. "Still, I thought it was something you should be aware of." He bit his lip, sighed again, tapped his cigarette on the edge of the ashtray.

"I don't want to talk about it," she said. Her stomach cramped with nausea; she felt it in her throat. "I can't believe you would tell me this. Who *cares,* Stewart? What difference does it make?"

She couldn't bear to look at him. Duz does everything. *Deliver me, Duz, from all evils.* Next door at the Laughlins' the radio was playing: dance music. Harry James's orchestra playing "You Made Me Love You," with that gorgeous trumpet solo. She closed her eyes, tapping her feet to the music, and it came back to her, all in a rush—like it or not—what it was like to dance with Ray. Lordy, how that man could dance. She remembered the night at the Club Dewitt when the floor was cleared for the two of them, everyone watching how he swung her out, and back, and the way her skirt looked, the violet-colored silk flaring like petals. *Why am I here with this sad gray man?*

But sex, oddly enough, was better with Stewart than with handsome, sexy Ray. Ray was always too rough, too quick, and he always wanted from her what she had no idea how to give. *Come on, come on, baby*—she hated him saying that, right in the middle of everything, in an impatient voice that clashed, to say the least, with the mood. And the first time, when he took her to the hotel, it hurt so much she pushed him off her, and he pulled his pants on and walked around the room swearing and kicking the furniture. She was a senior in high school. It was a long time before she would let him try it again.

Stewart said, "Oh honey," and she turned back to look at him. Tears in his eyes, hand raked back through his hair, trembling lower lip. "Listen to me for a minute. Try to understand. It was probably his, but it could have been mine," he said. "It could have been my child. I think back, trying to remember dates and figure it out, and I can't get anywhere, I can't put it together. And I can't stand it, Caro. I can't stand not knowing."

There was silence—no sound but the radio and a gurgle in her stomach from the Pepsi. What was she supposed to say? She understood that he was upset. All right, it was a shock, it made everything just a bit worse, she could see that. But profoundly, from the bottom of her heart, she didn't care. So what if Peggy had a baby? What difference did it make if the father was Stewart or Ray or the man in the meat market—which was not outside the bounds of possibility. Peggy was gone, Ray was gone. The baby was gone—who knew where? Adopted by some rich California friend of Aunt Alice's, no doubt. Water under the bridge. Water over the dam. What did it matter?

"I wonder if you would find out for me." He had better control of himself, and he spoke humbly, shyly—the voice he used when he wanted something or criticized her, a voice that was meant to calm and placate but always infuriated her instead. "What happened out there in San Francisco. You could write to your aunt, maybe. Or find out from your mother."

"I don't want anything to do with it," she said.

"Please, Caro. I just want to know. I don't want to *do* anything. But—if it's true, for one thing. If anyone knows—I mean, whose it was. And what happened to it. I only want information."

"I don't get it," she said. She stood with the window behind her, looking at his naked, saggy face. The sun was hot on her back, and sweat ran down from her armpits. "Why is it so important? These things happen. I can tell you this much—it's true, all right. I don't know why I didn't see it, I must have been blind. She had put on weight, I remember that now. She stretched out the elastic on my green skirt." What she remembered was glee, that Peggy was getting fat; she remembered that distinctly. Poor Peggy. Not that she didn't deserve everything she got. Well, not everything. But that—yes. The way she carried on.

He said, "I remember how she avoided me, those weeks before she left. Didn't want me to touch her. And her—" He made a rounding motion in front of his chest. "You know—her breasts were—"

"Oh, never *mind*, Stewart. I don't want to hear it." She finished the Pepsi and clutched the empty bottle. What if she just brained him with it? That thick greenish glass. He'd go down like a big old sawdust doll, too surprised to protest, too miserable. She said, "Maybe she avoided you simply because you were boring, you bored her to death, you bore everyone to death. Did that ever occur to you?" She turned her back on him and banged the empty bottle into the wooden case on the floor. When she stood up he was staring at her, stricken, his face flushed pink.

"I'm sorry," he said.

She sighed and went to him, put her hands on his shoulders, apologized, cradled his head against her. Oh Lord, it was wrong, it must be wrong, to hurt someone like this—when it was so easy. *She wolde wepe, if that she saw a mous caught in a trap.* "I didn't mean that, Stewart. I'm just upset."

"I know." His voice was muffled, his face burrowed into her waist.

He smelled of cigarettes. "I shouldn't have said anything. I was afraid it would hurt you. But I felt it was important that we share everything." He pulled back to look up at her. "And you've been so distant lately, Caro—as if you've got something on your mind. I don't know. Maybe I wanted to get your attention, shake you up a little."

Well: that was mildly interesting, at least. She stroked his hair, at the spot where she would have brained him with the bottle. He did have wonderful, wavy, thick hair—not really very gray. "Stewart, I really think you should forget this. I don't want anything to do with it—something some horrible man told you. It's disgusting, and it's— it's like an invasion of privacy. I mean, it's Peggy's business."

She remembered Peggy at the train—the lucky one, off to California, gloating, carefree, hugging everyone, laughing behind the new blue veil she'd bought for the trip. *All that time, she was suffering.* Caroline felt a brief, pure pang of sorrow for her sister—maybe her first one. She looked at Stewart's bent head and took a breath. "Besides," she said. "Stewart. Look at me." He looked up. A mouse in a trap. She said, "I really believe that anything you found out would only make everything worse. I don't mean just with you—I mean between us."

There was another pause. She hated scenes like this, full of pregnant silences, melodramatic declarations, tears. She had thought they were done with all that. But she forced herself to look into his eyes, blue like her own—what were called gray in the Middle Ages: the books she read, all the poems, were full of gray-eyed beauties.

"What do you mean?"

"Think about it, Stewart."

She stepped back from him and sat down, fanning herself with the morning paper. The heat in the kitchen was oppressive. She could not possibly cook dinner, even if they dragged the electric fan out of the bedroom and set it up in here. They could go out, drive over to Mother's. Stay home and eat crackers and drink beer, she

didn't care. Or would they be too upset to eat at all? Would this conversation go on and on, into the night?

She waited, with a detached curiosity, to see what he would say,
while the Laughlins' radio was drowned out by a car revving up
somewhere down the street. A horn blew. Stewart's cigarette burned
itself out in the ashtray. The headline on the paper was about the
Germans in Paris: she pictured cruel helmeted men goose-stepping
down the wide avenues. Stewart wouldn't be called up if America
got into the war, but what about John? What about Chip Maloney
and Hank Douglas and all the other men they knew? She put the
thought from her. She would go to the library tomorrow after her
appointment at the hairdresser. A book on medieval art, she thought.
Religious paintings. The Bayeux tapestry.

"You're not happy," Stewart said, startling her. She had almost forgotten him. He spoke sharply, so that she could tell the notion of her
unhappiness had just occurred to him, he hadn't had time to digest
it and find a nice way to talk about it. He took one of her hands,
clasping it between both of his; his hands were warm and sweaty. She
wanted to pull away. Draw a cold bath, fling off her clothes, immerse
herself up to her eyebrows, and then sleep, sleep. He said, "Caroline,
don't do this to me."

"I'm not going to do anything, Stewart. What on earth do you
think I'm going to do?"

"Don't leave me."

She knew she wouldn't leave him. It sometimes made things easier for her to imagine leaving him, but she knew there was no question of it. She had married him—why? Because they were linked,
because Peggy and Ray had died and thrown them together—yes,
that. But what else? She thought back, trying to sort it out. A
million years ago. That bleak winter and then the cold wet spring,
when everything was so awful at home. John drinking, out until all
hours. Jamie not talking to anyone, not even getting out of bed. Nell

looking desperate. The store sinking. She was sick of college, sick of her mother's short temper, sick of trying to get used to being poor— that, too, all of it. But when she really thought about it, it seemed to her that she had married Stewart because she had made him forget Peggy: in taking comfort from her, he had fallen in love with her. She remembered his face the first time he saw her naked. It was a face she decided she could love. And out of that mixture of triumph and gratitude and general disorientation, she had found the strength to marry him.

"If you left me, I don't know what I'd do," Stewart said. "I couldn't take it."

She said, "Of course I'm not going to leave you. It's not true that I'm unhappy, not one bit. In fact—"

"In fact what?" He was smiling up at her, gently, benignly. Already she had cheered him up. She assessed his good points. Not bad look- ing, that gorgeous hair, lovely steady deep voice, hard-working and responsible, devoted, stayed home at night, didn't drink much. She went through this list several times a week—always remembering something Nora Lyle had said to her in the ladies' room at Lorenzo's once when they double-dated. Nora was talking about her date. "I can't think of anything negative about him," she had said, blotting her lipstick in the mirror. "But there's nothing positive, either. And you know what that adds up to—no positives and no negatives. A big zero, that's what."

"In fact, what, sweetheart?"

"Maybe it's time we thought about having a baby."

As soon as she said it she saw how witless it was. What a farce: Peggy dictating babies to her from beyond the grave. But she per- sisted. "It's what you want, isn't it? Admit it." Smiling at him. "The patter of little feet around this place."

He couldn't get the grin off his face—like Jamie when he finally got the easel he'd been angling for. Stewart jumped up and kissed her and brought in the electric fan, set up to blow on her chair—

pampering her already. He opened another Pepsi and poured it in a glass, then got a cold beer for himself and sat down opposite her. "We've got to talk about this," he said. He was out of breath with happiness. "It's what I want more than anything, but you've got to be sure that you do."

She understood that it was already done. All that remained was the deed, the waiting, the pains, the life ahead. She sipped, drawing the cold Pepsi through her front teeth, trying to think what should come next. She had the strange sensation that she had just aged several years—like Stewart, when she came upon him in the kitchen, looking like an old man. She said, finally, "The only thing is, I thought I might go back to school."

"You can do that," he said, talking fast, gesturing with his big hands—spreading them out as if to indicate a wide path before her. "As soon as the children are in kindergarten. I'd be all for that, Caroline. With you all the way." *Children*. She saw him wrench his mind away from a roomful of blond darlings so he could ask her, "What do you think you'd like to study?"

She hesitated. She had no desire to talk about it, but she had to answer, so she shrugged her shoulders and said, "I've gotten interested in medieval history. I had that course, Tyler's Medieval Lit. course, I told you about it, my last semester—what? Two years ago. I started looking over my notes—up in Mother's attic one day, going through my old books and things, and I realized that what really intrigued me most was the history, not the literature so much, although of course I—" Abruptly, she stopped talking. Discussing it with Stewart was like a betrayal, though she didn't know of what. And yet what she was saying was important: it was, she knew, her life. She took a breath and went on, talking fast. "Anyway, I've been spending time at the library up on campus, reading. Afternoons, I go up there. I was there today."

Things she said to him often fell flat—wifely things like new curtains, or what the grocer said. The details of her life. When he feigned interest he wore the fake, posed, lively look of people in photo-graphs. But he was watching her closely, the way he observed clients. "Really," he said.

"I know it may sound strange."

"No—not at all," he said, which she knew was a lie. He did think it was strange, maybe even suspected an ulterior motive—meeting a man at the library, some old classmate or a stuffed-shirt prof like Tyler. Men always distrusted her, which was absurd.

"It's important to me. Sometimes I even imagine I'm living then. That I'm an actual medieval person."

He grinned at her. "You wouldn't like it at all, I guarantee. No electric fans. No radios. No canned food." He tipped his head back for a swig of beer, and she looked away from the pimply stubble on his neck. "But seriously," he said. "Go back to school and get your degree. Why not? Maybe you could teach, get a job at the high school. You'd have the same hours as the kids."

"Well." How could she tell him that all she wanted was the knowledge, the understanding? And what could she ever do with that? Distantly, she could see herself, like a tiny background figure in a medieval painting, writing a book herself. *Medieval Women,* she thought. She said, "I don't necessarily want to teach."

"Well—something. It'll work out." He leaned close to her across the table. Beer on his breath. The odd scent of his skin, not unpleas-ant, rather like something to eat though she could never figure out what. Chicken gravy? "I can't tell you what this means to me, Caro. I can't begin to tell you. I mean about the baby."

Standing up then, pulling her close to him, his erection against her, his skin hot. She closed her eyes and thought of cool empty halls and silent gardens, the bishop coming to dinner, the bell ringing for vespers. But it didn't work. They kissed. He put his hand between her legs, and she gripped it tight with her thighs, and then he let her go and they went awkwardly down the hall, their arms around each other, into the darkness of the bedroom.

She kicked off her shoes and he pulled at her dress, unzipped it, so eager he was clumsy, panting. "I don't deserve you," he said over and over, but she knew what had excited him: not her, but the idea of her as a vessel, something a baby could be pumped into. Why did that excite him? Perpetuating himself. Proving himself. And the thought of Peggy. She watched him throw his pants and shirt on the floor and pull off his shorts: oh yes, there it was, old reliable. She wondered, as she often did, why men weren't embarrassed by their penises, stuck out straight like something for a bird to perch on. She helped him with the clasp of her brassiere, and she lay back on the bed while he pulled her panties down. "I don't deserve you." *True,* she thought—her mind, again, free of her body, floating above it like the pictures of souls in the catechism—little white winged things. He kissed the insides of her thighs, and with his fingers pushed aside her pubic hair to find a place for his tongue. She opened her legs and stopped thinking. Let it happen, who cares anyway. She heard her own breathing, and there was his smooth long back under her fingers, his heavy body raised above hers, his mouth that tasted of herself, and it was as if she were slowly lighting up, she was a fire, she burst into flames—like the flames of hell that burn but never consume.

Peggy

1938

HE USED to push aside the green velvet drapes in the parlor, open the glass doors, and sit on the balcony watching for the mailman. Most days, that was how she spent the morning, starting around ten, when she had finished the breakfast dishes, made her bed, and washed out her underwear.

These chores weren't necessary, Aunt Alice had told her. Bernarda could take care of them. But Peggy continued to do them because they took up time, and when they were done she sat in the wooden folding chair on the wrought-iron balcony and looked two stories down to the palm trees on Laguna Street, smoking one of her aunt's Luckies, waiting the morning away.

The mornings in particular seemed immensely long. She tried to shorten them by sleeping late, but as her belly got bigger and the baby became more active, it was hard to find a comfortable position, and she would lie awake at dawn in her little room at the end of the long carpeted hall, listening to the foghorns out on the Bay, then the sounds of her aunt and uncle stirring, the arrival of Bernarda, the kettle whistling, her uncle humming on his way to breakfast. By October it seemed to her that she was hardly sleeping at all, so that she was always tired and sometimes dozed off in the parlor after supper—short foggy naps that left her sluggish and made it harder than ever to sleep at night.

When she had agreed to come to California, she hadn't understood that she would be alone all day—that, every morning but Sunday, Uncle Ralph would go to the Steele Ocean Transport and Shipping Company on Market Street, that Aunt Alice would leave shortly after he did—two mornings a week to teach sculpture at the California School of Fine Arts, the other days to work in her studio.

Peggy went to the studio once. Once was enough: a huge drafty room with an artist in each of its four corners. Besides Aunt Alice, there were Cora, Claire, and Frances—three painters plus her aunt, who worked in clay. They were cheerful women in young middle age, the wives of rich men. They all had short, filthy fingernails, and they wore green coveralls or paint-spotted smocks. They were old friends, affectionate or irreverent with each other. In their presence Peggy felt both disdainful and jealous.

The smells in the studio made her sick: paint, turpentine, clay, dust, and a stink of ashes from the fat black stove that stood in the middle of the room. The clay smelled like excrement, and the whole place made her uneasy. She didn't understand what drove these four women to come every day to a seedy old building—a top floor on Greenwich Street around the corner from the art school—to put paint on canvas or build strange shapeless things out of clay. She didn't understand Aunt Alice's sculptures, and she didn't like the paintings, even one her aunt told her she would love—a red-and-green painting of flowers that seemed to be trembling in a haze of heat, alive and out of control, almost sexual.

"It's very nice," she said. "But it makes me feel faint to look at it."

Aunt Alice said, "But you must admit that at least it looks like what it is—a nice bunch of anemones," and the women laughed—Cora, who had painted it, loudest of all.

Aunt Alice came home just before tea time every afternoon. If Peggy was sitting on the balcony, she would watch her aunt come up the street and turn into the cobbled sidewalk of the Clarion Apartments—a tall, strong-featured, slightly overweight woman in a split skirt and matching jacket, a flowered turban covering her wild gray hair. If she saw Peggy, she would call, "Hi there, kiddo," but mostly she walked as if she were lost in thought, seeing nothing but the pavement under her feet or, probably, the blobs of rough clay she had left behind.

Tea time was at four o'clock and Aunt Alice took it very seriously. As the weeks went by, Peggy too began to look forward to it with an eagerness that astonished her. The prospect of drinking endless cups of tea, eating pastry, and listening to her mother's sister talk about Frank Lloyd Wright, or Roosevelt, or the projects her students were struggling with was not something that would normally fill her with anything but mild dread. Now it was the highlight of her day.

When she was in the wrong mood, she considered this a tragedy, and she would write to Ray that her dependence on the small and insignificant had become pathetic. She thought about that often, how things she had barely noticed in her previous life, or taken for granted, were now the whole world to her. The arrival of the mail. A tray bearing a teapot and a platter of cakes. A chat with someone at the drugstore. Claire and Frances coming to tea. A new magazine. Once, when she was watching for the mailman, the sun came out from behind a cloud in a burst of white light and illuminated Laguna Street—the tile roof of the building across the way, the pots of yellow and rose lantana that lined the walk, the gleaming maroon chassis of a Buick sedan parked out in front. Even after the sun disappeared again, the scene stayed in her mind, its colors and clarity and brilliance, like one of Cora's paintings but infinitely more beautiful.

When she was aware of the baby kicking, even if it was the middle of the night, she got up and walked around to distract herself, and did her best not to imagine a little fist, or a foot with tiny toes jabbing at her. She tried not to think of the baby at all. It came into her head sometimes not as a living creature but as her old doll, Madeleine, whose smocked pink dress and real leather shoes with mother-of-pearl snaps had been the joy of her childhood.

They had arranged for her to see a doctor—a cold, painless act that she could endure with half of herself turned off. After her visit, she couldn't remember his name or what he looked like or the sensation of his gloved, Vaselined fingers in her vagina. He talked distantly about her general health and what she should be careful of—no mention of an actual baby. And, mercifully, Aunt Alice stopped talking about it after the first couple of weeks. Uncle Ralph never mentioned it at all, and kept his gaze off her middle: when he talked to her he looked fixedly into her eyes, his round face stiff with the effort of it. This would have amused her if she hadn't been so grateful to him.

At first, she wrote home critically about her aunt and uncle, making jokes, with exclamation points, about their dinner table conversation, which almost exclusively concerned shipping and art. She described Sunday mornings, when they all walked to Mass at Saint Mary's Church—a red-brick monstrosity, Peggy wrote, like a church in a horror story—and her aunt and uncle singing hymns at the top of their lungs, Aunt Alice in a shrill, off-key soprano, Uncle Ralph a rumbling monotone.

"They made 'Holy God, We Praise Thy Name' sound like a duet for mouse and freight train," she wrote to her friend Ruth, who appreciated such things.

Her letters were full of funny stories about Claire and Cora and Frances, and about Bernarda, the Mexican cleaning lady whose only English words seemed to be *clean* and *dirty* and whose lunch was a beer and a greasy tortilla wrapped in newspaper. She presented her life in California as if it were a play with a comic cast of characters— something like *You Can't Take It with You,* which she and Stewart had seen at the university with Ray and Caroline.

And yet this was her sanctuary, and she knew she'd better get used to it: the San Francisco home of her rich aunt, who had married late but enviably to a shipping tycoon, a man whose claim to fame in her family was that he made money during tough times. All through the last hard years, while Harper and Kerwin was slowly going down-hill, Steele Ocean Transport had been thriving, and Aunt Alice had not only tucked little checks into the letters to her sister Mary (purple ink on heavy rag paper with ALICE WOODRUFF STEELE printed across the top) but paid Peggy's and Caroline's bills at the university. At Christmas she shipped oranges—once, a case of champagne, most of which was still sitting down in the cellar on Hillside Street; and on birthdays she sent exotic, peculiar clothes like embroidered Mexican shirts, a red leather fringed vest, wildly colored Chinese silk shirts for the girls, lederhosen for John and Jamie. Aunt Alice fascinated the Kerwin children—she was their eccentric, lovable savior—and when California was proposed as a haven, Peggy seized on the idea of her wealthy and sensible aunt who would get her out of the mess she was in.

Because her mother, of course, had gone to pieces. She assumed the father of the baby was Stewart, and couldn't seem to understand that it wasn't—they had gone out together for so long, Stewart was so obviously crazy about her, why couldn't they just get married, how had she let it go so long, maybe it still wasn't too late for a wedding.

She finally convinced her mother it wasn't Stewart, and her mother became hysterical all over again. Some unknown seducer—

how much worse, worse than anything. Her mother had slapped her, called her stupid and stubborn, and then cried, horribly, like a child. Peggy endured it as silently as she could. She was surprised by the desire to tell the truth to someone. Not her mother. Nell, maybe? But Nell was so young, and she already disliked Ray. Ruth—but Ruth could never keep a secret. Louise? She would drop dead of shock. She had fantasies of telling Caroline, and imagined Caro's outrages, the breaking of the engagement, Ray's elation, the quickie marriage, the happily ever after—but at the heart of her fantasy was a knot of fear not only of her parents and Caroline but of Ray.

Meanwhile, there was her mother, lecturing her and crying and wringing her hands, and moaning about how Dad must never find out—all he needed was the disgrace of his daughter on top of his troubles at the store. If he knew, he would call her a whore and throw her out of the house: this her mother made clear. "We have to find a way to keep it from him," her mother kept saying, as if that were the important thing and not the baby growing inside Peggy, getting daily bigger and more insistent. And never a word of sympathy.

Finally, her mother pulled herself together and came up with her brilliant idea: she wrote to her sister, and Aunt Alice wired back that Peggy should come immediately. Peggy's mother broke down again. Alice was a saint, to take in a girl she hadn't seen since she was a child. Peggy didn't deserve such charity. Peggy should kneel at her feet.

Peggy refused to acknowledge her mother's resourcefulness or her aunt's goodness. She hardly spoke at all, those last days at home. She spent the evenings in her room with the key turned in the lock, reading magazines and sorting though her clothes, deciding what to pack, keeping her mind on details—ironing, mending, organizing her trunk. Ray was out in Ohio, on the road. Stewart kept calling, and she kept making excuses not to see him. In the back of her copy of *A Girl of the Limberlost,* she made a calendar showing the days left until November twenty-second, the date she figured she was due. Every night she blacked out a square with her fountain pen, slowly and carefully filling up every bit of it with a mesh of tiny inkblots. By the time she got on the Broadway Limited for Chicago, in August, there were a hundred and twelve days left.

Officially, she was going to California because childless Aunt Alice had expressed a wish to see one of her nieces, and Peggy was the one chosen to go.

"That's just great," Caroline said. "She gets rewarded for dropping out of college while I drone away at bio lab."

"She's the oldest," their father said. He accepted calmly the charity of his sister-in-law. He accepted everything calmly—his children's troubles, his financial crises, the state of the world—in studied contrast to his wife, who met life with hysterics. He put his arm around Peggy at the train and kissed her on the forehead. "It's a great opportunity for you, darlin'. See the world a bit. Find out what you want to do with your life."

She put her head on his shoulder and hugged him hard, sideways, keeping her thickened waist out of the way. She thought of what her mother had said, how his face would change if he knew the truth, what things he would say to her in his rage. She looked up into his gentle blue eyes and knew it was true, and it was her mother she clung to at the end, resenting the necessary conspiracies of women, the unreasonableness of men, the secrecy that had to accompany something as simple and good as her love for Ray. She wrote to him on the train and mailed it when she changed at Chicago:

I couldn't tell you. I didn't have the heart. I didn't know what you would say. I guess I was afraid you wouldn't want to see me any more. I'll stay in California until it's over and when I come back you can decide what you want to do. But at least the baby won't be there to make you decide on something you don't want. I couldn't bear for you to say I forced you. So this is good-bye for now, my dearest.

And then, after two more hot, sleepless days and nights in a roomette on the Forty-Niner, reading a blur of newspapers and magazines and Pocket Books she bought at the stations they went
through, she was in San Francisco, in the small oval-windowed spare
bedroom in flat 3-A of Clarion Apartments, where her blushing
uncle's first act when she arrived was to give her ten dollars as her
weekly allowance, and her large aunt who chain-smoked Luckies in
an ivory holder told Peggy about the new direction her sculpture
was taking since the European situation had become so serious.

It took her two days of moping in bed, drinking orange juice and
crying, to recover from the train trip. Uncle Ralph politely avoided
her whenever he could, and, when this failed, told her about California history—the Missions, the Gold Rush, the fire, the shipping
business, last year's opening of the Golden Gate Bridge. Aunt Alice
tried tactfully, dutifully, to talk about Peggy's "predicament," as she
called it, and Peggy hurt her feelings by refusing to discuss it.

After her first few disoriented days, the apartment, her refuge,
began to seem more like a jail, in spite of the overlapping Oriental
rugs on the polished floors, the new Frigidaire full of food, the
velvet-upholstered furniture, the flowers everywhere, the sparkling
clean bathtub where she took a long bath every morning using her
aunt's L'Heure Bleu bath oil. The quiet was overwhelming, and the
constant presence of Bernarda disconcerted her—her silent scurry-
ing with rags and mops, and the way she flattened herself against the
wallpaper when they passed in the hall, hissing a polite "*Señora*" and
showing her missing teeth.

A jail cell, Peggy thought compulsively. A convent. A hermitage.
A cage. She roamed the apartment, avoiding Bernarda, expecting to
see bars on the windows. Or to look out and see miles of ocean, as
if she were on one of Uncle Ralph's ships, trapped, isolated, in the
middle of nowhere.

Then, on her second Sunday afternoon, her aunt and uncle took

her out for a drive, first to Golden Gate Park to visit the Conserva-
tory and have tea at the Japanese Tea Garden, and then down Route
1, where below them they could see the terrifying surf crashing
against the rocks. She was shy with her relatives, and Aunt Alice did
most of the talking while Peggy sat, slightly carsick, in the Buick's
backseat and looked out the window at decaying adobe houses, fields
of flowers, trucks loaded with artichokes, rows of cypress trees, the
vast gray sky and brown hills. They ended up at Half Moon Bay,
where Aunt Alice bought vegetables from an Italian farmer and
Uncle Ralph, smoking a cigar, walked with Peggy down a dirt road
lined with fields of brussels sprouts, and told her that grizzly bears
used to live there. Then her aunt introduced her to the farmer and
his wife: *mia cara nipote da New York.* Mr. Mazzi smiled and bowed to
her over his clasped hands; Mrs. Mazzi gave her a mango, a fruit she
had never seen. It was Peggy's first hint that her aunt and uncle
weren't going to hide her away and be ashamed of her, and the
knowledge of this flooded her with the gratitude and affection she
had failed so far to feel.

She found herself becoming interested in the lives of her aunt
and uncle. She didn't understand her aunt's sculptures, but she
learned not to mind hearing her talk about them, and she began to
enjoy the tea table gossip about the art world and the students at the
School of Fine Arts. She became familiar with Uncle Ralph's ships:
the newest one, a fast freighter called the *Alice Ann* after her aunt, the
Cheney, which had been wrecked in the Indian Ocean, the *Einar,*
which brought back from China the very tea they drank every afternoon. There was a map on the wall in her uncle's study that followed, with colored flags, the course of the Steele ships across the
Pacific; weekends, they brought it up to date, her uncle consulting a
list of latitudes and longitudes he brought home from the office
every Saturday, Peggy moving the pins to their precise positions.

Her uncle gave her a street map, and with her allowance in her purse she began to spend the afternoons walking in the strange hilly city where palm trees lined the streets, and gaudy unfamiliar flowers bloomed everywhere, and there were so many beggars, so many foreigners—a city that was warm and sunny when she arrived, as August should be, but two days later became as gray and foggy as March. Her uncle quoted Mark Twain, who said that the coldest winter he ever spent was summer in San Francisco, and Peggy repeated that in letters to Ruth and Louise, with a certain pride.

She walked no matter what the weather, because staying inside oppressed her, and because walking tired her out and helped her sleep. She also had a vague idea that going up and down the hills would bring the baby on faster. And what else did she have to do? Map in her pocket, she marched slowly, methodically, up and down the straight, hilly streets, staring back at people if they looked at her, stopping sometimes at a cafeteria or a drugstore to rest and have something cold to drink. She walked rain or shine, wearing her gray raincoat even when the day was too warm for it, but her big belly was no longer possible to disguise. Women she encountered in shops and restaurants were always asking her when the baby was due, was it her first, did she want a boy or a girl. Once she had a long conversation with a waitress, telling her about her husband back east, the new house they had bought, how they were looking forward to their first child—Thomas Raymond if it was a boy, Judith Ann if it was a girl.

Her favorite walk was straight down Sacramento Street to Chinatown. She liked it there because, oddly enough, no one paid her the slightest attention. But she was afraid to eat or drink anything; the smells made her queasy, and the webbed feet and the pink pigs' corpses in the butchers' windows disgusted her. One day she stood for a long time in front of the window of an herb doctor's shop, wondering if, had she visited Aunt Alice last spring, the baby could have been disposed of by some small, wizened Chinese man with needles and potions. She closed her eyes and let tears come, seeing herself as a bulky, tragic figure in a gray raincoat in the midst of a thousand milling Chinese.

That was the day when, arriving home wet and exhausted and depressed, she opened the mailbox with the key Aunt Alice had given her, and there was Ray's beautiful angular handwriting.

She hurried upstairs with the letter. It didn't matter what it said. It was the fact of the letter that counted. He had written to her; he had compromised himself. She had proof in her hand if she wanted it: power. He had trusted her with that, had loved her enough to give it to her. "Oh Ray, Ray," she said softly, and ran her finger over her name: *Margaret Mary Kerwin, c/o Steele.* She was overcome, suddenly, with longing for him. She had thought pregnant women lost their desire for sex, and it astonished her how much she thought about it, wanted it—even dreamed about it, waking with such an ache between her legs that she had to relieve it, though that always made her cry, it was so sad, so pathetic to do it alone, and she only wanted him more than ever afterward.

The letter read:

My darling, I don't know if I can ever forgive you for stealing away like that. Surely you must know that I would have wanted to hold you in my arms and kiss you good-bye. Dearest Peggy, I never suspected this, all summer, you seemed just the same, not even sad, and I admire you more than I can say for being so courageous. I feel you have been wise and made the right decision for us. Our lives are too confused and unsettled now to add this complication to them. But my dearest I wish I could be with you. If there was any way I could get myself transferred to California I would! But in fact the territory here is booming, and I'm going to do especially well this fall. A case of Pepsi-Cola in every pot! That's our goal. Peggy, keep me posted on everything. Write to me often. I will be on the road a good deal, but your letters will be here when I get home. It would be best to use a plain envelope, with no return address. And I will write to you from all the hot spots of New York and Ohio! And I long to see you when you return, my darling. Ever your loving Ray

There could not be a more wonderful letter. She hugged it to her heart, kissed his signature. She got out her photograph, a snapshot taken by Caroline of her and Ray and Stewart the winter before. Stewart looked like Stewart, tall and long-jawed and dull. Ray looked like a movie star, better perhaps than he looked in real life, with his burning dark eyes and curly hair and clear-cut features, a faint smile on his lips. She loved the snapshot; she even loved the fact that she herself didn't look her best: she stood awkwardly between the two men, an arm on the shoulder of each; her stocking cap had slipped back, exposing her broad forehead, and she wore a goofy grin. She wasn't beautiful like Caroline, and yet she was the one Ray loved.

Beyond that, as always, she didn't go. Ray loved Peggy, but he was engaged to Caroline—formally and officially. It had been in the newspaper, and he was supposed to be saving up to buy her a ring. Their families were pleased. Caroline's father had gotten Ray the Pepsi-Cola job through his friend Bill Fahey. Caroline's mother and Ray's mother had become friends. Those were the facts. The situation was complicated. It would work itself out.

Peggy read the letter over and over, and she looked at the snapshot for a long time before she replaced it in the back of *A Girl of the Limberlost* with her calendar. Painstakingly, she blotted out another day. Then the baby began to kick, and she went downstairs for tea with Aunt Alice, giving her a hug that nearly knocked her over.

. . . . .

AFTER THAT, though she was often bored and uncomfortable in California, when she thought of Ray she was happy. It became easy for her to be kind to her aunt, patient with her uncle's stories, charmed by walks through their city, no longer oppressed but pleased by the details of their quiet, luxurious domestic life, by oranges and mangoes and avocados, by the scent of eucalyptus, by soft white sheets and wine with dinner and plenty of cigarettes. She became friendly with women in the shops she went to regularly, and enjoyed the imaginary life she constructed for their benefit. She and her husband were so broke, she always said, with a laugh. Times were still hard, at least in her husband's field, which was aviation. He had to stay with his parents until he got some money ahead and found them their own house. Then she and the baby would join him. Live with her mother-in-law? No sir! That battle-axe? Chatting over the counter, she could almost see her husband: a lot like Ray, maybe a bit taller, wearing a white scarf and a hat with earflaps, leaping into the cockpit of an airplane with a jaunty wave.

Ray kept his promise and wrote regularly, usually on hotel stationery from small towns in eastern Ohio and western New York State. She loved to think of him there, in places where there was nothing to do once he had performed his duty at the Pepsi plant. He would eat a lonely dinner, read a little, maybe take in a movie, occasionally get invited to the plant manager's house for a home-cooked meal, but mostly he'd be alone, a traveling man who inspected bottling plants, a man with nothing to do but think of the girl he loved and write her letters.

When he was home, back in Syracuse, she knew he saw Caroline. He never mentioned it, but she had occasional letters from Caro informing her that she and Ray had gone to the movies (they saw *The Lady Vanishes*) or Ray had had dinner up at the house. Her mother wrote regularly every Sunday, and twice she mentioned that Ray had been there. Nell wrote about him too, disapprovingly: Ray had drunk too much beer, Ray had hardly talked at all at Sunday dinner, Ray had promised to bring Mother some cheese from that place in Canandaigua but he forgot, wouldn't you know.

Peggy thought she would give anything to see him, just for ten minutes. And for him to see her. The worst of it, she sometimes thought, was that pregnancy was so becoming to her. Aunt Alice was always saying so—not in those words, just, "You seem to get prettier every day—doesn't she, Ralph?" Or Cora, or Frances, or Claire. In spite of the clothes she had to wear, the frumpy smocks and dark baggy dresses, Aunt Alice's old shoes because her own had become too tight, the voluminous gray gabardine raincoat, Peggy knew it was true. She had never had much color in her face, but now her cheeks bloomed. And her hair, which was always lank and wispy had, for some mysterious reason, acquired more snap; she was letting it grow, and it fell around her face in crisp waves. And her breasts were gorgeous globes as big as the melons they had at Sunday breakfast.

She used to adjust the tilting mirror in her bedroom so that when she looked into it she was visible only from the bosom up. She would drape her new black shawl around her shoulders, low over her breasts, and then let it fall, imagining Ray before her, imagining his face, imagining him touching her . . . *Without your letters I would die:* she wrote those words to him ten, a dozen times, and she knew they were true. But there were days she thought she would die anyway, in spite of the letters, in spite of the kindness of Aunt Alice and Uncle Ralph, in spite of the tea tray and the flowers and the weekly allowance and the sunlight bursting through the clouds. There were days—or, more often, nights, when, wide awake, she couldn't keep herself from thinking. There was one night in particular when her aunt and uncle were out late at a concert, and she was home alone. She crept down to the balcony and sat smoking in the dark, wrapped in her wool bathrobe. She could just glimpse the moon, blurry with fog, through the trees on Laguna Street. She sat there a long time, looking at it, keeping her mind blank, and was startled when people emerged from the house across the street—guests leaving a late party, talking and laughing on the front steps. When they were gone, the lights in the house went out, one by one. She thought she had never seen anything so bleak in her life as the slow darkening of that house, and when the lights were all extinguished she became aware that tears were rolling down her cheeks.

In late September, her aunt arranged for her to meet with a social worker from Catholic Charities who would arrange for the baby's adoption. Peggy took a streetcar and then a cable car to the office on Mission Street, where she was shown into a large shabby room, empty except for a desk and two chairs in the center. At the desk was a tiny woman in a tailored brown dress like a uniform. Mrs. Fitzgerald, she introduced herself. She was very brisk. She asked Peggy about her health and the health of her parents and siblings and grandparents, and wrote down the answers on a form that she kept covered with her hand so Peggy couldn't see it.

"And why are you giving up this baby?"

She had rehearsed her answer on the streetcar. Aunt Alice had said she would be asked. Her aunt had taken her hand and said, "Are you sure, Peggy? That you want to do this? If you really wanted to keep the baby, you know that Uncle Ralph and I would help you. You could stay out here in San Francisco, and we'd find you a job or send you back to college. And child care—maybe some kind of cooperative arrangement."

She had recoiled in dismay from these suggestions. To stay in California, far from Ray, living a Bohemian existence in some cheap apartment with a baby on her hands—that doll in the pink dress and the brown bonnet—no friends, no life, working at a job Aunt Alice thought suitable.

"I can't," she had said desperately. "I can't, I can't. I have to go back," and her aunt had squeezed her hand gently and said it was all right, she understood, but told her to be ready for questions from the Catholic Charities woman.

Mrs. Fitzgerald said, "I assume you've thought about this carefully."

"Yes," Peggy said. "I can't raise it myself. I'm too young. I'm too—

I have no money. I'm a college student. I have no other choice but to give it up."

Mrs. Fitzgerald wrote at length, turned a page. "No chance of marriage?"

Peggy blushed, and had to swallow hard before she could answer. Mrs. Fitzgerald looked up from her page.

"No," Peggy said.

The woman pursed her lips and continued to write, nodding to herself. Then she put down her pen and leaned forward, hands folded on the desk as if she were about to pray. "May I ask if you are a Catholic?"

"Yes, I—" Her voice echoed in the empty room, and she lowered it almost to a whisper. "Of course. That's why I'm here. I've always been a Catholic. My whole family is Catholic."

"I mean a *practicing* Catholic."

"Yes."

Mrs. Fitzgerald raised her eyebrows, stared at Peggy for a moment, and picked up her pen again. Peggy kept her eyes on the woman's small wrinkled hands. She wrote with her left; she wore a huge diamond with her wedding ring, and Peggy tried to imagine some man loving her enough to give her that ring.

Mrs. Fitzgerald said, "Now. About your associate." It took Peggy a moment to understand that it was Ray she meant. "Can you tell me anything about his health? The health of his family members?"

She said that his father had died—of what she didn't know. She had met his mother only a few times but she seemed in good health. He had an older brother. She knew nothing of his grandparents, aunts, uncles, cousins . . .

Mrs. Fitzgerald gave a tiny smile and said, "You don't seem to know this young man very well."

"Oh, I do—I mean—"

She rummaged in a drawer of her desk. "We have a form he really should fill out, since you're so unclear about all this. Would it be possible to send this to him?" She held it up, white paper with spaces to fill in on two sides. Signature of father, Peggy read at the bottom.

"I'd rather not do that," Peggy whispered.

"And why not?"

"I'd like to keep him out of this as much as I can."

Mrs. Fitzgerald sighed and tapped one fingernail on the desk. Peggy said nothing more. She sat looking down at the purse in her lap, a wooden-handled brocade one her aunt had bought for her. Inside it was a letter from Caroline that had come that morning. "Do you think Aunt Alice and Uncle Ralph will leave you all their money?" she had written. Classes had started, she said. She hated everything but French and Medieval Lit. Her French professor was really something: tall, dark, and handsome, and he called her *Mademoiselle Kair-veen* in a sexy voice like Charles Boyer's. She got an A on her first test. No mention of Ray.

"What about the future?"

Peggy looked up. "I beg your pardon?"

"You say that you and this person don't plan to marry, but do you intend to continue to see each other?"

"Oh, yes," she said. It was hard to know where to look. If she looked down, it seemed she was ashamed of something, and she had vowed she wouldn't be abject and apologetic. *I have done nothing wrong,* she had said to herself on the streetcar. She looked Mrs. Fitzgerald in the eye. "Yes. Of course."

"Really."

"Yes, we—actually, we do intend to get married when I finish school and his job is more stable." She blushed because this had never been said. And yet she knew it was true. "He's just starting out, and I'll be returning to school next semester."

"You have definite plans, then." Peggy hated the way she said it— a statement, with an undertone of disbelief, and her cold, pale eyes completely without expression.

"Yes, we do. Not right away, but—"

"Someday."

"Yes."

"I see." Mrs. Fitzgerald's lips twitched—in amusement or annoyance, it was hard to tell. "And what about birth control?"

"I beg your pardon?"

Mrs. Fitzgerald inclined her head toward Peggy. "Birth control, my dear. What steps do you plan to take to insure that this won't happen again? I'll give you a pamphlet on the rhythm method. I somehow doubt that you and your associate have abstinence in mind." She picked up her pen again. "But maybe I'm wrong. Maybe you've learned something from this experience?"

Peggy didn't know what to say. She wanted to get up and leave, but she was afraid the adoption wouldn't go through. Be very cooperative, Aunt Alice had said. These people can be rather moralistic. Just smile and say yes.

"Yes," she said. "I think I have."

"Well." Mrs. Fitzgerald wrote something down, then looked up at Peggy with a slightly more benign expression. "That's all we ask, isn't it?"

"And—just one thing," Peggy said. "My associate. I don't think of him that way. I mean—he's the man I love. I love him with all my heart, and he loves me."

Mrs. Fitzgerald's face became stern again. "Well, my goodness," she said. "I should certainly hope so, my dear. Considering."

. . . . .

SHE WAS sitting on the balcony one morning when Bernarda brought the mail up. There was a small brown-wrapped package: an Ohio postmark and Ray's handwriting. In the same post was a letter from her mother, and she made herself open it first. Her mother hoped she was being a good girl, that she was receiving Communion regularly, and that her health was good. She enclosed a holy card with a picture of Saint Catherine of Siena, who had cut off her beautiful long hair so no man would want her.

In the package was a ring wrapped in tissue. A note said:

> *This will have to do for now. When things get less confusing I'll do better. I bought it for you in this two-bit Ohio spa town because I'm feeling so blue without you tonight. Cold Springs, Ohio, and believe me that's a good name for it. I'm getting tired of these dumpy little towns and may be changing my mind about all this travel. I've heard of a job here, near Columbus, and I'm thinking about it. I'll keep you posted as to my plans. I miss you so much. It seems like years instead of months since we were together. Wear this and think of me. All my love, Ray*

It was a ring enameled in sky-blue, with a border of pink flowers and green leaves, and gold letters spelling out SOUVENIR OF COLD SPRINGS. She studied it carefully. It was basically a cheap metal band. She imagined the town—out of season in the autumn, few tourists, just trees shedding their leaves and a dusty wind blowing. A painted wooden sign pointing to the mineral springs: rotten, sulfurish water bubbling out of a hole. Ray bored to death, taking a walk down the main street, wearing his corduroy jacket, or maybe the tan cashmere sweater that looked so good on him. Thinking of her, he would step into the only store open, a gift and souvenir shop with a window full of doodads—desperate to buy her something, and this was the best they had. It was, after all, a ring. He had never given a ring to Caroline. It was cheap, but it was pretty, and it was the fact of it that was important: like his letters, the ring was more than it seemed. With difficulty—her fingers were swollen in the mornings—she put it on her engagement-ring finger and sat looking at it for a minute. It was the most beautiful sight she had ever seen: that ring on her finger. When she went inside she held up her hand to show Bernarda.

"*Es muy bonito!*"

"*Gracias,*" Peggy said.

"From you hahsbeend?" Bernarda asked, smiling.

"*Si! Si!* My husband. Very good, Bernarda." She nodded ecstatically. She would have liked to embrace Bernarda. They stood smiling and nodding at each other, admiring the ring, and then Peggy went down the hall to her room. With difficulty, she pulled the ring off her finger and held it in her palm. *Hahsbeend.* The quick tears slipped down her cheeks. Pathetic, she thought. You poor pathetic girl. She put the ring away in a drawer and went out for her walk.

By October, when there were forty-nine days left unblotted on her calendar, and when she was becoming embarrassed by her ungainly shape so that walking was no longer a pleasure, and the afternoons stretched out long and blank like the mornings, Aunt Alice asked her at tea time if she would like to come to the studio and pose.

"We'd get the stove fired up nice and hot," she said. "I know it's hard to sit still during these last months, but you could take plenty of breaks. And we'd pay you the going rate, of course." Aunt Alice smiled at her, sipped her tea, and said, "A pregnant model isn't something you come across every day. We'd all love to do you. We'd consider it a rare opportunity. And it would only be for a few days—a week at most."

Peggy stared at her. "You mean in the nude?"

"Of *course* in the nude." Her aunt leaned back in her chair, still smiling, and fitted a cigarette into her ivory holder. She exhaled a long stream through her nose. "We're all women, after all, and I promise you we'll keep it very tasteful and modest. And anonymous. We'll turn your head—like so." She clamped the holder between her teeth like President Roosevelt and reached out to tilt Peggy's chin. "After the first few minutes, you'll absolutely forget that you don't have your clothes on."

"How do you know I will?"

"Oh, I've done a bit of it myself." Aunt Alice tapped ashes into her special ashtray—a pair of green marble cupped hands—and her smile became reflective. "Posed for friends back in my student days. That sort of thing."

Peggy tried to imagine her matronly aunt arranged naked in some arty pose, surrounded by students. She laughed. "Aunt Alice, I'm shocked."

Her aunt said, "You'd be surprised at how natural it feels."

She couldn't imagine her aunt, but she could imagine herself: she had a vision of herself as a painting, naked, her skin gleaming, her head tipped back, her breasts lifted. She felt her heart begin to race.

"Think about it." Her aunt put down her cigarette and smeared jam on a piece of shortbread. "You don't have to decide now."

Peggy said, "No," and pressed her hands to her heart. "I've already decided. I'll do it."

. . . . .

SHE BEGAN posing at the studio every afternoon. In the cold bathroom, she changed out of her clothes into a silk kimono supplied by Claire, and sat as they arranged her, slumped on a sofa at one end of the room by the window. "Okay, dear?" Aunt Alice would say, and Peggy would let the robe fall. "Good," one of them would say. "Lovely. Just move that hand a little more forward on your—good. And tilt your head just—yes—up? Up a wee bit higher? Good."

She knew her aunt's friends better now; she was comfortable with them. And she no longer minded the smells; the nausea from earlier in her pregnancy was gone. She posed in half-hour shifts, sitting with one hand on her belly, one hand dangling, and her face turned toward the window. If she cast her eyes down she could see her hard brown nipples and the white swell of her stomach with its rivers of blue veins. Under her hand she could feel the baby move. When she saw it pushing out against her skin, a little bulge that came and went around her stretched-tight navel, she turned her eyes away again, watching the white sky and, in the distance, black and red rooftops, the Coit Tower, and the gray-green of the Bay. Out there, miles and miles distant, was Hawaii. She dreamed of going there with Ray on her honeymoon, the two of them browning in the hot sun, wearing flowers, eating fruit that dropped off trees at their feet.

Gradually, her pose would become less comfortable. Her back would begin to hurt, she would have to pee. She would hold out as long as she could, then say, "Could I take a rest?" There would be an apologetic flurry: the women plopping their brushes into jars of turpentine or water, Aunt Alice stepping back from the clay. One of them would pick up her robe and hand it to her, and they would cluster around her, telling her what a good model she was, what wonderful skin, what an expressive hand, what a good line from neck to shoulder. She would study their work—they didn't mind. She found it less strange than usual, as if her naked pregnant body had grounded them in reality. Claire's watercolors were quite pretty, really—all sort of misty and blue; and even Cora, though she painted in strident reds and purples, seemed to have captured something, some restless violence that Peggy understood. Her aunt's clay sculpture was clever, the way from one angle she looked heavy and awkward and from another dreamy, graceful, catlike. It was to be called *The Future.*

"Of course, I've barely begun it," Aunt Alice said. "But it's just a matter of proportion, once I get the masses down, then I—" She made a smoothing motion with her hand and stood looking at it, and Peggy would make a trip to the bathroom, drink some tea, walk barefoot around the room looking out of each window in turn, and then return to the sofa, let the robe drop, and listen to the dabble of brush in water, the desultory conversation of the women.

Don't tell anyone, she wrote Ray.

Not that you would—I can just see you telling everyone you had a letter from me! But here's my secret. I've become an artist's model.

*Aunt A. is sculpting me in clay, and the others are painting me, two in
oils, one in watercolor. Yes—in the nude! It's all very respectable, I
assure you, but I find it rather thrilling, I don't know why. Or maybe
I do. I seem to be one of those girls for whom this condition is particularly becoming. And it's very nice to be admired. Maybe I can get one
of the paintings and bring it back and show you what you're missing!*

While they worked, the women talked in little spurts. They talked
about the problems of German artists, the Munich conference, the
situation in the Sudentenland, and then moved gradually, inexorably
closer to home, to their husbands, their students, their children—all
of them except Aunt Alice had at least one child, mostly grown up.
As the days went by they drew Peggy into their conversation and it
turned, gently, to her *predicament*. Sitting in their midst with her
clothes off, she was another person—beautiful, brave, adult—and
one afternoon, all in a burst, she told them something about it. How
the man involved was unavailable at the moment. How marriage
was out of the question just now. How he stood by her, wrote every
week, missed her dreadfully. How good he was, such fun, and handsome—not unlike Cary Grant. How infernally complicated things
were.

There was a silence when she was done. She couldn't turn her
head to look at them, but she heard that their hands had stilled, their
brushes stopped. Then one of them—Frances—said, in a shocked,
hushed voice, "But the man is a heel!"

She did turn then, in confusion, and stood up without asking for
a break. She picked up the robe and put it on and faced them.
"That's not true," she said. "He's wonderful."

"Oh, yes—wonderful!" Frances twiddled her brush in the turpentine and wiped her hands on her smock. "My dear girl, I don't
know who this man is, but he's victimized you. Taken advantage of
you and abandoned you. What is he? Married?"

She flushed and said nothing. Let them think it. Frances came over to her and put her arm around her shoulders. "He's told you lies, you poor darling. Oh, it's so unfair what men get away with."

Peggy said, "No—"

Aunt Alice said, "Frances, dear—please. Don't start making assumptions. We don't know the whole story, and I'm quite sure Peggy doesn't want to tell it to us."

Peggy looked at her gratefully, then wondered how much her aunt guessed. Certainly she knew about Caroline's engagement to Ray Ridley, and knew he traveled for Pepsi-Cola, and she must have seen the mail for Peggy in envelopes from hotels.

"It's really none of our business," her aunt said.

"But it is infuriating," said Cora. "Not that it's necessarily true in your case, Peggy—that you've been seduced and abandoned, all those clichés. I don't mean to imply—but it does happen. Remember Helena Porter, Alice? Lord, she wanted to keep that baby. But she gave it away—what choice did she have? That's the real scandal, that society makes it impossible to keep the child. I'm sure you feel that, Peggy."

"Yes," Peggy said. "It's—" She made a vague gesture and excused herself to go to the bathroom. She sat on the toilet, her face burning. The baby: no: nothing could make her think about the baby. There was nothing to think. As far as she was concerned, the baby didn't exist. The bulges under her hand, the fluttering kicks that she knew were tiny, perfect fingers and toes, were not to be considered, were not to be seen as little Thomas or little Judith. *Ray,* she thought in a panic. She put her head in her hands. It was like the night on the balcony, all the lights going out, a mist over the moon. *Ray.* But what could he do? There was Caroline, and his promise to her. What had happened was never meant to happen, they were swept away, it was Fate, it was no one's fault, she had wanted it as much as he—more, *more . . .*

Tears rolled down her cheeks. It was partly that she was constipated and her back hurt and everything was so strange and she couldn't sleep enough. Oh, if only it could be over, so that she could go back home and fight for Ray on equal terms with Caroline. Or almost equal. Caroline was so beautiful. It was hopeless to compete with her there, she would never be pretty like Caroline, not if she worked on it for a hundred years. But Peggy knew she had something else: sex. She loved doing it, and would do it anywhere: in the backseat of Ray's old Dodge, in the woods, in Ray's ice-fishing shack on the lake, on the floor of his mother's garage—once, standing up, in one of the men's changing rooms at Sylvan Beach, while Caro and John and Nell sat on a blanket not fifty feet away.

She knew Caroline didn't like it because Ray had told her so. *She's cold,* he had said. *Not like you. All she cares about is how she looks.*

And all I care about is this, Peggy had said, and they had laughed, kissed, pressed their bodies together. *This this this—*

She wiped the tears from her eyes with toilet paper. She stood up and, breathing deeply, looked in the mirror over the sink, watching the frown between her eyes disappear. She made herself smile at her reflection: *pretty, so pretty,* everyone said it. Things would work out. It would all take time, but time was what they had: months, years— forever. Ray wasn't making enough money yet to marry anyone, and Caroline was only nineteen, still in college. Their engagement was vague, indeterminate. It would get more so as time went by. He and Caro would drift apart naturally. There was no need for a blowup, Ray said. No need to send everyone into a tizzy. Caro would become impatient with a fiancé who was always out of town, she would think twice about marriage to a traveling man. They were young. Time, time would take care of everything.

She came out of the bathroom red-eyed but smiling. The women were standing around the stove, looking her way with anxious faces, and she knew they had been discussing her. Frances came up to her and said, "Forgive me, Peggy. I have no right to meddle. I'm turning into a terrible old busybody."

"That's all right," Peggy said. "Really. I imagine it would seem hard for most people to understand." She lit a cigarette, shook out the match, and threw her head back to exhale. "Not for me, though. I mean, I know it's complicated."

"Well, it was especially rude of me, when you've been so kind about posing for us."

Peggy smiled. There was Frances's canvas, on which she was a vague rounded figure. The chair and the window, by contrast, were painted in photographic detail. *Everywoman,* Frances had said in explanation. The specifics don't matter, just the condition.

"I like posing."

"That's what makes you so good at it," Frances said. "You're so completely relaxed. That's very rare."

Cora put her hand on her arm. "It's true," she said. "You've been a gem. A wonderful opportunity for us. And frankly, I think you're very gallant, my dear. I have no doubt that you'll keep your young man in line. My personal opinion is that he'd be mad to let a sweet girl like you get away."

Peggy's eyes filled again with tears. She expected Cora to embrace her, but instead she gave her hand a hard, masculine shake, which made Peggy giggle, and then each of them shook her hand in turn, laughing with her, as if it were a ritual in Caroline's silly sorority.

Back in position, the robe at her feet, she felt happy again, and comfortable. They hadn't condemned her, hadn't called her stubborn and stupid and loose as her mother had. They had condemned Ray, and though they were wrong and didn't understand the situation, a kind of elation came to her because of it. She was appreciated, sympathized with, admired for her courage. And, yes, she would talk to Ray. Things must change. The situation had gone on long enough. He had to face it—behave like a man! She smiled, imagining this conversation. Poor darling Ray. She would be firm—yes— but she would say nothing until she was lying in his arms, sure of her power. And not in some freezing ice-fishing shack or backseat, either; he could damn well take her to a hotel. *You could ask me any-*

thing right now, he had said once, his trembling breath on her neck, their bodies linked. *I couldn't deny you.*

It occurred to her that she had never asked him for a thing. You've changed, he would say. California has changed you. Maybe they should just pack up and move, he should take this job he'd heard about in Ohio, take off and leave them all gaping. First Hawaii, then the job in Columbus, and a tiny apartment with a big bed . . .

Outside the window, there was sunshine, the day had turned warm. Claire complained about it—how harsh the light was. Peggy listened to them talk, talked a little herself, and felt that she could say whatever she liked, that what would have shocked people at home in Syracuse was here met with laughter and agreement. She told them a lot about Caroline, mimicking her affectations and absurdities, and made them all laugh, even her aunt, who said she recalled Caro as an unpleasant creature even at—what? Five? When had she last been east? 1923? Four? She could still remember little Caroline and her blond curls, how she showed off—dancing, reciting poetry— how she played up to people to get what she wanted.

The talk turned to sisters, to daughters, finally to people Peggy didn't know, then back to the situation in Europe, and she stopped listening. The troubles in Europe were like a hurricane far off. She sat quietly, head turned toward the window, but what she saw was home. Suddenly she missed everything—all the things she'd barely thought about all this time: her blue-flowered bedroom, her good black winter coat with the frog closings, the silver urn in the dining room, the jars of penny candy at Minetti's Grocery, Nell's kitten Dinah. The oil-and-dust smell of her father's hardware store. Her mother's corned beef. Dancing at Club Dewitt in her tight-fitting black dress with the slit skirt—how she'd love to get into that again! And snow: Nell had written to say they already had snow. The first thing she would do would be to make a snowman—no, make a snowball and throw it at Jamie! And then go sledding down the hill. There would be the sound of chains on the tires of cars laboring up

Hillside Street. And Mother would have cocoa waiting for them when they came in. And John would tease her about how red her nose got in the cold. And she would show them her California things—the half-moon pendant her aunt gave her, the embroidered black shawl from Frances, the funny old doll she found in Chinatown, the blue Mexican beads, the scarab bracelet. And she would put on the blue ring and meet Ray and they would have their talk.

She longed for home, with an actual pain that made her want to put her head in her hands and weep. But she sat quietly, eyes on the blue sky, blue bay, her belly hard under her hand. She wondered how soon, after it was all over, she could get on a train headed east. The Forty-Niner, then change in Chicago for the Broadway Limited. All those dull states, so dusty and shabby on her way out, would be covered with snow on the trip back, made beautiful and serene. She would enjoy the train ride this time. She wouldn't just sit sulking in her roomette, she'd be friendly and talk to people, wave from the window when they went through towns, dress for dinner every night, smoke cigarettes in an ivory holder and drink whiskey sours in the dining car with its round tables and handsome black waiters in white coats.

The women were finishing up their paintings; Aunt Alice pronounced *The Future* nearly done. A day or two more, they said. And there she would be, her likeness, ready for the San Francisco Art League Show in the spring—hanging on someone's wall or, in clay, up on a pedestal where people could touch her as they passed, think perhaps *who was this girl* . . .

But by then she would be home. She saw herself moving back across the country, freed of her cargo, sailing swiftly and gaily and brightly flagged, like one of Uncle Ralph's ships coming into port.

Epilogue . . . .

Nell

1988

ON HER WAY to the video store to return *Sid and Nancy,*
Nell detoured by the old house on Hillside Street to see what hor-
rors the new people had perpetrated since the last time she passed.
With the first signs of spring, they had enclosed the porch. Then they
put on beige aluminum siding and replaced the first-floor windows
with big staring casements unbroken by panes. Now they were
landscaping—sodding over her rose garden, ripping out the over-
grown rhododendrons and the lilac bush, widening the driveway,
and, from what Nell could see, turning the backyard into a massive
concrete patio.

"Not that I care," she wrote to Jamie and Sandra from her new
address—a neat little condo on Grant Boulevard. "I'm just glad to be

rid of the place. I should have unloaded it years ago, when Thea died. Four and a half rooms instead of ten! This is what those women in the diet ads must feel like after they've lost 150 pounds."

She hadn't even taken much with her. Photographs. Books. The afghan Thea had knitted. Jamie's painting, *Blue Number Eleven,* that she had lived with for over twenty years. One small truckload of boxes, and her new kitten, Dinah Number Six. The rest was auctioned off. Now her furniture was all new, and so was the VCR that was the joy of her life.

Nell always got her movies at the Video Bazaar, even though another place had opened up closer to home. *I have a good relationship with my video man,* she wrote to Jamie, then realized how odd it sounded and crossed it out. Sandra would consider it strange indeed to rent a movie every day: she'd use that to make some point about the degeneracy of American culture.

"So what did you think of it?" Randolph asked when she handed over the film.

"I loved it. It reminded me of Keats. And it made me cry, which I always like."

Margaret had recommended the film in one of her letters from California—letters that were so impeccably spelled and punctuated that Nell had sent her a fat check when the house deal closed. One of her great pleasures was sending money to Margaret, who had a job in a bookstore in San Francisco and was working furiously on her novel; she was planning to dedicate it to her great-aunt Nell, whom she considered a patroness of the arts. As another sign of her gratitude, she gave Nell pointers on keeping up with the times. When people retired, she said, they sometimes lost touch with reality. She hoped *Sid and Nancy* would help.

Randolph put the film back in its box, matched it up with the proper square white card, and stowed it away while Nell watched approvingly. She liked the finickiness of his system, and she liked

Randolph, who was short and trim and usually dressed in running clothes. Something about him, she didn't know what, always made her wonder if he was gay.

"So recommend something, Randolph," she said. "What's good?"

He stood with his hands on his hips surveying the shelves. "Let's put it this way. What haven't you seen?"

They discussed the problem at length, with digressions. There were seldom any other customers at that hour of the morning, so she and Randolph always had plenty of time to talk. Nell ended up with *High Noon,* which she had seen once already (not counting seeing it at the old Paramount in 1952 with Caro and the children) but wanted to see again. She loved watching movies twice. "But only if they're absolutely first-rate," she said to Randolph.

"This is definitely one of the greats," he said. "Not what you'd call an innovative film, except maybe for that literal-minded clock motif, but perfect in its own small way. And it has a lot in common with *Sid and Nancy,* come to think of it. Love and death—that's the name of the game." Randolph had been working on an M.A. in English when he decided to quit and open the video store; the rumor in the neighborhood was that the store had made him a wealthy man, but he still talked like a graduate student. He said, "Hey—is that a good topic for VB?"

"Too broad."

"Think so? Yeah, you're probably right."

VB was *Video Blast,* a publication edited, subsidized, and mostly written by Randolph, who handed it out to his customers. He gave her the new issue along with a receipt for the film. They had a private arrangement: two freebies a week, a better deal than he gave his other customers.

"By the way, if you liked *Sid and Nancy* you'll love *Stranger Than Paradise.* It should be back tomorrow."

"Save it for me. I think that's another one Margaret mentioned."

"Is she as big a videohead as her auntie?"

Nell flushed. "I hope you don't think I've given up reading entirely, Randolph, just because I watch so many movies." Though, if pressed, she would have to admit that she read less than she used to. All she really liked now was poetry; she kept Yeats and Eliot by her bed, and the bad romantic poems Joyce wrote in his youth. She said, "I couldn't stop reading any more than I could stop eating."

"That's the trouble with a lot of people," Randolph said, winking at her. "They read instead of watching movies. If you didn't read so much, you'd have time for two movies a day."

She gave him her tart schoolmarm smile and left, the film tucked in her canvas shopping bag. She was aware that Randolph was watching her go, that he found her quaint and amusing—a colorful little old lady—and she didn't mind that in the least.

Her morning pilgrimage up Grant Boulevard to the corner of Butternut Street was one of the high points of her day. She walked slowly, taking her time and looking about her, enjoying the fact that she was still healthy, she had strong legs, she could have walked miles if she'd chosen to. Retiring from teaching and moving out of the old house had given her a new perspective on the neighborhood she'd lived in all her life; it had become important to her in a new way. She used her leisurely mornings to walk its streets and grow fond of them, and she felt that she and the neighborhood were somehow one, that she encompassed its entire history within herself. The stores, the trees, the buildings, even many of the people she passed: she knew their histories, she saw them come and go, she had lived with them since the day she was born, and she considered them in a sense hers.

The drastic alterations in the neighborhood were all right with Nell. She found them interesting, and she believed that places, like people, needed to change with the times to survive. Minetti's Grocery was gone, and Clarice's, where Caro and Peggy used to have their hair done, and the drugstore with its marble fountain, and the sheet music store. The old Methodist church had evolved into the

True Light People's Deliverance Tabernacle and then into a failing kitchenware shop. The building that had once housed her father's hardware business had been knocked down years ago; an apartment house was there now, with dusty geraniums growing out of bare parched dirt in the front yard and an overflowing dumpster in the back.

The Video Bazaar was where Lily's used to be—the store where she had always shopped for the neat blouses and skirts and sweaters she wore to teach in.

"Don't you miss Lily's like crazy?" Pat Garvey had asked her once—Pat who still wore sweater sets and pleated skirts: disasters on her plump, elderly body. The loss of Lily's didn't bother Nell; she no longer cared what she wore, and Randolph and his store were part of her new life. So was the deli that had opened on the corner where Minetti's had been for years. Now it was called Glorious Food, and Nell stopped in regularly to get takeout for her dinner.

When she got there, she stood outside trying to remember what she had in the refrigerator. She was sure there were leftovers from the day before. She stood looking in the window, where a display of something called California Chili (All Vegetable, All Natural) reminded her of Margaret. Videohead indeed! She smiled. Margaret also recommended books: avoid *Less Than Zero,* she advised, but read *Anywhere But Here,* it's out in paperback.

Nell was flying to San Francisco in August to see Margaret—also to eat her way through Chinatown and feast her eyes on the Pacific Ocean and go to see two of her Aunt Alice's sculptures (one called *The Past,* one *The Future*) that Margaret had discovered at the art museum there. Maybe have dinner with Heather and Rob—find out if there was any truth in Margaret's improbable speculation that Heather was expecting. And something else. When she was cleaning out the old house, she had found a packet of letters in the attic, tied up with ribbon and stored, overlooked and forgotten, with Peggy's costume jewelry in an old tin candy box: PICKWICK INN

CANDY SHOP, SAN FRANCISCO. They were dated fifty years ago, letters to her sister Peggy from Ray Ridley—that two-timer, the man who had deceived Caro and lured Peggy to her death. Nell had unfolded one and glanced into it—*My darling I don't know if I can ever forgive you*—and tucked the packet away again, blushing and short of breath, as if she were being watched.

Sitting there on the attic floor, with her hands pressed to her heart, it had all come back to her. Struggling home in the blizzard to hear that Peggy hadn't returned from shopping, all her friends had been called, no one knew where she had gone. Then waiting through the night and the next day, when the snow stopped falling and a policeman came with the news, the horror of it. And Ray Ridley. After all these years, she had nearly forgotten his name.

Nell had already sent the jewelry to Margaret—she was Peggy's namesake, after all, and they were pretty pieces, just right for a young girl—but she decided to take the letters to California with her. She couldn't bear them alone, but she and Margaret could look at them together. There could be nothing shameful in reading them now; everyone involved was long dead. They were family history. She put the box away on the top shelf of her linen closet, back where she couldn't see it, but she was always conscious of it there, waiting.

California Chili: no, that didn't tempt her. She remembered that she had some leftover pasta carbonara and some broccoli salad in the fridge, but she went into Glorious Food anyway and bought a giant chocolate-chip cookie and a bottle of raspberry soda. For the first time in her life she was getting what Caroline used to call midriff bulge; Nell didn't mind that, either.

The girl who waited on her was new; Nell recognized her as an ex-student. Feathered hair, blue eye shadow on top and bottom lids, wristful of noisy silver bangles.

"How's it going, Miss Kerwin?"

"It's going just fine, thank you."

"You like being retired?"

She couldn't remember the girl's name. Debbie something? Or was she one of the Morrison girls? Nell did remember the class she'd been in, a bunch of alienated slouchers who refused to keep up with the readings in *Dubliners*.

"What do you think?" Nell asked.

The girl grinned at her. "I guess you like it pretty well."

. . . . .

SHE WAS eating the cookie with a cup of tea when old Mr. Fahey's son Jerry called to say his father was dying and wanted to see her.

"The doc says he won't last 'til morning, Nell. But he's still got all his marbles, and he keeps asking for you. Finally I told him, all right, all right, I'll call her. If it's not too much trouble for you to drive out here."

She changed from her jeans into a skirt and a clean blouse. At the last minute, she took off her Jesse Jackson button, which she knew wouldn't be appreciated by Mr. Fahey, who had been a knee-jerk Republican all his long life. Then she drove out Teall Avenue to Serenity House, the nursing home he had been moved to last winter when the quick work of cancer had begun to supplement the slow work of old age. Old Bill Fahey must be ninety if he was a day.

"It's the Pepsi that's kept me alive so long," he had joked the last time she visited him. That had been just after Easter; even then he was dying. His eyes were milky-blue, lost in wrinkles. His smooth spotted hands reached for hers, and when she held his dry fingers he gave his wobbly smile and fell asleep.

Serenity House was an old Tudor mansion set on a hill in a grove of trees. Nell parked and walked up the path. It was bordered with late tulips, the purplish black ones that always reminded her of Lent. Here and there on the grounds an old person sat in the sun accompanied by a nurse dressed in white. Where do they find them, Nell wondered. The ancient and dying, she knew, were plentiful, but there was a shortage of nurses. Maybe Serenity House paid them well. Jerry Fahey had told her once how much it cost them to keep his father there; he also told her that he and his wife were on the waiting list.

"But you're not even sixty, Jerry!" Nell had protested.

"I won't be young forever," Jerry said. "It won't be that long before I'm—" He jerked his head over at his father, who drooled placidly in his chair. "I don't want to find that there's no room at the inn when I need it."

He had hinted that Nell might do the same; a small annual fee would guarantee her a place when the time arrived. Nell always felt a faint sense of dread when she approached the door. The next time she came, would she be a senile old vegetable, struggling for breath? And would they turn her away?

We who were living are now dying. Eliot. Not exactly a comfort, but he tended to hit the nail on the head.

Mr. Fahey was on the third floor, in a sunny corner room; they had paid extra for the location, which had a view of treetops. Three folding chairs were set up outside the door. Jerry Fahey sat on one, his wife Rosemary on another, young Brendan on the third. Nell disapproved of them all. She felt they had neglected Mr. Fahey in his declining years. Alone in that house after Marge died. And all those Thanksgivings when he had to come next door and eat with the Kerwins while Jerry and his family went to Florida. Mr. Fahey hated to fly. It was something he had in common with Jamie—the old dour Jamie, pre-Sandra. Meeting in the driveway, the two of them liked to talk about air disasters.

Jerry and Brendan stood up when she approached. Jerry looked grave, Brendan embarrassed. Jerry was the manager of the Pepsi plant in Utica; young Brendan had been given a series of increasingly low-level jobs there, all of which he had botched. Nell had heard the predictable drug rumors, and something about his going back to school to get a degree in Recreation and Leisure.

"Well, this is it, Nell," Jerry said. He shook her hand, looking theatrically sad: a large, jowly, red-nosed, Irish ex–football player, twice as big as his father even when the old man was in his prime. "At his age, there's nothing else they can do."

Rosemary raised her head; under makeup, she looked weary and bored. "He's been asking for you. First he wanted to see Brendan. Bren won't tell us what he wanted." Brendan looked down at his shoes, shrugging his shoulders. Rosemary lit a cigarette and blew out smoke, raising her eyebrows and shaking her head to indicate perplexed disapproval. "Now he wants you."

"Should I go in?" Nell asked.

"He was asleep a while ago," Jerry said. "Let me just check."

He opened the door a crack. A voice said faintly, "Nell?" Jerry stepped back and nodded, and she started to go in. Jerry grabbed her arm and hissed, "Five minutes."

"Nell, is that you?"

"Yes, it's me, Mr. Fahey."

The door closed behind her, and she went over to the bed. It was cranked up to a sitting position, but Mr. Fahey was slumped with his chin on his chest. He rolled his eyes up to look at her, then managed to raise his head. "It's about time, young lady," he said—or something like that. His voice was thin and indistinct, as if he spoke on an inhale.

She went closer and took his hand; he slumped down again. Nell had no idea what to say. She thought of all the people who had died. Her sister Peggy, her brother John. Her mother, who died while Nell was in her Milton class. Her father, who had what was called a good death while she held one hand and Father Dwyer the other. Caroline's husband, Stewart, who died in unspeakable agony of emphysema. Caro herself, cold and quiet in her bed when Nell looked in to see why she was sleeping so late. Poor Aunt Alice, dropped dead of a heart attack in the shower, ninety-three years old.

And Thea, who died in the hospital alone in the night because the nurse persuaded Nell to go home and get some sleep.

I had not thought death had undone so many.

"Jerry said you were asking for me," she said.

"That's right." She waited, watching the old man's face, while he struggled to say more. He had cancer of the pancreas: a useless operation and now this slow decline. She wondered what it was like, how did it feel to have your body inside its shell consume itself. The old man's eyes closed, opened again, closed, opened. He had been old for so long. He looked the same as he had looked for years—just smaller.

"Nell?" His head was sunk into the folds of his neck like the head of a white turtle.

"Yes."

"Nell?"

"I'm here." She squeezed his hand in case he wasn't hearing her. "I'm here, Mr. Fahey."

"You were always my favorite, Nell. I always liked you."

"I know that, Mr. Fahey." She squeezed his hand again. She had never forgotten those two times, once in her backyard and once in the Faheys' kitchen, though she had forgiven him years ago. These same hands on her breasts and under her skirt, these frail old waxy fingers—younger then, eager, strong. The little moustache bristling against her neck. The voice muttering, "Don't tell."

"You were the one I always liked."

"I know."

He showed his yellow teeth and made a death-rattle sound that she knew must be a laugh. "I sent you Pepsi," he said.

"Yes. All those years." Mr. Fahey's Pepsi, in fact, had been one of the ludicrous, unsolvable problems of her life: the amused dread she and Thea used to feel when the delivery truck came lumbering up Hillside Street. She had left cases of it behind when she moved.

"Well—" Mr. Fahey sighed and closed his eyes. Nell wondered if she should leave. Her mind wandered. She thought about Jamie and Sandra, who were flying over from England with the twins for a show of Jamie's work in Boston, then to Syracuse for a visit. She wondered if they were planning to stay with her, and she spent some time trying to figure out how she could put them all up. Give Jamie and Sandra her room, take the tiny guest room for herself, put the babies in the dining alcove in rented cribs? Or put the cribs in the guest room and sleep on the sofa? Or maybe they weren't in cribs any longer, maybe they could just sleep on the floor in the—

"But I know you appreciated it, Nell."

What? Ah, the Pepsi.

"Yes. I certainly did. It was—"

It was what? He lay there peering up at her. The room was dim, the drapes closed against the light. She wondered if he would like them open, if a view of green trees would make dying better or worse.

"It was good of you," she said.

"Well, I wanted to give you something." His voice faded out.

She stroked his hand. "Do you want to rest now, Mr. Fahey?"

He opened his eyes and looked straight at her. "Rest? I'll be getting plenty of rest," he said, and made the terrible laughing sound again. "But you know, Nell—I always did like you. You and your. You and your." Nell's stomach fluttered. What on earth was he going to say? "Your lady friend," Mr. Fahey wheezed finally.

"Ah," Nell said. She closed her eyes, seeing Thea's face.

"Liked you both."

Nell wanted, suddenly, to get away, to go home and wrap herself in Thea's afghan. She was afraid she might cry, and not for poor old Mr. Fahey.

Jerry put his head in the door and lifted his wrist, pointing at his watch. Nell said, "I'd better get going, Mr. Fahey. I don't want to tire you."

He turned his head on the pillow and saw Jerry in the door. "Get out of here," he said fiercely, hoisting himself up. His voice was perfectly distinct. "Get out of here, damn you, I'm talking to Nellie."

Nell tried to withdraw her hand, but his grip was tight. "I probably should leave, Mr. Fahey."

His milky old eyes narrowed with anger. "You go on now! I'm talking to Nellie."

"Dad—"

Jerry turned, rolling up his eyes, to look at his wife out in the hall, and Rosemary joined him in the doorway. "Now, Dad, remember what the doctor said." She grimaced at Nell, half apologetic, half irritated. How unfair it is, Nell thought, to treat him like a nincompoop just because he's old and sick and out of it. Why shouldn't he be allowed to sit a while longer with an old friend? And yet she wanted desperately to leave.

"Dad, I'm going to have to get Dr. Granger."

"Get out of here, the whole bunch of you. I'm talking to Nell."

Nell bent close to him; he smelled of bad breath and disinfectant. "Mr. Fahey, I really don't want to wear you out. I'll come back. I'll come back tomorrow."

He clutched her hand, imploring her with his eyes. "I'm not long for this world, Nellie," he said. "Do you know that? I'm a goner. There's something wrong with me."

Nell remembered her mother: *there's something wrong with my head,* she had whispered. And then, before they could do tests, she was dead. A massive brain tumor. It was so long ago, and yet Nell could call it back so vividly it seemed to be happening all over again in some shadowy half-tangible world not far away. She squeezed her eyes shut again, opened them to find the old man staring at her. The look on his face, she realized, was fearful.

"Nellie?"

"You need to rest now, Mr. Fahey," she said. She felt close to tears. "I'll come back and see you again."

"Tomorrow," he said.

"Yes."

His grip on her hand relaxed. His face smoothed out. He smiled faintly. "Tomorrow."

"I'll be here."

She withdrew her hand. The chair creaked when she stood up. "You were the one, Nellie. The one I liked."

She watched him for a moment to make sure he was still breathing. His hand lay on his chest, and she covered it with hers; their hands rose and fell, rose and fell with his old sparse breath. How young and firm her hand looked compared to his. Mr. Fahey began to snore. She backed out of the room. Jerry was coming down the hall with the doctor—a tall, striding man in a flapping white coat.

"Wouldn't let you get away, eh?" the doctor said.

"He was my next-door neighbor for sixty years," Nell said stiffly.

The doctor said, "Amazing," and went into the room.

In the hall, Nell turned to Jerry and Rosemary. "I hope he doesn't wake him," she said. "He was just dropping off."

"Did he say anything?" Jerry asked her. She looked at him blankly. "Anything?"

"Dad. Anything special?"

"No. He just wanted me to know he—" She paused. "He considers me a friend."

Jerry looked at her doubtfully and then said, "Well, so do I," taking her hand and pumping it hard. "And I appreciate your coming, Nell. I know it meant a lot to him."

She shook Rosemary's hand, and took Brendan's limp grip. Then she went back down the hall, her heels clicking loudly in the silence. When she got to the elevator, the doors opened and a nurse pushed forward an empty wheelchair. For a strange moment, Nell imagined it was for her: she was supposed to ease herself down into it, let her chin sink to her chest, and be wheeled away to a sunless room to die. She stood staring at the chair. It took her a moment to realize she was in the way. She stepped aside. The nurse smiled at her and said, "Have a nice day now."

. . . . . .

SHE WATCHED *High Noon,* sitting on the sofa eating Gourmet Cheesy Popcorn and drinking raspberry soda. She had the afghan around her, Dinah curled up on her lap; whenever Nell touched her she began to purr violently. The movie was as satisfying as ever, though Nell wondered how much depended on that great theme music. She would have to discuss it with Randolph.

When the movie was over, she got into her nightgown. She usually read in bed for a while with a glass of wine. She fed Dinah and was about to settle down with *Video Blast* when the doorbell rang: Rosemary.

"I was practically around the corner at the undertaker's, Nell. Bogan and McKay." Rosemary came in and sat on the edge of the sofa. "I thought I'd stop in and tell you Dad passed away this afternoon not long after you left."

Nell would have preferred a phone call, under the circumstances—ten o'clock at night, Nell in her nightgown, popcorn crumbs on the sofa where Rosemary perched—but she knew Rosemary meant to be nice. "Was it peaceful?" she asked. "At the end?"

Rosemary hesitated. "Well—for a while he was kind of difficult, but the hospital chaplain talked to him and gave him the last rites and he calmed down quite a bit. Yes—I think he died in peace."

Nell didn't comment. She had a feeling the old man had asked for her again, but she didn't want to know. It wasn't fair that the dead were so needy, could still load you up with guilt.

"The poor old guy," she said.

"He lived too long," Rosemary said, and sighed. "Well. It comes to all of us, doesn't it?"

"We who were living are now dying, Rosemary."

"More or less, I suppose." Rosemary half opened her bag, shut it again. Nell knew she wanted a cigarette, but she didn't encourage her. "Nell," she said, and stopped, started again. "Nell, I think Dad may have left you something." Rosemary looked up, into her eyes.

"In his will, I mean. A little token of his remembrance. Did he—mention anything about it to you?"

Nell was surprised by a desire to laugh. She imagined the Pepsi truck pulling up once a month for the rest of her days to deposit a case on the doorstep of her condo. She said, "No, not a word." She looked at Rosemary's eye makeup, too much and freshly applied—imagined her ducking into the ladies' room at the undertaker's with her little zippered bag while Jerry negotiated the price of caskets. She decided that whatever Mr. Fahey had left her she'd turn over to Margaret. "He didn't have to do anything like that, Rose," she said. "But he was a very sweet man."

"Yes—he was." They sat there looking at each other sadly. Nell was impatient for Rosemary to go, but she offered her a cup of coffee, a glass of wine. Rosemary said, no, she was exhausted, she'd be off, she had to pick up Jerry at the funeral home and drive all the way home out to Fairmount. At the door, she hugged Nell and said, "You've meant a lot to our family." Nell was touched; she always felt bad that she could never warm up to Rosemary and Jerry. She said she'd see them all at the funeral, though she had no desire to go: funerals were for the living. What did Rosemary's mournful face have to do with all those Thanksgiving dinners, all those cases of Pepsi-Cola?

It seemed somehow disrespectful to poor Mr. Fahey not to tell someone he was dead, so she called Lucy in Boston. She described her last conversation with him, and Lucy said, "He sure was fond of you, Aunt Nell."

"Yes, he was." What would Lucy say if she told her? The creeping fingers, the fierce whispers. It was all so long ago; it seemed so harmless now. "He liked you, too," Nell said.

"Did he say anything about me?"

"He wanted me to tell you hello," Nell lied. What harm? He'd said that when she saw him in the spring: *say hello to that pretty little Lucy for me.* She said, "I suppose good-bye is more like it."

"Ah, the poor old guy. Should I come for the funeral? It would be difficult—I have to be in Vermont Thursday."

"I don't think you need to," Nell said. "I mean—Jerry and Rosemary. Really. I wouldn't bother. Go to Vermont."

"I was thinking that maybe on my way back I could cut over on Route 20 and see your new place—if you can put me up. I'm going with a friend, but we'll probably be taking separate cars." Nell knew all about Lucy's friend—Philip Talner, her old art professor. Not the first of her affairs, but it looked like he might be the last: it had gone on eight, ten years. The last time she saw Teddy and Marie, they had hinted that, this time, Lucy might even divorce Mark and marry the guy.

"Whatever you decide," Nell said. "I'm not going anywhere. You know I always love to see you."

The idea pleased her. She'd get some California Chili and give Lucy a vegetarian dinner. Things had been strained lately between them. Mark was still angry with Nell for financing Margaret's move to California. He had called her up and said that Margaret's whims shouldn't be encouraged, after what she'd put them through—that Nell had overstepped the bounds. Why should Margaret be rewarded for her behavior? Lucy had told Nell several times that she personally didn't agree with Mark, she was glad to see Margaret happy for a change. And certainly Margaret was an angel, a paragon, compared to some of her cousins: Ann somewhere in the East Village, calling her parents only when she wanted money, and Peter rumored to be living in some kind of paramilitary commune in Montana. But Nell knew Lucy missed her daughter, and she couldn't help feeling responsible. How complicated life was, especially when you tried to be good.

She poured herself a glass of wine and settled into bed. Dinah jumped to the foot and sat there washing herself. Nell took the volume of Joyce poems from her bedside table and opened it at random:

O cool is the valley now
And there, love, will we go—

Reading poetry always reminded her, pleasantly, of Thea, but tonight she couldn't concentrate. She looked across the room to the crowd of photographs on the dresser: the laughing snapshot of Thea, Peggy in spit curls, an ancient sepia picture of Caroline and John as children, little Teddy and Lucy holding hands, a sullen school photograph of Margaret, Teddy's three troubled kids in better times, her parents' wedding picture. So many. So much sadness. And in spite of everything, always a comfort, that collection of photographs. She never looked at them without an awareness of how much they had taught her, how much, still, she could learn from them, the living and the dead.

Nell sipped her wine, and when the wine was gone she turned on her side, and was instantly asleep. The window was open; from outside came the sound of traffic on Grant Boulevard and a drone from an airplane passing overhead. A car door slammed, a voice down in the street laughed and called good-night. Dinah quit washing and curled up at Nell's feet, nose to tail, with a sigh. Jamie's painting hung over the bed, and, in the dim light from the street lamps, the vague blue shapes—a woman bending forward, offering or pleading—were lost in shadow.